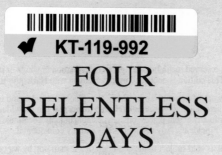

FOUR RELENTLESS DAYS

ELLE JAMES

IN THE LAWMAN'S PROTECTION

JANIE CROUCH

MILLS & BOON

First Published in Great Britain 2018
by Mills & Boon, an imprint of HarperCollins*Publishers*
1 London Bridge Street, London, SE1 9GF

Four Relentless Days © 2018 Mary Jernigan
In the Lawman's Protection © 2018 Janie Crouch

ISBN: 978-0-263-26592-7

0918

Elle James, a *New York Times* bestselling author, started writing when her sister challenged her to write a romance novel. She has managed a full-time job and raised three wonderful children, and she and her husband even tried ranching exotic birds (ostriches, emus and rheas). Ask her, and she'll tell you what it's like to go toe-to-toe with an angry 350-pound bird! Elle loves to hear from fans at ellejames@earthlink.net or ellejames.com.

Janie Crouch has loved to read romance her whole life. This *USA TODAY* bestselling author cut her teeth on Mills & Boon novels as a preteen, then moved on to a passion for romantic suspense as an adult. Janie lives with her husband and four children overseas. She enjoys traveling, long-distance running, movie watching, knitting and adventure/obstacle racing. You can find out more about her at janiecrouch.com.

Also by Elle James

Also by Janie Crouch

Discover more at millsandboon.co.uk

FOUR
RELENTLESS
DAYS

ELLE JAMES

To my editor, Denise Zaza—thank you for
your continued faith in me as an author
and for all your support and reassurance.

To my daughter Courtney Paige for helping
brainstorm plots. I love you so very much and
wish you great success in your own writing.

To my readers who keep coming back for more.
You're the reason I do what I do. Thank you
for being so faithful and encouraging.

Chapter One

First night back at the All Things Wild Safari and Resort in Kenya, Africa, and Harmon "Harm" Payne had trouble sleeping. Their commander had granted the team a bonus week of vacation. After a particularly difficult mission in South Sudan, cleaning up the damage done by a ruthless warlord bent on wreaking havoc with the locals and stealing their children for his army, the SEAL team deserved this time to unwind.

Though his week of rest and relaxation had begun, he couldn't rest or relax and paced the sleek wooden floors of his cabin, hoping to get sleepy, but so far, nothing was working.

As a US Navy SEAL, he was used to snatching some shut-eye whenever he had fifteen minutes to spare. Why couldn't he do it now?

He stood by the window, staring out into the darkness of night, studying the myriad of stars twinkling in the heavens. The setting was perfect, the mission had been a success, but he couldn't calm his racing pulse. Harm felt on edge, as if he teetered on the precipice of something.

He lay on the bed, forced his eyes to close and counted bullets, hoping the monotony of the numbers would lull him to sleep. Around fifty, he must have slipped into a troubled sleep. The numbers became the beat of a drum; the sleek bullets became gyrating bodies, shiny with sweat and paint, dancing in the flames of a bonfire. The rhythm grew stronger, the dancing more erratic, and a voice called out words in a language he could not understand. A flowing red scarf drifted through the dancers and into the fire, becoming part of the dancing flames.

What did it mean? Why was he there?

A movement in the shadows surrounding the fire caught his attention. The face of a coyote, wolf or jackal appeared, its golden eyes reflecting the glow of the burning embers.

For a moment, Harm's attention remained riveted on the jackal, his heart beating fast and furious, slamming against his ribs, as if eager to escape the jackal and the confines of his ribs.

Harm swayed with the drumbeat, his body drawn like a moth to the flames, his gaze captivated by the jackal's eyes, mesmerized in the effect of the dancing flames. His feet moved as if of their own volition, taking him to within reach of the blaze. He would have fallen in had an owl not swooped low, screeching loudly at just that moment.

The sound jerked him back from the fire. The jackal disappeared and Harm sat up in the bed, his heart racing at the close call in the dream. He rubbed his eyes, swung his feet over the side and stood, letting the night air cool his sweating body.

Obviously, sleep wasn't coming any time soon. At least, not the restful kind he sorely needed.

Closing his eyes now would only bring on a recurrence of the freaky nightmare. Harm pulled on a T-shirt, jeans and boots and left his cabin for the main house, hoping to find a sandwich or a beer. Maybe that would help settle his nerves and let him sleep...dream-free.

In the distance, he heard the scream of something that sounded like a big cat. The night sounds of the savanna were enough to make anyone a little nervous. He was glad he wasn't sleeping in a tent, exposed to whatever wild animal sniffed him out as a potential meal.

His buddy Buck had been on a recon mission with his doctor lady for a couple days, sleeping in the open, exposed to the elements and wild creatures of South Sudan. They'd managed to survive, with the worst threat being from the warlord they were determined to find and nail.

Surely Harm would be okay walking by himself between the cabin and the main lodge without being stalked by a hungry beast.

Talia had mentioned walking in pairs to discourage the wildlife from singling them out, but he didn't want to wake any of his teammates. They didn't have problems with insomnia, apparently.

Harm followed the starlit path to the lodge and climbed the stairs to the front door. As he reached for the door handle, a high-pitched scream pierced the night air, followed by a long wailing cry.

His hand jerked backward and he spun toward the sound.

"It's just a jackal," a feminine voice said from the shadows on the wide veranda. "They like to yodel at night."

Harm turned toward the sound.

Talia Ryan, the resort owner, rose from a porch

swing and leaned against the railing, the starlight glinting off her blue-black hair. Beside her lay the resort mascot, Mr. Wiggins, the long, sleek leopard they'd met on their previous visit.

The animal lay stretched out across the decking, completely relaxed and asleep.

"You get used to the sound of the jackals after a while," Talia said.

"Apparently Mr. Wiggins is unconcerned."

Talia laughed. "He feels safe here."

The jackals screamed again, making Harm start.

Talia looked out into the night. "And if it's not the jackals, it's the lions chuffing or the elephants trumpeting. There really isn't such a thing as a quiet night on the savanna." She turned toward him. "Are the natives keeping you awake?"

He chuckled, though the sound was strained, even to his own ears. Her comment hit far too close to home for comfort. He shrugged it off. "I wish I could blame it on the animal noises, but I just couldn't sleep. What's your excuse?"

She shrugged, the slight movement unaffected yet graceful. "Some nights I don't sleep well. There just happen to be more of them lately."

Harm admired the curvy silhouette of the beautiful woman, glad for something besides flames, dancing bodies and jackals swirling through his mind. "What would keep a pretty lady like you up at night?"

She stiffened, her gaze turned toward the night and the savanna where the jackal sang. "Nothing my guests need to worry about."

Harm should have left the conversation there and entered the main lodge in search of that snack, but something kept him on the veranda with Talia.

He liked the woman who owned and managed the resort single-handedly in a country where native women were often treated worse than cattle. "I imagine you have a lot of responsibilities, running a resort by yourself. Is this something you've always wanted to do?"

She laughed. "It wasn't *my* dream."

"No? Then whose dream was it?"

She hesitated for a long moment before finally answering, "It was my husband's."

"Husband?" Harm hadn't heard anything about a husband in connection with Talia during the several days they'd spent at the resort a couple weeks before.

"Michael was a freelance photographer. We spent so much of our time here in Africa, we decided to buy the resort and make it permanent."

"Where is he now?" Harm asked.

"He was killed by a rhinoceros over a year ago." Her voice was soft, quiet, almost a whisper. But the tone said it all.

The catch in her voice tugged at Harm's heart. "You miss him still?"

She nodded. "For the first few months, I could barely breathe. I knew life on the savanna could be dangerous, but I never thought I'd lose Michael to the animals he fought so hard to save. He always seemed so good with them. And they were tolerant and accepting of him."

"They don't call them wild for nothing," Harm pointed out.

She nodded. "Still, it was so sudden. One day he was here, the next he was gone. We'd been together since we were teenagers. I really had no idea how to go on without him."

"You seem to be doing fine now."

She shook her head. "I didn't take reservations for over six months, and when I did, I only invited a few guests at a time. My heart wasn't into it. Not without Michael."

"You always seem so upbeat around us."

"I never stopped missing him, but it's easier to get through the days now than it was after it first happened. The guests keep me from getting sad." She turned to him. "So thank you."

The starlight shined down on her face, illuminating her bright eyes, making them sparkle despite the melancholy droop to her lips.

Harm had the sudden urge to pull the woman into his arms, to hold her and make the hurt go away. But she was still grieving for her husband. It wouldn't be right for him to embrace her.

She dipped her chin. "I guess I miss him more at night, when I slow down from the day's activities. The past week has been particularly difficult with everything happening at once."

Harm couldn't resist. He opened his arms. "I'm not your husband, but I have strong arms."

She gave him a wobbly smile and stepped into his embrace. "Thanks." Talia rested her hands on his chest and pressed her forehead to his breastbone. "I didn't realize how much I missed having a hug."

"My pleasure," he said, his tone soft, gentle, as calming as he could make it. The moment she'd stepped into his arms, he realized his mistake. He'd gone a while without female companionship. Her body pressed to his made him hyperaware of that neglect.

She was the perfect height, the top of her head coming up to just beneath his chin. He rested his hands at the small of her back, amazed at how narrow her waist was in comparison to the swell of her luscious hips and breasts. His blood heated and his groin tightened automatically.

Yeah, holding this woman, who still grieved her husband, might not be his smartest move.

For a long moment, Talia stood in his arms. Eventually, she turned her head and laid her cheek against his heart.

He pressed her closer, fully cognizant of even her slightest move. Conscious of his own proximity and desires, he fought to hold himself back from making an idiot of himself.

"Why are you still here at the resort? Why didn't you leave when your husband passed?" he asked.

She shrugged. "I loved Michael. Leaving here would have been like leaving him all over again. I thought about selling, but I just couldn't. This was his dream. He saw beauty in every living creature. For the most part, so did I. But when one of his beautiful creatures killed him, I had a hard time seeing them as purely beautiful."

Finally, he set her at arm's length and brushed a strand of her dark hair off her cheek, tucking it behind her ear. "Are you okay for now?"

She nodded and then looked up into his eyes. "You're kind. Thank you."

"For what? I should be thanking you. It's been a long time since I've held a beautiful woman in my arms."

He clasped his hands together to keep from pulling her back against him.

"Look at us. All this talk about me and my lost love… what about you?" Talia asked.

Harm stiffened. "What about me?"

"You say you haven't held a woman in your arms for a long time." Talia pinned him with her wide-eyed stare. "Why not?"

His jaw tightened. "I have a job to do. Women aren't part of it."

"But you have to have someone to come home to."

"Why?" He waved his hand. "Don't answer that. My job precludes relationships. Besides, unlike you, I don't believe in true love. It doesn't exist."

"Oh, but it does." She touched his shoulder. "It's that feeling that you can't live without that person, that your life is better for having him in it."

"And when he leaves, sends you a Dear John letter, just walks out of your life or dies?"

She smiled. "You thank God you had him for the time you did."

"But you said you couldn't live without him. Yet, here you are." He raked her with his gaze. "You appear to be very much alive to me."

She chuckled. "I am. And I had to learn how to live without him, but I wouldn't trade my time with Michael for anything."

"If you believe in love, are you going to fall in love again? Knowing what could happen?"

"I don't know if love can happen for me again, but if it does, I'm not going to pass it up because I'm afraid of losing him. I'd be stupid to walk away when there is so much happiness to be gained."

"And so much sorrow..." he reminded her.

Talia nodded. "True, but feeling so deeply is a sign that we're very much alive. If I push past the sorrow, I remember the happiness and it's all worth it." She laughed. "I'm sorry. You're a guest. I shouldn't be bringing you down with my troubles."

"You didn't. I'm just curious. If you're finally getting over the sorrow, what's keeping you up at night? When we were here a couple weeks ago, other than the poachers, I didn't get the feeling you were unhappy."

"I wasn't." She stared out at the night again. "Everything seemed to be getting back on track. And then... strange things started happening."

He studied her silhouette, noting the frown pulling her brow lower. Normally Harm avoided deep conversations, preferring to remain uninvolved. But Talia had been through so much, and she seemed like a genuinely nice lady. He wanted to get to the bottom of her troubles. "Strange? Like strangers showing up? Or hinky strange?"

She laughed. "Hinky?" Her smile soon faded. "Actually, hinky kind of describes it."

"Really?"

"Yes." She stepped away from him and wrapped her arms around her middle. "As the locals would say, the resort has some bad juju going on."

Harm crossed to the swing and sat. He patted the space beside him. "Tell me about this bad juju." If it was anything like what he'd been dreaming a few minutes ago, he could understand her concern.

She hesitated before joining him. As she settled, her movement set the swing in motion, gently swaying in the dark.

Again, Harm might have been better off going into the kitchen alone.

Talia's warm thigh rested against his, and with every sway of the swing, he caught a whiff of her perfume.

"Yesterday, we found native paintings on the doors of the cabins."

"Graffiti?" Harm asked.

"In a way. Only the content was threatening."

"How so?"

"They'd painted an owl swooping down over several people." She snorted. "Stick figures, nothing too dramatic, but enough to scare away the guests who'd been staying in the cabins."

"Why?"

"I had hired new guards to protect the perimeter. They swear they saw no one sneak past them into the compound. They got to the guests before I did and spooked them by telling them about what omen the images foretold."

"And what does an owl mean in the local folklore?"

She stopped the swing with a foot on the board of the veranda and stood. "It doesn't matter."

Harm stood and rested an arm over her shoulder, cupping her arm with his hand. "You can't scare me. I'm a crusty old SEAL. I don't believe in bad juju. But I do believe in bad people who like to frighten women and children."

She squared her shoulders, shrugging off his grip. "I'm not easily frightened, either, but when it scares my guests, it threatens me and my livelihood." She lifted her chin and faced Harm. "Around here, if an owl flies close to you or a loved one, it means someone is going to die."

"You don't believe that hooey, do you?"

"Normally I don't." She looked back over her shoulder toward him. "I believe people painted the signs over the doors. But it's hard to discount the omens when they happen."

"What do you mean?"

"The night before my husband died, an owl swooped over my head." She sighed. "I shrugged it off as coincidence…until they brought Michael back to the lodge the next day. Then I went through everything I could have done to keep him from dying that day."

"But you couldn't undo what was done," Harm said softly.

"No."

"And you think it's happening again?"

"I haven't seen an owl this time around, but someone is planting those superstitions in the heads of my staff and my guests. I can't run this place by myself. If the juju threats continue, I won't have staff to take care of the guests and the guests will leave, like the ones who left the day your team arrived. I'll be out of business." Talia's voice lowered to a whisper. "My husband's dream will be lost."

Once again, Harm fought the urge to pull Talia into his arms. She had been so very upbeat and friendly from the day she'd first welcomed the SEALs to her resort.

Harm was a fixer. He liked to make things right. But he wasn't sure he could fix Talia's problems. He didn't have any experience with black magic and bad juju.

Chapter Two

Talia hadn't wanted to bring her new guest into the superstitious world of the locals. Granted, the SEALs seemed of stronger constitutions than her rich guests who'd left the day before, hurrying away because of a painting on their doors.

She stared up at the tall, broad-shouldered SEAL and wanted to laugh.

Harm would not be as easily frightened. Hell, he'd frighten those trespassers who'd dared to draw the omens on the doors. Perhaps having the SEALS there would keep the saboteurs from spreading their portents of bad juju on her property.

"Enough about my troubles." She pasted a smile on her lips. "Is there anything I can get you?"

"No. Like you told us from the beginning, we can make do for ourselves. I was heading for the kitchen, hoping to snag a sandwich."

"Do you mind if I join you?" she asked, not ready to be alone after everything that had happened. She'd found temporary comfort in this man's arms, something she hadn't counted on, especially after the loss of her husband. A tug of guilt pulled at her heart. At the same time, she felt a spark of something else. She refused to put a name to it. Not yet.

"I'd be honored." Harm offered her his elbow.

She slipped her hand into the crook of his arm and stepped through the door with him.

They had just crossed the threshold when a shot rang out. One of the cabin doors slammed open and Big Jake burst out running backward, wearing only his boxer shorts, cursing. He held his M4A1 rifle in his hand, pointed back into the cabin.

Pitbull, Diesel, Buck and T-Mac all ran out of their cabins in varying stages of undress, carrying their weapons.

"I heard a shot fired." T-Mac hurried toward Big Jake, wearing just his jeans, no shirt or shoes.

"Me too." Diesel joined him on the path, in shorts and nothing else.

"What's going on?" Pitbull asked, tugging a T-shirt over his head, his jeans pulled up but not buttoned.

Marly emerged seconds later, zipping up her flight suit. "Who's shooting?"

Harm leaped off the veranda and ran toward Big Jake. "What happened?"

Big Jake shook his head. "I've never seen one that big. It was curled up at the foot of my bed."

"What was curled up at the foot of your bed?" Harm asked as he arrived at Big Jake's side.

His teammate shook his head and pointed his rifle toward the door. "I was having this strange dream. Drums, painted dancers, incense... I was falling into a fire when I woke up, sat up and stared at a cobra coiled at the foot of my bed, his head up, hood spread and ready to launch himself at me. I did the only thing a good SEAL could do."

"You blew it away, right?" T-Mac shuddered.

"Damn right I blew it away." He shot a glance toward Talia. "I'm sorry if I also put a hole in the wall."

"Holy hell, I hate snakes," T-Mac said. "That would be one of my worst nightmares—forget the fire and dancers. Snakes are the devil."

Talia pushed past him, headed into the cabin, then paused at the door. "You did hit it, didn't you?"

"I'm pretty sure I did." Big Jake shoved a hand through his hair. "It was all pretty much a blur."

Harm caught her arm. "Let me go in first."

"Here." T-Mac handed him the pistol he'd brought from his cabin. "You'll need this."

Harm grinned. "Are you sure *you* don't want to make sure the snake is dead?"

T-Mac crossed his arms over his chest and shook his head. "No. I trust you to make it right."

"I can take care of this," Talia said. "We have the occasional snake enter the compound. Although not lately. The villagers see cobras on occasion. They like rats and chickens."

"And the occasional baby?" Marly asked, a shiver shaking her body.

Talia grimaced. "They don't usually eat the babies. But some children have been bitten on occasion."

"Nice," T-Mac said. "Nightmare, I'm telling you." He turned to Diesel. "Why did we decide a safari in Kenya was a good idea?"

"You wanted to come as much as the rest of us," Diesel reminded him. "At least you weren't stuck in the jungle along the Congo for several nights, sleeping in snake-infested trees."

"Enough talk about snakes." T-Mac raised a hand. "Who's for heading back to Djibouti and the friendly scorpions they have?"

"We're not going back to Djibouti," Harm said. "One snake is not a den of snakes."

"How do you know?" T-Mac asked.

"Shut up, T-Mac." Harm unlocked the safety on the handgun and stepped past Talia and through the door, switching on the light. "I'll let you know if there are more when I come out."

"*If* you come out alive," T-Mac muttered behind him.

Cobra bites were deadly if left untreated. But there was treatment, Harm coached himself. Although he wasn't horribly afraid of snakes like T-Mac, he had a healthy respect for them and the damage they could create with a single bite.

He edged his way into the sitting room, past an overturned end table and a twisted rug. Big Jake had been in a hurry to get out of the cabin. He couldn't blame the man. He probably would have reacted the same way if he'd awakened to a snake in his bed, much less a deadly cobra.

He searched every nook and cranny in the sitting room before entering the bedroom. As soon as he did, he noticed the long, sleek body of a serpent draped across the bed, its tail hanging over the side. A dark spatter of blood spread across the white comforter and the mosquito netting draped from the ceiling. He rounded the foot of the bed to the other side to check the other end of the snake before he could let go of the breath he'd been holding.

"Dead?" Talia asked from the door.

Harm jumped. "You were supposed to wait outside."

"You were taking a long time," she responded. "I got worried."

"I was making certain there wasn't another snake in the building. They can hide in the strangest places."

"You would know this because?" She arched her brows and crossed her arms over her chest.

"I grew up in a small town in Texas. We had our share of rat snakes, rattlers and copperheads. We'd find them in garages, barns and sheds. Sometimes they would make their way into the houses through an open door or window and curl up in the base of a flowerpot or shoebox."

"Nice." Talia studied the snake lying across the bed. "Looks like a spitting cobra. Big Jake's lucky the snake didn't spit in his eye—its spit can blind a person."

"Don't tell T-Mac. He'll have one more reason to be afraid of snakes, as if being bitten isn't enough."

Talia chuckled. "It's hard to imagine any of you SEALS afraid of anything."

"As a kid, T-Mac was traumatized by a snake. I think his mother made him hold one once. He's been terrified ever since."

"But you must have been in places with snakes before."

Harm continued his search of the room, dropping to his knees to check under the bed. He was careful, now that he was aware that cobras could spit. "Being a SEAL challenges every one of your fears, but thankfully, they don't stick you in a pit filled with snakes. I don't think the cadre liked snakes any more than anyone else, or they would have used them, too."

The space beneath the bed was free of snakes and surprisingly clean of dust.

"Do you keep all the cabins this clean?" Harm asked.

Talia laughed. "I'm worried about snakes and you're looking at how clean this place is?"

"I've been in hotels that don't clean as well as this. I don't see a single dust bunny, even in the corners."

"My staff keeps the entire compound clean. We pride ourselves in making it a beautiful place to stay for all visitors, not including deadly cobras." Talia opened the closet and checked inside.

Harm slipped up beside her, ready to shoot anything that moved. "Well, they'll have their work cut out for them, cleaning up snake parts."

"I'll probably handle it myself. I've had a hard enough time convincing them to stay after the paintings on the cabin doors. I had to scrub them off myself."

Harm could picture her cleaning the paint off the doors. "We'll help you get this place cleaned up."

"No way." She shook her head. "You are guests of mine. I won't have you doing the dirty work."

"We're kind of used to dirty work. It's what we do." He nodded toward the pillows. "If you don't mind sacrificing a pillowcase to the cause, I'll start by removing the offender from the premises."

"By all means." She shook a pillow out of its case and held it out for Harm.

He lifted the snake off the bed, dropped it into the case and then took it from her.

"Be careful you don't let the fangs touch you," she said. "They still contain poison."

Holding the bag away from his body, Harm checked all the closets, drawers and corners and then straightened. "I can take care of the cobra, just tell me where you want me to put him."

Talia shook her head and held out her hand. "I'll take him and put him in the freezer."

He kept his hold on the bag. "Please tell me you aren't cooking up cobra for dinner."

She laughed. "No, but I know they need antivenin. They might be able to milk a dead snake for its venom, which they use to make antivenin."

"You're a woman after my own heart." Harm followed her out of the cabin, careful not to touch her with the snake in the pillowcase. "Beautiful and practical." If he was in the market for a wife, she'd be an amazing catch. But then, he wasn't in the market for a relationship. Especially with a woman who had so completely believed in love.

Harm believed in lust, the natural, chemical reaction between a man and a woman. But love?

No. Absolutely not.

Oh, sure. Once upon a time he thought he had, but one Dear John letter cured him of that fallacy very quickly.

But that didn't keep him from wanting women. A man had urges, after all.

"IF YOU'LL FOLLOW ME..." Talia turned toward the lodge and then back to Big Jake. "And I have a room in the lodge for you, Big Jake."

He nodded. "Good thing, because I wasn't gonna sleep in there. No, ma'am."

She laughed. "I can't blame you. But no worries. We have a snake-free room upstairs with a comfortable bed."

"The cabin is clear, if you want to grab your gear," Harm said.

"Yeah." Big Jake frowned. "If you're sure."

"I'm sure. I even looked in your gear bag. No more snakes." He held up the bag. "And you killed the one on your bed. He's not going to bother you again."

"Damn straight." Big Jake sucked in a breath and eyed the cabin, as if the structure might assume a life of its own.

"Come on," Diesel said. "I'll go with you."

"I can do it myself," Big Jake grumbled. "I just need a minute."

Talia fought back a grin. Seeing a huge SEAL like Big Jake hesitant to enter a building was so unlike the man. She could imagine him charging in like a bull at a bullfight.

Diesel draped an arm over the shaken man's shoulder. "Take all the time you need, dude. It's not every day you wake up to a cobra in your bed."

Big Jake grimaced. "And I hope it never happens again."

"We've got your back," T-Mac reassured him.

"Good," Big Jake said. "Then why don't you go in and get my gear?"

T-Mac backed away, shaking his head. "I said I've got your back, not your *bag*."

"If it makes you feel better," Talia said, "I've been in the rooms and didn't see any more snakes."

"I'm going. I'm going." Big Jake sucked in a deep breath and followed Diesel into the cabin.

"Let's get that snake on ice," Talia said.

Harm followed her into the lodge and through to the kitchen. She flipped on light switches along the way.

Once in the massive, updated kitchen, Talia opened the door to the walk-in freezer and held it wide for Harm to carry the bag with the snake inside.

A cool blast of air chilled her hands and cheeks as she waited for Harm to step inside.

"Where do you want me to put him?" Harm asked.

"Let me get a box." Talia hurried to the pantry, found an empty box and returned to the walk-in freezer. "The far side has empty shelves. I'd like to keep him separated from the food we serve the guests."

Harm chuckled. "We'd like that, too. I wouldn't want your chef to confuse chicken and cobra."

"I'll warn them not to touch the bag in the box. I don't want the staff hurt by brushing up against the snake's fangs." Her lips twisted into a frown. "Maybe I shouldn't put the snake in this freezer."

"If there is a shortage of antivenin, saving this snake could help. You're doing the right thing," Harm assured her as he set the bag in the box and the box on a shelf in the farthest corner of the freezer.

When they emerged from the freezer, the kitchen was filled with the rest of Harm's team, plus Dr. Angela Vega and Marly.

Buck clapped his hands together. "Since we're all awake, we thought we'd come raid the refrigerator."

Talia smiled. "I can whip up a casserole in about forty minutes, or I had the chef prepare a ham earlier to make sandwiches for the safari tomorrow. I believe there's enough meat for snacks tonight and sandwiches tomorrow. It's up to you."

"Ham sandwiches sound great," Diesel said. "But we can help ourselves. You don't have to stay up on our account."

Talia smiled. "I wasn't asleep, and a sandwich sounds good to me, too." She pulled the container filled with ham slices out of the commercial refrigerator and set it on the counter. Then she laid out freshly baked bread, garden-grown lettuce and tomatoes, plates, utensils and condiments.

"We can take it from here," Buck said. "Thank you."

"While you are preparing sandwiches, I'll check the room upstairs for you, Big Jake." She turned to leave the kitchen, crossed the wide-open living area and mounted the stairs to the second floor.

Footsteps behind her made her turn back.

Harm climbed the steps a few feet behind her.

Talia stopped midway up the staircase. "Are you following me?"

He nodded. "With all the crazy things happening, I thought I'd check the room for uninvited guests."

"I can do that myself," she insisted. "I've lived here long enough to know what to look for."

"Would you have looked for a cobra in your bed?" he asked.

Talia shivered and pressed her lips into a tight line. "Probably not. We've never had that happen here at All Things Wild."

"Then humor me. Let me look first."

"You're not going to be around forever. I need to do these things on my own."

"I get that, but it would make me feel better to help, since I'm here already." He winked and waved her ahead. "Ladies first. At least to the bedroom door."

She led the way to the guest room she had in mind for Big Jake. "Maybe I should have all of you move into the lodge if things are getting…how did you say?"

"Hinky. If you have another room in the lodge, I'd like to snag it as well."

Talia paused in reaching for the door handle of a room. "Are you afraid of snakes, like T-Mac?"

Harm shook his head. "No, but I don't like that these things are happening to the resort. Someone is playing games with you. They might make it more personal."

In the back of her mind, Talia had thought the same thing, but she hadn't let the possibility take root until Harm voiced it. "You think someone is targeting my resort and me?"

Harm took her hand in his. "I don't know, but while we're here, let us help. Let *me* help."

"But you're my guests."

"In case you hadn't noticed, we're not your normal uppity clientele. We've slept in deserts, jungles and swamps. We've been shot at, had explosives go off nearby and nearly been killed so many times, you start to think you're invincible, or just that your number is not quite up yet."

"Yet," she whispered. "You never know when that might happen."

"Exactly. We could step on an improvised explosive device or be hit by a bus. We don't borrow trouble. We wait for it to come to us. But that doesn't mean we don't take precautions."

"Like?"

"We brought our own weapons. We're prepared to take on anything and anyone."

Talia smiled. "I'm kind of glad my guests left room for you and your team to stay." She nodded. "Thank you for offering to help. While you're here, I accept." She held out her hand. He engulfed it in his own, sending sparks of electricity throughout her body.

As quickly as she took his hand, she pulled hers free, heat suffusing her cheeks. "I'll just be a minute checking on this room and the one down the hall. Do you think T-Mac would like to stay in the lodge as well? Seeing as he's so afraid of snakes? I don't want him to be uncomfortable in one of the cabins. I can't imagine how that cobra got into Big Jake's room. These things never happened while Michael was alive."

Harm touched a finger to her lips. "I'll ask. In the meantime, let me check the rooms first."

Talia's lips tingled where his finger touched them. She fought to keep from puckering and leaving a kiss on that finger.

What was she thinking? It wasn't as if he'd want her to kiss him. He wasn't there to get involved, especially with a grieving widow. Harm was there to relax and enjoy his vacation.

Yet Talia couldn't deny those female parts that had been dormant since her husband's death had come alive when Harm had touched her. How, after only a year, could she be interested in another man? Knowing what it was like to lose the love of her life, she wasn't ready, nor was she certain she could handle the potential heartache again.

She'd been blessed with true love with a kind, gentle man who saw the beauty of the earth and shared it through his photography. Talia wasn't at all sure she could love anyone else. And Harm was completely different. He had harder edges and deeper scars. He wasn't anything like Michael.

But those hard edges called to her, making her want

to smooth them. When he touched her with his callused hands, she could imagine those hands skimming over her naked skin, bringing her body back to life when she thought it wasn't possible.

Talia stepped back. "Thank you," she said. Not sure whether she was thanking him for checking the room or for reminding her that she was still alive, a woman who had a body that required more than just food and sleep.

Harm faced her. "You'll wait here?"

She nodded.

As soon as he turned his back and entered the room, she pressed her palms to her heated cheeks.

Get a grip, woman, she chastised herself. *He's off-limits. You're not ready.*

You loved Michael.

Her last thought brought her back to earth with a thud. She'd loved her husband. Past tense. Michael was gone. But he wasn't forgotten.

Harm was back far too soon. "All clear."

"Good." Talia forced a smile and stepped through the doorway, past Harm and into the bedroom. After a cursory glance to make certain everything was clean and in order, she joined Harm in the hallway and led him to the room he'd sleep in. If it was the one closest to hers, she couldn't let that bother her. It wasn't as though she'd picked it intentionally. The room just happened to be available, with clean sheets and a fully equipped bathroom.

So why didn't you put Big Jake in it?

Talia shrugged off the nagging thought and waited until Harm emerged with the all-clear announcement.

"This will be your room, if you don't want to stay in the cabin."

"I'll grab my gear and move in tonight." He looked around the hallway. "Where do you stay?"

Talia hesitated.

"It's okay," he said with a slight smile. "I'm not going to put the moves on you. I just want to know which way to run if I hear a scream in the night."

"I'm not worried about that," she said. "I sleep with a pistol under my pillow."

Harm's eyebrows rose. "And I bet you know how to use it."

She nodded. "With deadly accuracy. My husband taught me how. I practice enough to be good at it. A lone female in the African bush is a natural target. Even when my husband was alive, I was alone quite often when he took groups on camera safaris."

"I'm glad to hear it. I really am surprised that you haven't moved back to the States by now."

She glanced away. "I don't have anyone back in the States. My parents died in a car crash shortly after I married Michael. It was part of the reason I didn't mind moving to far-flung places. I didn't have a home to fall back on. The world was our playground. I followed him around for the first few years of our marriage. Then we bought this place and built it up to what it is today. I couldn't just walk away when he died."

"I get it. I don't have family back in the States. Just my brothers."

"You don't have family, but you have brothers?" Talia frowned. "I don't understand."

Harm's chest swelled with the pride of belonging. "My teammates are my brothers. I'd do anything for them."

"And they'd do anything for you," Talia added.

"I know families with real brothers who aren't as close," Harm said. "I didn't understand the brotherhood until I became a SEAL. When the going gets tough, I know they have my back, and I have theirs."

In that moment, Talia envied Harm. When Michael was alive, she could rely on him to be there for her. But he'd died, leaving her without a support system. Yes, she had the staff of the resort, but they had their families, and lately, they were skittish and scared of coming to work.

"I'll tell you what," Harm said. "While I'm here, I'll have your back. You need something, I'm your man."

"Thanks," Talia said. "Again, I don't want to rely on anyone. You and your team are only here for a week. Then you'll be gone. Besides, I've dealt with rumblings before."

"What do you mean?"

"A while back, the local witch doctor stirred up my staff and the community. Ever since Michael died, Raila Gakuru has been campaigning against the All Things Wild resort, spreading rumors and innuendos. He started out whispering that the area would have very bad luck—bad juju—as long as the resort was run by a woman."

Harm's jaw tightened. "Nice guy."

"For the past year, when bad things happened, Gakuru attributed it to me. I ignored the claims, hoping the rumors would die down. And, for the most part, they had. Until a few weeks ago, when the poachers showed up stealing baby animals for sale to foreign markets." She smiled. "Thankfully, you and your team were here to thwart their efforts."

"Seems we didn't stop all of it."

Talia crossed the hallway to a linen closet, extracted two bath towels and turned. "My gut tells me this is totally different from the poachers who were stealing animals. I think someone is trying to scare me off."

"The witch doctor?"

"Maybe."

"I could have a talk with him, if you like."

She shook her head. "No. That only gives him more credibility. Ignoring him worked the first time. I'm leaning toward repeating that tactic, since it worked before."

Harm shrugged. "Seems like it didn't work well enough, if he's back at it."

Talia entered the bedroom and laid the towels on the end of the bed, then straightened. "Either way, it's not your problem. It's mine and I'll handle it. You're a guest." She gave him a lopsided smile and moved past him, back out into the hallway. "Enjoy your stay."

Harm threw a snappy salute. "Yes, ma'am."

She grinned. "That's more like it. Now, let me get back down to my kitchen and see if any of your friends want to move to the lodge." She headed toward the stairs only to be brought up short by a hand on her arm.

"If someone is trying to scare you away, you could be in danger."

"I have my gun," she reminded him, her arm tingling where he held it.

"Are you a good enough shot to kill a cobra in your bed?"

She nodded. "I'm that good." At least she hoped she was. But she wouldn't let him know she wasn't quite so sure.

Harm held her gaze for a long moment, his hand tight

on her arm. "What if whoever is playing these games gets more personal?"

Talia lifted her chin, her entire body tingling now. Why couldn't he let go of her and sever the electric current racing along her nerve endings? "What do you mean, more personal?" she asked, her voice breathy. She cleared her throat and continued. "I'd say attacking my clients is already pretty personal."

"What if someone corners you?" He backed her against the wall. "Are you prepared to fight for your life? Do you know how to defend yourself?"

Her body hummed with the electricity burning through her nerves and veins. "I think I can," she whispered, her gaze shifting to Harm's lips. Holy hell, she had the sudden urge to kiss them. What was wrong with her?

Harm shook his head. "There is a difference between thinking and knowing." He bent close. "I can show you some moves."

She ran her tongue over her suddenly dry lips. "I'm sure you can..." Sweet heaven, she was sure he had some sexy moves. And now wasn't the time to demonstrate. Not when she was steps away from the room she'd shared with her dead husband.

"I... I have to go now." Talia pushed her arms between them and raised them sharply, knocking his hands from where they gripped her shoulders. Then she ducked beneath them and made a dash for the stairs.

A warm chuckle followed her down the staircase, making her insides hot and feeling like liquid. She'd do well to stay away from the handsome SEAL. Harm could rock her world. And she wasn't ready for her world to be rocked. Though Talia suspected he was half-way there, and it scared the bejesus out of her.

could not read what was at the top, faded and illegible
Harm hurried, though, he could see the words at
was below the surface at the bottom of the cast
to mention that ad
Finally trusting expert contains

Chapter Three

While Talia was in the kitchen helping his teammates feed their late-night hunger, Harm stepped out of the lodge and hurried to the cabin he'd been assigned, wishing he had a flashlight to shine at the ground. Though he didn't have a deadly fear of snakes, the cobra in Big Jake's bed would shake him as much as it had shaken his friend.

Once he reached the cabin, he flipped on the light switch and made a careful study of the interior, just in case another cobra had found its way in while Harm had been away.

The question burning in his mind was how did a cobra get inside Big Jake's cabin? And why would it end up on the bed?

After a thorough search of his own cabin, Harm studied the bed. The comforter had been neatly fitted over the entire bed with a colorful throw draped at the foot. Someone could have stashed the snake in the throw. Until Big Jake slid beneath the comforter, the snake might not have felt the need to move.

Using a hanger, Harm lifted the throw off the end of the bed. Nothing lay beneath. He shook the fabric. Nothing fell from the folds. Harm released the breath he'd been holding and set his gear bag on the bed. He unearthed the flashlight he kept in an outside pocket of the bag and unzipped the main opening.

A few minutes later, he'd ascertained his bag was free of snakes, bugs or anything else that might keep him up at night. After he zipped the bag, he hefted it onto one shoulder and left the cabin, closing the door behind him.

The screaming howl of jackals filled the night. Harm didn't consider himself very superstitious, but Africa and the savanna lent itself to being creepy.

He hurried back to the lodge and up the stairs to ditch his bag before joining the rest of the gang in the kitchen.

His five teammates were seated at a large wood and steel kitchen table, digging into ham sandwiches and drinking beer.

"Would you care for a sandwich?" Talia asked.

T-Mac held up what was left of his. "You gotta try the ham. I don't know what the chef put on it, but it's damned good." T-Mac glanced at Talia. "Sorry. Didn't mean to curse."

She smiled. "No worries. I've heard worse. I think I've even said worse."

Harm's heart contracted at Talia's sweet smile. Curse words from her mouth wouldn't detract one bit from her beauty. Not wanting to leave the kitchen yet, he tipped his head toward the container of ham slices. "I'd like a sandwich, but I can make it myself."

"No need. Sit with your friends," she ordered. "It won't take me a minute."

"At least let me help." Harm washed his hands in the sink and returned to pull lettuce off a head on the counter.

Talia laid bread on the counter. "Mustard or mayo?"

"Both," Harm replied.

She spread mustard on one piece of bread and layered ham slices over it.

Harm laid the lettuce on the ham, while Talia slathered mayonnaise onto the other slice of bread. She laid it on top of the pile of ham and held it from falling off to the side. "Could you hand me the knife?"

Harm reached around her, his chest brushing against her back.

Talia stiffened, her hand freezing on the sandwich.

"I'll cut that," he said.

She held the sandwich with one hand.

Harm's arm curved around her, and he held the knife over the bread. About that time, he caught a whiff of her perfume and couldn't think past wanting to get closer to identify the scent.

"Are you going to cut it?" she whispered.

Entirely too aware of his hostess, Harm pressed the handle of the knife into her palm. "Maybe it would be best if you did the honors."

She nodded. "Right." Her hand shook as she sliced through the bread, ham and lettuce. With quick efficiency, she laid the two sides of the sandwich on a plate and poured potato chips beside it. "Here you go." Talia shoved the plate toward Harm. "You can help yourself to the drinks in the refrigerator. If you prefer tea or coffee, I'll make some for you."

"Thank you. I'll have a beer, but I can get it myself." He took the plate from her hands, his fingers brushing against hers, sending an electrical current up his arm and all the way down to his groin.

Talia snatched her hands away and tucked them into

the back pockets of her jeans. By the way she was act-ing, she might have had a similar reaction to his touch.

A smile tugged at the corners of his lips as he car-ried the plate to the table. He liked that he unnerved her as much as she did him.

Diesel reached out as if to snag Harm's sandwich.

"Touch it and I'll break your fingers," Harm warned. That sandwich meant more than something to fill his belly. Talia had helped make it. For him.

The other SEAL held up his hands in surrender. "Just kidding with you. I kind of like my fingers the way they are. Need them to shoot."

"You know better, Diesel. No one comes between a SEAL and his sandwich," Pitbull said. As if to prove his point, he stuffed the last bite of his sandwich into his mouth and grinned like a chipmunk with his cheeks full of nuts.

Big Jake stood, carried his plate to the sink and stopped at the refrigerator on the way back. He snagged two longneck bottles of beer and handed one to Harm. "Didn't think you'd want to leave your food unattended with these vultures around."

"You got that right." Harm shot a narrow-eyed glare at the others sitting at the table and then gave a chin lift to Big Jake. "Thanks, man."

"You're welcome." He patted his flat stomach and stretched. "I think I'll be hitting the rack."

"I'll show you the room," Talia offered.

Big Jake grabbed his duffel bag and followed Talia out of the kitchen.

Harm couldn't focus on his food until Talia had left the room. His pulse hadn't slowed since he'd touched her hand.

"I'm going to marry that woman," T-Mac said.

Harm's gaze shot to his teammate, and he nearly crushed his sandwich in his fist. "Why do you say that?"

T-Mac laughed. "Seriously?" He tipped his head toward the door Talia had disappeared through. "She makes a mean ham sandwich, she's beautiful, and most of all, she's not afraid of snakes."

Dr. Vega set her bottle of water on the table, a frown wrinkling her pretty brow. "And you think those are enough reasons to marry someone?"

"It's enough in my book," T-Mac said.

"You barely know the woman," Pitbull said.

"And how long have you known Marly?" T-Mac raised his eyebrows and smiled at Marly. "No offense, Marly."

She shook her head, her sandy blond hair swinging around her chin. "None taken."

Pitbull lifted Marly's hand. "We're different. There was a connection between us from the start."

Marly lifted his knuckles to her lips and pressed a kiss to them. "Well, not from the start, but shortly after. I was more interested in making him sweat in the co-pilot's seat of my airplane."

"And I did," Pitbull said.

"Yes, but you held strong." Marly smiled into his eyes. "Even when you were scared out of your mind."

Pitbull frowned. "I wasn't scared out of my mind."

"Uh-huh." Marly pressed his hand to her cheek. "Even when we landed in the middle of a herd of ze-bras?"

"Crash-landed," he corrected.

"I prefer to call it a controlled emergency landing." Marly lifted her chin. "I was in control the entire time."

"Yes, you were," Pitbull said and leaned across to kiss her lips.

Harm watched their public display of affection and found himself wishing he had that kind of relationship with a woman. His thoughts immediately went to Talia and quickly switched back to T-Mac.

He'd be damned if his teammate stole Talia's heart out from under him. Not that he held her heart. She'd loved her husband.

The tension ebbed from Harm's body. T-Mac didn't have a chance with Talia. For that matter, neither did Harm. It would take a very special man to win her heart after the love she'd shared with her husband. Harm wasn't sure he, T-Mac or anyone else on his team was that special. He loved them like brothers, but none of them were as creative or sensitive to the plight of the animals on the savanna. Yeah, they cared about their existence, but not to the point where they'd choose to give up their lives in the States to run a resort in Kenya.

Talia deserved someone strong, yet sensitive and creative, who would love her so very much he'd be willing to risk it all to keep her safe.

Harm bit into his sandwich, thinking about Talia's husband, Michael. Any man who would bring his woman out to the wilds of Africa without a backup plan had to be too focused on his own dreams and desires to think about the needs of the woman he promised to love, honor and cherish. Somewhere in those marriage vows should have been another promise…to protect. By dying, Michael had left his wife exposed to all the dangers inherent to life in Africa. He should have had a plan in place for her should he be injured or killed.

The man obviously didn't love her enough, or he

would have left instructions on what to do in the event of his death.

Talia was a lone woman in a country where she didn't have family or a support system. And from the sound of it, the local witch doctor was using her femininity against her and turning the community against her as well.

"T-Mac, you need to focus on women within your reach," Pitbull said. "Talia lives in Africa. What kind of relationship could you have if she's half a world away from you ninety-nine percent of the time?"

T-Mac shrugged. "Love will find a way. I mean, look at you and Marly. All she had to do was blow up her airplane and voilà!" He waved his arm to the side. "She's moving to the States."

"Let me get this straight," Harm said. "Are you planning on blowing up the resort? Because if that's your plan, you'll have to go through me to do it."

"Well, no, but my point is, things have a way of working out." T-Mac frowned. "You don't have to take me literally." He stared across the table at Harm, his eyes narrowing. "Wait. What does this mean? Do you have feelings for our pretty hostess?" His eyes widened and a smile spread across his face.

Harm's brow dipped. "I didn't say that. I'm just saying she's got enough problems without worrying about one of her guests destroying her livelihood."

T-Mac's grin broadened. "You like her." He glanced around at the faces of the other four men in the kitchen. "The most confirmed bachelor of all of us has a thing for Talia." He whooped. "Hot damn. This ought to be fun to watch. The harder they are, the bigger the fall."

"I thought it was the bigger they are…" Marly com-

mented. "And what do you mean, Harm's the most confirmed bachelor? I thought you were all pretty happy
being single."

"I thought we were, too," Pitbull said. "Then Diesel
met Reese, I fell for you, and Buck reunited with Dr.
Vega. Apparently, even the most confirmed bachelors
are susceptible to falling in love."

Harm shook his head. "Not me."

T-Mac laughed. "I'd be willing to give up my pursuit
of the beautiful Ms. Talia to see the cynical Harmon
Payne fall to the greater power of love."

Harm frowned at T-Mac. "Yeah, well, it isn't going
to happen. You know as well as I do that we're not cut
out for relationships. Not in our line of work." He cast
a quick glance at Dr. Vega and Marly. "No offense. You
might be the exceptions. Although what you see in Pitbull and Buck, I'll never figure out."

Thankfully, Marly and Dr. Vega laughed.

"It's finding the right woman who can handle the
long separations," Buck said. He took Dr. Vega's hand
and smiled down into her eyes. "It takes a very independent woman who is capable of standing on her two
feet. I think Talia meets that criteria."

"She's a business owner in a challenging industry
and country," Marly pointed out.

"She obviously doesn't need a man to function," Dr.
Vega said.

"And neither do either of you two women," T-Mac
said.

The ladies nodded.

"But we choose to be with our guys." Marly laid a
hand on Pitbull's arm.

"Not because we are dependent on them, but because we want to be with them," Angela Vega said with a smile.

Harm shrugged. "Again, I believe you ladies are the exception."

"Be careful, Harm," Marly warned. "You can't paint all women with the same brush. Many of us are of stronger stock."

Angela studied him with narrowed eyes. "What happened in the past that turned you against relationships? Did you get a Dear John letter that broke your heart? Or am I getting too personal?"

Harm stiffened. The doctor's words hit far too close to home.

"Yeah, Harm, who rocked your love boat?" T-Mac asked.

"That's it." Harm glared at his teammates. "My love life—"

"Or lack thereof," T-Mac inserted.

"—is not up for discussion," Harm continued. "If and when I have a love life, which is highly unlikely, you all will be the last to know."

"I have a feeling we'll know before you," Diesel said. "You'll be in a huge state of denial."

"Like you are now," Buck added.

"Whatever." Harm spun toward the door. "I'm calling it a night." He marched toward the door, ready to get the hell out of the conversation.

"You can run from the truth," T-Mac called out, "but you can't hide."

He was so intent on leaving the kitchen, Harm didn't notice Talia coming from the opposite direction until he plowed right into her.

She bounced off his chest and might have fallen if he hadn't gripped her arms to steady her.

Laughter erupted behind him.

"See? You can run…" T-Mac said.

"I'm sorry. I should have been more careful," Talia said, looking up at him with her clear blue eyes, a smile curving her soft lips.

"No," Harm said, his voice gruff. "My fault. I should have been looking where I was going." His first inclination was to pull her into his arms and crush her to his chest. But the lingering chuckles behind him reminded him of the conversation his teammates had subjected him to.

He wasn't in the market to find love. But if he were, Talia was an amazing woman. Strong, sensitive, loyal and beautiful. Damn. "I can't go there," he muttered and set her to the side.

"What do you mean?" she asked, her eyebrows forming a V over her nose. "Go where?" She looked past him to the crowd in the kitchen. "Did I miss something?"

T-Mac slapped a hand to his knee and gave a bark of laughter. "Boy, did you."

Harm had no desire to be humiliated in front of their hostess. "Good night." He continued toward the staircase and took the steps two at a time, laughter following him all the way up.

He hoped his teammates wouldn't share their discussion with Talia. He didn't want her to get the wrong impression. He wasn't interested in her. Even if her touch sent fire ripping through his veins and her smile made his knees wobble.

TALIA STOOD IN the doorway of the kitchen, her arms still tingling where Harm had gripped them.

His friends were laughing and grinning like fools. Even Marly and Dr. Vega were smiling.

"I feel like I'm missing out on a joke. Someone want to fill me in?"

T-Mac turned to the others. "Should I?"

"No," Buck said.

Diesel shook his head. "Just leave it."

T-Mac frowned. "You take all the fun out of poking the bear."

Talia stared from T-Mac to Diesel and back. "Bear?"

"Harm." T-Mac raised his hands. "That's all I'm going to say."

"Good," Marly said. "Now, if you'll excuse me, I could use some sleep."

"Me, too." T-Mac pushed back from the table and stood. "After I check for snakes." He carried his plate to the sink.

"You're welcome to stay in the lodge, if it will make you feel better." Talia gathered more plates from the table. "I'll happily make up a room for you and anyone else who wants to move in from the cabins."

"I'll risk the cabin." Buck slipped his arm around Dr. Vega. "If you're willing."

Angela smiled up at him. "As long as you go in first and make sure we don't have a cobra waiting in our bed."

Buck shuddered. "I can't imagine what Big Jake must have felt seeing that snake."

"I would have blown the bed and half the room away trying to kill that cobra," T-Mac said.

"Because you're a lousy shot." Diesel draped an arm over T-Mac's shoulder. "Come on, I'll help you clear your cabin so you can sleep without fear of being snake bit. And so you don't feel the need to put holes in the furniture or walls."

"Thanks, dude," T-Mac said with a twisted grin. "You're a real friend."

"I've got your six, man," Diesel said.

The two men left the kitchen, followed by Buck and Angela and Marly and Pitbull.

Though they poked and prodded each other, they seemed to be a tight-knit team, willing to do anything for each other.

Eventually, Talia was alone. She cleaned the dishes, dried them and put them away. She knew she was procrastinating, avoiding going to bed. Many nights she'd stayed up into the wee hours of the morning, finally falling asleep in one of the lounge chairs in the common area rather than going up to the room she'd shared with Michael.

A few months after Michael's death, she'd moved her things out of their room and into a smaller room to open up the master suite to guests. She'd told herself it was because she could charge a premium for the larger room. The reality was she didn't want to sleep in the room she had shared with Michael. Too many memories kept her awake at night.

But tonight, she wasn't awake because of her memories of Michael. She didn't want to walk past the room Harm was sleeping in to get to hers. The thought of only a wall standing between them as they lay in their beds seemed too personal. None of her other guests had that effect on her. Why would Harm?

She wrapped her arms around her middle and walked into the common area. Maybe she'd sleep in one of the lounge chairs. She always woke before her guests. In that case, she could be up and dressed for the day well before they came down for breakfast.

Talia sat on one of the long sofas and tucked her legs beneath her.

Wide-awake and wired, sleep wasn't going to come to her at once. The cobra, the poachers and other happenings were getting too close for comfort. Something had to give. Her chef had suggested she hire the local witch doctor to lift the evil spell from the walls, floors and grounds. She hadn't been keen on doing that.

First of all, Talia didn't believe in magic, but the people who worked for her did. Second, the witch doctor could be the one behind all of the shenanigans. He could be setting her up for extortion.

However, if things didn't improve soon, her staff would stop coming to work. She'd have to run the place by herself. She could do it during the slow season, but not when the lodge and all the cabins were full. Someone had to lead the safaris while another person cooked enough to feed the guests, tended to the cabins and maintained the grounds.

No, she couldn't do all those tasks alone. If her staff quit coming to work, she'd have to take fewer and fewer guests. If she couldn't bring in guests, she couldn't pay the bills. She'd be forced to close.

Then what? After Michael was killed by a rhino, she'd automatically assumed she'd continue on with the operation of the resort. Yes, it had been primarily Michael's dream, but while he was alive, she'd shared that dream. After his death, she'd been in such a funk, she couldn't bring herself to consider other options. Michael was buried in Africa. She hadn't wanted to leave.

This place, the lodge, the resort, the savanna, had

memories seared into every corner, every tree, every-where she looked.

Yet her thoughts continued to drift up the stairs to the man in the room beside hers. Guilt rushed over her like a heat wave. Only a year had passed since Michael's death. She shouldn't be feeling anything for anyone other than her husband. Should she?

Talia reached for one of the throw pillows on the cushion beside her and hugged it to her chest. She missed being able to hug someone. Not just a friendly hug, but one that involved body-to-body contact. A real, warm, lasting hug she never wanted to end.

Not like holding a pillow. A pillow couldn't return the sentiment. Someone with thick, strong arms was needed to make that connection. Someone who could return the pressure and make her feel safe and loved. And not so very…alone.

"Why are you sitting down here all alone?" a deep resonant voice asked.

Talia started and glanced up into the warm, deep brown eyes of the man she'd been thinking about.

He wore jeans and a well-worn T-shirt stretched tautly over the broad expanse of his chest. And he was barefoot.

Talia fought the urge to drool like Pavlov's dog. "I… uh…" She gulped hard to keep from squeaking. "… wasn't sleepy."

"Too much excitement?" He nodded toward the cushion beside her. "Mind if I sit?"

Excitement? Oh, yeah. She pretended a nonchalance she didn't feel. "Please. Sit where you like." Inside she fought a losing battle between self-preservation and desire. If he accepted her offer to take the seat beside her on the sofa, self-preservation didn't stand a chance.

Harm dropped onto the cushion inches away from Talia.

Her breath caught and her pulse kicked into high gear.

Sitting half facing her, Harm leaned his elbows on his knees. "The snake in Big Jake's cabin worrying you?"

"For a start," she admitted. No use telling him she was also worried by her feelings for him. He didn't need to know that little bit of information. If she thought witchcraft and bad juju were making her vulnerable, letting a man know he made her weak in the knees would expose her in a way she was nowhere near ready to handle.

Talia prayed he didn't try anything silly, like kissing her. She wasn't sure she had the power to resist.

Chapter Four

Harm had been in his room, listening for the sounds of Talia's footsteps on the landing outside his door. When he hadn't heard them and the lodge had quieted, he'd left his room and descended the stairs, going in search of the pretty hostess.

He'd been surprised to find her sitting alone on a sofa, a pillow clutched to her chest, her blue eyes staring into the distance.

Talia hadn't noticed his barefoot approach.

If he'd been smart, he'd have crept back up the stairs and gone to bed. But he couldn't leave her there. The tug at his heart refused to let him leave. So he'd taken the seat beside her, with no idea what to say or how to comfort a widow.

"Thank you for adjusting the room assignments for us," he said.

She shrugged. "I didn't have to do much. It's not like I have an entire lodge full of guests." She hugged the pillow tighter. "I can't continue to run this place without a staff or paying guests. If things don't turn around soon, I'll be forced to shut the doors, sell the resort and find employment somewhere else."

"Is it that bad?"

She nodded. "The staff thinks I'm the one causing the problems. Because I'm a woman trying to run the place, I'm creating bad juju."

Harm's jaw tightened. "That's a bunch of bull."

"You know that and I know that, but my staff is very superstitious. I wouldn't be surprised if someone else quits tomorrow when he or she finds out there was a cobra in one of the cabins." Talia drew in a deep breath and let it out on a sigh. "It just makes more work for me. But if I don't have guests, I won't need the staff and I won't have a reason to stay at the resort."

"Have you considered selling?"

Her lips pressed into a thin line. "Even when Michael was alive, I was in charge of the day-to-day running of the lodge and cabins. Michael took care of expeditions, entertainment and nature hikes."

She stared around the room at the photos on the walls of the animals in their natural habitat. "He always came back with the most incredible photographs." Her gaze stopped on Harm. "I took care of everything else. But the lodge and the cabins weren't why the guests came. They came to see what Michael saw. He sold his photographs worldwide. He was well-known for how beautifully he captured the animals and the savanna. The guests came from all over the world to see what had inspired him."

Harm snorted softly. "You didn't answer my question."

Her cheeks blossomed with color, and she glanced down at the pillow. "I'm sorry. What was the question?"

"Have you considered selling the resort?"

She looked away, gnawing at her bottom lip. "I guess most women who'd lost their husbands would have sold something like the resort by now." She glanced back at

Harm. "I didn't because I couldn't imagine anything else. What would I do?"

"You could go back to the States where it's less dangerous, for one." He leaned toward her. "You could start over and choose any career you want."

"But I love running the lodge and catering to the guests."

"Even now that your husband is gone?"

Talia's lips twisted. "I don't know."

"You don't know, or you're afraid to say the truth because you'll feel guilty for wanting something different from what Michael had in mind?"

She tossed the pillow aside and leaped to her feet. "It doesn't matter what I want. I have the resort. I'm doing the best I can. I just need to figure out who's behind the threats to me and my guests and take care of it. Life will go on as usual."

"Will it?" Harm stood and reached for her. He knew it was a mistake as soon as his fingers curled around her arms. "Michael's gone, you can't continue to live his dream. What about you, Talia? What do you want?"

She stared up into his eyes, her voice soft...breathy as she said, "I don't know." Her bottom lip trembled and her gaze shifted from his eyes to his mouth.

That moment was Harm's undoing. Talia appeared so vulnerable and confused. He wanted to wipe the concern from her face, to make her lips curl up in a smile. To kiss her.

Before he could think through his next move, he lowered his head and breathed against her lips. "What do you want?"

Her fingers curled into his shirt and she whispered, "You."

Harm claimed her mouth, his lips crashing down

on hers. He pushed his tongue past her teeth to sweep the length of hers, caressing, thrusting and demanding a response.

Instead of pushing him away like she should have, Talia raised her arms to lace them behind Harm's neck and pulled him closer.

Harm released her arms and ran his hands down her back, cupped her bottom and pressed her hips to his, his groin tight, swelling with a fresh rush of blood and heat. This was where he'd wanted to be all evening. Holding this woman in his arms, kissing her like there was no tomorrow.

She clung to him, her tongue working against his, her fingernails digging into the back of his neck, one leg curling around the back of his thigh.

Holy hell, she was hot, sexy and everything Harm had sworn off when he'd received that Dear John letter so long ago. But here he was kissing Talia, completely captivated by the woman and unable to release her.

When the need for oxygen forced him to come up for air, he lifted his head, dragged in a breath and let it go slowly, trying to calm his racing heart.

Talia pressed her forehead to his chest, her hands dropping to curl into his shirt. "What…just happened?"

He chuckled. "I don't know, but I want to do it again."

She shook her head. "No."

Harm's heart stuttered and then tripped all over itself to get going again. "No?" He touched his finger to her chin and tilted her face upward, making her look into his eyes. "Why not?"

"It's not right," she said, her voice catching.

"Why?"

"Michael…" she said, a tear slipping from the corner of her eye.

"Is dead," Harm said softly, not wanting to be insensitive to her loss. "But you aren't."

"Still," she said, her hands flattening against his chest. "I loved him."

"As sensitive a guy as you make him out to be, wouldn't he have wanted you to go on living?"

"I have." She pulled her chin free of his finger and looked away. "Just not like this. He—I wouldn't want you to do it again."

"No?" Harm's arms slipped around her. God, he loved the way she felt against him. "Are you sure you don't want me to kiss you again?"

She tipped her head back and stared into his eyes. "Please," she said, her lips still swollen from making love to his.

He lowered his head until his mouth was only a breath away from hers. "I won't kiss you if you don't want me to. But it seems there were two people involved in that last kiss."

Her breath caught and her body stiffened in his arms. Then she rose upward on her toes, closing the distance between their lips. Talia wrapped her arms around his neck and dragged him even closer until their bodies melded together, almost becoming one. The only way they could be closer would be if they were naked.

Harm clutched her body to him and deepened the kiss, everything else around him fading into a hazy background until the sound of a throat clearing jolted him out of the lusty haze.

Harm lifted his head and stared across the floor at the intruder.

Big Jake stood in his jeans and nothing else. "Sorry, I was just on my way to the kitchen for a glass of water." He hurried by. "Don't mind me. I saw nothing."

Talia pushed away from Harm and smoothed her hands over her shirt and jeans, her cheeks flaming. "I'd better go to my room." She spun and ran for the stairs before Harm could stop her.

Moments later, Big Jake emerged from the kitchen, his lips quirking on the corners. "Confirmed bachelor, eh? Isn't that what you always claimed to be?" He snorted and passed Harm, carrying a glass of milk and a couple of the cookies Talia had offered the group after dinner. "Yeah, right."

"Shut up," Harm grumbled.

"The harder they are, the bigger the fall," Big Jake called out over his shoulder as he ascended the staircase.

As much as Harm wanted to disagree with Big Jake and the rest of his team, he was afraid there was some truth in what they predicted.

TALIA SHOWERED AND combed the tangles out of her hair before slipping into a faded T-shirt and a pair of jersey shorts, her normal sleeping attire. After Michael died, she'd given away all her sexy nightgowns and started wearing old T-shirts and shorts to sleep in. If anyone needed anything, Michael wasn't there to run interference while she dressed. She had to be somewhat presentable at a moment's notice.

But tonight felt different. The soft fabric of the well-worn T-shirt rubbed against her beaded nipples, stimulating them even more. And it all had to do with that kiss.

She crawled into her bed and pulled the comforter

up around her, hugging the spare pillow in her arms. It wasn't another person, but the down-filled pillow was all she had. And all she needed, she told herself. Even as the thought crossed her mind, she knew it for what it was…a lie. She needed to be in someone's arms. Otherwise, why had she reacted so strongly to Harm's kiss?

Was a year long enough to mourn the loss of someone you loved? Was it long enough to forget what they'd had together? She shook her head, a single tear sliding down her cheek to plop onto the pillowcase. She'd never forget what she and Michael had. But was that all the love she was allowed to have in one lifetime?

SHE MUST HAVE fallen asleep, because the next thing she knew, someone was knocking on her door. "Mrs. Talia, Mrs. Talia, it's time to wake up."

Talia jerked to a sitting position and stared down at the alarm clock on her nightstand. She'd slept an hour past normal, and she didn't know whether or not she'd have a enough staff to get breakfast for her guests. "I'm up, Nahla. I'll be down in two minutes."

Talia slipped into khaki slacks, a white blouse and her leather hiking boots. Then she pulled her hair back into a sleek ponytail. Makeup-free, she hurried down the stairs to the kitchen.

Nahla was there, helping the rotund chef, Jamba, prepare breakfast and set the table.

"Where's Mshindi and Kamathi? They should be here by now," Talia said.

"Kamathi is out gathering eggs for the breakfast." Jamba shot a glance toward Nahla. "Mshindi isn't coming in."

Nahla reached to place plates from the dishwasher into the cabinet, refusing to meet Talia's gaze.

"Why isn't Mshindi coming in?" Talia asked, knowing the answer but needing to hear it anyway.

"She heard there was a cobra in a guest's room last night. That plus everything else going on has her too scared to come back to work," Jamba said. He set the skillet on the gas stove. "Gakuru performed his magic last night. He says very bad things will happen at the resort as long as a woman runs it."

Talia sighed. "Jamba, do you believe that?"

Jamba shook his head. "No, ma'am. You ran All Things Wild even when Mr. Michael was among the living."

Talia nodded and turned to Nahla. "And you, Nahla? Do you believe the witch doctor Gakuru?"

Nahla fumbled with a glass she'd retrieved from the dishwasher and it fell, shattering against the tile floor.

That was all the answer Talia needed. "Don't move. I'll clean up the glass." She grabbed a broom and a dustpan and scooped up the shards of glass. "Are you that afraid of me?"

Nahla's eyes filled with tears. "No, ma'am. Not afraid of you. But afraid of everything that's happened. I wonder when one of us will be hurt by the bad juju."

Talia couldn't begin to argue with the woman. A cobra in a guest's cabin could just as easily attack a staff member as a guest. Talia took the woman's hands and stared into her eyes. "Do you want to go home?"

The young Kenyan met her gaze, her bottom lip trembling. "Yes, ma'am."

"Then go. I'll take care of the dishes and setting the table."

"But you have to lead the safari today." Nahla shook her head. "I'll stay until you find someone else to fill my position."

Talia shook her head. "At this rate, no one else will come to work for me," Talia said. "Gakuru has the entire village afraid to set foot on the resort."

"That he does, Mrs. Talia," Jamba said.

"It's been a year since Michael died. Why is he so set on scaring me off now?"

Jamba bowed his head, shaking it from side to side. "I don't know, Mrs. Talia. I don't know."

A muffled scream sounded from outside the kitchen door.

Talia started, her gaze swinging toward the sound. "What the he—"

Kamathi burst through the door, her eyes wide in her dark face. "The chickens…" She doubled over, dragging in breaths to fill her lungs. When she could speak again, she faced Talia. "The chickens are all dead."

Talia's heart plummeted into her belly. "What do you mean?" she asked as she hurried toward the door.

"They're dead." Kamathi crossed her hands over her breasts. "The witch doctor was right. This place has very bad juju."

Anger filled Talia. She wanted to tell the woman there was no such thing as bad juju. There were bad people who did bad deeds, but bad juju? No. Instead, she hurried out to the chicken coop to investigate for herself.

What she found made her stomach turn. Inside the fenced-in chicken yard and coop, every last chicken lay dead, ripped to shreds, a bloody mess. As much as she'd like to blame a human for the carnage, a person wouldn't have done this.

"Hey." A large, warm hand descended on her shoulder. "My team will help clean up the mess."

Talia turned and stepped into Harm's arms. Even though she wanted to appear strong, at that moment, all she wanted was to lean on someone.

Harm enveloped her in a hug, pulling her close against his body. "Even from here, I can see paw prints in the dust."

"You can?" Though she'd rather bury her face against his chest, she pushed back enough to stare down at the dusty ground. "Where?"

The navy SEAL squatted on his haunches and pointed at an indention in the loose dust. "Here," he said. "You can see the outlines of the pads of the animal's paws. By the size and shape, I'd guess it was some kind of dog." He motioned toward the tip of the print. "You see the sharper points of the toenails?"

Talia bent closer, studying the imprints. "Couldn't it have been a cat?"

"I don't think so." He stared around at the other prints now clearly visible in the dust. "All of the prints have the toenails. Cats have retractable claws. Some of the prints would have been without toenails."

Talia straightened and walked back to the gate. "But how would a dog have gotten into the chicken yard? The latch on the gate isn't damaged." She glanced around at the fencing. "The fence is intact, and I don't see any holes or damage."

Harm joined her at the gate. "Could someone have left it open?"

Talia shook her head. "I fed the chickens last night and made sure I closed the gate securely. We've had other varmints get into the pen before. My husb—Michael—reinforced the pen and the gate." She shook her head. "I know I closed it tight last night."

"Could someone have come back after you?"

Talia shrugged. "I suppose anyone could have. But why?" She looked up into Harm's eyes. "Why would anyone leave the gate open? These poor chickens…"

Harm slipped an arm around her waist and pulled her against his side. "Whatever killed them didn't stay around to eat. It just killed."

"What a waste." Talia leaned against him, glad to have his strong, solid support. Yeah, she could get through this on her own. Hell, she'd been through worse. But it was nice to have someone there. "I'll have to buy eggs locally until I can get more chickens. Hopefully, I have enough eggs on hand in the kitchen for breakfast."

"Me and the guys are easy. We could eat ham sandwiches again and be perfectly happy." He smiled down at her. "At least it wouldn't be MREs."

Talia laughed, though the effort caught in her throat and lodged there with something that felt like a sob. "Why is this happening to me? You'd think someone was trying to scare me off."

"Given the circumstances, you could be right."

She straightened, her jaw firming. "Well, it's not going to happen. I'm not giving up All Things Wild."

"What we need is to find out who's behind all of the troubles."

"We?" Talia shook her head. "You and your team are guests. You shouldn't have to fight my battles for me. You did it once already when you were here a couple weeks ago. Those poachers could have gotten away with those baby elephants if you hadn't stopped them in their tracks."

"Could the same poachers be back? We stopped their buyers, but that doesn't mean they haven't found new buyers for the animals."

Talia frowned. "It's a constant struggle to protect the animals of the savanna. With so much money to be made in illicit trade of live and dead animals, there aren't enough enforcement personnel to go around. We do what we can by reporting incidents when they happen, but it always seems our efforts are just a drop in the bucket."

"You're doing the right thing. But maybe someone is tired of your doing the right thing."

"Yeah?" Talia sighed. "But who?"

Chapter Five

While Talia worked to calm Kamathi and help the chef prepare breakfast, Harm and his team slipped out to the chicken pen and cleaned up the carnage left by whatever animal had entered. They found one chicken hiding in a tree outside the pen, the lone escapee from the terror of the night before.

Big Jake managed to capture the chicken, much to the delight and ribbing of the rest of the team.

"You can't ignore the irony of Big Jake catching the chicken," Harm said after they'd secured it in the cleaned chicken pen and were on the way back to the lodge.

"How's that?" T-Mac asked.

"They both escaped certain death by a killer animal. It only seems fitting Big Jake caught the chicken and returned it to the relative safety of the pen."

"Didn't look like the pen kept the other chickens safe," Pitbull said, his mouth set in a grim line.

"What about Mr. Wiggins?" T-Mac asked. "Could he have gotten hungry and torn open the gate?"

"Mr. Wiggins was in my room all night," Talia said. "It wasn't the leopard."

"I get the feeling someone opened that gate and left

it open on purpose," Diesel said. "I didn't see any sign of forced entry by human or animal."

Harm felt the same. "Question is…who?"

The men continued on in silence. Not one of them had the answer to that question.

In the lodge, the smell of hash brown potatoes, bacon and fried ham slices filled the air.

Harm's belly rumbled despite the unsavory task they'd just performed.

One by one, the men filed into the downstairs bathroom to wash up before entering the dining room, where Talia and her staff had set up a sumptuous buffet of breakfast items.

Talia set a steaming platter of scrambled eggs on the sideboard and turned to face them. "I thought I was going to have to send out a search party for you."

"We had something to do before we could sit down for breakfast," Big Jake said and dusted a feather off his T-shirt.

Talia frowned. "You didn't go clean up my chicken pen, did you?"

The men held up their hands, all innocence.

"Who, us?" Harm shook his head. "I smell bacon." He clapped his hands together and sidestepped Talia to reach for a plate. "Don't let the food get cold."

"Don't take all the bacon," Buck said.

Talia crossed her arms over her chest, her lips pressed into a thin line. "You shouldn't have done it. You're guests, not staff."

"Done what?" Diesel plucked a crisp piece of bacon off his plate and stuffed it into his mouth.

"By the way," Big Jake leaned close to her and whispered, "you had one survivor. She's safely locked in the pen."

"We nicknamed her Lucky," Pitbull said. "You should have seen Big Jake chasing her around before he caught her."

"We're thinking of changing his call sign to the Chicken Whisperer," Buck said.

Big Jake swung at Buck, clipping his shoulder with a not-so-light tap of his fist. "No, you won't, if you want to live to see thirty."

"I'd risk it," Pitbull said. "Chicken Whisperer has a ring to it."

"Ah, leave the man alone." Marly handed a plate to Pitbull. "Or they'll be calling you Sky Baby or Chicken Little because you always think we're falling out of the sky when we fly."

"Chicken Little thought the sky was falling *on* him, not that he was falling out of the sky." Pitbull leaned over and kissed her on the temple. "Get your fairy tales straight, fly girl."

"My mother didn't read those to me when I was a little girl. I grew up studying books about airplanes." Marly grinned. "My father's influence."

"Any idea what killed the chickens?" Angela Vega asked as she set a plate full of food on the table.

Buck set down his plate and held her chair for her. "Harm seems to think it was canine. Who knew he was a born-again animal tracker?"

"I wonder if it was one of those jackals we heard howling last night." Harm shot a glance at Talia. "Have you ever had trouble with jackals entering your resort area?"

"No," Talia said. "We have had the occasional lion

pride wander through, and sometimes the elephants get close. But the jackals always stayed out of sight."

"Did you ask your staff if anyone went into the chicken pen after you last night?"

"I did, but those who are here claim they didn't." She fussed with the items on the buffet, straightening the serving spoons and covering what was left.

Harm placed his plate full of breakfast goodness on the table and waited for Talia to fill her plate and join them.

When she hesitated, he asked, "Aren't you going to have breakfast with us?"

Talia gave him a half smile. "I'm not sure I can eat after seeing all those dead chickens."

"They're all taken care of," Harm said. "We'd like for you to sit with us."

"Yeah, beats looking at Harm's ugly face," Big Jake said.

The other men chuckled.

"Don't wait on me. I'll grab something before we leave for the safari I have scheduled."

"We insist you eat, too," Harm said.

"Yeah, sit," Angela said with a smile. "A safari is an all-day affair, and you'll need your strength to keep up with this motley crew."

Buck gave Angela a teasing frown. "Hey, who are you calling motley?"

"You." She touched his hand. "But I mean it in the nicest way."

"Yeah, yeah." Buck's frown curved upward into a grin. He lifted the doctor's hand and kissed her knuckles. "You're going with this motley crew, aren't you?"

"No, actually, I think I'll spend some time in the village. Nahla said there are a few people who need medical attention and don't have the time or wherewithal to get to the nearest clinic."

Buck's frown was back. "I don't know that I like you running around without an escort. I'll go with you."

"I wouldn't hear of you skipping your safari to help me."

"And I'm not going to argue about it. If you go to the village, I go to the village." Buck squeezed her hand.

Angela smiled. "You're a stubborn man, Graham Buckner."

"Damn right I am." He grinned and dug into his food.

"Anyone else backing out?" Talia asked. "I need a head count to know how many sandwiches to pack."

"The rest of us will be going," Pitbull said. "Including Marly. She'll have to fly low today in the back of the safari wagon."

Marly laid down her fork and set her napkin beside her plate. "I'm looking forward to it. I usually only see the herds from over five hundred feet in the air."

"Unless you're crashing into the middle of one," Pitbull reminded her.

Marly gave him the stink eye. "I didn't crash. It was a controlled landing."

"Right. Whatever you say." Pitbull stuffed another piece of bacon in his mouth and grinned while chewing.

Marly rolled her eyes and pushed back from the table. "If you'll excuse me, I'd like to grab a hat and sunscreen before we leave."

"I'm coming." Pitbull jammed another bite of toast into his mouth, grabbed another piece of bacon and stood.

Marly gathered their two plates.

"Don't worry about your dishes," Talia said. "I'll take care of them."

"And lead a safari, and clean the rooms?" Harm stood. "You're amazing, but you can't do it all."

When Talia started to stand, Harm put a hand on her shoulder. "Sit. I'll gather the dishes and get them to the sink. You need to eat. You'll be of no use on the safari if you're passing out from lack of fuel."

"Pushy a little?" she said with a smile and remained seated while Harm, Marly and Pitbull collected the empty plates.

"Touch mine and I'll stab you with my fork," Big Jake said.

Harm chuckled. "I'll let you carry your own plate into the kitchen." He held up his hands. "When you're done, of course."

"Damn right." Big Jake's fierce frown didn't fool anybody. The man liked his food. But it was a standing joke that no one hurried him through his meal. As many meals as he'd missed when on missions, the man deserved to eat at his own pace when on vacation.

Harm, Marly and Pitbull carried the plates to the sink.

"I'll help wash up. You two go get ready for the day," Harm said.

"Going all domestic on us?" Pitbull queried. "Could you iron my boxer shorts for me?"

"Get out or I'll make you dry." Harm popped Pitbull with a dish towel. "Besides, you don't wear boxer shorts."

"Just testing you." Pitbull backed away. "I'm going."

Jamba was busy making ham sandwiches for the day trip. Nahla was nowhere to be seen.

Harm filled the sink with warm soapy water and went to work washing the dishes.

"I have an electric dishwasher, you know," Talia said behind him.

The warmth of her presence filled Harm in a way he'd never experienced before. He liked it when she was around.

"Let me take over. You need to get ready for the safari." Talia slid up next to him and tried to take the washcloth from him.

He held it out of her reach. "If you want to help, you can dry."

She frowned. "You shouldn't be doing my work."

"A few dishes won't kill me," he said. "I might get dishpan hands, but it's a chance I'll take."

Talia laughed and grabbed a dish towel. "You're a very stubborn man."

"I thought that was Pitbull."

"I'm sure you and each of your teammates have a stubborn streak a mile wide, or you wouldn't have made it through BUD/S."

He glanced at her, amazed. "Look at the safari girl knowing about SEAL training."

Her cheeks filled with color. "We have satellite internet here. We're not complete troglodytes." With a shrug she continued, "I have to admit, I did some web surfing after you left the first time."

His heart swelled. "Curious about what we do?"

She took a clean plate from him and ran the cloth over it until it was dry. "I am. I also watched an old DVD of *GI Jane*. Every one of you went through hell to earn the privilege of being a SEAL."

Harm didn't say anything, just dipped his head in

acknowledgment and kept washing the plates, cups and flatware until every last item was clean. His time at BUD/S was something he could never forget, nor would he want to. Yes, he'd earned the right to call himself a SEAL, through blood, sweat and more blood and sweat.

Talia kept up with his washing, putting the dishes away as she dried them. When they were finished, the kitchen was clean and their lunches were packed into a sturdy wicker basket.

Harm carried the basket out to the truck wagon. Talia settled it on the floor of the cab on the passenger side. The truck had been rigged with four rows of two seats each in the back and a canvas awning.

The SEAL team gathered around the truck, joking and shoving each other. Harm recognized the raw energy they exuded. It was like this when they were preparing to leave for deployment. On edge and yet keeping it light.

"Are you ready?" Talia asked.

"Yes, ma'am!" the men replied in unison.

Angela and Marly laughed. "We're ready, too," Angela said.

They climbed into the truck. Harm was quick to get in first and took one of the seats closest to the cab. Big Jake took the other.

Marly and Pitbull were next. Diesel and T-Mac claimed the back seats.

Harm knew they'd be packing weapons. He had his nine-millimeter pistol strapped to his calf and his Ka-Bar knife in its scabbard, clipped to his belt.

Pitbull carried a gear bag with his rifle disassembled inside. He could assemble the rifle in five seconds and be ready to take on any threat, be it animal or human.

The last time they'd tried to go on safari with Talia, they'd had to fight off a group of poachers attempting to steal baby elephants. They would be even more prepared this time.

Once they were all in place, Talia spoke with the driver and the truck pulled out of the resort compound and onto a gravel road leading into the grasslands.

They bumped along for the first thirty minutes without stirring up more than a few birds. The air had warmed with the rising sun, promising to be a blistering day on the savanna.

Harm was beginning to think it would have been nicer to sit in the cabana with a fan twirling overhead, drinking chilled beer.

The warmth and the steady rocking motion of the truck lurching over potholes lulled Harm into a sleepy state.

He'd just closed his eyes when the truck jerked to a halt.

"What the hell?" Talia said from the front seat. She lifted her binoculars to her eyes and studied the path ahead.

Harm squinted, wishing he had the binoculars to see what Talia was seeing. From where he was, all he could make out was a flock of birds circling over an area of the grassland.

"Go," Talia urged the driver as she lowered her binoculars to her lap.

The driver hesitated. "Are you sure, Mrs. Talia? What if someone is there? Someone with guns?"

"If there are buzzards, there aren't people," she assured him. "We have to know what they're circling."

"Yes, ma'am," the driver said and pulled ahead, picking up speed as they headed for the circling birds.

"What's going on?" Big Jake asked.

"My bet is those birds are circling something dead," Harm said.

Marly and Pitbull leaned over the backs of Big Jake's and Harm's seats.

"Those are some big vultures," Marly said.

"I bet they could carry off a small child," Pitbull agreed.

"Let's hope that's not what they're hovering over."

"It wouldn't be something as small as a child," Talia said. "That many vultures means there's a big meal down below. They're all waiting their turn. Pecking order is strictly enforced."

Harm admired how calm and in control Talia remained in the face of potential danger. Yeah, his team had it right. She was the kind of woman who could handle the rigors of being the wife of a navy SEAL. She could hold her own. Though she'd lost her husband, she continued to operate a posh resort and manage all the staff. Harm could easily fall for a woman with so much grit.

TALIA'S HEART THUNDERED as they neared the spot. The vultures on the ground lifted on long, awkward wing-spans and rose into the air. They didn't go far—just far enough to be out of range of the approaching vehicle.

The driver pulled to a halt in front of a large carcass.

"It's a black rhino," Talia said, her jaw tightening. "Damned poachers."

The group dismounted from the truck.

"Based on the smell, I'd say the animal has been dead for at least a day in the heat," Angela said.

Talia nodded toward the dead rhino's head. "They cut off the two horns. Together, they're worth between forty and sixty thousand dollars."

"That much?" Harm asked. "No wonder the poachers are willing to risk their lives doing that."

"Oh, they don't get that much," Talia said. "They might only receive a fraction of that amount, but it's still a heck of a lot more than what they'd earn herding cattle for someone else. The wildlife is being devastated. When these animals are gone…they're gone forever." She took out a satellite phone and punched buttons.

"Who are you calling?" T-Mac asked.

"The local park rangers. They'll want to investigate and see if they can determine who is responsible and where they've gone."

"Will they capture the men?" Diesel asked.

Talia shrugged. "Sometimes they get lucky. But even if they do capture this bunch, there will be others to take their place. The money is too good, and the middlemen and kingpins are never captured. They'll always be around to lure more men into doing their dirty work."

The dispatcher answered and took down the GPS coordinates Talia supplied, along with the time and date of the discovery. He promised to send out a ranger immediately.

Talia reached into the truck, pulled out a small camera and snapped pictures of the dead animal. Sometimes the rangers took a long time to get out to the carcass. By then, the scavengers could have picked the bones clean, and much of the evidence would have been lost.

She took several pictures before pocketing the camera and turning to her tour group. "I'm sorry you had to see this, but I can't just drive by."

"We wouldn't expect you to," Harm said.

"Now that I've reported to the rangers, we can be on our way. I promised to show you some of the wildlife. Preferably the living, not the deceased. If you'll climb aboard, we can be on our way."

After they loaded into the truck, the driver continued along the dirt road across the savanna, heading deeper into the national preserve.

Soon, they came across a herd of zebras and cape buffalo.

Talia slowed for them to take pictures while she explained how zebras' stripes were like fingerprints, individual and unique to each animal. She also explained how their stripes made it harder for their predators to single one out, confusing them enough to allow them to escape. But as always, the small, weak and infirm were usually the ones to be preyed upon.

An hour later, they stopped beneath the broad branches of an acacia tree, where they were shaded from the harsh noon sun.

Talia pulled out the basket at her feet and distributed the sandwiches to the hungry guests. "You can help yourself to the bottles of water that have been keeping cool in the ice chest on the side of the truck."

Harm grabbed two bottles of water and sat on the ground beside Talia, handing her one. "How are you holding up?"

She tilted her head slightly. "I'm fine. It's the animals of Africa that have it bad. How do we get through to the poachers? They need to understand how bad it is."

"The demand has to be stemmed before the supply dries up," Harm said.

Talia nodded. "In the meantime, we lose thousands of rhinos and elephants to greed each year. At that rate, it won't take long before the animals are extinct."

"You have a big heart, Talia," Harm said.

Talia laughed. "I don't know about that. But I care what happens." She glanced around at the others. "I only hope to share what I know with my guests. It's up to them to take that information back to where they come from and help on a more global scale." Talia could have left when her husband died, but she'd stayed. Partially because this had become all she knew. She had no family back in the States. No one needed her.

But the animals did. Someone had to help them, or they would become extinct.

She glanced toward Harm. "You do understand how important it is to save these animals, don't you?" She waited, praying he was the man she thought he was.

HARM NODDED. "I GET IT. I'll help spread the word. I'll even write my congressman when I get back to civilization and send my dollars to the conservation groups. I'd hate to see these animals wiped off the face of the earth, or be confined to zoos as their only safe haven." Harm finished his sandwich, downed the bottle of water and pushed to his feet. He held out a hand to Talia.

She placed her palm in his and he pulled her up, the spark of electricity tearing through him all over again. The woman made him want so much more than a touch of her hand.

She didn't pull free immediately. Instead, she stared

up into his eyes, her own wide, her tongue swiping across her lips.

"Thank you for taking care of the chicken yard this morning."

"It wasn't all me," Harm said. "The guys were more than willing."

"It saved me a lot of time." She tugged at her hand.

Harm released it, albeit reluctantly. He liked holding her hand, but more than that, he wanted to kiss her.

Talia turned to the men. "Thank you for helping with the chickens this morning."

"We should thank you," T-Mac said. "It gave us a new nickname for the Chicken Whisperer."

Big Jake shook his head. "I'll never live that one down."

"Don't worry." Buck clapped a hand to the big guy's back. "We won't let you."

They climbed into the truck and continued on their trek to find more of the wildlife indigenous to the African savanna.

Not long after lunch, they came across a pride of lions lounging in the shade of a baobab tree.

Again, Talia had the driver slow the truck so the guests could take pictures of the animals without getting out. A few minutes after leaving the pride, they came across a group of cheetahs walking along the dirt road coming toward them.

The driver stopped, but the cheetahs kept coming.

Talia laughed. "Don't be alarmed. This group of cheetahs is notorious for visiting the visitors."

Moments later, two cheetahs leaped onto the canvas roof. A third, smaller one jumped onto the seat beside Harm.

Harm moved away as far as possible, hoping the animal was just being curious. "He's not going to rip off my face, is he?"

"I don't think so. *She's* never tried to before," Talia said softly. "Just be very still. Don't make her feel at all threatened."

Harm snorted quietly. "Her...threatened? I think you have that backward."

"Hold that pose, Harm." Big Jake held up his cell phone, snapping picture after picture.

"It's not like I'm going anywhere," Harm said.

The cheetah sniffed at Harm's hand and then his face.

"No, I'm not your lunch," Harm said in a whisper.

The two cats on top of the canvas roof leaped to the ground. The female in the seat with Harm turned and studied the other two.

"That's right. Follow the leaders," Harm said.

In one fluid movement, the cheetah leaped to the ground.

Harm released the breath he hadn't realized he'd been holding.

Big Jake pounded his back. "Wow. That was amazing. I got some great shots. You're gonna love them."

"I'm going to love the fact that the cat didn't rip my face off." Harm scrubbed his hands across his cheeks as if testing to be sure they were still there and intact.

"Well, that was a little tense." Talia laughed nervously. "I can't say that I've ever had big cats jump into the vehicle with my guests."

"Harm loves being a first for things," T-Mac said. "Don't you, Harm?"

"Yeah. I love it," he said, his tone flat.

Talia winked. "You're a good sport, Harm." She

looked to the others. "If you're ready, we should be heading back to the resort. The sun will be setting soon," Talia said. "And I have an appointment in the village tonight."

She didn't give him a chance to ask about her appointment. But he would ask before she left the resort that evening. With the way things had been going lately, she'd need an armed escort to see her there and back. He planned on being that escort. What kind of meeting could she have in the village? From what he knew, the village wasn't all that big.

No matter. He'd find out what it was all about and how big the village was. Plus, it would give him an opportunity to question the locals about the poachers. More than likely, one of them knew who they were. Perhaps the poachers would even be at the meeting.

Chapter Six

The sun sat like a blob melting into the horizon as the truck pulled into the resort compound.

Talia was the first person out. She had a lot to do before she could bug out to attend the meeting in the nearby community. She couldn't miss the meeting, as she'd been the one to start the community watch group Women Against Poaching.

In the year since Michael's death, the poaching problem had doubled in size and in disastrous effects. One of the local teenage girls had started working for Talia part-time while she attended the school missionaries had established nearby. Eriku had been a quick study with the tasks Talia had asked her to do. She was good with numbers and even smarter at coming up with graphics for advertising the resort on social media.

As part of her duties, Talia had asked Eriku to research the plight of the African animals. That's when Eriku learned of the impact of poaching on the different species. She'd been so appalled, she'd come to Talia with her concerns. Not content to sit back and do nothing, Eriku had let Talia know she wanted to help.

Together, they'd formed the Women Against Poaching group and had meetings once a month to discuss the progress of educating members of the community. The women had gone out with the intention of helping others, including suspected poachers, to let them know they were being used by the kingpins and middlemen and that once the animals were gone, they'd have nothing. Tourism was the lifeblood of the region. No animals, no tourists, no money. Their people would starve.

That night would be the first meeting after the women had promised to talk to community members and leaders.

It wasn't lost on Talia that the troubles she'd been experiencing had—suspiciously—begun shortly after the formation of the Women Against Poaching group. The poachers had probably gotten word she was in charge. Though she really wasn't. Yes, she'd helped with the education part of it, but Eriku had taken the lead with her friends and neighbors. Her passion and determination were hard to beat.

Talia needed to be there tonight to see how the campaign was going. Women of Kenya had taken more and more leadership roles in the local and national government. Yet, what the group was attempting could have negative repercussions on the females of their society. The men might view them as taking away their only source of income.

Talia gave the SEAL team a tight smile. "I'll see you at dinner. Remember, we're dressing formally tonight, and we could have music and dancing if you'd like."

Harm caught her arm. "Since you have a meeting, let us help you get tasks accomplished."

"Please, that's not how the resort is supposed to work."

"And we don't know how to relax. So, give us something to do or we're likely to cause trouble from boredom." He winked.

"Speak for yourself, Harm," T-Mac said. "I could use a nap before dinner."

Pitbull elbowed the man in the gut. "You can sleep when you're dead." He turned his attention to Talia. "What can we help with?"

"Yes," Marly said. "What can we help with?"

Talia stopped fighting the inevitable and grinned. "Thank you all so very much. I could use a little help. If someone would check out the music and line up what you'd like to listen to, that would be great."

T-Mac held up a hand. "I can do that."

Talia nodded and went on. "Could someone check on the chicken?"

"That would be Big Jake," Diesel said. "On account of he's the Chicken Whisperer."

"Shut up." Big Jake glared at Diesel but smiled at Talia. "I'll feed the chicken."

"I could use a little help setting the table."

Buck and Angela raised their hands. "We can do that."

"I can ice glasses or put the beer on ice," Harm offered.

Talia smiled. "Thank you all. But first, I know we all need showers. I'll meet you in the lodge in thirty minutes. We can take it from there."

Those who were staying in cabins hurried toward their respective units. Big Jake split off to take care of the lone chicken, Lucky.

Harm fell in step beside Talia, making her feel safe and protected. After everything that had happened over the past twenty-four hours, she still hated to admit it, but she liked having the man around. But she couldn't get used to it. He'd leave at the end of the week and she'd have to rely on herself again.

"What is this meeting you're attending tonight?" Harm asked.

"It's an organization I helped found called Women Against Poaching."

Harm grabbed her arm and brought her to a stop. "Are you kidding me?"

She frowned. "No. It's a worthy organization that's trying to stop the poaching by educating the communities as to the impact. One of our local teenagers, Eriku, was so inspired by what she'd learned about poaching from the internet, she wanted to make a difference. I promised to help."

"And when did your troubles start?" Harm asked.

Talia glanced away. "Right after our first meeting a couple weeks ago."

"Holy hell, Talia." Harm shook his head. "Don't you see?"

"That it could be the poachers behind all that's happened?" She nodded. "Yes, it could be the poachers. But I can't stop what has grown into a movement of women. They're doing their best to educate the men, letting them know what will happen if the animals all disappear to the poachers' bullets and machetes."

"You're setting yourself up as a target."

"But I'm not the one going around telling the men-folk they shouldn't kill the animals. Their wives and daughters are doing it."

"Are the men resentful of what the women are doing?" Harm asked.

"They might be. The girls in the village have been

attending the missionary school. They're learning so much. Before long, they will be going on to college or university, and after that, they will hold positions of influence."

"If they choose to return to their humble beginnings after being in a city," Harm said, "they might give the menfolk a run for their positions of leadership."

"It might not be quite as easy as that," Talia said. "But I'm glad they're heading in the right direction."

Harm lifted Talia's hand. "In the meantime, the men will know that you had something to do with organizing the group of women. If they have issue with the group, they'll target you, if they haven't already."

Talia nodded. "I understand. But I can't miss the first feedback meeting since we organized and developed our mission."

"All I can think is that you're sitting on a powder keg in a region where poachers sometimes rule communities."

Talia pressed her lips into a tight line. "I realized that, and I expressed my concerns to the girls." She bit down on her lower lip. "That's the main reason I need to be at that meeting tonight—I need to know what we're up against."

"Okay, then. You'll be there." He took her hand and guided her toward the lodge. "And by the way, I'm coming with you."

She opened her mouth to protest but thought better of it. Having Harm along might also give her some clout in the male-dominant society.

Harm held the door for her as she entered the lodge.

"I'm going to check on meal preparation and head up to shower."

"I'll go with you." He grinned. "To the kitchen. And the shower, if you want me to." He winked.

Talia's heart skipped several beats and then thundered against her ribs.

Harm smiled down at her. "I'm kidding and just trying to be helpful." He lifted her hand to his lips. "But when you're ready, you let me know. I'll be there."

"How? You won't even be in the same country," she whispered.

"I'll find a way," he said, his gaze locking with hers for a long moment. "But for now, let's check on dinner. I could eat an entire side of beef."

Talia laughed, though the sound that came out was more a hysterical giggle. She had loved Michael with all of her heart. How could she be entertaining thoughts of showering with this stranger she barely knew?

HARM FOLLOWED TALIA into the kitchen.

Jamba was working over the stove. Alone.

"Where's Nahla?" Talia asked.

"She left after you did this morning," Jamba said.

Harm's gut tightened. He was sure that news wasn't good for Talia.

"Damn," Talia muttered under her breath. "And Kamathi?"

"Same." Jamba's mouth formed a straight, tight line.

"You've been here working all day on your own?" Talia asked.

Jamba nodded. "Eriku came by after school and made beds and replaced towels."

"Thank goodness." Talia touched a hand to the chef's arm. "Thank you for staying, Jamba."

The older man nodded. "I am not as buried in superstition as others of the village. While you are at the meeting tonight, you might see some of the others."

"I hope to speak with them and reassure them it's safe to come back to work at the resort," Talia said.

"Don't expect them to return until the witch doctor deems All Things Wild clear of bad juju," the chef warned her.

Talia snorted. "And when will that be? Is he asking for a donation to help resolve the bad karma?"

"He hasn't mentioned a price to cure the resort." Jamba snorted. "But if you offer, I'm sure he'll take your money."

Harm stood back while Talia and Jamba conversed.

Jamba frowned. "Do you want me to go with you to the meeting? You shouldn't go alone." The chef seemed loyal and concerned for Talia's safety.

Harm had to admire the man for wanting to take care of Talia. But while Harm was there, he would fill that need to protect her. "I'll go with her tonight," Harm said.

Talia frowned. "There's no need for either one of you to take me. I can get there and back by myself." She raised a hand. "I don't want to argue about this. You've both done enough."

Harm met Jamba's dark gaze and nodded. "We won't argue. But I'm coming. It will give me a chance to ask questions of some of the villagers about who the cobra handlers are among them, and who are the people with trained dogs."

"You think you'll find the saboteur among the villagers?"

"Doesn't hurt to try," Harm pointed out. "They could be acting under instruction from the poachers. We entered a village in Afghanistan where the women and children had been threatened by the Taliban. They were so fearful, they were ready to take a bullet from us rather than have the Taliban slit their throats in the night."

"That's awful."

It had been awful. He'd had to shoot a woman and her child running toward them, loaded with vests full of explosives. He still had nightmares from it. Yet, had he hesitated, he and his team wouldn't be alive today.

"It might be a boring meeting," Talia warned.

"We can only hope it's boring," Harm said.

Talia nodded. "Jamba, if you have everything under control for the moment, I'll run upstairs for a shower. I'll be down in time to set the table and make a tray of cheese and crackers for an appetizer."

"Take your time. Dinner won't be ready for another forty-five minutes," the chef said.

Harm and Talia left the kitchen and climbed the staircase to the second floor. All the while, Harm remained completely aware of Talia's every move, from the sway of her hips to the way she pushed stray strands of hair back behind her ears. He would have followed her into her room, closed the door and kissed her until she begged for more, but he still wasn't sure where he stood with her. He could sense mutual attraction, but she didn't seem ready to get into another relationship so soon after her husband's death.

And Harm wasn't sure he wanted to start something that would only end when he left. He stopped at his door and rested his hand on the doorknob. "I'll be in the kitchen when you're ready."

"Thank you," Talia said and scurried past him to the

next door along the hallway. "Thank you, again, for all you've done for me."

"I haven't done much. No need for thanks."

She smiled. "We may have to agree to disagree. I'll see you in a few." With that parting comment, she went into her room and closed the door between them.

Harm twisted the doorknob and entered his room. Knowing Talia was only feet away on the other side of the wall made his heart beat faster. She'd be stripping out of her dusty clothes and getting into the shower, where water would run over her naked skin.

Harm groaned, his groin tightening with his lusty thoughts. What he needed was a cold shower and some clean clothes. With efficiency born of practice, he stripped, showered and dressed in his nicest black slacks, a button-down white shirt and the tie he'd purchased at the post exchange in Djibouti for the first time they'd been to All Things Wild. Talia had made it clear that dinner was formal. She'd even helped Marly find a dress to wear on two separate occasions when they were there before.

Harm was certain Marly had never worn a formal dress before in her life, but she'd come down dressed to kill. But Talia could outshine any woman in the room, with her rich black hair and her sexy curves. But more than her stunning body, it was her laughter, the smile and the light shining from her eyes that made her so attractive.

After wiping the dust off his dress shoes and strapping his pistol to his calf beneath his pants, Harm straightened his tie and exited the room. He could still hear the shower going in the room next to him. If he hurried, he could get ahead of Talia and do whatever needed to be done before she came down. He found himself wanting to relieve some of her burden. Being down several staff members made it hard for her to keep up. And she'd spent the entire day entertaining them on the savanna, away from the resort that still needed work.

Back in the kitchen, Harm asked Jamba, "What can I do that would help Talia the most?"

"All of the plates, cutlery and napkins are on the table. You could start there."

"We volunteered to set the table," Angela said behind him.

Harm turned to see her and Buck scrubbed and dressed for the evening. Angela wore a long white dress with narrow straps on her shoulders. Her wet hair had been pulled back into a tight bun at the base of her skull.

Buck wore dark slacks, a black button-down shirt and a bright red tie. The contrast of him all in black with Angela's all-white outfit was striking.

Harm grinned. "I feel like I'm staring at the angel and the bad man."

Angela laughed. "We didn't plan it that way, but I kind of like it." She tugged on Buck's tie to straighten it and leaned up on her toes to kiss him. "He makes a great bad man."

"The settings are on the table, ready for you," Harm said.

Buck clapped his hands together. "We're on it."

"There are several types of cheese in the refrigerator," Jamba said. "And the crackers are in the boxes in the pantry." He set a serving platter on the counter. "Cut up the cheese and arrange it on the platter with the crackers."

Harm was just placing the crackers around the cheese when Talia entered the kitchen. She'd pulled her damp black hair up into a loose bun on her crown, exposing the length of her neck.

Harm had the sudden urge to trail kisses down to the base of her throat where her pulse beat rapidly.

"Oh, thank you." She smiled and glanced around the kitchen at the steaming platters piled with steak, baked potatoes and a variety of vegetables. "Is there anything I can do?"

"Ice the glasses, since these are Americans we're serving and they like their ice." Jamba chuckled and shook his head. "I'll never understand why Americans always want to water down their drinks with ice."

"I wouldn't do too many iced glasses. The guys will want cold beer if you have it." Harm twisted his lips. "No ice."

Talia laughed and checked the refrigerator, counting the beer bottles. "Should have enough cold ones for the evening."

Moments later, the rest of the team arrived, raiding the refrigerator for the beer. Soon, they were all seated around the table digging into the platters of food Jamba provided.

Harm sat beside Talia, aware of the warmth of her thigh brushing against him every time she moved.

He downed the amazing steak, half of his potato and a heaping helping of brussels sprouts.

"You like those things?" T-Mac grimaced. "My mother tried to get me to eat those when I was a kid. I swore I'd never touch another when I got old enough to make my own choices."

With a chuckle, Harm popped one into his mouth

and chewed. "My grandmother served these at the Thanksgiving table. I don't think I liked them at first, but I eat them now because they remind me of my grandmother."

T-Mac shook his head. "Nope. Not a good enough excuse to eat mini cabbages. Not for me, anyway."

"You were close to your grandmother?" Talia asked.

"She raised me when my parents decided traveling was more important than spending time with their kid."

"I'm sorry."

"About what?" Harm pushed one of the morsels around on his plate. "My grandparents lived on a small farm in south Texas. They were retired, so they took me to all my school and sporting events. And we went to the beach a lot during the summer."

"What made you want to join the navy?" Talia asked.

"Yeah, Harm, why did you join the navy?" Big Jake echoed.

"I saw a recruiting video about the Navy SEALs," Harm answered and ate another brussels sprout.

"That's it?" Big Jake frowned. "You weren't trying to prove anything to your parents, a friend or a woman?"

Harm shook his head. "No. I liked challenges. I set records for my high school on the track team and swim team, and I lifted weights. I thought I'd give it a shot. I was pretty sure I could make it through the training."

"And you did." Big Jake clapped a hand against his back. "Like we all did."

"Yeah. I got recycled and almost didn't make it through," Harm said.

"That's right. You got sick or something," Pitbull

said. "I remember you telling me about that. In the middle of Hell Week."

"I would have stayed the course, but the docs pulled me."

"Wow, I can't imagine doing Hell Week twice. I'm not sure I could have done that."

"Yeah, well, by then you know what you're capable of and that it will end eventually. You just have to make it to lunch, then dinner, then breakfast the next morning until you get all the way through."

"That's how I survived BUD/S," Diesel said. "One minute, one hour, one day at a time. I lived in the moment, telling myself it wouldn't last forever."

The other members of the team nodded solemnly.

"Well, we're all glad you made it." Marly glanced around at the people at the table. "Otherwise, we wouldn't be where we are today. I might have been sold to the highest bidder in a sex trade business."

"And I might have been captured by a Sudanese tyrant," Angela added. "And who knows what would have happened to me?"

"And Reese could have died in the jungle when she was kidnapped and taken to the Congo," Diesel said.

"Have I said thank you for choosing All Things Wild for your vacation? You guys have helped me in more ways than I can ever repay you for. The last time you were here, you helped find and bring down the poacher stealing baby animals. I couldn't have done it."

"Don't underestimate yourself," Harm said. "By reporting what you find, you help the rangers keep tabs on poaching activities."

"Maybe so, but it doesn't stop them," Talia argued. "I think some of them are in cahoots with the poachers or their middlemen." She pushed back from the table. "I'm sorry to duck out on you, but I have a meeting to go to in the village. T-Mac will make sure there is music, and you're welcome to push the furniture around in the great room for dancing. Help yourself to the liquor in the lounge. Basically, make yourself at home. I'll be back later."

"You're not going by yourself, are you?" Big Jake said. "What happened to your hired guards?"

Talia grimaced. "I had a hard time hiring guards after two were killed the last time you guys were here. With the witch doctor stirring up rumors, it's impossible to get anyone to help at the resort."

"But don't worry, Talia's not going alone," Harm said. "I'm going with her."

"Do you need more of us to escort you?" Big Jake asked.

Talia shook her head. "I don't anticipate any problems. Having Harm with me will be more of a bonus than a necessity." She smiled. "Thanks anyway. I'm sure you all are tired from the day in the field."

"Ha," Buck said. "That was a walk in the park compared to what we're used to. I could use a little exercise." He grinned at Angela. "Feel like cutting the rug with this salty dog?"

The doctor smiled up into Buck's eyes. "It's been a long time since you've taken me dancing."

"Then let me remedy my failings." Buck stood and held Angela's chair for her. "Madam, would you honor me with a dance?"

"I'd love it." Angela took the man's arm and let him lead her from the room.

T-Mac scrambled to his feet and grabbed a dinner

roll from the basket on the table. "Let me get the juke-box going."

"Pitbull and I will clear the table," Marly said.

"You can leave the dishes," Talia insisted. "I'll take care of them when I get back."

"No worries," Marly said. "Just go, or you'll be late."

Harm hooked his hand through Talia's elbow and led her toward the front door.

Talia grabbed the keys for the safari truck from a hook on the wall and smiled up at Harm. "Thank you for going with me, but you really don't need to."

"I'll let you drive, since you know where you're going." And it would keep his hands free in case he needed to draw his weapon.

Chapter Seven

Darkness had settled in and all the stars in the sky were shining brightly, illuminating the dirt road leading away from the resort.

Harm kept a close watch on the road ahead, looking for movement from the sides as well. With as many wild animals as there were on the savanna, he wouldn't be surprised if they ran across a herd of something…cape buffalo, wildebeests, zebras or impala. And at night, many of the big cats roamed, searching for prey. Ranchers also ran their cattle on the grasslands bordering the preserves.

The village was a collection of huts and shacks made of mud and stick with thatched roofs. Some were constructed of sheets of plywood and tin. At the center of the village, someone had built a fire. Women had gathered around the fire, sitting cross-legged, apparently waiting for Talia's arrival.

When Talia pulled into the village and parked several yards away from the gathering, small children ran up to the truck, calling out her name. "Mrs. Talia! Mrs. Talia!"

Talia stepped down from the vehicle and bent to hug each child and say something nice to them.

"My, you have grown since last I saw you!" she said to the smallest boy.

He grinned and exclaimed, "I can count. Wanna hear?"

"Of course I do." Still squatting in front of him, she nodded. "Go ahead."

The little boy held up one finger. "One." He worked his chubby fingers until he had two up and the others still curled together. "Two." Another finger flexed upward. "Three." Then he grinned, a white flash of baby teeth.

"That was so good." Talia hugged the little boy.

Harm's heart tightened in his chest. He couldn't help thinking that this woman would make a great mother to her own children.

Talia straightened and glanced around the gathering. She strode to one of the women standing near the fire. "Have you seen Eriku?"

The woman nodded and pointed toward the far end of the glowing fire.

A young woman with a head full of tight braids smiled and raised her hand. She made her way through the throng, carefully stepping over those seated on the ground.

When she finally reached Talia, she laughed and hugged her. "I didn't want to start without you."

"You didn't have to wait on me," Talia assured her.

Eriku shrugged. "You are much better at public speaking."

"Only because I've been doing it longer than you."

"Whatever the reason, you're much more convincing than I am. They will listen to you."

Talia touched the young woman's arm and smiled

into her yes. "You just have to remember why you're here, and what good you can do by standing up for what's right."

"Yes, ma'am." She stared toward the women seated around the fire. "But there have been problems," Eriku said softly.

"Problems?" Talia asked, her brows drawing together.

Harm leaned closer to hear what the girl was saying.

"Some of the men didn't want to hear what the women had to say." Eriku led Talia over to a woman who sat huddled on the edge of the group, a bright red scarf wrapped around her head and part of her face.

Eriku squatted next to her. "Show Mrs. Talia," she commanded.

The woman slowly lowered the scarf, displaying a dark purple bruise on her right cheek. Her right eye was swollen shut.

Talia gasped. "Who did this?"

The woman shook her head and drew the scarf back up over her face.

"It's bad juju, Mrs. Talia," another woman said. "Gakuru said it's so. He said if we continue to behave as we have, we will be struck barren and our children will become sick."

"It's true," another woman whispered. "My boy is sick. All because I spoke to one of the tribal leaders about the poaching."

"Talking won't make your children sick," Talia said. "The witch doctor is trying to scare you silent."

"We are afraid for our children." A tall, thin woman walked out of the shadows, carrying a baby on her hip.

"We can't continue to educate our men and risk our children in the process."

"No, we can't risk our families," Eriku said. "But if we do *nothing*, the animals will die. Without the animals, we will have no tourism. Without tourism, we have no way to buy food to feed our families. We will die of starvation."

The woman with the baby on her hip raised her chin and stared down her nose at the shorter Eriku. "If we do *anything*, our families will die. The poachers will kill us. If not them, the bad juju will poison our water and kill our crops and livestock."

Eriku stared at the woman for a moment longer. "We can't let things continue as they are. We have a responsibility as humans to save our environment, to protect the animals and the land they live on."

"When we can protect our children without fear of attack by poachers, we will work on protecting the animals. Until then, we can't."

The woman with the bright red scarf pushed to her feet. "I am done here."

"As are we," another woman said. She was surrounded by several more women, some gathering children around them.

They moved toward the huts, leaving only a few women left standing near the fire.

The sound of vehicle engines filled the night, and suddenly headlights glared from one end of the road, running through the village.

"Run!" Harm yelled. He grabbed a child and herded his mother toward one of the huts.

Talia swung another little one up in her arms and ran alongside him.

The women screamed, gathered their children and ran for the relative safety of their homes.

Even before all of the women and children had cleared the road, trucks, SUVs and Jeeps careened into the village center.

Men carrying AK-47s leaped to the ground and began firing rounds.

More screaming filled the air.

The boy Harm had pulled out of the way ran into his mother's arms and they raced into the darkness, farther away from the roaring engines and flying bullets.

Harm's heart leaped into his throat when he couldn't find Talia. Then she appeared at his side, carrying a small child.

The kid was crying, tears streaming down her face.

"I don't know where her mother is." Talia held the child clutched to her breast, breathing hard from her mad dash. "They came so fast, I had to get her out of the way or she'd have been run over."

"You did the right thing." Harm pulled them behind one of the stick-and-mud huts on the far edge of the village. "Wait here. I want to find out what's going on."

More sounds of gunfire ripped through the air.

Talia ducked lower, shielding the child's body with her own. She reached out and touched his arm. "Don't go. They might shoot anyone standing."

"I'll stay in the shadows. They won't see me."

"Maybe not, but they don't seem too concerned about where they're shooting. They might hit you with a random shot."

"Trust me. I've done this before." He stared down at her. "As for you, stay in the shadows. I'll be right back."

She huddled with the child, both looking small and vulnerable.

Harm couldn't leave them for long. But he had to know if others needed help getting away from the attack. The women were defenseless, unarmed and burdened with the care of their children.

Harm pulled his pistol from the holster strapped to his calf and moved from shadow to shadow, working his way back toward the village center.

A toddler staggered between the buildings, crying hysterically.

Harm made his way toward the child and would have scooped him up, but a woman ran out of the darkness, snatched the baby up into her arms and turned to run back into the shadows, when a man wielding a rifle stepped in front of her and shouted, pointing his gun at the woman.

Harm didn't hesitate—he charged the man with the rifle, coming at him from his left side. The man didn't see him until Harm hit him in the side like a linebacker. At the same time, Harm grabbed the rifle, shoving the barrel toward the ground.

The attacker pulled the trigger, a bullet spitting up dust at their feet as they both crashed to the ground.

The man struggled beneath Harm's weight, but he couldn't wiggle free of Harm's hold.

Once the woman and her child got away, Harm knew he had to extricate himself. He didn't dare kill the man when he didn't know if he'd actually harmed anyone else. Every instinct told him to take the man out, but he wasn't on a mission. He wasn't authorized to use deadly force. For all he knew, the man could be one of the local rangers or some other authority. If he killed the man, he could set off an international incident involving the US Navy where they had no business fighting. Until he had a better grasp on the situation, he had to free his captive and let him go.

Harm silently counted to three, sprang to his feet, ripped the rifle out of the gunman's hands and flung it into tall grasses near the edge of the village.

The gunman staggered to his feet and ran toward the village center, yelling at the top of his voice.

"Time to leave," Harm muttered. He hurried back to where he'd left Talia.

She was there, but the child was gone.

"Oh, thank God." She flung herself into his arms.

He held her for only a second. "Where's the child?"

"Her mother found us and took her into the brush."

"We have to leave," Harm said. "Now."

"But how? The vehicle is at the end of the village. We have to get to it."

"Then we'll get there." He took her hand. "Stay with me and keep to the shadows." By freeing the gunman, he'd made his presence known. That he was at the Women Against Poaching rally would probably make it worse for the participants. Or he could be the bait to lure them away from the village. But if he was bait, that made Talia just as much of a target.

"It might be better if you hide in the brush and I come back later for you. They'll be after me."

"Why would they be after you?" Talia leaned into his body, her fingers holding tightly to his.

"I might have roughed up one of their own," he said

and eased to the corner of a hut. "Any reason the truck might not start on the first try?"

"No. It's always turned over immediately. Why?"

"We'll need to get out of Dodge faster than the gunmen can shoot."

"That doesn't sound very promising."

"You're right. I'm going to stash you in the brush and come back for you after I lose these goons."

"You're not leaving me anywhere. We came to this dance together, we'll leave together. My mother always told me to leave with the one who brought me." She squeezed his hand. "I'm not letting go, so you might as well get used to it."

Harm liked that the woman had backbone, but he didn't like that they might be surrounded and not get out of the village on their own steam.

TALIA RAN TO keep up with Harm, afraid she'd slow him down and get them both killed. By the time they reached the other end of the village, she was breathing hard.

She'd parked her truck beside a hut, but they had to cross the road to get to it.

The men in the trucks and SUVs were still at the center of the village yelling and firing off rounds into the air.

As far as Talia could tell, they hadn't taken any hostages, or she'd have insisted on staying to see if there was anything she could do to help. The best thing they could do now was to lure the gunmen out of the village. If that meant setting themselves up as targets, at least that would redirect the violence away from the women and children who'd scattered into the brush to keep their families safe.

"Ready?" Harm asked.

She nodded and then realized he couldn't hear that. "Yes."

"On the count of three."

She bunched her muscles, ready to run.

Harm was silent for a second and then whispered, "Three."

He took off running, pulling her along with him.

They'd made it all the way across the road and had their hands on the truck door handles when a shout sounded. Gunfire sounded like so many tiny blasts, filling the night.

Harm sent Talia around to the other side of the truck, putting the bulk of the vehicle between her and the bullets.

He dived into the driver's seat and reached for the key.

The ignition was empty.

"Here." Talia shoved the key in and twisted it.

The engine fired up and roared to life.

Harm whipped the shift into gear and kicked up gravel and dust behind them as he spun away from the hut and onto the road. "Stay down!" he yelled.

Talia ducked low in her seat as bullets pinged against the metal truck body. Her heart raced and her hands shook as she remained bent double in the passenger seat, worrying about Harm, who had to sit up high enough to see over the dashboard.

A round pierced the back seats and flew all the way through the middle of the truck to hit the front windshield, leaving a jagged marble-size hole.

Talia's breath lodged in her throat and she gulped back the fear threatening to overwhelm her. She couldn't lose it now. She wasn't in as much danger as Harm. The least she could do was not panic and make his job even harder.

But it was hard not to panic. Those maniacs were still shooting at them.

The truck picked up speed, putting distance between them and the attackers.

Harm didn't say a word. His jaw was set in hard lines and his eyes shifted between the road ahead and the side mirrors. He pushed the accelerator all the way to the floor, rocketing them away from the village.

Talia dared to glance up into her side mirror. It had been hit by a stray bullet and the glass was cracked, but she could still see that the vehicles that had entered the village were now leaving—following them!

Go faster, she urged Harm silently. *Much faster!*

The road twisted and turned through acacia trees and brush and around termite mounds. Soon they'd be hitting the wide-open spaces of the savanna, where they'd be easy to shoot at and nothing would stand in the way.

They still had a long way to go to reach the resort, and when they did, the rest of the team would have no warning to let them know to be prepared to stand and defend. Besides, this attack wasn't the SEALs' responsibility. Unfortunately, Talia didn't even have any armed guards left to protect the resort. Perhaps she had overestimated her ability to run All Things Wild without a man to lean on. Nothing like this had ever happened when Michael was alive. Why was it happening now?

The engine coughed and sputtered.

"What's that?" she asked.

"We're losing oil pressure. One of those bullets probably hit the oil pan."

"Without oil, the engine will burn up." As the words left her mouth, Talia could smell the acrid scent of something burning. "Seriously? Why can't we limp along fast enough to reach the resort? At least there, we have more weapons. We stand a chance of defending ourselves."

"Sorry, darlin', but that's not going to be one of our choices."

"Figures." She sat up and stared into the side mirror. "We might not have more than a minute to come up with a plan."

"I'm ditching the truck. We can hide in the brush."

"That will be the first place they look."

"They will be looking for us to hide next to or ahead of the truck. We're going to backtrack in the direction of the village. Right now, I need to ditch the truck and hope they don't find it. Hold on." He shut off the headlights and shifted into Low to slow the vehicle without pressing the brakes, which would shine the brake lights, giving away their position.

For a few hundred more yards, he let the vehicle decelerate until it was going slowly enough to roll off the road without flipping and killing them.

Talia gripped the armrest on the door as they bumped off the dirt road into the tall grass. She glanced behind them. Anyone with half a brain would see the trail they left in the grasses the truck mowed over. Hiding the vehicle would be impossible. They had to get out and hide themselves.

Once the truck came almost to a complete stop, Harm glanced over at her. "Jump."

Talia shoved open her door and threw herself out of

the rolling vehicle. She hit the ground on her side, rolled and came up on her feet, searching for Harm.

The truck continued to roll forward. Once it had passed, the light from the stars overhead shined down on Harm's head.

Talia breathed a sigh and stepped into his arms.

He held her for a brief moment and then took her hand. "We have to get as far away from this truck as we can before they find it."

She nodded and fell in step with Harm as he jogged through the tall grass back toward the village. They ran twenty yards from the road but parallel to its path, hunkering below the tips of the tall grasses.

Harm raised his head over the tops of the grass fronds every so often to gauge where they were in comparison to the dirt road and the oncoming headlights.

Within two minutes of them abandoning the truck, the convoy of five vehicles roared past. Talia's heart leaped to her throat.

Harm grabbed her arm and pulled her down to her haunches until the last vehicle had gone by.

Harm slowly straightened, peering after the vehicles. "They blasted past, missing the point where we drove the truck off into the grass."

Talia breathed a sigh of relief.

"No, wait. One of them is backing up." He bent over and parted the fronds slightly. "Make that two…no, all of them have come about."

Talia tugged on his pant leg. "We should go."

Harm helped her to a crouching position and led the way, hurrying away from the truck and the gang of gunmen. They hadn't gone far when the rapid report of gunfire made them drop down to hug the earth.

Harm covered Talia's body with his own, pressing her harder into the dirt.

She could barely breathe, he was so heavy on her. If they were firing at them, Harm's body would take the bullets. "Don't." Talia squirmed beneath him, her voice lost in the noise of the barrage of bullets being expended.

Harm shifted and lifted his body off hers, then rose to check out what was going on.

"Are you crazy?" Talia whispered. "You'll get killed."

"They aren't shooting at us. I'm sorry to say this, but they're killing your truck."

"My truck?" Talia sat up and parted the grass.

From what little she could see, the men stood in a semicircle around what she assumed was her truck—she couldn't see it for the tall grass and the gun-toting men. But they were firing every round of ammunition they owned. One man even expelled his magazine and loaded another to shoot all the bullets in that one as well.

"My truck," Talia moaned. "Do you know how hard it is to get a good one for a reasonable price?" She sat back on the ground, feeling tears welling in her eyes. "Can't catch a stinkin' break."

"They're turning around. Get down." Once again, Harm threw his body over hers as bullets peppered the grass and brush in a 360-degree radius around the doomed truck.

When the gunfire ceased, Harm remained on top of her, facing the direction of the gang. "They're spreading out, trampling the grass. Time to move again," he said.

On hands and knees, they crawled away from the men searching for them.

When they'd gone a couple hundred yards, Harm

rose to a crouch, clasped Talia's hand in his and led her farther away at a faster pace.

Talia glanced back to see headlights coming their direction. "They're on their way back toward the village."

"Hopefully just to pass through this time. They made their point the first time they came."

"What if the villagers have returned to their huts? We need to get there and warn them."

"Without a vehicle," Harm said, "we won't make it in time. And my bet is the truck is totaled."

"Then we shouldn't try to go back to the village. We might as well head home." Talia turned back and trudged toward the All Things Wild Resort, her feet already tired and her spirit tattered. When they came abreast of the truck, she fought back the tears, telling herself it was just an inanimate object, not a person. She had no reason to be as upset as she was.

Harm slipped an arm around her waist and pulled her against him. "I'm sorry about your truck," he said in a low, resonant tone that warmed the cool night air. She felt something warm against her hair and realized he'd pressed his lips to her head. *Why stop there?* she wanted to say. Instead, she tipped her head up to him and stared into his eyes, shining in the starlight.

He cupped her cheeks in his palms and brushed a tear away with the pad of his thumb.

Talia hadn't even realized the tears had fallen until Harm swiped one away.

"You can replace a vehicle," he said. "Don't let it get you down." He kissed her forehead.

Again, Talia wanted more. She lifted her chin higher. If he tried to kiss her forehead again, he'd have to settle for her lips.

For a long moment, he stared down into her eyes and then his gaze shifted lower.

Her breath caught and held in her throat. This was the moment of reckoning. If he didn't kiss her, she'd already decided to make the move herself. Her curiosity and the raging fire inside would not let him walk away again.

"I have no right to do this," he whispered. "You've already lost so much."

Beyond patience, Talia rose up on her toes, hooked the back of Harm's neck and pulled him down to meet her lips in a kiss that could only be described as a coming together of two very hungry people.

It started out desperate and raw, and several long, mindless minutes later, it ended just as it began—raw and edgy.

Chapter Eight

Talia pressed the back of her hand to her throbbing lips, her eyes wide, her breath coming in shallow gasps. "What the heck just happened?"

"I don't know. You tell me," Harm said.

Talia squeaked, her cheeks burning with embarrassment. "Did I ask that out loud?"

Harm chuckled. "You did."

She turned her hand over and touched her lips. "I've wanted to do that for too long."

"And now that you have?" He slipped his hands around her waist and pulled her hips against his.

She could feel the hard evidence of his desire dig into her belly and an answering response burn all the way to her core. "I want to do it again."

He bent his head, his mouth hovering over hers. "What are you waiting for?"

She shook her head, her desire pushing the guilt to the back of her mind. Again, she rose up on her toes, only this time she didn't have as far to go. Harm met her halfway there, his lips claiming hers in a kiss so hot, it left Talia burning for more.

His tongue traced the seam of her lips until she

opened to let him in. He pushed past her teeth and caressed her tongue in a long, sensual sweep.

Talia melted into him, her knees weak, her heart racing. If Harm hadn't been holding her around her waist, she might have slipped to the ground in a boneless heap. Standing in the middle of a field, with the potential of bad guys returning to finish them off, Talia didn't care and she didn't want the kiss to end.

Too soon, the need to breathe superseded her desire. Talia tipped back her head and dragged in a shaky breath. "What are you doing to me?"

He chuckled, the low resonance of the sound reverberating in her chest where it touched his. "I should ask you the same question."

She laid her cheek against his shirt and listened to the pounding of his heartbeat. He was as affected by the kiss as she had been. For some reason, that made her strangely happy.

Talia drew in another deep breath and let it out before she stepped back far enough that he was forced to relinquish his hold. Immediately, she wished his hands were back around her waist, dipping low on her backside. How she wanted to be much closer. But they were a long way from the resort. By the time they walked there, it would be the wee hours of the morning. Another day would be upon her and, with it, all the chores and duties of a business owner with only the chef to help. The happiness of moments before was weighed down by the extent of her responsibilities.

"Are you ready for a stroll in the starlight?" Harm held out his arm.

Talia smiled and took it. "It's too bad we can't call a cab." As soon as she spoke the words, she remembered.

"Wait. I might have a solution. If it wasn't destroyed." She strode to the bullet-ridden truck and dug in the console between the front seats. At the bottom of the storage compartment was the satellite phone she'd placed there earlier that day when they'd gone out on safari.

"Can you believe it?" She held it up triumphantly. "It doesn't have a single scratch."

Harm laughed. "I could kiss you."

"What are you waiting for?" she said, parroting his words of a moment before.

He pulled her into his arms and dropped a quick kiss on her lips. Then he set her at arm's length. "Make that call."

She hit the numbers that would connect her with the resort. Jamba answered on the fourth ring. "All Things Wild Resort."

"Jamba. What are you still doing at the resort? I thought you'd have gone home by now."

"I stayed to prep for the meals tomorrow. I was about to step out the door when the phone rang. What's wrong, Mrs. Talia?"

Talia told him what had occurred in the village and then on the road home, and how they were stuck without transportation back to the resort. "Could you bring the spare truck to pick us up?"

"I'll try. I was going to take it home, if it would start."

"Are we still having trouble with the starter?"

"Yes, ma'am. If I can't get it going, I'll call someone to come get you two."

Talia told him approximately where they could be found and ended the call. The silence of the night surrounded her again. "Jamba will make sure someone comes to collect us."

"In the meantime, we might as well get comfortable." Harm glanced around. Shell casings littered the ground around the truck, like so much shiny confetti that could easily twist an ankle.

"It might be a good idea to stay away from the truck in case the gunmen return to look for us," he suggested.

"Agreed. But we can't go too far, since this is where I told Jamba to come."

They settled in the grass the length of a football field away from the destroyed truck, but closer to the road. From where they were, they could see headlights coming long before the drivers or occupants could see them.

Harm sat on the ground beside Talia and slid an arm around her. "You can lean against me and sleep, if you'd like."

"After all that's happened today, I don't think I'll ever sleep again." Nevertheless, she leaned into his hard body. "I'm glad you insisted on coming with me tonight." Despite the chaos of the evening, a yawn overtook her and she closed her eyes. "I don't know if I would have tried to make a run for it in the truck. Because of your decision to leave, I'm sure the village women had a better chance of escaping once we led the gunmen out of the village."

"I'm glad I came, too. The thought of you dealing with what happened by yourself would have made me sick with worry."

She laughed. "You wouldn't have known it was happening."

"Which would make me even more worried, imagining all the possibilities." He sighed. "Not that I would have come up with any imaginary scenarios close to the reality of what went down tonight."

"What a disaster. The women of the village will never want to stand up to anyone again. Not when there are gunmen shooting at them and their children."

"We need to come back during the daylight and ask questions. I want to talk with the witch doctor and the men of the village. They seemed suspiciously absent tonight."

"Hopefully, the gunmen were only there to scare the women into submission."

"Shooting up your truck and then firing into the field went beyond scare tactics."

Talia nodded. She prayed they hadn't returned to the village to do more damage. Perhaps when Jamba arrived with the spare truck, she'd head back to the village and make certain the women and children were all right.

HARM SAT IN the starlight, holding Talia. Not long afterward, he could feel her relax against him, so much so that she had to be asleep.

He studied her slight frame in the meager light, wishing he could do more to protect the woman. She was brave beyond measure, but he feared she was careless about her own life.

Less than an hour after Talia placed the call to the resort, headlights appeared, coming from the direction they'd been heading when their truck had given out.

Though he was expecting the truck from All Things Wild, Harm still wasn't taking any chances. He squeezed Talia's shoulder and whispered in her ear, "We need to move."

She startled awake, her gaze shooting to his. "What? What's happened?"

He laughed. "You fell asleep. But someone's coming."

She glanced toward the oncoming orbs and rubbed her eyes. "That will be Jamba."

"I'm not taking any chances. When I know for sure, I'll let him see me. Until then, I want you to stay here and lie low." He pushed to his feet.

Her hand caught his. "You're not staying with me?"

"I'm going to get closer to the truck. He will stop there first, because that's where he expects to find us."

"I'd rather stay with you."

Harm shook his head. "It's too dangerous."

She tilted her head to the side and narrowed her eyes. "I could be attacked by lions, you know."

Harm thought for a moment and then sighed. "You're damned if you do and damned if you don't." He jerked his head to the side. "Come on."

Talia leaped to her feet and hurried after him.

Together, they hunkered below the tall grass fronds and ran toward the pickup. The headlights were moving fast, closing in on them.

By the time the vehicle came to a halt near the road where the grass had been mowed down by the truck, Harm and Talia were safely concealed in the thick grass, several feet away from the damaged truck.

Jamba dropped down out of the driver's seat at the same time as the entire SEAL team leaped to the ground.

"Harm! Talia!" Big Jake called out.

Harm chuckled and straightened. "Over here."

Talia stood beside him, grinning. "You really do have each other's backs, don't you?"

"Damn right, we do." Harm strode out of the grass onto the road where the SEALs stood, each holding a weapon.

"You look like you're on a mission," Harm said.

"We are," Diesel responded. "A mission to rescue one of our own."

"You're a little late."

"The story of our lives." T-Mac circled the truck. "It appears we missed all the fun."

"Damn, Harm, you could've saved some for us," Buck said.

"Would've if I could've." Harm pulled Talia close. "But we were too busy trying to survive."

"Then I suppose we'll cut you some slack this time." Pitbull whistled. "They did a number on Talia's truck."

"You weren't in it at the time, were you?" Big Jake looked away from the truck to study Harm and Talia.

"No, thank goodness," Talia said.

"The main thing is, you came." Harm held out his hand to Big Jake. "Thanks."

Big Jake took his hand and pulled him into a hug. "Wouldn't have let Jamba go on a mission by himself." He released Harm and grinned at the chef. "We're thinking of making him an honorary SEAL. He drove like a bat out of hell to get here as fast as he could."

"I would have been here sooner if the starter hadn't given me troubles," Jamba said. "That's why I haven't turned off the engine."

Talia shook her head. "I guess that's at the top of my to-do list."

"Between Marly and T-Mac, they ought to be able to help you," Pitbull said.

"I ordered a spare starter. It should be in any day now." Talia yawned. "I'm sorry. I guess I'm more exhausted than I thought." She leaned into Harm.

He tightened his hold on her, loving the way she felt pressed against his body.

Talia yawned again. "And I'm sorry we disturbed your evening to come rescue us."

"No worries," Big Jake said. "There weren't enough womenfolk to go around on the dance floor, and some of the guys weren't sharing. We needed a little excitement."

"Speak for yourself," Buck said. "I had excitement in my arms and will again, when we get back to the resort."

"Speaking of which," Harm said, "let's get back. I'm sure Talia has an early morning planned."

"If it has to be because of us, don't worry. We can fend for ourselves," Big Jake assured her. "We've been doing it for years."

"Yeah. I can make toast," Pitbull said. "And we've all been trained to make our own beds."

Buck puffed out his chest. "I can bounce a quarter off my sheets when I put my mind to doing it right."

Talia laughed. "I might take you up on that. But I do need to get back, and you all need a good night's sleep. We're supposed to go out on safari again in that truck tomorrow."

"If it's all the same to you, we could use some downtime," T-Mac said. "We have yet to use the pool, and my tan is woefully pale."

"I'm up for a swim and a long nap in the sun," Pitbull agreed.

Big Jake nodded. "We can save the safari thing for when we're sure the truck won't leave us stranded somewhere in the middle of a herd of angry cape buffalo."

Harm smiled at his team. He couldn't have asked for

a better group of men to fight, live and play at his side. He loved being a part of this brotherhood.

He took Talia's hand in his and squeezed it gently. "Then it's settled. No safari tomorrow. That frees up the truck—once it's fixed—for me to go into the village in daylight and ask a few questions."

Talia grinned. "Thanks." She let him help her up into the passenger seat next to Jamba.

"What about you, Jamba?" she asked. "You need a way to get home tonight."

"I can stay at the resort. As late as it is, it doesn't make sense for me to drive home, turn around and drive back just a few hours later."

"Jamba, you really are a gentleman," Talia said.

"An honorary SEAL." The chef lifted his chin and waited while the others climbed aboard.

Talia laughed, the sound filling Harm's heart with hope.

She was an amazing woman. To have lived through what had happened tonight and still be able to laugh showed what stern stuff she was made of. The more he saw of her, the more Harm liked. If he wasn't careful, he could fall in love with the woman.

On the trip back to the resort, Harm kept a vigilant watch over the road ahead, on alert in case the men who'd attacked them earlier had circled around to head them off. By the time they arrived in the resort compound, Harm was wound tighter than an old-fashioned top. He was out of the truck before it came to a complete stop.

Talia pushed open her door. Before she could drop down, Harm caught her around the waist and lowered her to the ground.

She remained in his grip, her body pressed against his for a long moment.

"Anyone up for a beer?" T-Mac asked.

Talia pulled away and pushed her hair back from her face in a nervous gesture.

"Not me," Pitbull said. "I'm hitting the sack."

"Me, too," Buck said.

"That's right, rub it in." T-Mac shook his head. "You have women. We don't." He turned to Big Jake. "Beer, big guy?"

"Not me. All the excitement today wore me out."

"Seriously? Dude, you're getting old." T-Mac slung an arm over Diesel's shoulders. "Looks like it's just the two of us. Care to play a friendly game of pool? I'll spot you two balls."

"Keep your balls, I'm calling it a night," Diesel said. "I gotta rest up for the sunbathing I'm going to tomorrow."

Harm chuckled. T-Mac turned to him, his brows raised.

Harm shook his head. "I'm looking for a shower and pillow." He wasn't really sleepy, but he wanted to keep pace with Talia. If she was headed up to her room, he was, too.

"Talia?" T-Mac asked, his tone that of a man who already knew the answer.

"Sorry. I'm dirty and sleepy. Maybe tomorrow night, when I haven't been used for target practice."

T-Mac's shoulders slumped. "Then I'll call it a night."

"If you ask me nicely, I'll check your cabin before you go in," Diesel said.

"Diesel, sweet cheeks, will you snake-proof my cabin

for me?" T-Mac asked in a falsetto that had the other guys laughing out loud.

Diesel rolled his eyes. "Yes, but keep the girl talk to a minimum."

"Aye, aye, sailor." T-Mac popped a salute and then ruined it with a wink. "Night, all." He left the group with Diesel bringing up the rear.

Jamba claimed one of the empty cabins for the night. Buck and Pitbull hurried off to their cabins, where their women waited for them.

Big Jake was already halfway up the stairs when Harm and Talia entered the lodge.

Which left Harm and Talia alone on the ground floor.

Talia glanced toward the kitchen. "I should check to see that everything is in order for breakfast in the morning."

Harm gripped her arms. "Give Jamba a little credit. That man runs a tight kitchen."

She sighed and rested her hands on his chest. "You're right. Besides, I'm too tired to care right now."

He liked how warm her fingers were through his shirt. "Then go to bed," he said, his voice husky.

She stared at her hands where they rested, as if avoiding his gaze. "It's hard to walk away without knowing exactly what I'll have to deal with in the morning."

"I'm sure you can handle anything. But you'd do it even better on a decent night's sleep." He released one arm to brush a strand of her hair back from her forehead.

She laughed, the sound breathy and maybe a little shaky. "Okay, okay, you don't have to twist my arm. I'll shower and then go straight to bed."

Still, Harm couldn't bring himself to let go. He could

still feel the panic that had overtaken him when he couldn't find her in the village. "I'm sorry about what happened in the village tonight."

"It's not your fault," she said. "I'm just glad you were there to help." She finally glanced up, meeting his gaze.

He felt as if he were teetering on the edge of a precipice, on the verge of falling into the deep, blue depths of her eyes. "About that kiss," he said without thinking.

"You don't have to apologize," she hurried to say.

"I wasn't going to." Harm chuckled. "What would you say if—" he lowered his head until his lips hovered a breath away from hers "—I asked if I could kiss you again?"

"I might regret it later, but I'd probably say, what are you waiting for?" She raised up on her toes, wrapped her arms around his neck and pressed her lips to his.

The moment her mouth touched his, a storm of desire ripped through his body, spreading fire along every nerve ending, pooling low in his groin. He wanted her in the most primal way.

Harm buried his fingers in her thick, luxurious hair, dragging her head backward, exposing her neck. He left her mouth to trail kisses down the length of her throat to the base, where her pulse beat like a snare drum in a marching band.

Footsteps on the stairs behind him finally pierced the haze of longing and made Harm lift his head.

Talia stepped back and pressed her palms to her cheeks.

Big Jake stopped halfway down the stairs, his lips twsiting. "I seem to be making this a habit. I didn't know you two were still down here." He started to turn around.

Talia hurried toward him. "No, don't go. It's okay. We were just…" She glanced toward Harm.

"Saying good-night," Harm said. He grabbed her hand and led her up the stairs and past Big Jake.

"If you need anything in the kitchen, you can help yourself," Talia called out over her shoulder.

The rumbling sound of Big Jake's chuckle followed Harm and Talia all the way up the landing and to Harm's bedroom door.

Now that they were out of Big Jake's sight, Harm pulled Talia into his arms again.

She shook her head. "We shouldn't."

"Name one reason why we shouldn't," he challenged her.

She opened her mouth to speak, but nothing came out.

"I can give you at least a dozen reasons why we should." He kissed the tip of her nose. "Because you're beautiful. Because I can't seem to resist you. Because I like the way your nose wrinkles when you frown. Because your eyes turn a darker shade of blue just before you kiss me. Because we're not getting any younger. Because there's something happening I can't explain. And because you can't go through life second-guessing yourself. Sometimes you have to go with your gut." He pressed his forehead to hers.

"And what is your gut saying to you?" she asked.

"It's telling me to make love to you. Now. Before my brain engages and tells me otherwise." He lifted his head and brushed her forehead with his lips. "What's your gut telling you?" He closed his eyes and wished for the answer his heart desired.

"It's telling me to go for it, but my mind is telling me to get a shower and go to bed. Alone."

"We could take this one step at a time." He swept his knuckles down her cheek and the length of her neck, stopping to rest on her beating pulse.

She leaned back her head, giving him better access. "What do you mean?"

"You need a shower." He poked his thumb to his chest. "I need a shower. We could conserve water and take one together."

Her lips curled upward. "You make a good argument. And we always need to conserve water on the savanna."

"Then what are we waiting for?"

She pulled her bottom lip between her teeth. "We're waiting for my gut to overrule my head."

Harm drew in a long, slow breath and let it out a little at a time. "As much as I want to throw you over my shoulder and march with you into the shower…if you're not ready, you're not ready. And I won't take advantage of you."

He kissed the tip of her nose and leaned away from her.

"Wait." She touched a hand to his chest. "I didn't say I wasn't ready."

"I can read your body language. You're hesitating. I don't want to be the focus of your regrets. Whatever we have between us must be based on our own attraction, the merit of the two of us…together."

She stared up into his eyes for a long moment. Then she took his hand. "One more reason to fall into this relationship is because you're willing to wait when I can't find the words to express how I feel. Because when you kiss me, I can't think of anything else besides getting completely naked with you and making love until the dawn rises on the eastern horizon."

Before she could say another word, he was leading her into his room and the connecting bathroom. Once there, he slipped her shirt up over her head and tossed it over the towel bar. He ripped his own shirt over his head and let it fall to the floor.

Her fingers wrapped around the button on his jeans. She gripped the zipper and eased it downward until his staff sprang free of the tight confines. Talia wrapped her hand around his erection and squeezed gently.

Harm moaned and leaned his head back, savoring the feel of her warm hands on his hardness. He didn't want her to stop. The only thing that could feel better was to be buried deep inside her.

He reached for the button on her jeans and slipped it loose, not wasting any time removing the remainder of her clothing. As soon as he'd stripped her, he shucked his own clothing and turned on the faucet in the tiled shower stall. He held out his hand to her. "It's up to you. Come or go. Leave or stay. I won't be mad, or think any less if you decide now isn't the right time."

"Seriously?" She laughed and placed her hand in his. "I thought the time to back out was before we got naked."

Harm laughed with her. Not only was she beautiful, she had a sense of humor. Could the woman be any more perfect?

Chapter Nine

Harm smiled into her eyes, the rumble of his laughter a quiet echo in the room.

Talia loved that he could joke as they stood next to the shower in nothing but their birthday suits. He didn't make her feel awkward or insecure. Since she hadn't been out on a date or with another man since before she married her husband, the whole business of getting to know each other was fairly new to her.

"No kidding, Talia. I can still be swayed by a simple no. But mark my words," he said. "I won't give up easily. I go after what I want. And I want you."

Her gaze slipped from his eyes to his mouth. She didn't want to say it, but she couldn't help herself. "You haven't mentioned a word about love."

Harm shook his head. "That might take a little longer. You see, where you think you might not be ready, there's an equally big hesitation on my part. When my fiancée dumped me for another guy, I swore I wouldn't fall for that kind of relationship again. What I feel for you is purely physical."

Talia's chest tightened. She'd bet he was afraid of love and commitment. She spread her hand over his heart, her fingers warm against his skin. "Are you sure?" she whispered.

"Sweetheart, I know I want you. That's a one hundred percent certainty." He looked away. "Anything else, I can't say for sure. Can we leave it at that? I'm not asking you for commitment, nor am I promising the same. If that's a deal breaker, speak now."

With a sigh, Talia slid her hand up to circle around the back of his neck. "It's not a deal breaker. It's just that I've never been in a purely physical relationship." She leaned up on her toes and touched her lips to his in a feather-soft kiss. The caress was over almost before it began, yet she wanted more. "How do you guard your heart, to keep it from breaking?"

"You leave your heart out of it," he said in a harsh tone. "This is all about the needs of a man and a woman."

Someone really must have hurt the man to make him so cynical. Though she still had love in her heart for Michael, she couldn't deny her attraction to Harm. "Mmm. I have needs. But they aren't all physical." She pulled him down for another teasing kiss. Her breasts brushed against his chest, causing electricity to shoot straight to her core.

It must have hit him, too, because his shaft grew longer and harder. She'd bet he could drive nails with it. Her lips quirked at the image in her mind.

"Shouldn't we get under the water before it grows cold?" she prompted.

Harm sucked in a steadying breath and stepped under the spray, bringing Talia with him.

The water drenched them, running in rivulets over their shoulders.

Talia studied the paths the little tributaries took as

gravity led them downward. Across the massive planes of his chest, down the rock-hard abs to where his shaft jutted out, strong and full.

Her breath caught and held in her throat. As if of their own accord, her hands rose and wrapped around Harm's thick erection.

He sucked in a sharp breath and surged up into her grip.

She loved how he responded to her touch. It gave her a sense of power. Slowly, she stroked him, sliding her fingers the length of him and back to the base.

He closed his eyes and tilted his head back, letting the warm water glide over his body and hers.

Then he poured shampoo into his hands and rubbed it into her hair.

Talia almost moaned at the wonderful feeling of someone massaging her scalp. She basked in the attention. Michael had never washed her hair for her. They'd been too busy running the resort to slow down long enough to think much about the other's desires.

Harm rinsed the bubbles free and applied conditioner.

Almost giddy with delight, Talia couldn't help but wonder what man remembered that long hair needed conditioner in order to ease out the tangles?

Once Harm finished washing her hair, he grabbed the bar of soap, worked up a lather and slid his hands along her neck, over her collarbone and across the swells of her breasts.

She pushed into his palms, urging him to take more.

He did, lightly pinching the tips of her nipples between his thumbs and forefingers.

Her body answered with a resounding tug low in

her belly, her core tightening with every move. Soon, she realized that foreplay took far too long. She wanted him. Now. Having gone more than a year since she'd been sexually satisfied, she didn't have the strength to wait any longer.

She resumed her grip on his erection, tightened her hand and moved faster, until she was pumping along like a piston engine.

"Can't do this." Harm grabbed her wrist and lifted her hand free of his shaft. He spun her around and doused her beneath the water, rinsing all the suds from her body.

She soaped him and traded places. Once they were both clean and suds-free, Harm turned off the water and wrapped Talia in a towel. He lifted her out of the shower and set her on the bath mat, then stepped out to stand beside her.

They dried each other off, laughing when arms and legs got in the way. Still damp in some places, they came together in a soul-defining kiss Talia never wanted to end.

But it did, with better things to come.

Harm scooped her up in his arms, carried her into the bedroom and laid her on the bed.

She scooted back and made room for him, her heart pounding, her nerves stretched. This was the moment of reckoning. A year was a long time to go between lovemaking. What if she'd forgotten how to please a man? What if the only man who could please her was Michael?

Her breathing grew strangled, and her body stiffened.

"Hey." Harm pressed a kiss to her forehead. "We

don't have to take it any further. You can back out now, if it will make you feel better."

"No, that's not it. I'm just nervous." She laughed shakily. "I feel like this is my first time, all over again."

"And it is…with me." He nibbled her earlobe and trailed a line of kisses along her jaw until he reached her lips, where he paused. "Are you feeling it yet?"

"Uh, no?" She stared up at him. "Maybe this will help." She curled her fingers around the back of his neck and closed the short distance between their mouths.

Yes. This was where she'd wanted to be.

He leaned over her, his chest pressing against hers, warming her in the cool of the air-conditioned room. Where his body touched hers, she could feel the fire building, burning a path to her center. "Better," she said against his lips.

He left her mouth to press kisses down the side of her neck to the base, where her pulse pounded against her skin.

Harm's hands led the way across her breasts, cupping each orb as if weighing it in his palm. Then he rolled her nipple between his fingers. He followed quickly with his mouth, taking the nipple between his teeth, nipping gently and then flicking it with the tip of his tongue.

Talia's back arched, her breasts rising up, urging him to take more.

He sucked the tip into his mouth and more, pulling hard and then letting go with a popping sound. While he treated the other breast to the same teasing, his fingers led the way again, sliding down her torso, skimming across her ribs, dipping into her belly button and coming to a stop over the mound of hair covering her sex.

Talia sucked in a breath and held it. Would he stop there? Oh, she hoped he didn't. Already her channel was slick and ready. He could take her now and she'd welcome him.

His mouth left her breast and followed his fingers' path down her body.

Her body on fire, Talia writhed beneath him. "Please," she moaned.

He chuckled. "Please what?"

"Enough with the appetizers. I want the whole enchilada."

Harm laughed out loud. "Way to kill the mood by talking about food."

"I'm sorry. I told you I was rusty." She still couldn't breathe, her body poised for his next move. And if he didn't make it soon, she might have to do it for him.

The SEAL parted her folds and blew a warm stream of air onto that heated strip of flesh.

Her body trembled, on the verge of something monumental. She raised her knees and let her legs fall open, willing him to come to her.

One big, callused finger dipped inside.

Talia almost cried out her relief that finally they were getting somewhere.

Then his tongue flicked her in just the right spot.

She dug her heels into the mattress and raised her hips. "There, oh yes. There," she called out.

He chuckled and flicked her again, then settled in to lick, stroke and tease her into a frenzy, all the while pumping his finger into her damp channel. He added another finger, then another, stretching her, hopefully for when he came inside her.

Which couldn't be soon enough.

Talia couldn't get air into or out of her lungs, but she didn't care. If she died then, she'd be completely satisfied.

Then he hit the magical sweet spot and sent her flying to the moon.

Talia grabbed the hair on his head and cried out, "Harm! Oh, yes! Oh, yes! Oh, yes!" Her body shook with her release, the spasms shooting through her in waves until she finally sank back to earth and the mattress. But she wasn't done yet. Nothing would be complete without Harm filling what had been empty for far too long.

Instead of slipping into her, the man rolled off the bed and stood.

"Holy hell, you can't leave now," she cried.

"We're in my room." He grinned and smoothed his hand over her fevered brow. "We need protection, and my wallet is on the dresser."

"Don't just stand there…get it," she commanded, her body already cooling in his absence.

Within seconds, Harm was back in the bed with a foil packet. He ripped it open and would have applied it himself. But Talia, already impatient beyond control, grabbed the condom from him and rolled it over his erection.

Harm nudged her knees apart and positioned himself between her legs. "You can still say no."

"No. I. Can't," she said in short, clipped tones. "I want you, Harmon Payne. If I have regrets in the morning, I'll deal with them then. For now, all I need is you. Inside me. Now."

He pressed his shaft to her entrance and eased into her. Talia dragged air into her starving lungs and let it out slowly, letting her body adjust to his girth and the feeling of being full in the best possible way she could imagine.

Harm eased back out. Before he could slip free, she pulled him back.

He set a steady pace, increasing the speed and force with every thrust until he pounded in and out of her.

When she thought it couldn't get better, he thrust one last time and buried himself inside her, so deep she couldn't fathom where she ended and he began. It all felt so good and so…right.

When his shaft stopped throbbing and his body relaxed, Harm sank down onto her and rolled them both to their sides.

Talia inhaled a shaky breath. "Wow."

"I agree. Wow."

"It really is like riding a bicycle."

Harm's bark of laughter filled the room. "What?"

"You never forget. You just get back on and it all comes back. Only it's better than memories. It's real and visceral." She cupped his cheek and smiled. "Thank you."

He shook his head, his lips twitching at the corners. "That has to be the first time anyone has ever compared having sex with me to riding a bicycle."

Laughter bubbled up inside her. For the first time in a year, she felt young and alive again. "I'm sorry if it took the wind out of your sails, but you made me feel alive again. And if we never see each other again, I have you to thank for that."

HARM PULLED TALIA into the curve of his arm, where she rested her head on his shoulder and her cheek against his chest. She fit him perfectly. Not too tall, but small enough that she made him feel like he should protect her.

"Why do you think we'll never see each other again?"

She traced her finger around his nipple. "When would we have the opportunity? You have your job as a SEAL. I have the resort. I can't leave it to run by itself. Especially now that my staff has been scared off."

"But you could. Once we figure out why someone is putting the screws to you."

She shook her head. "In the eight years we've owned the resort, we haven't had a real vacation. We got away for a couple of weekends, but that was it. When you're a small-business owner, you live, eat and breathe the work."

Harm shook his head. "I can't imagine you being shackled to the resort for the rest of your life when there are so many more places to see and visit."

"But I'm not shackled. I can come and go as I please."

"If you have staff to do the work."

She sighed. "There's always some drama. This too will blow over. This has been my home for so long. I can't imagine leaving. I have nowhere else to go."

Harm's gut twisted. "I'm sorry. I know how hard it is to lose loved ones. My father was killed by a drunk driver while I was in BUD/S."

Talia touched his cheek. "That's awful."

"I think the loss was what made me sick, but my mother insisted I stay and gut it out. She wouldn't let me quit, any more than I wanted to quit."

"She was right. You wouldn't be the man you are today if you quit. Your father would have been so proud of you."

Harm nodded. His father had grinned from ear to ear when Harm had told him he was going to BUD/S training. As a former marine, he knew what it took to make it through that training. Even to be selected for it, each candidate had to meet the highest standards.

"What about your in-laws?" Harm asked. "Where are they?"

"Michael was ten years older than I am. His parents died before we met."

"Siblings?"

She shook her head. "We were both only children."

"What about children?"

"None."

"Never wanted them?" Harm asked.

Talia gave him a sad smile. "Never got around to it. We were always so busy with running the resort, photography and safaris, there was never time to slow down and raise a child."

"You would make a good mother."

Talia laughed. "Why do you say that?"

"You have a big heart. I saw you with Eriku. You want so much for her. You gave her a job, taught her there was a world bigger than just her village. You have a lot to give to children."

"But to be a parent, you have to have the time to be with the children, to nurture and teach them what's important in life."

"Sometimes all it takes is showing them by example. Both my parents worked, but when they were with me, they loved me wholeheartedly. I learned so much from them by watching how they handled people, work and life."

"I always wanted to have children, but there never seemed to be the right time."

"I learned from other members of the SEAL brotherhood that you can't *plan* children. They just happen, and you adjust your life around them."

"Yeah, well, I'm sure that's what other people do. My husband is gone. I'm alone now and I'm getting too old to have children."

Harm had never thought to ask how old Talia was. She seemed so young and vibrant. "At the risk of being rude, just how old are you?"

"I'll be thirty-three next February."

Harm laughed. "Thirty-three? And you're too old to have children?"

Talia's eyes narrowed. "Most of the people I went to high school and college with have children almost in their teens."

"And I know more people who are waiting until they're in their forties to have children." Harm brushed a strand of her hair back behind her ear. "Trust me, you're not too old."

"I'm sure I'm older than you," she said. "I'm probably robbing the cradle. A cougar stalking a man child."

Harm frowned. "You're only two years older than I am."

"In dog years, that's fourteen years."

"Since when are you a dog?" He pressed his lips to hers. "You must be beyond exhaustion, because you're babbling and not making any sense."

"I make a lot of sense. I'm too old for you and I'm too old to have children, and I own a resort that needs me. My staff need the jobs the resort provides. I can't desert them. They depend on that money to support their families."

"If you don't make money, you can't afford to pay them."

"I know. I know." She closed her eyes. "Perhaps you're right. I need to sleep. Everything will work out in the morning."

Harm smoothed a hand over her hair. "That's right. Sleep. Knowing you, you'll be up at the crack of dawn, and that's only a few hours away."

Talia yawned, covering her mouth with her hand. "Harm?"

"Yes, sweetheart?"

"Will I see you again?" she whispered.

"I'm here all week," he replied.

"That's not really what I asked, but I guess you gave me your answer."

He would like to have said more, but the reality was, he'd leave at the end of the week, and he had no idea when he'd ever be back to Kenya, much less to the All Things Wild Resort.

The night seemed to get shorter, the possibilities drying up, only making him more depressed by the moment. The more he was with Talia, the more time he wanted to spend with her. A day wasn't enough. The week would be too short. A lifetime didn't seem enough, at that point.

Was it possible? Had he succumbed to love?

Chapter Ten

Too tired to keep her eyes open, and too comfortable and safe in Harm's embrace, Talia fell into a deep sleep, the likes of which she hadn't experienced since the death of her husband.

When she awoke, the sun shined in through the windows, bathing her in a warm, golden light.

She lay for a moment trying to get her bearings. The room didn't look right. It took several seconds for everything from the night before to rush back into her mind. She sat up straight in the bed and realized she was naked.

The door to the bedroom opened.

Talia yanked the sheet up over her bare breasts and stared wide-eyed at the man backing into the room, carrying a tray smelling of food and the rich aroma of coffee.

"I thought you might be hungry and in need of caffeine." Harm turned with a smile. The tray was laden with everything from scrambled eggs to pancakes and bacon, along with steaming mugs of coffee and two small glasses of orange juice.

"What time is it?" she asked.

"After seven o'clock."

"What?" She flung her legs over the side of the bed, hugging the sheet to her body. No matter how hard she pulled, she couldn't get the sheet to come untucked from the foot of the bed. If she wanted to stand, she'd have to abandon the sheet altogether and go naked.

Harm set the tray on the dresser. "Now, don't go getting your panties in a twist."

"I'm not wearing any panties," she hissed. "I think we left them in the bathroom."

With a chuckle, Harm crossed his arms over his chest. "Well, then I think you're in a pickle."

"Could you please hand me my clothing?" she asked. "I have a lot of work to do."

"As you can see, I'm quite busy serving a pretty lady her breakfast in bed. Otherwise I would comply." His lips twitched as if he was holding back a grin.

"Harmon Payne, you are no gentleman," she declared.

He nodded. "That's one thing we can agree on." Turning back to the tray, he asked, "Do you prefer sugar and cream in your coffee, or do you drink it black?"

Talia hefted a pillow from behind her and threw it at the back of Harm's head. "You're so…so…" She struggled for the right expletive.

"Handsome? Thoughtful? Sexy?" He retrieved the pillow from the floor and tossed it back to her. "Now, how was it you liked your coffee?"

"Dressed in my own clothes."

"Maybe you'll take it black instead." He handed her the mug of coffee. "Be a good girl and sip it slowly. It's piping hot."

She glared at him but took the mug, the aroma too tantalizing to resist. As she reached for the mug, the sheet slipped, exposing one breast. Talia struggled to pull the sheet back in place, nearly spilling the coffee.

Harm tucked the sheet beneath her arm and winked. "You know, I've seen all of you."

"At night. All wet," she countered and took a sip of the coffee, careful not to burn her tongue. "And it's different."

"How so?" He tilted his head to the side, studying her. "You're the same person today as you were last night."

"Last night I was…" Again, words escaped her.

"Beautiful." Harm kissed her forehead. "Sexy." He kissed the tip of her nose. "Amazing." His lips found hers. Without breaking the lip-lock, he took the coffee mug from her hand, set it on the nightstand and kissed her thoroughly.

He tasted of coffee and bacon, making her tummy rumble. Talia couldn't fight what her body wanted. She raised both arms, wrapped her hands behind his neck and pulled him down to her.

Harm lay on the bed beside her and dragged her into his arms, his hands gliding over her skin, warm, rough and igniting every nerve where he touched.

Talia forgot to be shy or embarrassed as her body awakened to Harm.

His kiss deepened, his tongue pushing past her teeth.

Talia opened to him, loving the taste, feel and strength of the man. She tangled her fingers in his hair in an effort to get even closer, but he was dressed for the day, not naked like her.

Harm's hand slipped down the small of her back to her bottom, where he smacked her lightly and pushed to a sitting position. "There's nothing I'd like better than to spend the day in bed, making love to you, but I'll bet that within the next twenty minutes or less, someone will come searching for you."

She sighed and pulled the sheet back up over her body. "I suppose you're right."

He stood, handed her the mug of coffee and pulled a long T-shirt out of his duffel bag. "You can wear this to get to your room and your own clothing."

Again, he took the mug and set it on the nightstand, then held the shirt over her head.

Talia raised her arms, letting the sheet drop around her waist. Part of her hoped it would be enough to entice the man to throw caution to the wind, strip naked and join her.

The shirt slipped over her head and arms and pooled around her hips. So much for dreaming lusty thoughts.

Harm brought the tray over and set it on the bed beside her. Together they ate the food Jamba had prepared, feeding each other like lovers.

Talia couldn't remember the last time someone had served her breakfast in bed. Probably her mother, bringing soup when she'd been a sick child.

She liked being treated like a cherished princess, if only for an hour. The man was chalking up a pile of points in his favor. Talia would have to guard her heart well or risk losing it to the SEAL.

Once they'd finished their breakfast in bed, Talia gathered her clothing and ran for her room down the hall. She had barely dressed when a knock on her door forced her to finish quickly.

"Mrs. Talia, Mrs. Talia, you have a visitor," Nahla's voice called out through the paneling.

Talia looked one last time at what her life had been

and laid the photograph facedown on the nightstand. She crossed to open the door and found Nahla wringing her hands and staring over her shoulder at the staircase. When she realized Talia had opened the door, she gushed, "Mr. Krause from Pinnacle Ranch is in the great room. He wanted to talk with you. What do you want me to tell him?"

"I'm coming down. Did Jim say what he wanted?"

"No, ma'am. He just wanted to talk to you. He's down there now with the guests."

Talia's lips quirked. She could imagine Jim sitting among the navy SEALs. They'd overwhelm him with their size and the breadth of their shoulders.

Jim wasn't a small man, but he wasn't built like the SEALs. She wondered what they'd find to talk about.

With one last glance at her room, she hurried out the door and down the stairs to the great room where Jim Krause sat with the six navy SEALs, Angela and Marly.

Harm saw her first and stood. The rest of the men rose to their feet. Jim was last. He strode to her and extended a hand.

"Jim, it's good to see you. What's it been? Three months?" she asked.

"At least. We seem to be so caught up in our own businesses, it's hard to get out and pay our respects to the neighbors." His grip on her hand was cool and a little clammy, but firm almost to the point of hurting.

When he released her fingers, she moved her hand behind her back. "Would you like a cup of coffee?"

"No, thank you. I came by to see how you were. I understand there was some trouble in the village last night."

Talia nodded. "Apparently the village idiots don't

like the idea of the women protesting the slaughter of protected animals."

Jim shook his head. "I don't know what it will take to get everyone on the same page for conservancy."

"The demand has to dry up or be jailed before the poachers will quit poaching." She was stating the obvious, but Jim knew the stakes. "The poachers don't understand that when these animals are gone, there won't be any more to replace them. Not only will they become extinct, but the tourism industry will dry up and the locals will have no way to make enough money to feed their families."

Jim nodded. "The money is far too good to stop them now."

Talia knew this to be true. The danger to the animals was real, and not enough of the right people seemed to give a damn. "Yesterday, we came across a dead rhinoceros in the national preserve."

Jim's eyes narrowed. "Horns removed?"

Talia nodded, pressing her lips together in a tight line. "Such a waste of an animal, all for its horns and superstitious nonsense."

"When you can get thirty thousand dollars for a single horn, the money talks," Jim said.

"Yeah, but the poachers aren't getting that much. The middlemen are." Talia wrapped her arms around her midsection, aware Harm was standing close to her. His mere presence made her feel somehow protected.

"Still, the poachers are getting more for the horns than they can make in a year working at one of our resorts or ranches," Jim pointed out. He looked at her closer. "But how are you since Michael passed? I'm surprised you haven't sold this place and moved back to the States where it's much safer. Let me know when you're ready to sell. I'd be interested in taking the place off your hands."

"Thanks, Jim, but I haven't made that decision yet, and I'm not sure I will." In her peripheral vision, she could see Harm. She'd shared a heated moment with the man, but was it enough to leave behind her hopes and dreams for All Things Wild?

"Michael loved this place, but without him, you're exposed. Though Kenya is becoming more and more modern, it's still a country where women aren't as valued as men."

Talia bristled. "Maybe because they haven't stood up for themselves. The village women are taking strides in that direction."

Jim's eyes narrowed. "And what came of it? I understand they were raided during the middle of their little meeting last night, putting them and their children in danger."

Jim was right. The women had taken a stand, but the danger was real.

"They're trying," Talia said. She lifted her chin. "What brings you out this morning?"

"Just checking on my neighbor. It's past time. I'm sure Michael would have wanted me to take a more active role in ensuring your safety." Jim glanced around at the men assembled in the great room. "Although it appears you have guests who can more than assume the role of protector."

Harm stepped forward an inch, his arms crossed over his chest. "We're looking out for Mrs. Ryan," he confirmed.

Jim nodded. "I'm glad to see she has someone look-ing out for her well-being. How long will you be here?"

"A week," Big Jake confirmed.

"A week." Jim faced Talia, his eyebrows rising. He glanced around. "What happened to your hired body-guards?"

As much as she hated answering, Talia couldn't be rude and ignore the man's question. "I haven't been able to hire new ones since the last shooting."

Jim swept his arm to encompass the room. "And when these fine gentlemen are gone? Who will protect you from poachers or rebels?"

Talia stood straighter, her shoulders pushed back, her chin raised. "I have a gun. I know how to use it."

"If you see them coming and they don't outnumber you." Her neighbor shook his head. "Face it, Talia, you need to sell and move on with your life. This was Mi-chael's dream, not yours."

"It was both of our dreams," Talia insisted. Some-thing about Jim's insistence made her back teeth grind. The fact that she was a woman shouldn't have any bear-ing on her ability to run the resort. She'd done just fine for the past year. Only for the last couple of months had she been plagued with troubles.

Two of her guards had been killed the last time the SEALs had been her guests. She frowned. Could it be they were the draw? As quick as the thought surfaced, she put it aside. They'd been gone a couple weeks, and the troubles had continued in their absence. The local witch doctor was blaming it on her being a woman, run-ning a resort without a man to protect her.

"For the record," Talia said, "I have no intention of selling, now or anytime in the future."

Jim held out his hand to Talia. "I understand. If you should change your mind, I'll do what I can to help you out." He tipped his head toward the men in the room, his glance lingering longer on Harm. "Nice to meet you gentlemen. I hope you enjoy your stay in Kenya before your return to duty." With that, he turned and left the lodge.

Talia followed him to the door and closed it behind him. Then she turned and leaned back against the wood paneling, letting go of the breath she'd been holding.

Harm reached for her hand. "Are you all right?"

She nodded. "It doesn't seem to matter how well I run this place, there are more doubters than supporters around here for a woman running a business alone. It makes me so angry. I'm fully capable of owning and operating this resort. I don't need a man to back me, and I don't want to sell."

"And you shouldn't feel like you have to. This is your place. No one should tell you how to run it or to leave."

"Damn right." Big Jake joined them in the front foyer. "From all we've seen, you do a helluva job and have every reason to be proud of your accomplishments."

The other SEALs gathered around her, along with Marly and Angela.

"You're amazing, running an operation like this," Marly said. "All I had to do was fly a single airplane. You manage an entire army of people to keep this place running."

"I *used* to manage a lot of people." Talia sighed. "Lately, I can't keep them. They're bailing on me like mice on a sinking ship."

"Because of rumors and witch doctor mumbo jumbo," Angela added.

"Still, if I can't get help, I can't run this place. I might as well sell it." Talia tugged on her hand to release it from Harm's grip.

He didn't let go. "You just told Krause you weren't selling."

"And when I told him that, I meant it. At least not selling it to him."

"Why not him?"

Her cheeks heated. "He makes my teeth grind. He tried to buy the place from my husband on several occasions, but Michael refused to sell to him. He didn't trust the man."

"Why?"

She shrugged. "Gut feeling." Talia pasted a smile on her face. "So, what's on the agenda for the day? Are you certain you don't want to go on safari?"

T-Mac raised a hand. "I'm all for a beer and the swimming pool."

"I have my eyes on that hammock I saw in the garden," Diesel said. "After I call Reese."

"How's she doing back in the States?" T-Mac asked.

"She's landed another bodyguard gig. Apparently, Secretary of Defense Klein spread the word that she's one tough cookie and can handle any job, big or small."

"And how do you feel about that after your trek in the jungle?" Harm asked.

Diesel shrugged. "She'd be good, and it's what she wants to do. I'll take any time I can get with her."

"It'll be tough keeping up a relationship with both of you on disparate missions," Harm said.

"We'll make it work. I love that woman." Diesel

grinned. "She's everything I didn't know I was look-ing for, and then some."

Talia's heart squeezed in her chest. She'd had that with Michael, and they'd been together all their mar-ried life. Until Michael died. Now, the thought of start-ing over with another relationship was daunting to the point of terrifying.

"What if she's injured or—God forbid—killed on the job?" Talia asked.

Diesel's lips thinned. "Then I will have had her for as long as I did and loved every minute of it. It goes both ways. I could be killed on my job and leave her alone. We both know the risks and are willing to ac-cept them. We don't know how long we have on this earth, but we want to spend as much of that time as we can with each other."

Harm's hand tightened on Talia's.

She didn't dare glance in his direction. She wasn't sure what she'd see, nor was she sure she was ready for whatever came next between them.

For now, she had her own issues to face, dealing with the troubles at the resort. She had to focus on them, not on a potential love affair that would only end in heartbreak.

Chapter Eleven

Diesel's words hit Harm square in the chest. His teammate knew he wouldn't be able to spend much of his time with the love of his life, Reese Brantley, but he was willing to commit to her nonetheless.

Relationships for SEALs were usually doomed to failure because of the nature of the job. They were seldom home and, when they were, they were on call for whatever emergency or mission arose. They had to be ready to bug out at a moment's notice. What woman could handle that kind of uncertainty?

His hand tightened on Talia's. This was a woman who faced hardships head-on and didn't back down. She'd stood up to her neighbor when the man suggested she give up and move on. As a lone woman in what could be a hostile country, she had enough difficulties to face without being burdened with a long-distance relationship—one in which the man would rarely make it back to Kenya to see her.

Wait. What was he thinking? He wasn't considering a long-term relationship with Talia, was he? The thought of walking away at the end of the week was looking less and less appealing. The woman had managed to crawl beneath his skin and straight through to that hardened muscle in his chest.

It wasn't so hard anymore, was it?

Like Reese was to Diesel, Talia was everything Harm hadn't known he was looking for in a woman. She was smart, tough, beautiful and loyal to the man she loved with all her heart. She'd love her husband… deeply.

Harm hadn't known he was looking for someone who could love so hard and fiercely. But that's what he wanted. Someone like Talia.

What was he thinking? Anything between the two of them would never work. She was tied to this resort in the heart of Kenya, a world away from the place Harm called home in Virginia.

He couldn't promise her anything, and he couldn't expect her to promise him love and commitment when he wasn't sure when he'd be back in Africa again.

It was pure insanity to even think he could be with Talia. He'd have to quit the navy. Then he'd be jobless. What woman wanted a man who couldn't pull in a paycheck?

No, he'd be better off sticking to his original idea of a quick fling and leave at the end of the week. No strings. No commitment.

Still, he couldn't bring himself to release Talia's hand. In the few days he had left at the All Things Wild Resort, he had to help Talia figure out where the threat originated and nip it in the bud. Or blow it out of the water. Whatever left her safe and made him feel better about leaving her alone.

"Buck and I are going to the village to see if anyone needs any medical attention after last night's raid," Angela said.

"I promised one of the local ranchers I'd stop by and check out his plane," Marly said.

"You're not considering buying another plane, are you?" Big Jake asked.

Pitbull chuckled. "No, she doesn't need any more target practice."

Marly elbowed him in the side. "I didn't use my plane as target practice. I couldn't let that monster get away in it and continue dealing in exotic animals and human trafficking. My choices were let him go free or sacrifice my plane." She lifted her chin. "As far as I was concerned, there was no choice. I saw some of the animals and women he'd stolen. He was a monster. Blowing up my plane was a small price to pay for ridding this planet of that scum."

"And you did the right thing." Pitbull kissed her and hugged her close. "I know how much that plane meant to you."

"Damn right." She kissed him back.

Pitbull hooked an arm around her and faced the others. "And I'm going with Marly today. Unless you need me to pound on some poachers."

Talia laughed. "I wish we could find them and let you pound on them. Unfortunately, they always manage to slip away before we can nail them with the goods."

"What about you, Big Jake?" Harm asked. "Are you hanging out here? Or do you want to ride with us into the village to do some questioning?"

"I think I'll tag along with you. I'm interested in finding out who busted up your party last night."

"Great." T-Mac headed for the door. "Call if you need backup. Otherwise, you can find me at the pool."

"I left my weapon in my room. I'll be ready to go in a few minutes," Big Jake said and sprinted up the stairs.

The great room slowly cleared of everyone except Talia and Harm.

"What do you need help with first?" he asked.

"I need you to enjoy your vacation," she said. "I can handle things on my own."

He held up his hand. "You might as well save your breath. I'm sticking to you like a fly to flypaper. We need to get to the village to question the ladies about who crashed their party."

"I have to take care of things around here first. Give me an hour and I'll be ready to go to the village." She marched into the dining room and frowned.

"Looking for the dishes?" Harm asked from behind her.

Talia frowned. "Well, yes."

"The guys cleaned up after themselves, washed and put away their dishes." Harm chuckled. "They might be hard to house-train, but they're familiar with KP."

"KP?" Talia asked.

"Kitchen patrol." Harm followed Talia into the kitchen, where the chef was pulling a roast out of the oven.

The scent of roast and seasonings filled the air and made Harm's mouth water.

"Um." Talia sniffed the air. "That smells wonderful."

"I made it for lunch," Jamba said. "The men can make sandwiches, or I can cook a pot of rice and make gravy."

"Sandwiches will be fine," Harm said. "They won't care, as long as it's easy and satisfying."

"Good, then I'll help clean cabins and make beds," the chef offered.

"Don't," Talia said. "I've got that covered."

Harm shook his head. "The guys assured me they made their own beds. They won't need service in their rooms or cabins."

"But they'll want fresh towels," Talia insisted.

Harm shook his head. "They're all about reusing and saving the environment. They can use them one more time, and then we'll gather them and bring them to the laundry room tomorrow."

Talia tapped a finger to her chin, the frown still in place. "That doesn't leave much for me to do."

"Good." He touched her arm. "Then we can get into the village and find out who's behind the troubles."

"Yeah, about that," she said. "I've been asking around for the past couple of weeks and have yet to locate the instigator."

"You have me to help now." He held up his hands. "Not that you couldn't do it on your own. Woman power and all. I'm just saying two heads could be better than one on this effort."

She laughed. "All right, then. Give me a minute to check on the truck—"

He grinned. "I had Marly and Pitbull install the starter this morning before breakfast. It's running like a champ."

Talia's lips twisted into a wry grin. "You've thought of everything."

"I try." He held out his arm. "Ready?"

Her eyes narrowed. "I'm not sure."

"Not sure about what?" he asked, all innocence and charm.

"Not sure I trust you." But she hooked her hand through his arm anyway.

"What's not to trust?" He winked and led her through the kitchen door to the front entrance.

Big Jake met them there and followed them out to the truck.

Harm offered to drive but said it would tie up his shooting hand if he did. Jake did the same, so Talia took the wheel. The truck behaved itself and started right up. The drive into the village was blessedly uneventful.

By all appearances, nothing untoward had occurred the night before. The bonfire in the middle of the square had been reduced to a pile of ashes. Small children scampered between the huts, crying out in excitement. Mothers worked over smaller cooking fires, wove baskets or pieced together beadwork for sale to the tourists. If Harm didn't know better, he'd think it was just another day in rural Kenya.

Talia parked the truck on the edge of the village.

Big Jake got out and headed one direction while Talia and Harm went another.

His pistol tucked beneath his light jacket, Harm took Talia's hand as they walked into the center of the buildings.

Talia greeted several of the women and knelt to hug a couple children. She appeared to be looking for someone. After a few minutes, she leaned into Harm. "I don't see Eriku."

"And we haven't asked about the events of last evening," he reminded her in a quiet voice only she could hear.

Beneath her breath, she answered, "I'm sensing the women are a little more closed off than usual."

"How so?"

"Normally, they rush to greet me and ask how things are at the resort. They used to all want to work for me. But now…" She shook her head. "I feel like they will shut down altogether if I start asking questions."

"Then let me," Harm said. He started toward one of the elderly women who squatted on her haunches over a cooking pot, stirring the contents slowly.

"Excuse me, ma'am," Harm started.

She glanced up at him through glazed eyes with a disturbing white film over her pupils. Was she blind? If so, she wouldn't have seen anything that had happened the night before.

Already committed to conversing with the woman, Harm was shocked when she cleared her throat and said, "Eriku is not here. She went with Jolani to the preserve because she'd heard poachers were after the elephants for their tusks. If she is killed…" Her rheumy gaze shot to Talia, who was walking toward Harm. "Why did you have to turn Eriku against her own people?"

"What do you mean? I didn't turn her against her own people," Talia said. She squatted on her haunches beside the older woman. "She learned what was happening to her country, to the animals in Kenya and all of Africa. She decided to do something about it."

"We were happy before you and your husband arrived. We were not fighting among ourselves." A frown deepened the grooves across the woman's forehead. "Now, you will cost us the lives of our young people, our children and our men."

Talia sighed. "I'm not the one poaching. Nor am I the one attacking your people like last night. I'm as much a victim as the women and children were last night."

"But the men wouldn't have attacked if you had not come to the village," the old lady insisted. "It's you. Gakuru is right. A lone woman can't run a resort. It creates bad juju. Nothing has been right since your husband died. You must leave before our village loses anyone else."

"Anyone else? Who have you lost?"

The old woman's lips clamped shut, and she turned away from Talia.

Talia straightened. Harm cupped her elbow and led her away from the crotchety old villager. "Don't listen to her. You didn't cause the problems around here. The poachers know what they are doing is illegal. Someone would eventually catch them in the act. The fact that you turned them over to the sheriff isn't a reflection on you making life worse for the villagers. Their actions—killing protected species—are what's causing the rift among their people."

"I know that. But if you hear the same thing over and over, you start believing it to be true. Maybe I am bad juju."

Big Jake hurried over to them. "No one's talking or naming names of the people who attacked last night. However, the few people I spoke to all said they think Eriku is in trouble."

Talia touched Big Jake's arm. "Where did she go? Did they say?"

Harm wanted to know the same. The savanna contained a vast number of wide-open acres of grass, watering holes and massive herds of wild animals. Finding Eriku in all of that would be close to impossible without a direction to head.

Big Jake frowned. "The people I spoke with said she

was heading for the elephants' favorite watering hole." His eyes narrowed. "Do you know where that is?"

Talia grinned. "I do. But we better get there in a hurry. If Eriku is there to stop the poachers, I fear she's in trouble. She won't have a weapon to protect herself, even if the poachers took the teenager seriously."

The three headed back to the truck and jumped in.

Talia spun the vehicle around and punched the accelerator to the floor, heading north toward the savanna and the elephant watering hole.

Thirty minutes stretched by in excruciating slowness, no matter that Talia had the accelerator all the way to the floor, kicking up a plume of dust behind the truck.

Harm held on to keep from being thrown into the dash or ejected from the vehicle altogether.

In the seat behind the cab, Big Jake grunted and bounced around, tossed like a rag doll on the bumpy, rutted road across the savanna.

"I assume you know where you're going?" Harm yelled over the roar of the engine and the noise of the tires hitting the ruts.

Talia nodded, her grip so tight on the steering wheel that her knuckles turned white. "I just hope we're in time to help Eriku. She shouldn't have gone out alone."

"She's with Jolani? I take it Jolani is a man?" Harm asked, his teeth rattling with the effort.

Talia nodded. "But they're no match for the poachers. They'd just as soon shoot them than have witnesses to their destruction. Foolish girl," Talia muttered and held on as the vehicle lurched violently into a hole and the steering wheel was almost jerked out of her hand.

Harm would have offered to drive, but changing drivers would slow them down, and Talia knew where she was going. He didn't.

After twenty-five minutes of being beaten up by the road, they rounded a curve in the path and emerged from a stand of trees, arriving at the edge of a large muddy pond.

A herd of zebras scattered in all directions and cape buffalo shifted from hoof to hoof, but retained their lazy stance near the life-giving liquid.

"This is the elephants' watering hole?"

Talia nodded. "They usually show up here." She sat behind the wheel, her hands still gripping it tightly.

No elephants and no Eriku in sight. "I don't know where else to look. Unless…" She stepped on the accelerator and spun the truck around, heading back to the rutted road and straight for a stand of acacia trees. "They hang out in the shade sometimes!" Talia yelled.

Harm was glad to know it, but his teeth were banging together so hard, he didn't bother to respond. He hoped they found the elephants and Eriku before he chipped his teeth down to nubs.

TALIA'S HEART RACED and her arms hurt from manhandling the steering wheel of the old pickup, heading straight for the copse of trees she'd known the elephants to retreat to when the sun got too hot. If they weren't there, she wasn't sure where she'd look to find Eriku. The girl needed to understand how dangerous it was to chase after poachers.

As she pulled into the shadows of the grove of acacia trees, she saw the huge silhouettes of elephants standing in a circle.

"Oh, no." Talia's heart sank to the pit of her belly. She

slowed the vehicle and eased up to where the elephants stood, swaying slightly from foot to foot.

One of the largest of the elephants nudged at something on the ground and then raised her trunk in the air and trumpeted. The other elephants joined her, trumpeting so loud, Talia had to cover her ears.

One of the pachyderms shifted just enough that Talia could see between them to the animal lying on the ground in a pool of blood, its tusks missing, hacked out of its head.

Bile rose in Talia's throat. She swallowed hard to keep from losing it in front of the men.

Harm swore softly beside her. He'd pulled his gun from the holster beneath his light jacket and scanned the area.

Talia focused her gaze on Harm rather than on the dead elephant.

The herd gathered around their fallen member. Now silent, they paid tribute to their dead, a giant ring of solidarity in the face of the tragedy.

"We should go," Big Jake said. "Apparently, we're too late for the elephant."

"Any sign of Eriku?"

"Without getting out on foot, we can't comb the brush to search."

"It's not safe to get out," Talia said. "After what happened here, we can't guarantee that the elephants won't mistake us for the poachers who killed their friend." She shifted into Reverse and backed slowly away. The truck backfired, the sound like that of a high-powered rifle in the silence of nature.

The big elephant who'd trumpeted her sadness swung

around at the sound. Seconds later, she was running toward the truck, building up to full speed.

"Go! Go! Go!" Harm shouted, holding on to the dash and the armrest.

Talia was afraid to turn around and lose the lead she had on the not-so-gentle giant, who seemed to be in a rage to trample the occupants of the truck.

Talia pressed hard on the accelerator, sending the vehicle hurtling backward. For several long seconds, she didn't think they'd get away before the elephant slammed into the front of the truck.

"We can't afford to lose this truck, too," Talia muttered, staring over her shoulder at the field of grass behind them.

"More than losing this truck, I think we can't afford to let that elephant catch up to us." Harm stared out the front of the vehicle at the monstrous pachyderm pounding the ground, racing toward them.

Judging her direction by glancing in the side mirrors, Talia blasted backward, refusing to slow down before the raging cow elephant. Though she didn't focus on the animal, Talia could see her movements in her peripheral vision. The sheer size and anger in those dark eyes had her heart thundering against her ribs and her palms sweating on the steering wheel.

Soon the elephant slowed, tiring after a mad dash across the savanna.

Talia kept going, determined to get as much distance between them and the herd as possible. When she could afford to safely turn around and drive away without being trampled, she did. And they were on their way back toward the village, tragedy averted.

Harm and Talia watched each of the side mirrors.

"She stopped running," Harm said.

"Whew!" Big Jake leaned over the seat and pounded Harm on the back. "Talia had me worried for a moment. That elephant could have stomped the crap out of this truck, with us in it." He laughed. "I never should have doubted our driver. She's amazing."

"Yes, she is." Harm reached across the cab and touched Talia's shoulder.

Talia's insides warmed until she thought again about the elephant brutally murdered by the poachers.

The killing had to stop. But first, she had to find Eriku and make sure she wasn't as much a victim as the elephant lying dead on the Kenyan savanna.

Chapter Twelve

Harm didn't like the carnage he'd witnessed. And the vision of solidarity in the pack of elephants' grief stuck with him long after he'd left the scene of the crime.

"How can people do that to an animal and call themselves human?" Big Jake asked.

"For money," Talia replied, her lips thinning. "My biggest question right now is where the hell is Eriku? If they did anything to hurt her..." Her hands tightened on the steering wheel until her knuckles turned white.

Harm held on as they bumped along the dirt road back to the lodge. "Who else would know where to find Eriku?"

Talia shook her head. "I don't know. The people in the village told us what they knew. The only people who might know are the poachers who killed the elephant."

"Where to from here?" Harm asked.

"Back to the lodge. I need to call in the park rangers to document and investigate the kill. This can't continue."

The ride back to the lodge was considerably slower than the ride to the elephant watering hole, but still bumpy. Harm held on to keep from being thrown from the open-sided truck.

They arrived after noon. No sooner had they pulled into the compound than the other four members of the SEAL team emerged from the lodge, along with Marly and Angela.

Harm hurried around to the driver's side of the truck, but Talia had already slipped from her seat onto the ground.

"Did you find Eriku?" Angela asked.

Talia shook her head. "No. But we found another dead animal."

"Another rhino?" Buck guessed.

T-Mac stepped up beside Buck. "Or was it an elephant?"

Harm's eyes narrowed. "What makes you think it was an elephant this time?"

"Buck and Angela said you'd gotten word from the villagers that Eriku had gone out to stop poachers at the elephant watering hole." T-Mac's jaw tightened. "But that's not the only reason I guessed elephant. You have to see what I found online."

Harm's gut knotted. "What?"

"Just come inside and see. It might be a coincidence, or it might have some bearing on what's going on around here."

Harm reached for Talia's hand and followed T-Mac into the lodge. He caught up with Diesel and leaned close. "Do you know what he's talking about?"

Diesel shook his head. "It's a mystery to me. T-Mac's been holed up in the study since he came in from his swim. Can't keep that man away from computers for long."

All he could figure was that T-Mac had found something on the internet, but he couldn't imagine it would help them resolve what was happening in Kenya. The troubles there were deeper and more prevalent than a SEAL team on vacation could eradicate in the few days they had left there.

T-Mac sat in the chair behind the desk and ran his fingers across the keyboard.

The rest of the SEAL team, Marly, Angela and Talia crowded around him as an image appeared on the monitor. In the middle of the screen was a rhinoceros lying on its side. A man with a rifle stood with his foot on the animal's neck. The proud hunter had killed the animal and was posing over his dead conquest. The rhino was intact, still in possession of his two horns.

A collective gasp rose from everyone in the room.

"That could be an old photograph," Talia suggested.

"I looked up the stats on it. It was posted yesterday."

"Still, it could be an old photo," Angela said.

"I thought of that, too, but look here." T-Mac enlarged the image and pointed to the hindquarters of the rhino. A distinctive scar could clearly be seen. A scar exactly like the one on the rhino they'd found dead the day before.

Talia cursed beneath her breath. "If what I'm seeing is true, the poachers didn't kill the rhino. They only scavenged what was left." She lifted the telephone. "I need to report this to the park rangers. They need to know someone is illegally hunting on protected land."

"Wait, you'll want to see this." T-Mac clicked a few keys, and another image appeared.

This time it wasn't a rhinoceros lying on the ground. It was a larger animal. Again, a hunter stood with a big rifle, his foot on the neck of the dead animal. The dead elephant still had its tusks.

"This photograph was posted last night." T-Mac glanced toward Harm. "Was that your dead elephant you found today?"

"We didn't get close enough to identify specific details," Harm admitted. "Its friends were gathered around and didn't like being interrupted in their grief."

"Who posted the pictures?" Talia demanded.

"I'm working on that," T-Mac said. "I can trace it back to an IP address. If you give me a little more time, I might be able to get the name of the owner of that IP address."

"Get it." Talia lifted the telephone and punched numbers on the keypad before she looked up again. "The more ammunition we have to give the rangers, the better off they'll be in locating the hunter and the outfitter who brought him to the preserve to kill."

Talia gave the information to the Kenya Wildlife Service and promised to be available to answer any further questions and take them out to the site when they could send a ranger. When she hung up the phone, she appeared tired and disheartened. "Why can't people understand these animals are a finite quantity? The more they kill, the fewer there will be until they become extinct." She jabbed a finger toward the man in the image. "And I'll bet that man is educated, has a degree and probably a lot of money. He, of all people, should know what his sport is costing the world." She backed away. "I'm sorry. This isn't your problem. I have to keep reminding myself you all are here on vacation. You shouldn't be burdened with our issues." She turned and walked away.

Harm's heart squeezed hard in his chest.

"She doesn't understand that this is what we do," Diesel said. "We fight for what's right."

"I don't know about you, but I feel like punching someone," Pitbull said. "Namely, the guy in that picture."

"You and me both," Buck said. "He can't be too far from here, if we're finding his trophies." He leaned over T-Mac's shoulder. "There has to be some connection to this area."

"I'm working on it," T-Mac said. "Like I said, it takes time."

"Well, we might not have time. He could be out there now taking aim at another animal."

"We have to find him before he succeeds," Big Jake said.

"Exactly," Diesel agreed. "And we have to find whoever is leading him there."

Big Jake shook his head slowly, his eyes sad. "You should have seen those other elephants. It was downright heartbreaking the way they rallied around their fallen comrade."

The other occupants of the room fell silent.

Harm heard all their comments, but his gaze followed Talia from the room. She was in a bad spot with what was happening. If she called the wildlife service every time an animal died, soon the rangers would be camped in their area, which would put a damper on the killing and on whoever was leading the hunts. Harm would bet there was a lot of money paid out to go on one of those hunts. And money was a huge motivator. People would kill for money. Sometimes not even a lot of money.

Could it be the troubles Talia was having were all motivated by money?

Harm would like to question the witch doctor in the village. What if someone was paying him to scare Talia away from the resort? Paying off a witch doctor had to be a drop in the bucket compared to the amount a rich hunter might pay for a chance to bag exotic game.

Harm followed Talia across the great room and into the kitchen. She had to be hurting and scared for Eriku.

He wanted to take away her pain and help her in any way he could. She was in danger, and they had yet to resolve who was at the root of the problem. The end of the week loomed, seeming to speed toward him. How could he leave her when his time there was up?

TALIA WAS GOING through the motions of running the resort. She had rooms to clean, guests to see to and meals to plan. None of these things took the edge off her worry for Eriku. The teen had likely stepped into the middle of a hot spot. Poachers were ruthless and wouldn't hesitate to kill a girl bent on shutting down their operation.

And she couldn't begin to guess how ruthless the man leading hunters to the kill was. Her stomach roiled at the images of the rhino and the elephant running through her mind, like a film reel stuck on replay.

Jamba was at the stove, stirring something in a pot. The aroma made Talia's belly tighten and growl. They'd missed lunch while out on the savanna.

"Roast's warming in the oven," Jamba said. "But if you wait an hour, dinner will be ready early."

"Thanks, Jamba." Talia turned to Harm. "Would you like to split half a roast beef sandwich?"

"Only if you let me make it. I'm sure you have a dozen things you need to be doing."

She smiled. "I'm tired just thinking about all the things I should be doing."

"Then sit and let me make the sandwich. I might not be the best cook, but give me bread and meat and I can make a mean snack." He winked and led her to the industrial-style table in the corner of the kitchen and pressed her into a chair. "Sit for a minute. You did all the hard work driving today."

She started to rise. "Yeah, but I was sitting then."

He pressed his hand on her shoulder. "And it took a lot of muscle to manhandle that truck through all those ruts. You could probably beat any one of us in arm wrestling."

She laughed. "Not hardly."

He opened the refrigerator and retrieved a bottle of water, unscrewed the cap and set it on the table in front of her. "Hydrate."

Talia popped a salute. "Yes, sir." But she took the bottle and downed half of it before she took another breath. She hadn't realized how thirsty she was until Harm had set the chilled bottle in front of her. "Thank you."

"You're welcome." With her directing, he collected lettuce, tomatoes, mayonnaise and mustard and set them on the counter. Then he sliced off two thick slices of the homemade bread Jamba baked daily and pulled the roast from the warming oven.

Talia sat mesmerized by his every move.

Harm had shed his jacket, working now in a T-shirt that was stretched taut over his chest and arms. Every move caused his muscles to flex, every sinew well defined beneath his smooth skin.

Talia couldn't help comparing Harm to her late husband. Michael had been lean and strong, but not bulky. He'd been a running back in the United States and he walked a lot in Kenya, but he hadn't been as well built as Harm. Every time Harm touched her, she could feel the sheer strength in his fingers. If he wanted, he could crush her in his grip. But he didn't. He was very careful not to hurt her. For such a big guy, he was gentle and considerate of her every need.

By the time Harm finished making the sandwich and cutting it in half, she was very hungry. But not for food. Along with her desire came a healthy dose of guilt. Was she being unfaithful to her husband's memory by lusting after another man under the roof she'd shared with Michael?

Michael wouldn't have wanted her to spend the rest of her life alone, but had she mourned him long enough? How long was long enough? Judging by the fact that she was questioning the length of time one should mourn, was it a clear indication she was ready to move on?

Harm placed the two sandwich halves on small plates and carried them to the table. He grinned at her and sat directly opposite her.

His grin made her feel warm and liquid all over. If she'd been standing, her knees would have wobbled, suddenly boneless.

He lifted his sandwich and waited for her to take hers. "I hope you like mustard and mayo."

"Love them both." Talia held up her snack. "Thanks."

"Don't thank me until you try it. Could be the worst thing ever."

She bit into the moist roast beef, slathered in mustard and mayo. The explosion of flavors filled her mouth and she moaned. "Mmm." With her mouth too full to voice her opinion, she chewed and swallowed first. "Amazing."

"In a good way?" he asked.

"In the best way." She pushed aside her feelings of guilt and basked in the intimacy of sharing a sandwich with a sexy SEAL.

For a few minutes, they ate in silence. Then Harm asked, "Who do you know around here who runs a hunting outfit?"

She shook her head. "No one. It's illegal to hunt endangered animals. Especially when they're on a national reserve."

"What other groups offer safari treks?" Harm asked between bites of his sandwich.

"There are several resorts like All Things Wild. Tourism is big business in Africa. There's the Campfire Adventurers, African Explorers, Go Africa and other smaller outfitters like Krause Tours, us, Heart of Africa Safaris…" She smiled. "I could go on."

Harm held up a hand. "No. No. I get the idea. There are a lot of outfitters leading safaris in Kenya." He shook his head. "I guess I didn't realize how big the business was."

"All you have to do is go online and key in 'African safaris in Kenya' and you'll be overwhelmed."

"Remind me to thank Marly for recommending you. I could get stressed just by the overwhelming number of outfitters to choose from."

"Exactly." Talia finished her sandwich and gathered their plates. "Since none of my cleaning staff came in today, I need to pull laundry duty." She held up her hand. "And no, you can't help. You've already waited on me for lunch. I won't let you enter the laundry room."

"In that case, I'll check out what T-Mac's looking at. Do you want me to head to the village and ask around about Eriku?"

Talia shook her head. "If they'd known anything, they would have told me."

"Even given the bad juju you supposedly have?" He smiled, dulling the hit.

With a wry twist of her lips, she sighed. "You're right. They could have sent me on a wild goose chase this morning, just to get rid of me."

"But you did find evidence of poaching."

She nodded, a frown pushing her brow downward. "I just hope Eriku is okay." Talia squared her shoulders. "In the meantime, I've got work to do. Help yourself to anything else you might want to eat or drink. I'll be back in the kitchen in time to set the table for dinner."

Talia would rather have stayed with Harm, but the more she was around him, the more she wanted to be with him. The end of the week would arrive before she knew it, and she'd find herself lonely and wishing he'd never left. She'd be better off weaning herself off his company before she got too used to having him around.

AN HOUR AND a half, two loads of towels, three loads of sheets and a shower later, she returned to the kitchen, her cheeks warm from the laundry room. The table had been set with cutlery, plates and glasses, and the SEALs were gathered in the kitchen trying to help but only getting in Jamba's way.

"Shoo," Talia said. "Jamba is a master chef and needs

his space to prepare such wonderful dishes." She sniffed the pot on the stove. "What are we having tonight?"

"Roast lamb shank and my special sauce, potatoes au gratin and brussels sprouts," Jamba replied. "And I made a special dessert of cherries jubilee and home-made ice cream."

"I'm for skipping right to dessert," Buck announced.

"Out." Angela herded him toward the door. "You heard the lady. Jamba needs his space to prepare his culinary delights."

Buck kissed her on the lips and grinned. "Yes, ma'am. I'm going."

The rest of the SEALs and Marly exited the kitchen, all except Harm.

Talia's heart warmed. In the short time she'd been away from him, he hadn't been out of her thoughts for a moment. "You, too."

"I'm here to carry food to the table. We can't expect you and Jamba to handle everything."

"Yes. You. Can." She drew in a deep breath and let it out. "Don't you understand? You're the guest, for heaven's sake."

"What you don't understand is that we don't mind helping. In fact, putting us to work keeps us out of trouble." He raised his brows, a smile tugging at the corners of his lips. "And let me tell you, those guys can get into trouble if they don't have something to keep them busy." He jabbed a thumb to his chest. "Including me."

Jamba set the lamb shank on a platter, sliced through the meat, poured his special sauce over it and handed the platter to Harm. "If you want to be useful, take this to the table."

Harm took the platter and smiled at Talia as if to

say, *See, I told you so.* Then he marched into the dining room to the loud cheers of his friends.

Talia stared after him, shaking her head.

"You like him, don't you?" Jamba said.

Jerked back to reality and the kitchen, Talia responded automatically, "I don't know what you're talking about."

"I might be older than you, but I'm not blind. You like that one." Jamba indicated Harm with a lift of his chin. "It is possible to fall in love again, you know."

Talia's cheeks burned as she busied herself pulling the dinner rolls out of the oven and placing them in a basket. "Who said I was falling in love again?"

"You loved your husband, but he's gone. A beautiful woman like you can't go through the rest of her life alone. If you find love, you should go after it."

"I have my life here. Anyone I might love would have to be willing to stay here and work like a dog to keep this place running. A man would have to be a fool to sign up for that kind of punishment."

Jamba chuckled. "Men have been known to be fools in love."

Talia cast a sideways glance at the chef. "Including you?"

He shrugged. "I, too, have been in love."

"You?" she asked, too stunned to hold back. When she realized it might have sounded rude, she added, "When?"

He turned off the burner on the stove, poured the brussels sprouts into a bowl and carried them to the door of the kitchen. He paused before leaving the room and said, "I fell in love with a woman at culinary school. But she was heading one way and I was coming home."

"And you wish you'd followed her?" Talia asked, her gaze softening.

He nodded. "Sometimes I wonder if she'd still be interested." Then he pushed through the door and left Talia standing in the kitchen, her heart hammering against her ribs as she caught a glimpse of Harm laughing with his friends. What would it be like to give up everything she'd worked for and dare to start over?

The door closed between the kitchen and the dining room. Was it an omen? If she waited too long to go after what she wanted, would the door close on the possibility?

She slipped her hands into oven mitts, pulled the potatoes out of the oven and carried them into the dining room. As she crossed the threshold, her cheeks burned again and her heart thundered against her ribs. She felt like she was standing on the edge of a precipice. Should she back away, or jump?

Throughout the meal, she remained quiet, afraid she'd blurt out something stupid, like declaring her undying love for a man she'd only known a short time. The thought left her tongue paralyzed and she refused to look up, lest Harm see her thoughts reflected in her eyes.

By the time dinner and dessert had been consumed, Talia's insides were tied in a knot and she couldn't think, other than to offer the guests an after-dinner drink and the use of the game room. Then she excused herself, claiming a headache, and ran for her room.

As she strode through her bedroom, she passed by the photograph on the nightstand of her and Michael standing in front of the first truck they'd purchased and had modified to conduct the photography safaris.

They'd been so proud of their accomplishments. They'd worked hard, investing sweat equity into cleaning up the old resort that had been established in the late 1960s. Michael had purchased the place for a song, convinced the old safari hunts would be better served as hunting for good shots—as in camera angles, not bullets.

Not all of the neighboring outfitters had been happy about their attempt to educate the tourists on the dangers of hunting the animals into extinction. Some still had the ability to purchase the right to hunt certain game, if they paid enough money to the right government officials. Those kinds of hunts had been outlawed in Kenya. But some said they still happened.

Talia lifted the photo frame and stared down at the smiling image of Michael, eight years younger and full of passion for the animals, his work and life in general. He'd been an amazing man.

She still missed him, but the pain of loss had faded to a dull ache. Up until a few weeks ago, Talia had been going through the motions, living one day to the next, as if in a fog. When the navy SEALs arrived, all that changed.

Those men had seen the horrors of war, had suffered the loss of their brothers in arms and continued to live life to the fullest. When things had gotten rough at the resort, they hadn't run in the opposite direction. They'd jumped in and attacked the problem. She admired their resilience and determination. They'd inspired her to pull her head out of the haze of her own loss and get on with life and living.

Maybe she was on the rebound from Michael's death, or tired of being lonely, but there was something there when she touched Harm. Something she'd never expected to feel again. That sense of wonder in a new relationship. The hope she'd felt when she was younger. That hope of finding the love of her life, that someone she could share her hopes and dreams with. Someone she could come home to and grow old with.

But Harm had been very clear with her. He was interested in a physical relationship, nothing else. Somewhere along the line of his life, he'd been hurt by a woman, causing him to be cautious when committing or giving his heart.

Talia suspected the man was holding back, maybe even lying to himself. Otherwise, he wouldn't have gone to the trouble of fixing breakfast for the two of them to share in bed. He'd have ditched her and gone down to eat at the table with his buddies.

But he'd chosen to come back to her. And he'd had the opportunity to make love to her again, and opted out to give her time to dress and be ready for her duties as hostess. If he'd been that interested in a physical relationship only, wouldn't he have taken her up on her offer of her body before breakfast?

Talia realized she was thinking of making love to Harm while she held a photograph of herself and her late husband.

A surge of guilt washed over her, making her stomach roil and her chest hurt. She could never forget how much she'd loved Michael and wished he was still there to share all of life's joys and challenges with her.

But the fact was, he was gone, and she had to find her new normal. She wasn't old enough to be put out to pasture. And, as Harm had pointed out, she wasn't too old to start over. Maybe fall in love again and have those children she'd put off because she and Michael had been too busy saving the animals to think of themselves or anyone else who might come along.

Talia reached out to touch Michael's face, only to come into contact with the cold, hard glass covering the image. Michael was gone. Talia had no other option but to continue living, breathing and making decisions that only involved her.

But to fall in love? With a stranger? No way. Jamba was wrong. Falling in love couldn't happen that fast. She'd dated Michael for several months before she knew he was the one for her. He'd been her best friend before he'd become her lover and then her husband.

With Harm, he'd gone straight from stranger to the person she lusted after. Successful relationships weren't founded on such shaky structure. They needed mutual understanding and respect, as well as time to get to know each other.

Harm was only there for a few more days. Why start something that could only be short term?

Talia ducked into the shower and rinsed off. Though she'd showered the dust of the savanna off her body earlier, she felt the need to cool her skin. Since before dinner, she'd alternated between cool and hot. She'd begun to wonder if she'd started early menopause with the accompanying hot flashes. But each time she got hot, she could trace the temperature increase to thoughts about Harm or glances exchanged with the man.

Yes, a cool shower might go a long way to restoring her balance.

Afterward, she slipped into a lightweight silk nightgown. Still overheated by the relentless fantasies swirling in her head, she dimmed the lights and stepped through the French doors leading out onto her balcony.

The cool night breeze brushed across her skin, calming her when nothing else seemed to do the trick.

The sound of a door opening and closing in the room beside hers made her jump and pushed her pulse into overdrive again. Harm's room shared the balcony with Talia's. If she really didn't want to see the man, she'd step back into her room and close her door.

But something made her stand her ground and stare out at the night. A shooting star flashed across the dark sky. Talia found herself making a wish. A wish for happiness. Whether it meant living her life alone at the resort…or falling in love with someone else…well, she left the wish open-ended. Let the chips fall where they would.

The French door from the room next to hers opened and Harm stepped out on the balcony. At first, he didn't see her standing there, giving Talia a moment to study him in the light from the room behind him.

He'd removed his shirt and stood in his jeans, barefoot.

Talia's mouth went dry and she swept her tongue across her lips.

"How long have you been standing there?" he asked without turning toward her. His warm, husky tone seeped into her skin like melted chocolate.

She gulped, heat filling her face and traveling south to pool in her core. "I was here before you."

Then he turned and opened his arms.

Talia didn't hesitate—she closed the distance between then and melted into his embrace. Who was she trying to kid by thinking she could ignore him until he left? This was where she'd longed to be all day. In this man's arms, pressed to his chest and all other parts of his body.

He pressed his lips to the top of her head. "I've wanted to do that since before I got out of bed this morning."

She laughed and wrapped her arms around his waist. "I am afraid…" she admitted.

"Afraid?" He leaned back and stared down at her. "Of me?"

She shook her head, staring up into dark eyes reflecting the light from the moon. "Of me."

"Explain that so a mere man might understand. Please." He tipped her chin up and brushed his mouth across hers in a featherlight kiss.

"I was afraid that the more time I was with you, the more I'd want to be with you. Then when you're gone, I… I didn't want to think about that." She sucked in a breath and let it go. "You're only here a few days. I didn't want to get too attached."

He gave her a lopsided grin. "I guess I understand. We live worlds apart. It doesn't make sense to start something we can't finish."

Talia nodded, her eyes stinging with red-hot tears she refused to let fall. "No sense at all."

He kissed her again, just enough to tease her and make her want more. "Do you want me to leave?" he asked, his breath smelling of cherries jubilee and sweet vanilla ice cream.

She'd be smart to tell him to go.

"No. Please, stay."

A cool breeze made Talia shiver. Or was it in anticipation of what might come next?

Harm rubbed his hands over her arms. "Are you cold?"

She lifted one shoulder. "A little," she lied. Why tell him he made her shiver with longing? He'd think she was desperate. And she was. Desperate for him to run his hands over her body, to make her feel alive all over again.

Harm captured her cheeks in his hands and guided her face up to his. Then he claimed her mouth, pushing his tongue past her teeth to tangle with hers in a kiss so deep and profound, it left her weak in the knees and trembling.

"You are cold," he whispered against her lips. Then he bent, scooped her up into his arms and carried her into his room, kicking the door closed behind him.

Talia wrapped her arm around his neck and leaned into the hard muscles of his chest. She loved that he carried her as if she weighed nothing. He didn't groan or break a sweat as he strode across the room and laid her on the bed.

She stared up at him as his hands reached for the button on his jeans.

Again, she ran her tongue across her dry lips. "Protection?"

A slow, sexy smile slipped across his mouth. "Got it." He nodded toward the nightstand, where a foil packet lay.

Her pulse quickened. Had he come to bed with bedding her in mind? Her belly tightened, and warmth spread from her core outward. She sat up and helped him push the button loose on his jeans.

Then they were falling into the bed naked, kissing, touching and holding each other in a frantic attempt to get as close as possible. They came together in a hot, dynamic, pulsing explosion of lust.

After her pulse returned to normal, she lay against Harm's side, basking in the afterglow.

"I could get used to having you lying naked beside me," Harm admitted.

Talia trailed a finger over his hard chest. "Wouldn't you get tired of a purely physical relationship?"

He chuckled. "I think we've gone past that."

She leaned up on her elbow. "I thought you didn't want anything else."

He smoothed the hair out of her face and tucked it behind her ear. "I was wrong. You make me want more."

Her heart swelled as she sank into the curve of his arm.

He tightened his hold on her, his hand sliding across her bare skin. "I want you for more than just the sex."

"Why?" Talia demanded.

"You're smart, strong and determined." He kissed her temple. "In my line of work, I need a woman who can hold her own when I'm away." He slipped his arm from beneath her and leaned over her. "I need a woman who doesn't need me."

"That doesn't make sense," she said, her voice breathless, her heart pounding.

"I need a woman who wants to be with me, but who can function on her own." He kissed her forehead, her nose and finally her lips. "I need you."

"I don't need you," Talia said. "But I want you."

"Exactly."

Then she shook her head. "But that wouldn't be true. I find myself needing you, the more time I spend with you." She lifted her head and pressed her lips to his.

"We are a mess, aren't we?" Harm claimed her lips with his.

Then they were making love all over again, in a fevered frenzy. Hot, hard and passionate, as if neither could get enough of the other.

When Talia had temporarily slaked her thirst for Harm, she drifted to sleep, happy for the first time in long time and hopeful of the future.

A few hours later, she awoke, thirsty. Not for making love again, quite yet, but really thirsty.

"What's wrong?" Harm asked, his voice gritty with sleep.

"Nothing. I'm going down for some water. Do you want anything from the kitchen?" she asked.

"No, thank you." He lay with his arm over his eyes. "I think you sucked every bone out of my body. I can't even move to turn off the light."

She laughed and rolled out of the bed.

He moved his arm, opening his eyes long enough to rake her body with his gaze. "You're beautiful. You know that?"

She slid her nightgown over her head and stepped into her panties. "No, but I do now. Mind if I borrow one of your shirts? Or would you rather I went to my room and got my robe?"

"Take my shirt hanging in the wardrobe," he said and closed his eyes. "Let me go get that drink for you."

"No. You stay put. I'll only be a moment." She pulled on his long-sleeved shirt and padded barefoot from the room, closing the door softly behind her. She didn't want to wake Big Jake, though she wasn't sure their lovemaking had been all that quiet. Big Jake could be awake at that moment, cringing.

Her footsteps were so soft, she couldn't hear them herself as she tiptoed down the staircase and out to the kitchen. Once she had a bottle of chilled water in her hand, she headed out into the hallway. The front door of the lodge stood ajar. Thinking perhaps Mr. Wiggins, the leopard, had nudged the door open, she poked her head through the door and glanced out into the night. "Mr. Wiggins?" she called out softly.

The sound unique to the leopard came from close to the steps leading up onto the front porch. He sounded stressed, possibly in pain.

Her heartbeat kicking up a notch, Talia hurried out onto the deck and down the steps. "Mr. Wiggins? Where are you, sweetie?"

Again, the animal called out to her. This time she determined the sound came from the corner of the lodge, near the bushes rimming the porch.

She ran barefoot across the grass and around the side of the building, where she almost tripped over the leopard.

Mr. Wiggins lay on his side. He didn't get up and wrap himself around her legs as was his usual greeting. Instead, he lay still, barely lifting his head to stare up at her in the starlight.

"Hey, big guy." She knelt beside him and laid the bottle of water on the grass. "What's wrong?"

He gave his deep-throated rumble that turned breathy on the end, and he coughed.

Talia rubbed her hand over his neck. "Are you sick? Did you get hurt?" She ran her hands over his body, but couldn't find any sign of injury. She'd worked with sick animals before, but she didn't have any idea what might be wrong with the big cat. "Wait here, I'll get help." She straightened and was about to turn back to the house when something hard and heavy hit her on the back of the head.

Before she could make a sound, the stars blinked out and she sank to the ground, the sound of Mr. Wiggins's rumbling growl the last thing she heard.

Chapter Thirteen

Sated from making love into the wee hours of the morning, Harm must have fallen asleep. When he woke, the gray light of early morning edged in around the curtains over the French door.

He stretched and reached for Talia. The bed beside him was empty, the pillow dented from where she'd been sleeping. She must have gotten up early. Harm hadn't even felt her come back to bed after getting a drink from the kitchen. The woman could slip in and out of a room making very little noise.

He climbed out of the bed, pulled on jeans and dragged a T-shirt over his head before he left his room in search of Talia.

Knowing her, she was probably in the kitchen, helping Jamba start breakfast for her guests.

Padding barefoot down the stairs, Harm paused in the foyer and stared at the front door, which was open.

The door was never left open.

A trickle of apprehension slithered across his skin, raising gooseflesh. He walked outside onto the porch and looked around.

A beat-up old truck rumbled up to the lodge and

parked near the corner of the house. Jamba pushed his large frame out of the driver's seat and stood, stretching in the morning light as the sun eased up over the horizon. He gave Harm a friendly wave and then frowned. Jamba hurried toward the bushes and squatted on his haunches.

Harm walked to the edge of the porch, curious as to what Jamba was staring at. There appeared to be something lying on the ground.

"Mr. Payne!" Jamba straightened and waved Harm over. "Mr. Wiggins is not well."

Harm jogged to where Jamba hovered over the resort mascot, the long, spotted leopard Talia had named Mr. Wiggins. The animal lay on its side, taking short, shallow breaths.

"What do you suppose is wrong with him?" Jamba asked.

Harm ran his hand over the cat, searching for an injury and not finding anything obvious. "I don't know. He seems to be in some kind of respiratory distress."

"What's going on?" Buck called out from the cabin he shared with Angela.

"The leopard's down. We don't know why," Harm answered.

Angela leaned through the door. "Want me to take a look at him?"

"Yes," Harm said. "He doesn't look well at all."

"I'll be right there." Angela ducked back inside the cabin and came out a minute later, dressed and carrying her doctor's satchel.

Diesel, T-Mac, Pitbull and Marly wandered out of

their cabins and gathered around the leopard. Big Jake came out on the porch. "What's going on?"

"The big cat is down," Diesel said. "Has anyone told Talia?"

"Big Jake, could you get Talia?" Angela called out. "She needs to know what's going on. I'm not sure I can be of any help. I'm a human doctor, not a veterinarian."

"I'll get her." He ran back inside. A couple minutes later, he was back on the porch. "She's not here."

Harm's heart skidded to a halt. "What do you mean, not here?"

He shook his head. "She's not anywhere in the lodge. I looked everywhere."

About that time, Harm noticed something lying at the base of a nearby bush. His gut clenched and he sucked in a harsh breath. Then he bent to retrieve a plastic bottle of water that had never been opened.

"What did you find?" T-Mac asked.

Harm couldn't tear his gaze off what he held in his hand. "A bottle of water."

T-Mac chuckled. "Do you suppose the cat went for a bottle of water and was on his way back to bed when he took ill?"

Realization dawned on him, spreading like a brushfire through his consciousness. "Talia went downstairs for a drink of water," he said softly.

T-Mac's smile slipped. "When?"

Harm pushed his empty hand through his hair. "I don't know. I must have fallen asleep. It was maybe a couple of hours ago." He looked around at the cabins and the main lodge.

Big Jake put the team to work. "Diesel and Pitbull,

check the outbuildings. Buck and T-Mac, go through the entire lodge from top to bottom. I believe there's a wine cellar and an attic. Make sure I didn't miss anything. Harm and I will check the truck, the grounds around the cabins and out toward the landing strip."

"Find Talia," Harm said. He could kick himself for not going down to the kitchen for the water. At the very least, he should have gone with her.

Big Jake stared at the bottle of water. "She probably came out to check on the cat."

"If she did, where is she now?" Harm asked. He took off at a run, circling the cabin, calling out her name. "Talia! Talia!"

He checked the truck where they'd parked it the day before. Talia wasn't in it. Even more disturbing, she hadn't taken it. After checking the grounds all the way out to the landing strip where Marly had landed her plane the last time they were at the resort, he was all-out alarmed. He ran all the way back to the resort, where he met up with Big Jake.

"Anything?" Harm asked.

Big Jake shook his head. "Nothing."

The others all converged on the lodge's sweeping veranda, each reporting he'd found nothing.

"We need to get Mr. Wiggins to a vet," Angela said. "Marly and I will do that while you guys find Talia. She wouldn't want us to leave the animal in this shape." She glanced around, caught Jamba's attention. "Could we borrow your truck to get Mr. Wiggins to the nearest veterinarian? I'd take Talia's, but the guys will need it to find our hostess." She leveled a narrowed glance at Harm. "And you *will* find her."

Harm's jaw hardened. "Damn right, we will."

Jamba nodded. "You will have to take Mr. Wiggins into Nairobi. He'll stand a better chance there."

Marly sat on the ground with Mr. Wiggins's big head in her lap. "I hope he makes it. He's in pretty bad shape."

The men helped lift the leopard into the bed of Jamba's truck. Marly and Angela climbed in with Jamba, and he drove them out of the compound, headed for Nairobi.

Harm ran back into the lodge and up to his room, where he pulled on his boots, slipped his shoulder holster over his arms and secured the buckles. Then he checked his pistol, slipped it into his jacket and added a couple loaded magazines to his pockets. He didn't know what he would be up against, but he wanted to be ready.

Back outside, he joined the other members of his team around the resort safari truck. T-Mac and Pitbull had brought along their gear bags, indicating they were packing longer-range rifles. Good. Pistols were only good for close range.

All six men climbed into the truck. Big Jake took the wheel, which was fine with Harm. He wanted his hands free in case he was forced to shoot someone. And he'd shoot a lot of someones if it meant getting Talia back. Alive.

The road to the village seemed longer than before. About fifteen minutes into the ride, Harm spotted another truck ahead. The men getting out appeared to be armed. "Slow down." Harm pulled out a pair of binoculars Talia kept on board for spotting wildlife and focused on the men piling out of the truck. All were armed with military-grade rifles, possibly AK-47s. And they were aiming at the oncoming truck.

"Stop!" Harm yelled. "Take cover!"

Big Jake slammed on the brakes and slid the truck sideways on the road. Even before the vehicle came to a stop, the five men not driving leaped out on the side of the truck, away from the men firing on them.

Bullets slammed into the side of the truck, but so far, no one had been hit.

T-Mac and Pitbull pulled from their gear bags the M4A1 rifles with the SOPMOD upgrades they'd had built specifically for special operations. Each man took up a position on either end of the truck and aimed at the men firing at them.

"Give them a warning shot first," Big Jake said.

"Like hell. They tried to kill us," Harm argued.

"We're not supposed to be armed and operational in Kenya. We don't have clearance," Big Jake reminded them.

"They don't know that," Harm said, but he waited and let T-Mac and Pitbull work their sniper magic.

They aimed and fired almost simultaneously, kicking up the dust at the gunmen's feet.

Apparently, it didn't make a difference. They continued firing, peppering the truck with more bullet holes.

All six SEALs hunkered behind the relative safety of the big metal truck. They had distance on their side. Their rifles were modified to fire accurately at much longer distances than the AK-47s being used by their opponents.

"Okay, they got their warning. Make them believers," Big Jake said.

Harm wished he was the one with the sniper rifle. Waiting was hard. But he knew the two men on it were the best on the team.

Pitbull and T-Mac took aim and fired.

Two of the men who'd been showering them with bullets from their thirty-round banana clips suddenly stopped. One dropped to the ground, his weapon clattering to the dirt. He lay still. Probably dead.

The other screamed, flung his rifle to the side and fell, clutching at his leg.

Five other men turned and ran, scattering across a broad field.

"Should we take them down?" Pitbull asked.

"No. They're not stopping to set up defensive positions. My bet is they're not trained military men." Big Jake waited a few more minutes to make sure no one else was going to fire on them. Then he climbed into the truck and started the engine. "Let's go see what we caught."

The men climbed aboard, rifles and pistols trained on the truck ahead as they closed the distance between them.

The man on the ground who had been clutching at his leg crawled toward the rifle he'd thrown, wincing and moaning as he pulled himself through the dirt.

Harm leaped out of the truck and stepped on the weapon before the man could lift it and fire at them.

"Don't shoot!" he yelled and raised his hands high. "Don't shoot."

"We'll shoot if anyone else shoots at us," Harm said, pointing his pistol at the injured man.

"They're all gone." The man went back to clutching his leg. "I'm bleeding to death. They left me to die."

"Hey, guys, get a load of this." Diesel stood at the rear of the broken-down truck, lifting a tarp with the barrel of his pistol.

Harm remained where he was, with his foot on the

rifle, while the others crowded around the truck and peered into the bed.

"Holy hell!" Big Jake exclaimed. "We should have shot every last one of those guys."

"Why?"

"They're the poachers." Big Jake lifted an object out of the truck and held it up.

Harm's gut twisted.

The long ivory tusk had to belong to the dead elephant they'd come across the day before.

"Where were you taking this?" Big Jake carried the tusk to the man on the ground.

"I don't know. They tell me nothing." He pressed his hand to the wound on his leg to stanch the bleeding.

"I'm not buying it," Harm said and aimed his pistol at the man's uninjured leg. "Where did they take Talia Ryan?"

The man stared up at him, a blank look on his face. "Mrs. Ryan?"

"Yes. Mrs. Ryan. Where did they take her?"

"I've heard nothing of this," the man on the ground said. "When did this happen?"

"Sometime in the middle of the night," Big Jake said. "Who else would take her if not the people she's trying to stop?"

"I swear, I know nothing."

"Then tell us who you sell the tusks to," Harm said. He wasn't convinced the man knew nothing about Talia's whereabouts. "Where were you taking the tusks?"

"I don't know," the man said, though he wouldn't meet Harm's gaze as he spoke.

"You're lying." Harm pointed the muzzle of his pistol at the man's good leg. "Try again."

The injured man on the ground pressed his lips together, refusing to utter another word.

Harm leaned close the man's ear and spoke softly, yet firmly. "I suggest you start talking, or I'll shoot the other leg."

"Don't shoot! Don't shoot!" The man ducked his head and scooted away from Harm.

Diesel, T-Mac, Buck and Pitbull stepped up behind him, blocking any escape route.

"You don't understand," the injured man cried. "They will kill me."

"Or we will," Harm reminded him. "Your choice. My finger is getting really tired of resting on the trigger. All it will take is for me to jerk that finger and I'll put a bullet in your other leg. At close range, it won't be as easily treated as the other gunshot wound."

"No, please, don't shoot." He cast a glance in the direction his comrades had gone. "We were to meet with our contact tonight."

"Where?"

"Outside the village, near the ruins of an old fort."

"Who is your contact?" Big Jake asked again.

"I don't know. None of us know. He wears a mask and pays us well."

"He will be there tonight?"

"Not if he hears we have nothing to trade." The man shot a glance toward the truck. "He will not come if we have no tusks or horns to deliver."

Big Jake turned toward the team medic. "Buck, fix this man's leg. He has goods to deliver."

Buck flushed the man's wound with bottled water, dug out the bullet, sanitized the wound and glued it with liquid bandage.

Meanwhile, Diesel and Pitbull looked into the engine compartment of the truck and fiddled with the wiring. A few minutes later, they were able to start the engine.

Harm lifted his chin slightly toward T-Mac, the team electronics guru. T-Mac gave an answering chin lift and hurried to his gear bag. He returned moments later, circled the truck once and then helped Buck half carry the man into the driver's seat.

"He should be good enough to get the tusks to his buyer tonight," Buck pronounced. "He lost blood, but the bullet didn't hit any major arteries." Buck faced the man. "You need to see a doctor soon and get on antibiotics to reduce the chance of infection and possibly losing the leg."

"I will." The poacher frowned. "You are letting me go free?"

Big Jake nodded. "On the condition you deliver your goods to the buyer."

"How do you know I will deliver them?" the poacher asked.

"Because we will be watching you," Harm said. "And we won't hesitate to kill you next time." Harm narrowed his eyes. "And we'll make it very painful."

"Unless you are with me, how will you know if I delivered?" The wounded man winced as he adjusted his position in the truck's seat.

"We have ways," Big Jake said. "So, make sure you take your goods to the buyer. Your life depends on it."

Diesel and Pitbull loaded the dead poacher into the back of the truck with the tusks. The wounded poacher shifted into gear and drove the truck toward the village.

Harm stood beside T-Mac as the poachers' truck left in a cloud of dust. "You tagged him?"

"Tracker in the truck, on the tusks and in the poacher's clothes. We should be able to find them." He held up the tracking device reader. "Ready to roll?"

"Don't worry," Big Jake said as he started the truck. "We'll find Talia."

Harm wasn't as certain. "We don't know that the poachers are the ones who took her."

The men climbed into the back, and Big Jake took off after the poachers' truck, heading for the village.

T-Mac called out from the seat behind Harm. "The poacher turned off the main road." He leaned over and showed Harm the display. They were coming up on the road the poacher had taken.

"As long as we can track him," Big Jake said, "we should be able to find him again."

The big SEAL passed the turnoff and continued toward the village.

Harm spun in his seat, looking over his shoulder at the dirt track the other truck had taken, his heart hammering. "Aren't we going to follow him?"

"No, he needs to meet up with his compadres and make good their handoff. They were supposed to meet with the buyer tonight."

"Aren't we taking a risk they'll make the handoff early?" Harm asked.

Big Jake smiled, a thin, dangerous smile. "If so, the tusks are marked. We'll find him. I didn't get the impression our little poacher dude knew anything about Talia's kidnapping. I think we need to talk to the witch doctor."

"Good." Harm sat back in his seat and stared at the road ahead. "I have a feeling the witch doctor is more involved than just spreading rumors."

"My thoughts, too."

As they pulled into the village, women and children moved out of the road to keep from being hit. Big Jake parked in the village center.

Before the men piled out, Jake said, "Harm and I will handle this. The rest of you stay put. We don't want to overwhelm the locals."

Big Jake headed for an elderly man seated on the ground in front of a mud-and-stick hut.

Harm spotted the old woman Talia had questioned the day before and headed straight for her. He squatted beside where she sat weaving a basket with her gnarled hands. "Where can I find Gakuru?" he demanded, his tone harsher than he intended. The more time that passed and they hadn't found Talia, the more worried he became.

The old woman didn't look up, nor did she speak.

Swallowing his frustration, Harm started over, lowering his voice to a softer, gentler tone. "Mrs. Talia is missing. I need to find her. Please…help me."

This time, she looked up, her eyes widening. "Mrs. Talia?"

He nodded. "She was taken in the night. I need help finding her before it's too late."

The old woman shook her head. "Gakuru warned her. He said she was bringing bad juju to our people. She should have left when her husband was killed."

Again, swallowing the burbling desperation he could barely contain, Harm spoke in an even tone. "We can't change the past. But I have to find her. Gakuru might know where I should look. Do you know where I can find him?"

The woman's fingers continued to weave the basket,

threading the strands in and out as if by memory. When Harm thought he'd hit a wall, she finally spoke. "His home is the building south of the village, a ten-minute walk by foot. You will know it by the mask on the door."

Harm joined Big Jake at the truck and climbed in.

"The village leader didn't have much to say," Big Jake reported. "However, he said head south to find the witch doctor."

"The old woman Talia spoke to yesterday said the same. She said the witch doctor warned her to leave and that by being here, she was spreading bad juju."

Big Jake snorted. "Yeah. A bunch of horse hockey, if you ask me."

The ten-minute walk south took less than a minute in the truck, and soon they were pulling up to the hut with the mask on the door.

A short, dark man sat on the ground in front of a cauldron, alternating feeding sticks into the fire beneath and stirring the contents.

Again, Big Jake asked the others to wait in the truck while he and Harm climbed down.

Harm reached the man first. "Are you Gakuru?"

The man glanced up, his eyes rheumy and bloodshot. "Who wants to know?"

"I'm Harmon, a guest at the All Things Wild Resort." Trying to keep the desperation out of his voice, he went on. "Mrs. Ryan is missing. We thought you might have an idea of where we can look for her."

"Why would I know where she is?" He continued to stir the contents of the pot. "Perhaps she finally heeded my warning and left Kenya."

"Why should she leave Kenya?" Big Jake asked. "This has been her home for many years."

A sneer curled the witch doctor's lips on one side. "With her husband dead, she brings bad juju on the people of the village."

"She offers jobs and brings in tourists for those people to sell their goods to. How is that bad juju?" Harm asked.

"A lone woman needs a man to bring balance to her life and those around her."

"Mrs. Ryan doesn't need anyone. She's strong, has a big heart and helps others." Harm couldn't hold back. "She certainly didn't deserve to be singled out by you as bringing bad luck to the people of the community." He stepped closer, all pretense and niceness gone. "What do you know about her disappearance?"

The witch doctor straightened to his full height, coming up short of Harm by at least eight inches. "I know nothing, other than the fact that she should have left long ago. This country is no place for a lone woman running a resort by herself."

"If you are lying to me—" Harm reached for the man, but Big Jake stepped between them, placing a hand on each man's arm.

"He's of no use to us." Big Jake let go of his grip on the witch doctor and tightened his hand on Harm's arm. "Come on, we have work to do."

"If you've done anything to hurt Talia, I'll be back. Without my guard dog." Harm glared at the witch doctor before turning to follow Big Jake.

As the two men climbed into the truck, T-Mac leaned over the backs of their seats and showed them the tracking monitor. "The poachers' truck stopped a couple miles out of the village."

"We need to get back to the resort and see if Talia turned up there. If not, we'll plan the coming evening accordingly."

"You think the poachers have something to do with Talia's disappearance?" T-Mac asked.

"No, but I think we might find out who's behind all the troubles she's had at the resort and on her safaris." He nodded toward the side mirrors. "Our witch doctor is on the move."

Harm studied the small, gnarled man in the mirror as he mounted a motorcycle and sped away. "Shouldn't we follow him?"

Big Jake shook his head. "I tagged him with one of T-Mac's tracking devices. My bet is he knows something and we'll find out soon what that is."

Harm sat back in his seat, his fist clenched. Too many threads remained loose, and they still had no idea where Talia had been taken or who had kidnapped her.

TALIA OPENED HER eyes to dark gray light filtering beneath the door of the room where she lay on a dirt floor. Her vision blurred, and she fought to keep from losing the contents of her belly. When she moved her head, a shooting pain radiated from the back of her neck through her skull. She gasped and lay still until a wave of dizziness passed.

When she tried to move her hands and feet, she couldn't. They were bound together with what felt like duct tape. Keeping her head and neck as still as possible, she flexed her legs, and her feet bumped into something soft.

A moan rose from somewhere near her feet.

"Who's there?" Talia said into the darkness, her voice rough and gravelly.

Another moan sounded, and the soft form at her feet shifted.

"Who's with me?" Talia asked again, the words hard to form, the sound coming out more of a whisper.

"Mrs. Talia?" a shaky, feminine voice said.

Talia's heartbeat stirred a little faster. She fought off the gray fog of semiconsciousness, trying to hang on for the sake of the other woman in the room. "Eriku?"

"Yes," she answered as if it took a lot of effort to force the word out. "Where are we?"

"I don't know," Talia answered.

Voices sounded outside the door. Men. They were speaking in angry tones.

Talia tried to turn her head and wished she hadn't. The stabbing pain made her stomach roil and her head spin. She fought the encroachment of fog seeping in around her vision, but it was a losing battle.

The door opened, but she couldn't stop her eyes from closing. In an in-and-out state of consciousness, she recognized one of the voices but could do nothing to call out. She felt her body lifted by rough hands, and she was flung over a man's shoulder. They carried her from the room and out into the cool night air. With her hands bound, she was unable to steady herself, nor did she have the energy to try. Her head flopped and the pain sent her into a black abyss.

Her last thought was of Harm and the joy he'd brought back into her life. She wished he was there, and she wished she could tell him how he made her feel. Too bad he'd never know.

Chapter Fourteen

"I count eight tangos, two trucks and a motorcycle in the center of the camp," Harm reported. He'd taken point on their mission to infiltrate the poachers' transfer of the illegal goods.

The camp was nothing more than a few tents, sheltered beneath camouflage netting and several stacks of crates that had been unloaded from the trucks. One of the trucks there was the one they'd allowed to leave earlier that day.

The injured poacher limped around the camp, leaning on a long stick, his gaze darting left and right. The man had to be scared out of his mind. Harm hoped so. He hoped they'd scared him so much he'd get out of the poaching business and go legit.

"We have another vehicle approaching," Pitbull said from his position observing the dirt track leading into the camp.

A shiny black SUV bumped along the ruts and entered the camp. A man climbed out of the vehicle, surrounded by four big burly men with AK-47 rifles. The five men entered the tent along with four of the poachers, the injured man being one of them.

"The gang's all here," Big Jake whispered into their headsets. "Let's move."

Harm waited for the others to come online with him. They took out the few poachers who'd been set up as guards on the perimeter. Not a shot was fired, but the men were silenced, gagged and tied. If all went as planned, they wouldn't be poaching anything ever again. The SEALs would turn them over to the authorities, they'd be tried and sentenced.

One by one, Harm and his team took out the men around the camp, carefully keeping it quiet so that the men inside the tent would not be aware of what was going on outside.

One of the SUV bodyguards stood at the front of the tent, his weapon at the ready. Another stood at the rear.

"Ready?" Diesel said, in position near the rear. At the same time, he and Harm moved, taking out the guards.

No sooner had he dispatched the man guarding the door than another bodyguard stepped out of the tent. He almost stumbled on his teammate on the ground. Harm slipped up behind him and clamped his arm around the man's throat, choking off his vocal cords and air.

The man slid silently to the ground, unconscious.

Voices sounded from inside the tent. Harm recognized the witch doctor's muttering, though his words seemed slurred.

"Remember, we need some of them alive to answer questions," Harm said quietly into the radio. Then he motioned for the others of his team to move in. When they had the tent surrounded, Harm, Big Jake and Pitbull slipped through the door and behind the guards gathered inside.

Shots rang out.

Harm pressed a knife to the throat of one of the burly bodyguards and held the man in front of him as a human shield. The only light came from a battery-operated lantern hanging from the center pole. It rocked violently as the struggle within ensued.

By the time they had the occupants inside subdued, three were dead and the others were incapacitated.

Harm performed a head count of his teammates. Everyone was there. All the SEALs were alive and uninjured. He breathed a short sigh of relief and concentrated on what they had in front of them.

The poachers had been quick to throw down their weapons after three of their compatriots had been knocked out. And the witch doctor lay in the fetal position, covering his head with his hands, mumbling in a language Harm didn't understand.

The man in the mask knelt on the floor, his hands cinched behind his back in zip ties T-Mac had brought from his gear bag. The two remaining bodyguards were secured with handy duct tape.

Big Jake grabbed the mask and yanked it off the man's head.

"Don't kill me!" he begged. "I wasn't even supposed to be here. I was just filling in for someone else. He said it was an easy way to make a lot of money. All I had to do was pay for the goods and leave."

"Who sent you?" Harm demanded.

The man glanced around the inside of the tent, his eyes wide, his fear evident. "I can't say."

"Yes. You. Can." Harm pressed the tip of his Ka-Bar knife to the man's throat.

The man moaned, his entire body shaking. "He said I'd be killed if anyone found out."

"Well, you've been found out and you will be turned over to the authorities," Big Jake said. "Are you going to let the man who sent you get away while you go to jail?"

The man glanced around at the poachers still alive and glaring at him. "What about them?"

"Oh, they're going to jail, too," Big Jake bluffed.

Harm didn't have any idea what happened to poachers and middlemen in Kenya. But Big Jake was probably close enough to right for them to believe him.

"Did you stop to think that whoever sent you knew this would be a bad night?" Harm leaned close to the man. "He sent you to take the fall for him. Are you going to let him get away with it? He'll be a free man, while you languish in some hellhole of a prison."

"No." The man shook his head. "He wouldn't do that."

"But he did." Harm waved a hand around the room. "Look around you. You should be dead right now, if we didn't let you live. *He* would have been dead had he come."

The man hesitated, his gaze shooting back and forth as if he was searching for an escape. Finally, he stared at Harm and said, "Krause sent me."

"Jim Krause?" Harm frowned. "Mrs. Ryan's neighbor?"

The man nodded. "He wanted me to negotiate this deal while he took care of other business."

"What other business?" Harm asked, his tone low, strained. His heart hammered against his ribs. He knew the answer without the man actually saying it.

"He wanted to get Talia Ryan out of the way. She was messing up his operation by stirring up the local women."

Harm's heart squeezed hard inside his chest. "What operation?"

"He takes rich people on safari hunts for a lot of money and then turns the dead animals over to the poachers to scavenge what they want."

"The bastard," Harm bit out.

Big Jake picked up the thread and unraveled it further. "And then he masquerades as this silent middleman brokering the illegal goods from the poachers and sells them to the Chinese?"

The man nodded. He glanced at the poachers. "He makes it look like the poachers are the ones killing the animals, not the rich hunters."

Harm grabbed the man by the collar and half lifted him off the ground. "Where is Krause now?"

"I don't know. He said he was going to take care of the women and make sure no one could take over the resort when they were gone."

The witch doctor moaned and muttered, "The only way to rid a place of pestilence is to burn it. Cleanse the bad juju with flame."

At the old man's words, Harm's blood ran cold through his veins. "He's going to destroy the lodge." He ran for the door. "God, I hope Talia's not in it."

"Don't leave without us," Big Jake called out. He pointed to the SEALs. "More duct tape. Pronto!"

While the team remained behind to apply liberal amounts of tape to their captives, Harm ran for the truck, sprinting a mile to get to it. He raced back to the camp in time for the rest of his crew to jump on board.

He would have driven on without them, but chances were he'd need them to help save Talia. Now wasn't the time to go rogue and do it alone.

Once he had all the men on board, he floored the accelerator and sent the truck down the rutted track toward the resort, thirty minutes away.

Talia might not have that much time.

WHEN TALIA WOKE AGAIN, her head ached with a different kind of pain and her vision blurred no matter how many times she blinked. When she lifted her head, the room spun and she could swear she smelled smoke.

She forced herself to stay awake and not slip back into the dark fog of drug-induced sleep. "Where am I?" she asked aloud, not expecting an answer.

"In your wine cellar," a female voice responded.

Talia glanced around, glad she'd had the foresight to have motion-sensor lights installed at the top of the stairs. At the moment, they shined down on her and her companion.

"Eriku," Talia said. "Are you all right?"

The woman nodded. "Yes, ma'am, for now. But I don't know what they have planned for us."

Talia sniffed the air. An acrid scent assailed her nostrils. Her heart leaped into her throat. "Do you smell smoke?"

The other woman lay on her side, her hands bound with duct tape behind her back. She sniffed the air and then nodded. "That's what it smells like. Did Jamba leave a pot burning on the stove?"

"He would never do that." By then her head had cleared and her heartbeat had kicked into high speed. "You don't think…whoever did this to us…holy hell."

She struggled to free her hands. "We have to get out of here. Now!"

"I can't move my hands or feet."

"Me either, but maybe we can if we work together." Talia inched over to where Eriku lay on her side, her hands secured behind her back. "Let me see if I can tear away the tape on your wrists."

Eriku scooted until her back was to Talia.

Using her fingernails, Talia worked at the tape, searching for the end, praying she could find it and easily unwrap it to free Eriku. Why did it have to be so difficult? She scrambled furiously as the smoke thickened. Just when she was about to give up, she found the end and tore at the tape, clumsily unwinding it from around the young woman's wrists.

She had the tape down to the last wrap when the door to the cellar opened.

"Play dead," Talia whispered and went limp, closing her eyes and then opening them just a slit to see a man standing at the top of stairs, silhouetted against the light from the kitchen above. She couldn't make out his face, but she'd bet her last dollar it wasn't Harm.

A flashlight clicked on and the man descended, carrying a stick with a wad of cloth on the end. As he moved closer, the biting scent of gasoline filled the air.

When he reached the bottom, he stood next to Talia and nudged her with his foot. "You should have listened to the witch doctor and left when you could."

The voice belonged to Jim Krause.

He reached into his pocket, pulled out a cigarette lighter and lit the gasoline-saturated cloth wrapped around the stick. He started for a stack of empty cardboard boxes.

Talia couldn't keep quiet. Her life and Eriku's depended on her actions. "Don't do it, John."

He turned, his eyes narrowing. "Didn't give you enough of that drug, did I?" Her neighbor shrugged. "Oh, well. Can't be helped now." He tossed the torch into the stand of boxes. "You'll die of smoke inhalation before the fire takes care of the rest."

"You can't do this." Talia pushed to a sitting position. "At the least get Eriku out of here. She's just a child."

"Like you, she's interfering in my operation."

"What operation?" Her eyes widened as realization dawned on her. "You're behind the illegal hunting expeditions."

"You're partially right. My clients pay a lot of money to hunt big game. But my other clients are just as eager to pay me for the prizes. You realize I can get tens of thousands of dollars for each rhino horn and elephant tusk?" He shook his head. "And it all looks like poachers doing the dirty work." He smiled. Flames licked at the boxes behind him, giving him the appearance of the devil rising up from a burning hell.

Fear gripped Talia's heart. "Killing animals is bad enough. Killing humans is murder. You don't want to do that."

"Hell, I already have. That rhinoceros that ran over Michael was the front end of a pickup truck. He got too close to the truth. I couldn't let him blab it all over the country. He was a damned bleeding heart, always sticking up for the dumb animals."

Talia closed her eyes, the pain of her loss hitting her again. "You killed Michael."

"I did what I had to do. He was in the way, like you and Eriku are in the way. I thought Michael's death would have been enough for you to sell and leave Kenya. But you didn't. I paid the witch doctor to scare you away. You didn't leave. I finally had to take care of it myself."

"What did you do to Mr. Wiggins?"

"I gave him some tainted meat."

"Tainted?"

"With rat poison. The cat was protective of your compound. I couldn't let him get in the way. As it was, he made it easy for me to grab you."

Smoke was filling the room, making it more and more difficult to breathe, but rage burned brighter inside Talia. "Bastard!"

Krause snorted. "Maybe so, but I'm not letting some holier-than-thou women stand in the way of my profits." He started past her, heading for the stairs.

Talia lurched to her feet, swayed when she couldn't balance and launched herself into the man who'd killed her husband and was destroying the only home she'd known for all these years.

With wrists and ankles bound, she didn't have much control over her direction and speed, but she managed to clip the man in the backs of his knees.

Talia hit the floor on her shoulder. Her forehead bounced off the concrete and she nearly passed out.

But she didn't. And she witnessed Krause falling toward the stairs. He didn't have time to put out his hands to break his fall. His head hit the first step, and he lay still.

Eriku coughed. "We have to get out of here." She scooted over to where Talia lay on the ground. "You can't pass out now. Finish untying me so that I can free you, too."

Talia's head swam and her eyes and lungs stung, but she worked the rest of the tape free of Eriku's wrists.

When she pulled the last strand off Eriku's skin, the young woman gasped. But she didn't stop to cry at the pain; she tore at the tape on Talia's wrists.

"Don't," Talia said. "You don't have time. Get out before you're overcome by smoke."

"I'm not leaving you." Eriku coughed, pulled her shirt up over her mouth and nose and finally found the end of the tape. With quick efficiency, she unwound the tape from around Talia's wrists and ripped it free of her skin.

Talia bit down hard on her lip to keep from crying out. Losing a little skin was better than losing her life. As soon as her hands were free, she worked at the tape around her ankles while Eriku worked hers.

Talia freed herself sooner and helped Eriku work hers free. By then, the cellar was thick with smoke. The only thing saving them was that they were lying on the floor.

Talia pulled her shirt up over her mouth and blinked. Tears streamed from her eyes, the smoke making it impossible to see and breathe. But if they didn't get out of the lodge in the next minute, they'd die. She crawled past Krause and motioned for Eriku to go first up the stairs.

Eriku scrambled upward, disappearing into the kitchen above.

Talia started after her and had gone up several steps when something snagged her ankle and pulled her back down the steps.

"No! You have to die," Krause said, his voice hoarse.

He coughed and yanked harder at her ankle, dragging her back down into the smoke-filled cellar.

Talia screamed and kicked, but she couldn't free her ankle from the man's iron grip.

Chapter Fifteen

Harm's heart ached in his chest. He could see the flames reaching into the sky well before Big Jake pulled the truck into the resort compound. "Hurry!"

"I'm going as fast as I can," Big Jake said. As he brought the truck to a screeching halt in front of the burning lodge, a woman stumbled out of the main building and fell to the ground. Silhouetted against the flames, her face wasn't visible.

Harm leaped from his seat and ran toward her. When he reached her, he realized it wasn't Talia, but Eriku.

He rolled her onto her back and gripped her face between his palms. "Where's Talia?"

Eriku coughed and pointed toward the lodge. "In… the…wine cellar." She rolled to her side and coughed uncontrollably.

Harm yelled for Buck. "This woman needs help!" And he ran for the lodge.

Pitbull, Diesel, Big Jake and T-Mac raced up alongside him.

Big Jake grabbed his arm. "You can't go in there. It's an inferno."

"I have to. Talia's in the wine cellar. I have to get her out."

"Then come around the back. Take the shorter route to the kitchen and the cellar door." Big Jake led the way around the burning structure to the rear entrance, where the supplies were unloaded into the kitchen.

The back door was open. Flames rose up inside the kitchen, and the heat was staggering.

Harm stopped Big Jake at the door. "I'm going in. Don't follow." He didn't wait for his teammate's response but dived into hell, determined to come out with Talia or not at all.

On his way through the kitchen, he grabbed a dish towel, quickly soaked it in the sink and pressed it to his nose. Hunkering low to avoid the thickening smoke, he felt his way to where he remembered seeing the door that led down into the wine cellar.

It was open, and he could hear sounds coming up from below.

"Let go!" Talia yelled.

His pulse racing, Harm ran down the steps. The smoke was so thick. At first, he couldn't see Talia. Then through the haze, he noticed a jumble of arms and legs twisting about on the floor.

John Krause had her pinned to the ground. He pulled back his fist, ready to punch her in the face.

Rage ripped through Harm. He threw himself at the man, knocking him over before he could hit Talia.

"Talia, get out!" Harm yelled.

Krause swung at him.

Harm dodged the hit and landed a fist in the man's gut.

When Krause doubled over, Harm brought his knee up sharply and hit him in the face, breaking the man's nose. Krause crumpled to the ground, limp.

Smoke choked Harm, but he couldn't give up now. Talia wasn't moving.

He scooped her into his arms and ran up the steps and into what appeared to be a wall of flames. He didn't stop, racing through the fiery kitchen, his lungs burning, his eyes stinging. He couldn't remember which direction to run. The smoke made it impossible to see.

Hands reached out to guide him, pulling him through the maze of counters and islands and out the back door into the blessedly clean, smoke-free air.

Pitbull took Talia from Harm's arms and laid her on the ground, away from the flame-engulfed building.

Harm stumbled along beside him and collapsed in the dirt beside Talia. He coughed, trying to get the smoke out of his lungs. Then he leaned over her. "Sweetheart, tell me you're alive. Please."

She didn't respond.

He cupped her cheek and brushed his thumb across her lips. "Please don't die. I want to get to know you better. I want to take you out on a date. I'll quit the SEALs and stay with you in Africa, if that's what you want. I'll do anything, just don't die on me."

Harm watched her face in the light from the burning building.

Her eyelashes fluttered.

Harm's heart stopped beating and he held his breath. "Talia? Did you hear me?"

"Every word," she whispered, her voice hoarse, her eyes opening. Then she doubled up, coughing.

Buck arrived and squatted on the ground beside her. He handed her a bottle of water. "Drink a little of this."

Talia took the bottle and swallowed a sip. Then

she coughed again, tears streaming from her eyes. "I thought I would die in that cellar," she said finally.

"You almost did." Harm smoothed her sooty hair from her forehead. "Welcome back." He pressed his lips to hers in a featherlight kiss and then sat up.

Pitbull knelt in the dirt beside them. "I put in a call to Marly on the satellite phone. They made it to Nairobi. She'll inform the authorities about the fire, and the wildlife management folks will collect the men we left tied up."

Talia frowned. "You left men tied up?"

"The poachers, the witch doctor and Krause's substitute middleman," Harm said. "We thought they might know where you were."

"And they did?" She glanced around at the SEAL team. "You found me."

"The witch doctor gave us the clue. He said the only way to cleanse the juju was to burn it." Harm pressed his lips into a tight line. "I figured Krause would torch the resort."

Talia glanced at the burning lodge. "He succeeded."

"A building can be rebuilt." Harm tucked a strand of her hair back behind her ear. "There's no replacing you."

She captured his hand in hers and pressed a kiss to his palm.

Pitbull leaned close. "You'll be glad to hear that Mr. Wiggins is going to be okay. Whatever poison was in him wasn't enough to kill him."

"Rat poison," Talia said and closed her eyes. "That bastard Krause poisoned the cat. He's behind all the poaching around here."

"We got a full confession out of Krause's stooge."

"He killed Michael." Talia pushed up to a sitting position. "Michael wasn't trampled by a rhino. He was run over by Krause's truck."

"Bastard," Big Jake said.

"I hope he rots in hell," Diesel agreed.

"He will," T-Mac said. "Right after you got Talia out of the lodge, the ceiling in the kitchen collapsed. We couldn't have saved Krause if we'd wanted to."

Harm rose to his feet. Talia raised her hand to him.

He helped her to stand and slipped his arm around her waist to steady her. "I'm sorry we didn't get here in time to save the lodge."

She shook her head. "You got here in time to save me. That's all that matters." She leaned into him. "Thank you."

"We almost didn't make it." Harm's arm tightened. "It made me realize something."

"Oh, yeah?" She looked up at him in the light from the blaze. "What's that?"

"I know we've only known each other for a short time…" He drew in a deep breath and continued. "But what I know, I fell in love with." He smiled down at her. "I don't want it to end."

Talia wrapped her arms around him and held tight. "Me either. Staring death in the face made me want to live. And I wasn't living, holding on to the past."

Harm stared at the fire, imagining a future rising out of the ashes. A future with Talia.

"I never thought I could love someone as much as I loved Michael," Talia said softly. "Until I met you."

"And I never thought I'd fall so hard for someone that I'd give up my career to be with her. But I would."

He turned to her and looked into her eyes. "I'd leave the navy and find work here in Africa, if it meant being with you."

She cupped his cheek and smiled into his eyes. "You'd do that for me?"

He nodded. "I want to be with you, to love you, raise a couple little girls with black hair and blue eyes that sparkle in the sunshine." He laughed. "Listen to me. The curmudgeon bachelor talking about love and children."

Big Jake snorted beside them. "Another one bites the dust." He glanced over at T-Mac. "That leaves the two of us. The hold-outs for retaining our bachelorhood."

T-Mac sighed. "I could have gone for Talia, but she only had eyes for Harm." He patted his chest with both hands. "Talia, you don't know what you're missing by choosing Harm over me."

Harm swung a fist at T-Mac, clipping him lightly in the shoulder. "Face it, T-Mac, you never had a chance with her."

Talia laughed and coughed. "Your soul mate is out there. You just have to wait and recognize her when she comes along."

"Like Harm recognized his?" Big Jake asked. "I don't think he knew it at first. He should have. I could see the fear in his eyes. The fear of falling for someone. But he seems to be okay."

"It didn't hurt as bad as I thought it would," Harm admitted. "But then, I didn't lose her. If I had, it would have hurt a helluva lot more." He leaned down and kissed Talia.

"You are my soul mate. I never want to let you go."

"Sweetie, you don't have to. I'm yours, if you want me."

"Oh, hell yeah," he said.

"And you don't have to give up your career in the navy."

"No? But what about the resort?" Harm waved his hand at the burning lodge. "We can rebuild. I'm pretty handy with a hammer."

She shook her head. "I can donate the land and what's left of the buildings to the reserve. The animals need more space. The acreage that goes along with the resort might not be much, but it's something."

"Will you stay here in Africa?" Harm asked.

She shook her head. "I'd like to go to the States and back to school."

"There are some great colleges and universities in Virginia. Close to our home port," Harm suggested.

Talia smiled up at him. "I'd like that very much. Maybe I'll become a veterinarian."

"You're good with animals," Harm agreed.

"But before I go, I need to make sure Mr. Wiggins has a home at a refuge that will take care of him. He'd never make it out in the wild."

"Absolutely. I'd offer to let him come live with us, but I'm not sure about the laws governing wild animals in Virginia."

Talia shook her head. "He needs to stay in Africa where he belongs."

"Are you sure you don't belong here?"

"I can live anywhere my heart belongs." She touched her hand to his chest. "And my heart belongs with you."

Harm captured her hand and brought it up to his lips. "I love you, Talia, more than I ever thought possible. I promise to do my best to make you happy."

"And I love you, Harmon Payne. You proved to me that my heart is big enough to love again."

* * * * *

IN THE
LAWMAN'S
PROTECTION

JANIE CROUCH

This book is dedicated to Mills & Boon. This is my twentieth book with this great publishing company, something I never thought would happen even in my wildest dreams. Thanks for taking a chance on me and being the driving force behind romance for readers all over the world.

Chapter One

For a dead woman, Natalie Anderson was pretty paranoid about security.

She rested her forehead against the back of the heavy wooden door. The closed, locked and completely bolted, heavy wooden door. And even though she hated herself for it, she reached down to double-check the security of the locks again.

Double-check, ha. Double-checking could be forgiven. This was more like octuple-check. And it wasn't just this door. It was every door in the house. And every window.

And she was about to start round nine. She had to stop herself. This could go on all night if she let it; she knew that for a fact.

"Get your sticky notes, kiddo," she muttered to herself. "Work the problem."

She'd discovered the sticky note trick around year two of being "dead." That if she put one of the sticky pieces of paper on each window and door after she was one hundred percent certain the locks were in place, she could finally stop checking it again. Didn't have to worry she'd accidentally missed one. Otherwise it was hours of the same thing over and over, just to be sure.

She grabbed the knockoff sticky papers she'd gotten from a discount store and began her process. She checked every single door—*again*—then every single window. The little yellow squares all over the place gave her a sense of security.

Although she had to fight the instinct to check them all one more time just to be absolutely sure.

She hadn't needed sticky notes in a while. Her tiny, threadbare apartment—not even a full studio, just a room and bathroom that was part of a garage—only had two windows and one door. That didn't take a whole lot of stationery to make her feel safe.

Agreeing to house-sit a gorgeous beach house in Santa Barbara had seemed liked such a great idea two weeks ago. Something different. Beautiful sunsets on the beach. A place where she could get out her paints, ones she'd caved and bought when she couldn't afford them, even though she hadn't painted in six years. Yeah, house-sitting had seemed like such a great idea.

Olivia, a waitress friend at the bar where Natalie worked in the evenings, had talked Natalie into it. Olivia was supposed to have been doing the house-sitting, but her mother had had a stroke and she'd had to go out of town.

So here Natalie was, in a million-dollar home with a view of the Pacific, and instead of cracking the doors to hear the sounds of the ocean or getting out her paints, she had every drape pulled tight and every door battened down enough to withstand a siege. Did she really wish she was smelling the motor oil that permeated everything in her apartment on the far east side of town rather than the brisk February California night air?

She turned away from the front door and forced herself to cross to the living room and sit on the couch. Once there the exhaustion nearly overwhelmed her, settling into her bones. Seven hours at her cleaning job today, then another six washing dishes at the bar.

That was her life almost every day. Seven days a week. For nearly the past six years.

None of the jobs paid even minimum wage. But they all paid in cash, and that was what mattered. She hadn't filled out any tax papers or had to show any ID. Because anyone who tried to pay Natalie Anderson Freihof would find out rather quickly that Mrs. Freihof died six years ago, caught in a freak shootout between law enforcement and some bank robbers.

The irony of that entire situation wasn't lost on her. Law enforcement had come for the robbers, never knowing there was a much bigger criminal—her husband—trapped right in the lobby with all the other victims. They could've made the world a much safer place by leaving the thugs with guns and masks and taking the man in the impeccable three-piece suit into custody. Would've saved a lot more lives.

Including Natalie's.

But she had made it away from Damien, thanks to some idiot bank robbers, gung-ho SWAT members and a freak biological hazard scare at the local hospital, which required the immediate cremation of all corpses that day.

In other words, chaos on multiple levels. But Natalie had taken the chance and run.

Whatever the reason it had all worked out, she wouldn't question. She was just glad it had. Just glad she had gotten away from the hell she'd been trapped in. If she had to work under the table, doing low-paying junk jobs for the rest of her life, she would do it. At least she was alive.

Most people would probably think staying completely under the radar even after all this time would be overkill, not that she had ever told anyone about her situation. That after a funeral and burial—even if it had been an empty casket—her husband would accept that she was dead. Wouldn't be searching for her.

But Natalie would put nothing past the methodical bastard that had systematically controlled her life and tortured her for years. Checking to make sure she wasn't drawing a paycheck years after she'd been declared dead? She could totally see Damien doing something like that. Then casually strolling through the door of her place of employment the next day.

She should probably move to Nebraska or Missouri where the cost of living wasn't so high or somewhere that wasn't SoCal so she wouldn't have to work so hard. Even the rent on her tiny apartment was ridiculous.

But California was the only place *he'd* ever said he hated. That he never wanted to step foot in again. Natalie had been praying that was true for six years and, so far, it had been. So she would stay here, even if she was tired. Even if fear was her constant companion. Even if half her salary was spent on sticky notes.

Agreeing to house-sit had been a mistake. The view was nice, as was the coffee machine she used to brew her cup in the mornings. And the linens were at least a three times higher thread count than she was used to. But the unfamiliarity of it all just added to her stress.

More windows to check. Longer bus rides to and from work.

The feeling like eyes were on her.

She'd fought that compulsion so often in the early days. The fear that she would get home and Damien would be there. Or that he was watching her from across the street. Ready to take her back into the hell he'd trapped her in for so long.

The feeling that she was being watched had to be just the unfamiliarity. The exhaustion. She needed sleep.

She wished she could convince herself that was the case.

It was so hard to know. In the early days, she'd so often given in to the panic. Let it dictate all her moves. She tried not to do that anymore, tried instead to make logical decisions based on actual circumstances rather than gut feelings.

Gut feelings couldn't be trusted. Her gut had told her that marrying Damien was a wise move, that he would provide her a happily-ever-after.

So she didn't trust her gut to tell her what to do now. Especially when she knew exhaustion was playing such a large factor in everything happening inside her head.

She hoped.

But she stood up and began checking the locks on all the windows and doors once more, despite the sticky notes. Trusting her gut or not, she knew sleep would not be coming. Not tonight. She couldn't shake the feeling.

Someone was watching out in the dark.

REN MCCLEMENT STRETCHED his long legs out in front of him in an attempt to get comfortable inside the Dodge Stratus. He was forty-one years old and one of the highest ranked members of Omega Sector, arguably one of the most prestigious law enforcement groups in the world. Hell, he'd *created* Omega Sector.

He should not be on a damned stakeout.

Any one of his colleagues would tell him the same thing: that there was other important work he could be doing. Although Ren didn't have an office at either the Critical Response Division HQ in Colorado or in Washington, DC, where the Covert Operations Division was located, at any given time he was a part of a dozen different operations, almost all of them clandestine. He'd advised two separate presidents on operational strategies in both foreign and domestic events.

And he'd been undercover for months at a time in some of the ugliest hellholes on earth—both geographically and situationally. He'd taken the ops nobody else wanted or could do. Stepped up to and over lines no one else was willing to cross in order to get the job done. Deep-cover operations where the line between who you were and the psychopath you pretended to be got pretty blurred.

He had to be able to live with that.

Ren McClement lived in darkness. Not only lived, *embraced* it. The dark was home for him. The dark was what allowed him to become whoever he needed to be in order to get the job done. To trick the worst of the worst into trusting him so he could make sure they could never harm anyone else again.

And if he sometimes forgot who he really was—the boy who grew up on a ranch in Montana with loving parents and a fierce need to be outdoors—he just considered that an occupational hazard.

If losing the real Ren meant that the world was a safer place, then so be it. He would sacrifice his past childhood so that future childhoods would endure.

But normally stakeouts weren't part of his world-saving undertakings. Some grunt with much less experience and responsibility would be tasked to watch the very quiet beach house in Santa Barbara and could report back.

Not that there would be much to report.

This was night number five of watching Natalie Freihof inside this damn almost-mansion. Every night she came home late from the bar she'd been partying at, went inside and didn't come out until the dawn hours.

He had to admit, she was smart. Conscious of keeping a low profile. She kept her head down as she came in and out, always wearing nondescript jeans and a T-shirt, and caught a bus to get wherever she was going so it was much more difficult to follow her.

She went into one office building just after dawn on Mondays through Thursdays, and an entirely different one Fridays through Sundays. Both offices were in the process of being thoroughly investigated by Omega. He imagined at least one of the businesses in them was being used as a shell company of some kind. A front so Natalie could provide resources for her husband. It was just a matter of time before Omega found out exactly what she was doing with which business.

Then some nights she would go to a bar a few miles away. Once more dressed in the jeans and shirt to go from place to place, which proved again how smart she was. If she needed to run, the clothing would allow her to blend in quickly and easily to almost any crowd. The comfortable athletic shoes would allow her to run.

He had no doubts she changed clothes once she was inside the bar for whatever it was she was doing. Meeting other clients or contacts? Or maybe just having a good time. She tended to stay until well after midnight on the nights she was there.

Evidently the dead Mrs. Freihof didn't require much sleep. Or partying, wining and dining were more important to her than rest. Either way, every time she left the bar, she was again changed into her nondescript clothes, her head was down and she was back on the bus.

The multi-million-dollar beach-front house was more along the lines of what Ren expected of Damien Freihof's wife. The deed wasn't in her name, of course, and the owners were also being investigated, although on the surface even Ren had to admit they looked clean.

The entire thing was smart. Savvy. Natalie had the weary bus commuter look down to a science. If Ren hadn't known it was all fake—that she lived in the lap of luxury while assisting a monster who had made it his mission in life to kill innocent people—he might have felt sorry for her. Something about the tall, willowy blonde brought out his protective instincts.

But Ren viciously tamped that down. What brought out his protective instincts more? The need to stop a killer before he struck again.

They didn't have a warrant to get inside the house, but that hadn't stopped Ren from going in while others were following Natalie to work. He'd been disappointed in what he'd found in the house.

Nothing.

But what had he been expecting? Natalie had successfully convinced the world she was dead for six years. Omega Sector had only discovered she was alive by sheer accident. Their photo-recognition software— part of it programmed to run 24/7 searching for any known associates of Damien Freihof—had tagged her in the background of a newspaper photo. She'd happened to be walking out of a building when a photographer snapped a picture of a group of teenagers receiving a science award.

Ren hardly expected to find anything now that was going to provide irrefutable evidence that she was working with Freihof or providing him assistance. The only thing he'd seen that provided any evidence she'd been there at all had been the small indentation on the very edge of the king-size bed.

Natalie definitely wasn't rolling toward the middle of the bed, reaching for her husband. Of course, Damien would have to be called her ex-husband since he remarried after Natalie's "death."

That poor woman had died in a car accident just a year later. Dead wife number two. When Omega had found out that Natalie was in fact alive, they had exhumed two grave sites. One coffin had contained a body. Natalie's had not.

Legally, Natalie was no longer officially married to Freihof, due to his second marriage. Omega lawyers had already checked into that to make sure laws about testifying against one's spouse wouldn't come into play.

But married to him or not, if Natalie Freihof was helping Damien—which Ren had very little doubt she was—he would take her down.

Five days he'd been watching her, hoping she would slip up or get complacent and lead them to Freihof. The phones at the house were tapped, but she never used them. And if she had a cell phone, it was a burner that she didn't use at the house. No cell signals ever came from there.

So they were basically at a dead end. A place Ren didn't like to be and didn't find himself at very often.

It was time to shake things up. If they didn't put pressure on ex–Mrs. Freihof, she was never going to do anything reckless. It was time to force her hand.

Ren grabbed his phone and dialed a number. It wasn't even dawn here yet, and Colorado was only an hour ahead, but Steve Drackett still answered and sounded like he'd been awake for hours. Given that the man had a new baby it was entirely possible.

"Ren. Any change?" The head of the Omega Sector Critical Response Division skipped all formal greetings.

"Nothing. And no sign that she's going to do anything anytime soon. We need to prod her into action. Watching just isn't cutting it."

"I've had Brandon Han and Andrea Gordon-Han working on this. They're both pretty adamant that Natalie may be a victim, not an accomplice."

Ren glanced at the house again. Quiet. Almost deathly still. "Maybe." He doubted it. "But either way she's our best shot."

"There's something else you should know. Six of the canisters in law enforcement offices around Atlanta have gone missing."

Ren's muttered curse under his breath was foul. Saul Poniard, the traitor inside Omega Sector who had been working with Freihof, had planted biological weapons in law enforcement offices throughout the country. He'd come within seconds of releasing them all and killing tens of thousands of law enforcement personnel two weeks ago.

"I thought we'd gotten all the canisters back into safe hands?"

"Finding them all has been more tricky than we anticipated. These were scheduled for pickup. And they were picked up and signed for, just not by the agents who were supposed to get them."

Ren cursed again. Six canisters of the biological contaminants was enough to take out half a city.

"The icing on the cake?" Steve continued. "Signed for by a D. Freihof. Bastard didn't even try to hide it, Ren. And we got an affirmative ID on him from a traffic cam in South Carolina. I've got some of my best agents there now."

Freihof with biological weapons was damn near the scariest thing Ren could imagine.

"We move tomorrow, Steve. We can't wait any longer. I know it's a complicated operation, but it's our best bet."

"Roger that. You still want Brandon and Andrea to talk to her? Keep you out of the picture? If so, I'll send them out in a couple of hours. They can be at Natalie's doorstep by this afternoon."

"Yes." Ren could feel all the details of the plan floating around in his mind. "I'll watch from the surveillance truck. And I'll have everything ready. If this plays out the way I think it will, Natalie Freihof will be running into my arms soon enough."

Chapter Two

Natalie was getting home from work at two o'clock in the afternoon rather than two o'clock in the morning. Only seven hours of work rather than fourteen. She smiled wryly as she put the key into the lock of the beach house door. Practically a vacation.

And damn it, she was going to enjoy the beach. This house. Not let it make her feel panicked and trapped like last night. The sun was shining outside and she was going to revel in it. She'd fight the darkness tonight when it arrived.

She dropped the smaller backpack, the one she took with her everywhere, on the ground inside the bedroom door and opened the larger one resting next to it. She hadn't unpacked any of her clothes here at the beach house, but then again, she didn't have anything unpacked even when she stayed in her apartment. She'd trained herself to be ready to leave at a moment's notice.

And if she was tempted even for a second to let her guard down, to unpack and get comfortable, all she had to do was stretch her arms out over her head and feel the ache in her shoulder from where Damien had dislocated it not once but twice during their marriage.

Or go up on her tippy toes and feel that one ankle

couldn't support her because of how it had broken when she'd fallen down the stairs, courtesy of her husband's shove.

Burn marks on the inside of her arm. Scars from restraints on her wrists and ankles.

And the fact that she still couldn't stand the snow.

Snow would haunt her until the day she died.

She ripped off her cleaning uniform of khaki pants and solid navy polo shirt, threw them over the back of the couch and put on a tank top and shorts. Damn it, Damien wasn't here. Couldn't hurt her. There was no snow. There was only California sunshine and a view of the beautiful Pacific Ocean. He would not steal this from her like he'd stolen so much. She would sit out on the deck and do nothing.

She was successful at that for all of ten minutes.

The knock on the door had her bolting from her lazy sprawl in the hammock, her heart a hammer against her ribs. She looked at the front door, then at the stairs that led from the deck down to the street below. Should she run?

Her backpack was still inside. If she ran, she would have to leave everything behind. Money. Clothes. It wasn't much, but it was all she had.

The knock came again as she fought to decide what to do.

Damien wouldn't knock. She calmed a little as the words flowed through her. If Damien had found her he would not be knocking politely at the door.

This wasn't even her house. Chances were it was someone for the owners. Easy to get rid of. She walked inside to the front door, collecting herself.

As soon as she opened the door she knew she'd made a mistake.

Everything about the Asian man and smaller blonde woman, both dressed in carefully cut suits, screamed federal agents. Natalie should've chosen to take the stairs at the deck, to get out while she could. Leaving behind everything would've been better.

She forced herself to breathe at an even, normal pace. She eased the door more slightly closed, hoping if she needed to slam it and run she'd be able to.

"Can I help you?"

"Natalie?" The woman, four or five inches shorter than Natalie, with hair almost the same color blond, spoke.

"I'm sorry," Natalie said, avoiding the question. "This isn't my house. I'm just house-sitting for a friend."

Oh, crap, Natalie realized she didn't really know anything about the owners. She had their names written down somewhere on the instructions Olivia had given her, but didn't remember them offhand.

"But you're Natalie, right?" the woman asked again softly. The man moved slightly closer to the woman, almost as if he was going to step in front of her to protect her if she needed it. Like Natalie was going to jump out at her kicking and clawing. That was the last thing he needed to worry about.

She had to stay calm. "I think you have me confused with someone else. Like I said, this isn't my house, but I promise I'm not here illegally." She inched the door farther closed.

The woman just reached down into her bag and pulled out a photograph, sticking it directly in front of Natalie's face.

Fear closed around her throat. It was a shot of her and Damien on their wedding day, smiling at one another. Natalie's hair had been much longer, her cheeks fuller, her smile genuine.

She felt the room begin to spin.

"Whoa, are you okay?" It was the man this time. He pushed the door open and grabbed Natalie's arm before she could fall. "Just take a breath, all right? We just want to ask some questions."

Natalie's knees couldn't hold her anymore and the guy helped lower her to a sitting position on the floor leaning back against the wall next to the door. Both he and the woman took advantage of Natalie's moment of weakness to enter the house, closing the door behind them.

"You shouldn't be here," Natalie said again. "This isn't my house."

The two people looked at each other, the man giving the woman a slight nod. Some sort of secret agent code, for sure. Then they both looked back at her, squatting down so they were closer to her, eye to eye.

"I'm Andrea," the woman said. "And this is my husband, Brandon."

No last names. No credentials. Natalie didn't want to push, but at least they weren't reading her her Miranda rights.

Of course, the afternoon was still young.

"I'm sorry, I'm not feeling well," Natalie finally responded. "I appreciate your help, but I'm going to have to ask you to leave. Like I said, this isn't my house and I had express instructions that I wasn't to have anyone else here while the owners are away."

"Just let us help you get over to the couch," the man, *Brandon*, said. "Just to make sure you're okay."

If that would get them to leave, then great. "Fine."

She took the hands both of them outstretched and rose. They walked her over to the couch, and she sat back down, feeling the shirt and pants she'd thrown over it rub against her back.

"Thanks. If you guys don't mind seeing yourselves out, that would be great." Natalie would be seeing herself out as soon as they were gone.

Out of the entire state.

"It's obvious you don't want to talk to us," Andrea said, taking a seat in the chair across from Natalie, much to her dismay. "We'd just like you to listen for a few minutes."

What could she do? Natalie nodded slowly.

"We're trying to find Damien Freihof," Brandon said, coming to stand next to his wife, still staying within a protective reach.

Natalie fought not to blanch, not to give anything away, when it was all she could do not to bolt. "I'm sorry. I think you have mistaken me for someone else."

It was just as flimsy the third time, but it was all she had—hanging on to the possibility that they weren't exactly sure who she was. Although the wedding picture was pretty damning.

But at least if they were looking for Damien, they hadn't been sent by him.

"Falsifying a death report is illegal," Brandon continued, but then stopped with just the slightest touch on his arm by Andrea.

Just a single touch. What would it be like to have someone respect you and care for you so much that the touch of fingertips communicated something both ways? Something Brandon obviously respected.

Natalie had never had that in her entire life.

"It's imperative that we find Damien Freihof," Andrea said. "Lives are at stake."

Natalie just stared. She couldn't help them even if she wanted to. She'd known better than to keep tabs on Damien—the man was near genius with a computer. He would've found out.

She shrugged. "I can't help you."

"Maybe we can help *you*," Andrea continued. "Keep you safe, if that's part of your concerns."

Natalie just shrugged again.

"We're talking about more than just Brandon and me, of course," Andrea continued. "An entire team. A very strong group of people who would help you."

For just a second Natalie wanted to cave, to find out more, to trust someone so she wouldn't have to live in fear all the time. But she squashed it down. She couldn't trust anyone. All she could do was run.

Because the truth was, if these people had found her, Damien could, too. She needed to get them out of here.

"Look, I'm sorry. I know I look a lot like that woman in the picture. Quite the doppelgänger." She gave a laugh that sounded fake even to her own ears. "But that's not me. I can see how you would think that it is, but it's just not. I've never been married."

She stood up and walked toward the massive kitchen that was open to the living room, gripping the island to try to steady herself. "I don't want to be rude, but I've got appointments and stuff scheduled for this afternoon. So I'm going to have to ask you to leave."

What was she going to do if they didn't leave?

Threaten to call the police? Natalie wasn't capable of that kind of bluff.

"Falsifying your own death is illegal," Brandon said again. Natalie just stared at him unflinchingly.

Her choice had been between faking her own death or eventually ending up actually dead. She had no doubt the course she'd been on with Damien would've led to her eventual death.

So no matter how crappy her life was now, how many jobs she had to work to survive, how many sticky notes she had to put on windows to convince herself she was safe and how accusingly this law enforcement agent looked at her now...she'd definitely made the right choice.

"I'm sure it is, Officer..."

The two looked at each other again, secret agent code with some husband/wife telepathy thrown in. They got up and walked closer to her in the kitchen, where she was filling a cup with water from the tap.

"My name is Brandon Han," he finally said. "I'm an agent with Omega Sector's Critical Response Division."

They were both staring at her as if this would cause some big reaction. Natalie had no idea what they were talking about. She'd never heard of Omega Sector and wasn't about to ask any questions.

They were cops. They could bring to light the fact that she was still alive, if they hadn't already. And maybe she might do a year or two in prison for faking her death, but that would be nothing compared to what she would face after she got out.

"Okay, Agent Han. I'm still not who you think I am. I'm sorry I can't help you. But I'm still going to need to ask you to leave."

"Omega Sector can protect you," Agent Han continued as if she hadn't spoken. "We can make sure the slate is wiped clean. No jail time for you for falsifying. If there is something else, we can maybe make a deal for that, too."

Something else? What the hell else illegal did they think she'd done? Maybe they were talking about taxes or something. That could add up to more jail time.

Which would *still* be safer than being out on the streets if Damien knew she was alive. God, she had to get out of here. The panic was crawling all over her body, slimy and slick. She couldn't get rid of it. Just needed to get out of here. Right. Now.

"Please go." She forced the hoarse words past her throat and nearly buckled in relief when they turned toward the door without further argument. Brandon reached into his pocket and grabbed a card. Natalie took it, although she never planned to even so much as glance at it again.

"Call us if anything changes," Brandon said as Natalie opened the door and allowed them to walk through. "Anything. At any time. And especially if you happen to see Damien Freihof. And remember, the earlier you get us information, the better it will go for you. Deals for keeping you out of prison are only good when they help both sides."

"I'm still not your person. Sorry." She smiled in as friendly a manner as she could manage.

She was closing the door behind them when at the very last second Andrea stopped her with a hand on the door. It was only open a crack and Natalie had stepped behind it so she couldn't see them. She considered just shutting it until she heard Andrea's words.

"Damien Freihof got remarried to someone else two years after his wife Natalie died. Because no body for Natalie was ever identified, he was required to file for divorce before he could remarry. So no matter what, according to state laws, his marriage with Natalie is null and void even if she magically reappeared alive somewhere."

Marriage was null and void. Natalie gripped the door, barely able to contain a sob.

"Call us, Natalie. We want to help." Andrea took the pressure off the door and it slid shut, leaving Natalie alone. She turned and slid her back all the way down the wood until she reached the ground, tears streaming out of her eyes.

She wasn't married to Damien anymore. No matter what, she wasn't married to him.

Until this moment she'd had no idea that had even been a concern, but now she realized it had been a huge one. That if she was discovered alive she'd be returned to her *husband*. The man who had abused her for years.

But that would never happen because they weren't married anymore. She took a shuddery breath, pulling that fact deep into her soul. Damien would never be her husband again.

That didn't mean he wouldn't kill her if he found her.

She got up off the ground. She had to get going right now.

Because lack of an official piece of paper calling them married was not going to stop Damien from hunting her if he found out she was alive. California was no longer safe.

She needed to run.

Chapter Three

"Did you get what you needed?" Brandon asked as he and Andrea stepped into the surveillance van that was parked farther down the block from the beach house.

Ren shrugged. "I didn't get a location on Freihof, so not exactly."

He'd had both audio and partial video of Andrea and Brandon's discussion with Natalie. The questioning had gone down like he'd expected it would: without any co-operation from her.

"Maybe we should've pushed harder," Brandon said, sitting in the van's only other seat and pulling his wife onto his lap.

"No." Ren shook his head, glancing at the feed they had of the front of the house. "We needed to keep the situation open. Make Natalie think that she has options, can still get word to Freihof if she wants to. Maybe run to him and both of them flee the country."

Whatever she did, they would be watching.

"I don't think she's working with him," Andrea said. "I should've brought up the not-married aspect earlier. That was key, I realize now. If I had been able to see her when I said that, I'd be able to tell a lot more about her."

Andrea was a gifted behavioral analyst. Her abilities to read people's nonverbal cues were uncanny.

"Do you think she was upset that she's not legally married to him anymore?"

She gave a small shrug. "I don't know for sure, since I wasn't able to see her. But the news definitely affected her. Her knuckles were white in her grip and she stopped pushing on the door because she wanted to hear what I had to say."

"She could've been upset because Freihof hadn't told her about the divorce. Any wife would be pretty miffed to get that news."

Andrea nodded. "That's possible, certainly."

Ren studied her. "But you don't think so."

Brandon curled his arm around his wife in support. Out of everyone in Omega Sector, these two had had the most contact with Damien Freihof. Freihof had written letters to Andrea while in prison, then had come after her once he'd escaped.

"Freihof is obsessive. Controlling," Brandon said. "Hell, the man once saved Andrea's life just because he wanted to kill her himself."

Andrea nodded, leaning into Brandon. "Freihof is a master puppeteer. He's been collecting people who have some sort of gripe with Omega for months. Inciting them to violence. Getting them to do his dirty work for him. Or at least trying to."

The number of people connected to Omega who had been hurt or killed by either Freihof or one of his *puppets* over the last few months had been pretty staggering. Omega was still reeling. It was the reason Ren was on this case personally.

"Agreed." Ren nodded. "But what does this mean

with Natalie? She didn't even admit to being Natalie Freihof much less give any info on him."

"There's something we're missing," Andrea said. "Honestly, I'm not sure exactly what it is, but I know it's important. We don't have all the information."

Ren didn't need all the information to make his move. "It doesn't matter. Your presence shook her up. She'll do something now. Hopefully lead us directly to her not-husband husband."

Andrea tilted her head to the side. Ren could feel her studying him. Gauging his nonverbal behavior. "And if she doesn't know where he is? If she's been *dead* all this time to get away from him?"

"She's been running three businesses without anyone even knowing she's alive. She's either one hell of a businesswoman or she's doing it for Freihof."

Andrea shrugged again. "All I'm saying is that we're missing pieces of information. Important pieces."

"That's why I'm going to be ready for anything. She's going to run. Hopefully trying to get somewhere where she thinks it's safe to contact Freihof. Where she's *forced* to contact Freihof. We're just going to make sure we control that spot when she does."

"And if she really doesn't know where he is? If she's been trying to stay away from him all this time? Hide from him?"

Highly unlikely, but Ren was willing to consider it. "Then we go to plan B. If she can't take us to Freihof, then we use Freihof's obsession to get him to come to her."

"That may be risking her life," Andrea said quietly.

"Natalie is a criminal here. Let's not forget that. She could've gone to law enforcement if she wanted to get away from her husband. It's much more likely that the two of them have been in on this together the whole time. That Freihof is trusting her to run her businesses to get him money."

"She didn't recognize Omega Sector at all when we mentioned who we were with," Brandon said. "Even I could tell that, and I'm not nearly as gifted at reading people. If she's working with Freihof, he's keeping huge chunks of information from her."

Or maybe she was just a much better liar than they were giving her credit for. Trained by Freihof to completely school her nonverbal reactions so they couldn't read her. "Look, I don't have all the answers. All I know is we're out of time, especially now that Freihof has those canisters. We shook things up, caught Natalie unaware. That's good. Now I suspect that tonight or early tomorrow she's going to make a break for it. We watch carefully and—"

Ren's words were cut off by Brandon's muttered curse. He pointed at the screen. "Actually, looks like she's already on the run."

The screen showed Natalie, the small backpack she always carried over one shoulder and a larger one over the other, already on the move, coming out her front door.

"Damn it, I wasn't expecting her to move that fast. Get Lillian Muir on the phone and tell her to get in place down at the bus station."

Andrea stood and grabbed her phone.

"There weren't any calls from the house phone or the taps would've automatically turned on," Ren said. "She must have already had an emergency plan in place.

Which doesn't strengthen the case for her being an innocent party."

"Unless she's just that scared," Brandon reasoned.

"Lillian will be at the downtown bus station in fifteen minutes," Andrea said, disconnecting the call. "It might be cutting it a little close if Natalie goes straight there, but Lillian should make it."

"Good. Muir is a good choice. If you don't know her, her size helps her come across as very nonthreatening. Natalie will respond to the suggestion more easily."

They needed to direct Natalie's path without making her suspicious.

"Brandon and I want to stop Freihof more than anyone," Andrea said, staring at him. "Trust me, I can still feel the explosives he strapped around my neck. So I hope you can get what you need from Natalie, Ren. And in a lot of ways I hope you're right and she is working with Freihof."

"You do?"

"Yes. Because if not, we're about to ruin an innocent woman's life."

NATALIE HAD BEEN taking the bus from the Santa Barbara oceanfront to downtown since she started house-sitting two weeks ago. She'd always been cautiously aware of anyone around her.

Now she was downright suspicious.

Were some of these people cops? Were they following her? Did they work for that Omega-whatever that Brandon and Andrea mentioned?

Nobody seemed to be paying any attention to her, which she hoped was a good sign. Maybe she had gotten out faster than the cops had expected. She'd grabbed her bug-out bag and left.

That was the point of a bug-out bag, right? So you could bug-out the instant you needed to.

Her bag wasn't a true survivalist kit, but it had changes of clothes, all her spare cash, some nutrition bars and a bottle-size water filtration system. It even contained a high-end sleeping bag that folded into the size of a bowling ball, but only weighed a pound and a half. She'd balked at the price at the time, but now took comfort in knowing that if she needed to walk or hitchhike out of California, she could. Although her paints would have to go if she did that, which she hated to even consider, hoping to one day get the courage to use them again.

But there was no way she was staying here, even though she was losing her only means of employment. There had to be somewhere she could go where law enforcement wouldn't find her. She wasn't a violent criminal. Her picture wasn't going to show up on some Most Wanted list at the post office.

But she wanted to get as far away from here as possible. She would start heading to the East Coast—Boston or New York or Atlanta—somewhere where she could get lost in the crowd.

Flying was out since that required an ID, but she was hoping to get a jump on her escape by catching the first bus out. Hopefully it would take a day or two before the agents came back—and Natalie had no doubts they'd be back—and discovered she was gone.

Fifteen minutes after she left the beach house she was stepping off the bus in downtown Santa Barbara. The bus station, pretty tiny and nondescript, was another quarter mile down the main drag, far enough away from the tourist section to not be an eyesore.

The station was really just a large room with a series of benches and hard plastic chairs, and a small office where the ticket seller sat behind a glassed-in counter. The room was empty and the man working behind the counter was reading a magazine.

The first thing she needed to decide was where she wanted to go. But honestly, she didn't care. She would just see what was available.

"Can I help you?" the guy asked without looking up from his magazine as Natalie stepped up to the counter.

The door opened behind him. "Hey, George. Need you out here."

George turned from Natalie. "What? Who are—"

"The main office is on the line and some bigwig asked for you by name." The dark-haired woman in her midthirties, wearing the same uniform as George, walked into the small office and squeezed his shoulders, obviously urging him to stand. "Dude, just go. Rick's got the call on hold in his office. He sent me in here to relieve you."

George just looked confused. "But who are—"

The woman glanced over at Natalie and rolled her eyes with a look that screamed, *Men. Am I right?* "George, honey, I don't know who it is. But I'm thinking promotion, so just go."

George stood. "Yeah, okay. A promotion would be good. Um, you're okay here?"

The woman rolled her eyes again before shooing him out. "No need to mansplain it. Lily's got it handled." Once George was out the back door, Lily turned back around to Natalie. "Okay! What can I do for you now that we've got the dead weight out of the room?" She winked at Natalie again.

Despite the panic crushing down on her, Natalie had to smile at the pocket-size woman who'd handled George so deftly.

"I need a ticket."

"That I can do. Where're you headed and when do you want to go there? We've got some great sales coming up next week if you want to go north."

"No, next week won't work. I know it will cost me more, but I need to go today."

Lily smiled. "No problem. Where to?"

"What are my options?"

"We have daily buses that go to Los Angeles, San Francisco and Las Vegas. From any of those you can get to just about anywhere. Where are you ultimately trying to get to?"

Natalie shifted back and forth, finding it difficult to look the friendly woman in the eye. "East Coast. Honestly, anywhere. But I was thinking Atlanta or maybe Philadelphia. I just need to get out of here today."

"I see. Well, do you prefer Atlanta over Philadelphia?"

Atlanta would be less cold and didn't tend to get snow. "Sure. Atlanta. But just…it's important that I leave as soon as possible."

Lily nodded, a little more solemn. "Okay, hon. Let me see what I can find."

Natalie waited as Lily began typing. After a few moments, a frown marred her forehead and a minute after that she began to grumble.

"Is there a problem?" Natalie finally asked.

"There's a California drivers' strike affecting buses

from both LA and San Francisco. So neither of those are available for the next few days."

"Okay. What about Vegas?"

Lily nodded. "I'm checking that now."

The woman's fingers flew along the keyboard. Her grimace didn't reassure Natalie. "Completely full until Saturday. I'm so sorry, honey. What about flights? I know our municipal airport isn't much, but they have some flights. Or renting a car?"

Natalie could feel the panic clawing up inside her again. Neither of those would work; both required identification that would put her in the system, making note of where she started and where she ended.

To her utter dismay she could feel tears welling up in her eyes. God, she could not lose it in the middle of this tiny busy station. She just needed to get out. She would hitchhike or walk.

"No, that won't work. Thanks for your help," she muttered, trying to wipe her eyes before the tears fell.

She was almost to the door when Lily called out. "Hang on there a second, hon, do you have any problems with trains?"

Natalie stopped and turned slowly. "Trains?"

Lily motioned for her to come back to the window and she did. "Look, you can't mention this to anyone here, and we need to handle it before George gets back from his big promotion or whatever."

"The bus station sells train tickets?"

She shook her head. "No, but we have access to information and ticketing about flights and trains in case of emergencies. Normally I wouldn't even mention it, but since you need to leave today and can't get out on a bus..."

"I didn't even know there were trains around here."

"Yeah, this one is a little weird. It's actually a freight train, but it has one passenger car. Sells up to twelve seats that can recline for sleeping. It's no frills...you have to bring food or grab some at the scheduled stops. One shared bathroom. But it's not too bad. My cousin took it a couple months ago—she's afraid of flying— and enjoyed it. Goes from here to Saint Louis. Takes four days."

A train. Natalie had never even thought of that possibility.

"What would I need to get a ticket?"

"Just cash or a credit card, just like a bus ticket." Lily quoted the price, which wasn't much more than a bus. "It only runs on Wednesdays, so you're pretty lucky. But if you're really trying to get out of here today, it sounds like it's your best bet. As long as you don't mind not having many people to talk to."

"Actually, that sounds kind of perfect. I just need some time to myself."

Lily grinned. "Every woman does at one time or another, sweetie."

Within five minutes Lily had printed her a ticket and given her directions to the train station. Natalie had to walk quickly to grab a sandwich and snacks at the grocery store and make it to the south side of town in time for departure. She was pretty nervous when she arrived at the train yard, hoping she hadn't made a huge mistake. But an employee pointed her in the right direction and a few minutes later she was climbing into the passenger car with just five minutes to spare.

She could barely believe her luck. It was perfect. Wide seats in groups of four—two each facing each other—with a table in the middle. They would be much more comfortable than the cramped constraints of a bus. Plus large windows where she'd be able to see as they crossed the country. There were three groups of seats, and Natalie's ticket was for one of the empty groups. Even better. Maybe no one else would get on.

There were only three other passengers. Across the aisle was an older woman reading a book and a younger man in a hoodie with headphones on sitting across from her. Natalie shifted so she could see the seats behind her.

Her breath caught in her throat at the man sitting in the seat. He looked up from the papers and computer on the table in front of him to glance out the window as a whistle blew, giving Natalie a view of his carved jaw and strong chin. His brown hair was thick and full, a little messy like he'd been running his fingers through it.

She knew she was staring but couldn't quite help herself. There was a ruggedness about his face that drew her. He looked away from the window, catching her ogling, his green eyes pinning hers. Before she could look away with embarrassment, he nodded slightly, then resumed the reading of his papers.

At that moment the train gave a little jerk as it started forward. Natalie took her seat and watched out the window as she left Santa Barbara behind.

No one knew she was here. No one knew where she was going.

Then why did she feel like she was in more danger than ever?

Chapter Four

Lillian Muir deserved an Oscar. Ren had watched as the woman quite deftly handled George even though Natalie had beat her to the bus station by a couple of minutes. If Lillian hadn't been able to get George out of the office she would've never been able to lie to Natalie about all the buses and get her on this train.

Score one for Omega Sector. And given how Lillian Muir didn't usually do undercover—she was a kick-ass SWAT team member who could kill any given person a dozen different ways with her tiny bare hands—she truly had been amazing. The perfect blend of friendly and business that had sold Natalie on this venture.

A venture that wouldn't have even been an option without the funding of Joe Matarazzo, another member of Omega Sector who also happened to be a multimillionaire. Joe wanted Freihof caught and behind bars so he and his pregnant wife could live in peace without worrying that they were next in line for a madman to attack. Funding this little field trip had been a nobrainer for Joe.

They'd been on the train nearly thirty-six hours. Natalie had kept to herself all of that time, mostly just staring out the window. The other two people in the car were both Omega personnel. The older woman, Madeline, was a retired agent who now worked as an analyst. The younger guy was Philip Carnell, not Ren's first choice, but he was someone who wanted Freihof off the streets pretty badly after getting stabbed a few weeks ago by one of the villain's cronies.

Natalie hadn't spoken to either of them. And, after looking at Ren that one time as the train left Santa Barbara, hadn't interacted with him, either. Not that he'd expected her to be the life of the party.

The train had stopped once at its scheduled point, east of Las Vegas. Everyone had gotten out and bought food and any supplies they needed. Agents had been following Natalie discreetly in case she bolted, but she'd actually been the first one back on the train.

They hadn't gotten very far before Philip, still dressed in a hoodie, swung casually across the aisle and sat right next to Natalie. Ren leaned a little toward them so he could see what was happening more clearly. She had already stiffened and was leaning away from Philip, not looking at him at all.

Exactly what they had been hoping for when they'd come up with the plan of Philip turning on the obnoxious.

"Hey, you want some of my sandwich?" He was barely understandable over his chewing.

"No, thank you." Natalie didn't look away from the window. "I bought food at the stop."

Philip just leaned in closer and waved the sub sandwich in front of her face. "Are you sure? It's really good."

"No, I just want to be left alone."

"Aw, c'mon," Philip whined, slurring his words a

little as though he'd been drinking. "It's getting dark. There's nothing to look at out the window. Why don't you talk to me instead? I'm tired of sitting by that old lady. Tell me a little about yourself."

Ren could see Natalie growing stiffer with every word. She didn't respond to Philip, just kept staring out the window.

"All I want to do is chat," he continued. "We've got a long way to Saint Louis. Just talk to me."

She finally glanced at him before immediately moving her gaze back to the window. "I'm not interested in talking. I just want to be left alone."

"Really?" Philip sneered. "You think you're too good to talk to me, is that it? Well, that's okay, I can just stay here and get close to you. How about that?"

Natalie's spine was ramrod straight as Philip drew closer. She was all but pressed up against the window, but Ren caught a glimpse of one little fist tightening into a ball. He wondered what she would do if he wasn't about to intervene for the sake of the mission. He almost wanted to find out.

"Just leave me alone."

"I'm not talking about anything crazy, baby, unless you're interested in a little alone time in the bathroom or something like that." Philip leaned even closer.

That was Ren's cue.

He stood and crossed over to their seats. "Look, I think the lady has made it pretty clear that she doesn't want to talk to you."

Natalie peeked up at him, concern flashing in her blue eyes. Philip just kept staring at her. "Step back, man. This has nothing to do with you."

"Considering how small this train car is and that

you're a little drunk and pretty loud, I think it does have to do with me."

Philip snickered. "Fine. We'll be quiet. Won't we, sweetheart?"

He reached toward Natalie and she flinched. Ren found it took much less acting than he'd thought to reach over and grab Philip's wrist and yank it backward away from her.

"Dude!"

Without effort, Ren bent Philip's arm into a position that wouldn't take more than a flick of his wrist to break it. "I'm pretty sure the lady doesn't want you to touch her." Color had leached from her face. "Is that right, ma'am?"

She nodded.

Ren released Philip's arm, and slapped him on the shoulder almost good-naturedly. "Why don't we just get one of the train officials to come back here and sort out the seating arrangement?"

If possible, Natalie's face lost even more color. "No, that's not necessary. I'm just not interested in talking to anyone."

Ren looked at Philip. "Why don't you just go on back to your assigned seat? Like she said, she's not here for conversation."

"I don't think it's fair that you both get your own sets of seats and I have to share with the old lady," Philip whined.

Ren glanced over at Natalie, who was still looking like she wanted to find some way to jump off the moving train, then back to Philip, who was doing a pretty damned good job of staying on script.

"Why don't you take my seat for a while? That way

you'll have your own set and can spread out and get comfortable." His eyes flickered to Natalie. "I'll sit here if that's okay since I have work to do and am not looking for any conversation. Would that be okay?"

She looked back and forth between him and Philip. She didn't like it, he could tell. But when her eyes rested on Philip it was in distaste. When they rested on him it was in...*fear*.

Either he was projecting his intent in some way he wasn't aware of, or Natalie was very astute. Regardless, he was going to need to handle her with the utmost care if he was going to get her to trust him.

"Um..." She bit on her lip.

Ren gave her a friendly smile. "I understand. Just hang on a second and let me make a call up to the conductor." There was a phone near the front of the car that allowed passengers to make calls to the train officials if needed. Train officials that were all, for the most part, Omega Sector agents for this journey. "We can get this sorted out so you don't have to worry."

"No," she said quickly. "No, it's fine. If you don't mind giving up your seat, it would be fine with me if you sit here."

Ren raised an eyebrow at Philip. "Okay with you?"

Philip looked over at Natalie and shrugged. "Your loss." Then got up and sauntered over to Ren's seats.

Philip winked at Ren as he followed him and grabbed his stuff. Ren gave the younger man a little nod. So far, everything was going as planned. Hopefully Ren's gesture of help would soften Natalie slightly toward him.

A few moments later he had his papers and laptop in hand and moved to the set of seats facing Natalie.

He chose the seat near the aisle so both of them could stretch their legs without hitting each other.

She gave him a soft smile. Looking at her like this for the first time—not a photograph of her or through a recording device—Ren was almost struck dumb by her beauty. Straight blond hair that was in a braid that fell over her shoulder, wide crystal-blue eyes.

Lips so full and pouty they made him forget for a moment that she was most likely working with a man who had killed multiple innocent people and planned to continue.

No matter how angelic she looked—whatever air of innocence and fragility she gave off—Ren could not forget she was the enemy.

He smiled at her. "I promise, no talking."

She gave a little laugh. "You don't have a sandwich you're going to wave in my face, do you?"

"No, left all my sandwich weapons at home."

"Ah, hope we're not ambushed, then, or else you won't be much help." She gestured toward his computer. "I'll let you get back to work. Thanks again for the rescue."

She turned back to the window but Ren could see her checking him out in the reflection. And once it got dark she didn't have the excuse to stare out it anymore. She just sat there for a long time, looking at her hands folded in her lap.

"Do you not get cell coverage on your phone out here?" he finally asked. He could understand if she didn't want to contact Freihof, but surely there was something more interesting to do than just stare at her hands.

Her eyes flew to his. "I'm sorry?"

"People are on their phones all the time. It's unusual to see someone without one these days. I thought maybe yours just doesn't have coverage."

She shifted a little in her seat. "Oh, yeah. That's it. No coverage."

"No games or anything? E-reader?"

She shifted again, looking away. "My phone…isn't working right. So, not having coverage doesn't matter. And it's not much use for anything else."

He gave her his friendliest smile. "Going to be a long trip without anything to do. Or maybe you just prefer paper books?"

That got him a real smile. "Actually, I love paper books. But I didn't have a chance to buy any before I left."

"Sudden trip or are you like me, a last-minute packer?"

She relaxed just the slightest bit. "A little of both, I guess. Wasn't planning on taking the train, but the bus was full."

Ren nodded. "Yeah, the strike. What a mess." He shut his computer, watching to see if she would tense and turn away, pleased when she didn't. "I suppose you're going to mock me now."

Those blue eyes flew to his. "I am? Why?"

"Because of my fear of flying. I just can't stand the thought of being in an airplane. Therefore, my life involves a lot of buses, driving or, in this case, trains."

"What do you do?"

"I have a sheep and dairy farm in Montana."

Damn it, where the hell had that come from? A small auto parts store owner in Saint Louis. That was supposed to be his cover, something nondescript and not very memorable.

Why the hell had he told her the truth? He did have a sheep and dairy farm in Montana. His parents and brother lived and worked there. Ren had been itching to get back there himself.

But he definitely had not been planning to tell his suspect about it.

"Oh, wow, like cows and sheep?" She sounded a little excited before laughing harshly at herself. "Of course cows and sheep. I'm an idiot."

"Nah, don't say that. But yes, cows and sheep. We sell wool to some boutique stores out in California and across the country."

Damn it, more truth. But he was committed to it now, so he'd have to stick with it.

"That's pretty interesting. I've always loved animals, but…"

Only when it became obvious she wasn't going to finish did he prompt her. "But what?" he asked gently.

She looked back out to the blackened window for the longest time. "But having a pet or being around them just never worked out for me."

"Did you know that during WWI President Woodrow Wilson had a flock of sheep trim the White House lawn?"

She laughed, then looked surprised by the sound. "You're making that up."

"I'm not, Scout's honor." She liked animals? That he could give her. "My family got into sheep and dairy farming because my mother loved animals and couldn't stand the thought of slaughter. So sheep and dairy cows it became."

He told her some more entertaining stories about growing up with his brother on the farm, about getting chased around by chickens when he was a toddler and how his brother, Will, had thought that black sheep were dirty and tried to wash one when he was young.

And damned if he hadn't used Will's real name. A pretty common name, but still.

By the time he'd finished she almost looked like a completely different person. Her face was more relaxed, unguarded. Her long legs were tucked up under her as she'd turned to the side to listen to him, head against her seat, playing with the braid over one shoulder.

Every time he'd stopped telling a story, tried to get the conversation turned back to her, she'd asked another question about his life. Some downright insightful.

Had his father considered becoming a large-animal vet at one time? Yes, until he'd realized he wanted to own his animals and farm.

Did his mother ever knit them anything from a particular sheep they'd loved? Yes. Ren still had a sweater she'd made him from a sheep he'd once carried home after it had broken its leg.

Had he and his brother both reached a point where they'd felt trapped by the farm and wanted to get away?

That one wasn't as easy to answer. Yes, Ren had left just after high school, deciding he'd preferred the excitement of joining the army than staying there any longer. The army had fast realized his ability to pick up new skills quickly, as well as his natural strength and intelligence. They'd fast-tracked him into special forces.

Ren had loved the army but had gotten out after six years when he was approached to start a special law enforcement task group that would be made up of the best agents and ex-soldiers the country had to offer. He'd birthed Omega Sector. And had been fighting bad guys ever since.

Like the bad guy sitting across from him now, with alabaster skin, her blue eyes drooping. She would've fooled him, he had to admit. If he hadn't already known what she was capable of, he wouldn't have believed it.

So yeah, he'd left the farm because it had made him feel trapped. Like nothing ever happened there. But he was beginning to realize how wrong that was. Maybe shootouts and arrests didn't happen there, but life did.

Light did.

He'd been living in the darkness so long that light was starting to seem damn more appealing.

"You going to go to sleep there, Peaches?"

One eyebrow cocked. "Peaches?"

He shrugged. "Your skin. Just looks smooth, like peaches and cream. My mom used to make it for us." Damn it, the truth. Again.

"Yeah, I'm a little tired. My name's Natalie, by the way."

He smiled. "I'm Warren Thompson, but generally go by Ren. Get some rest. I'll make sure no one attacks you with a sandwich. We've got a long way to go."

Plus, it would make it much easier for him to do what he was about to do if she was already out.

Her nod was full of trust, and just for a second guilt ate at Ren. It didn't get any better when she tucked herself into a tighter ball on her seat a few minutes later, one small hand curled under her chin.

He forced the feelings away. He wasn't dragging her into the darkness; she already lived there.

He just hoped he'd be able to find his way back to the light when this was all over. After what he had to do. Because the light had never seemed so far away.

Chapter Five

Natalie dreamed of sheep. All kinds. Baby lambs, adults heavy with wool and some that had just been shaved. She dreamed of sweaters and yarn and of a special sheep that had to be carried back to the safety of the farm.

She sat and watched as the man she'd listened to for hours, would've listened to for the rest of her life if she could've, ran around her with the sheep. Would ask her to count them, to make sure they didn't get lost in the darkness.

It was a crazy dream, because she knew she was dreaming, knew this wasn't real. She felt funny, like she was moving.

She was on a train, her tired brain remembered, but her eyes refused to open. But the movement felt different. Like she was being carried somewhere.

But she didn't want to go anywhere else; she just wanted to stay here on the nice farm with the sheep.

"No, please," she murmured.

"Shh," someone said. "You're just dreaming."

That voice, that smoky, sexy voice again. She didn't want it to stop. Ren's voice.

"Sheep," she said, hoping he'd understand. She wanted him to tell her more stories.

"Yes, the sheep. Stay with the sheep, Peaches."

Peaches. That made her feel warm. So nice and warm. She just lay there and basked in it.

But soon the warm became hot. Too hot. What was happening? The sheep were nowhere around anymore. Just the heat. A fire. It was burning her.

Natalie forced her eyes open only to find she was surrounded by smoke. She coughed and sat up. Where was she? What was happening?

And why in the world was she outside sitting in half a foot of snow?

"Natalie, stay there." It was Ren again, somewhere nearby but she couldn't see him through the smoke. "There's been an accident."

"A-an accident?" She tried to clear fog from her brain but couldn't.

"Yes, the train derailed or something. Crashed." Suddenly he was there kneeling beside her. She could still barely see him through the smoke, but could see blood streaming over his temple. She coughed again.

"There's a fire." She still couldn't figure out what was going on. "You're bleeding."

"I'm fine. But yes, the train is on fire. You need to stay back. I'm not sure what sort of materials the freight sections were hauling. Could be combustible."

She tried to focus on his words, to understand them, and she did, but it was like they had to wade through mud to get to her brain. She put her hands up to her head.

"Are you okay?"

"My brain is so slow. How did I get here?" She couldn't remember any of it.

"I carried you. I'll tell you the whole story later, okay? But right now I need to go back."

She grabbed his wrists. The thought of him leaving her alone in the dark and smoke and snow, when she couldn't process anything, scared her.

"Am I hurt?" she asked. "I can't seem to figure things out. I feel almost drunk."

"Maybe you hit your head. But I've got to get back in there."

It finally became clear to her. "Oh, my God, the other people. I'll help you." She tried to stand up but dizziness assaulted her.

Ren's hand fell on her shoulder. "No, you just stay here. Trust me, in the shape you're in, you'll do more harm than good."

"But that elderly lady…"

He gave a curt shake of his head. "She's gone, Peaches. She and the guy who was hitting on you. The way the train car flipped when we derailed…if I hadn't changed spots with the guy it would've been me dead. No one could've survived."

Natalie bit back a sob. "Oh, no."

"Just stay here, okay? I'm going to see if I can find the train engineers, although, honestly, I'm not holding out much hope. But just don't move. We're not far from a ravine, and I don't want you falling. Plus, it'll just put us both in more danger if I have to look out for you, too."

He was right. She couldn't even stand up on her own. "Okay. Be careful."

She felt like he was gone for hours, although she knew it couldn't be more than a few minutes. She was shivering and clenched her jaw as her teeth started chattering. Her stomach revolted every time she moved. She touched all around her head gingerly to see if she could find any lumps that would signify some sort of concussion, but couldn't find anything.

How the hell did someone just sleep through a train crash that killed at least two people? She remembered dreaming about sheep. About feeling like she was being carried and hearing Ren's voice. Had that been after the crash? When he was getting her out?

Her brain just felt so sluggish. She knew sitting in the snow wasn't helping—physically or mentally—but was afraid to move in case she couldn't find Ren again. The dark and smoke just seemed so all-encompassing. And until her brain started working again, she didn't want to be alone.

But Ren had already been bleeding before he went back to try to help the train engineers. What if he was hurt worse than she thought? What if he was trapped somewhere right now and couldn't get out without help?

She couldn't sit here and do nothing.

She took a few steps into the smoke, coughing as it became thicker. The fire seemed to be getting louder.

"Ren?" she yelled between coughs. "Where are you? Let me help!"

She couldn't hear or see anything. The smoke was too thick.

"Ren!"

Which way should she go? She took a few steps in the direction of what she thought would be the front of the train and where he had headed but she couldn't be sure.

"Natalie!" She'd only gotten a few more steps before

she heard him behind her. She turned and ran back in the direction she'd come, arms in front of her in the smoke.

"Ren. I'm here!"

She felt his arms come around her. "Thank God," he whispered against her hair. "I didn't know where you were."

"I couldn't just stay and do nothing. I was worried you might be hurt." She reached up and touched the blood that had dried on his temple.

He kept one arm around her as he led her farther away. "I'm fine. But we've got to get out of here. There's definitely some explosive materials, not to mention we're going to have to find some shelter."

"Is everybody…" She couldn't bring herself to say it.

"They are. I'm sorry, Natalie. It looks like everyone was killed in the initial impact. Somehow we both made it, but we're going to have to get moving if we're going to keep it that way. We've got to go. Right now."

He pulled her, half walking, half running, before wrapping his arm around her and leading them into darkness. She had no idea where they were going, but Ren was determined to get them away from where they'd been.

She understood why a few moments later when a loud fireball burst behind them. Natalie let out a little shriek and fell forward, only saved from falling face-first into the snow by his arm around her.

"Oh, my gosh, was that the train?" She could finally see him a little more clearly now that they were coming out of the smoke.

"Yes, that's why I wanted to get us out of there. But I didn't expect the explosion to be quite that big. Are you okay?"

It was so out of character for her, but she just wanted to lean into him. Into his strength. She didn't know this man at all. Didn't know if he could be trusted. But it didn't stop her from resting her forehead on his chest for just a moment.

They'd almost *died*. Surely it was okay to take just a second and rest here against him.

After a breath she pushed away. She realized he had both her larger backpack and the smaller one.

"I found both your bags—they got thrown from the passenger car. I couldn't find mine, but at least I got my coat."

He set her backpacks on the ground, and Natalie immediately knelt and opened the bigger one, pulling out a dry sweater. No point in putting on dry pants, they were just going to get wet again as they walked.

But at least they were alive. Unlike the others. Tears filled her eyes.

"Hey, you okay?"

"Yeah, I just can't believe this is happening. That everybody's dead and we're not."

He nodded. "I know. Me, too. But we'll have to process it later. Right now survival is the most important thing."

He was right. She would cry for these strangers, but it couldn't be right now. Like he said, survival was the most important thing. That thought helped cut through the fog in her brain a little more.

Survival.

She had been doing that for six years. She had survived everything Damien had done to her, and she would survive this crash. That was what Natalie did: *survive*.

Already, she felt a little better, a little clearer, a little stronger. She clenched her jaw against the chattering of her teeth.

"You're right. Survival is the most important thing." She began digging through the backpack again.

"I don't guess you have hiking boots in there?" Ren asked.

"No, only the tennis shoes on my feet."

"Yeah, me, too. But that's better than nothing. Get as warm as you can, and if you've got an extra sweater to wrap around your head, that will help, too. The body loses a lot of its heat from the head. I have an extra pair of gloves, so use those."

She did as he suggested and handed him a second sweater. He looked a little surprised before taking it and wrapping it around his own head.

"Thanks."

"Do you know where we are?" she asked. "I have no idea what state we're even in."

"I've taken this trip a few times, and based on how long we've been traveling since our stop, I'd put us just over the Utah/Colorado line. But it doesn't matter what state we're in. Either way we're high altitude and not near anything. This was the worst possible place this could've happened."

"Should we stay near the train? Won't someone come looking for us?"

He gave her the smaller backpack and put the larger one on himself. "Eventually they'll come when we don't show up at our next scheduled stop. But that is more than eighteen hours from now. Then by the time they figure out something's actually wrong and get someone out here...we'll die from exposure."

"Oh." Natalie fought not to get overwhelmed. One hour at a time. She just needed to take it one hour at a time.

And at least she was in absolutely no danger from Damien up here. That thought made her smile.

"Want to share your happy thoughts?" Ren tapped the corner of her lips. "I wouldn't mind a little good news."

"Nothing. We're alive. That's what matters. But I guess I shouldn't be smiling."

He pinched the tip of her chin gently. "No, it's okay to smile. We *are* alive. Let's just keep it that way. We need to find shelter for tonight and we'll take stock of everything tomorrow. Food. Water. Figure out a plan."

"Okay. I have a sleeping bag, some protein bars and a water filtering system."

"You do?" Incredulity painted his tone. "Were you on your way to a camping trip or something?"

Yeah, explaining camping equipment when she had no clothes that could be used for that type of activity wasn't easy. "I was sort of relocating and had this stuff in my bag."

"It'll definitely come in handy. Let's get going."

Natalie took a couple steps, then had to stop as dizziness assailed her again.

"You all right?"

"Yeah. I must have hit my head in the crash, although nothing feels tender. I'm just woozy."

He began to walk again, but kept her close to him as they moved. "Shock. Altitude. Cold. A lot of things could be affecting you. And yeah, I'm sure we'll both be totally sore tomorrow."

"Better sore than dead."

She felt his arm tighten around her waist. "Always."

Chapter Six

Ren led them, in a slightly roundabout way, to the overhang he'd found when setting up for this operation last
week. He and the team had cleaned it out—not wanting to accidentally find themselves bitten or attacked
by something—then carefully made it look as if it had
been undisturbed.

Not that Natalie would notice. He didn't think she
would notice if there was a couch and television in the
small cave. The drugs he'd given her, a tiny injection
once she'd fallen asleep to make sure she wasn't conscious when the train "crashed," had affected her a little
more than expected. She still seemed woozy and confused, clinging to him a lot more than he suspected she
normally would.

Ren would continue to foster that closeness as long
as he could. Maybe by the time the drug was completely
out of her system her body would already be used to
his nearness somewhat. The closer he could get to her,
the more information he'd be able to glean.

He'd planned on wrapping the both of them within
his coat inside the little cave. That, along with the random pieces of dry timber he and the team had placed

inside that would allow him to make a fire, would've made for an uncomfortable but not miserable night.

She had a damn sleeping bag. She'd definitely caught him off guard with that one. Were she and Freihof planning to go on the run, *literally*, where they would need camping gear? A water purifier? Who carried that around if they didn't plan to use it?

Of course, she'd also had stuff that made no sense if she was going somewhere on foot. Paints and brushes. He'd just left them in the bag.

They stepped in a particularly deep drift of snow and it came past her knees. Natalie stiffened almost to the point where her back was bowing. Ren looked over in concern.

"Natalie, what's wrong? Are you hurt?" The drug shouldn't be causing a reaction like this. She looked like she was in pain. Not just pain, but complete agony.

"I just... The snow hurts. It hurts." Her voice sounded odd. Distant. "Please. I'm sorry. I'll be good, just let me out of the snow. It hurts."

What the hell?

He pulled her a few steps forward until she was out of the drift, trying to figure out what was going on. He'd been monitoring their time in the snow, knowing frostbite was a possibility, especially in tennis shoes. But they hadn't been walking long enough for it to be an issue—it shouldn't be causing her pain. She hadn't said anything about it until the drift.

He ripped off his gloves and grabbed his phone to turn on the flashlight. He leaned Natalie—who still looked dazed and frightened—against a tree. Lifting her foot, he checked for any holes in her shoes that he hadn't known about or some sort of wound that had caused her such distress. She was still breathing so deeply she was in danger of hyperventilating.

There was nothing on either her leg or foot that should be causing her pain. And while she was cold, she definitely wasn't anywhere near numbness or frostbite.

He shifted the light back up to look her in the face. Her lips were pinched with pain, her eyes closed. "No more snow. Please, no more snow. I was wrong. You were right."

"Natalie." He put his hands on either side of the sweater she'd wrapped around her head. "Tell me what's wrong."

"No more. It burns so bad. Please," she whispered. Tears were streaming out of her eyes.

Ren didn't know exactly what was happening, but he knew it wasn't part of his plan. They weren't far from the cave so he whisked her up in his arms and cradled her against his chest.

"Okay, Peaches, no more snow. I've got you now. You're not in it anymore."

Her arms came up to wrap around his shoulders, and he pulled her more tightly against himself and farther from the ground. He began walking quickly toward the cave.

Was this some sort of weird phobia? Maybe just a reaction to stress? After all, she thought five other people had died tonight and they'd narrowly escaped with their lives.

She definitely didn't know that if she'd taken another couple dozen steps toward the train when she'd decided to come help him with the "rescue" that she would've seen Ren talking to Philip and Madeline, both very much alive. The three-member train crew? Also totally unharmed.

As a matter of fact, if she'd come out of the circle of smoke, she would've seen the train hadn't crashed at all. It was all a very elaborate smoke and light show. One car had been burning so she could feel the heat, and be scared enough not to come closer.

Damned if she hadn't come anyway, trying to help. Ren had barely caught her in time.

After blowing the carefully laid explosives once he'd given them the signal through a single text, the rest of the team had left and were probably already down in Riverton, the Colorado town that was only about six miles away.

Ren just hoped he didn't have to bring them immediately back up here because Natalie was having some sort of nervous breakdown or allergic reaction to the drugs. The first he could possibly still use to his advantage as long as it didn't get too murky. But the second would require immediate medical attention, effectively bringing the mission to a halt.

She still had her arms wrapped tightly around his neck, trying to hold as much of her own weight as she could, as if that was very significant to begin with. He'd regularly carried more weight for much longer in the special forces. Ren just kept her close and moved quickly toward the cave.

"Here we are, Peaches," he said. He set her down inside the overhang that sheltered them from the wind on three sides. He'd planned to make a big production of searching it to make sure it was safe, but she seemed much more concerned about the white stuff on the ground outside than she did about anything else. He clicked his phone flashlight back on to make sure nothing had taken residence in the last few days.

"Yeah, this will be good," he continued. "Get us out of the elements so we can get some sleep."

She looked around, slowly taking everything in, one of her hands still grasping his shoulder.

"See?" He took the sweater covering her head and pushed it down slightly so she had more freedom of movement of her head. Strands of her light blond hair flew everywhere. "No snow in here. Do you think you can crawl in?"

She nodded and let go of him to slide inside. He took off her backpack and pushed it toward her. She wrapped her arms around it and pulled it up to her chest. But at least she had lost that utterly hollow look in her eyes.

"I think there's enough dry wood in here for us to start a fire. It won't be much of anything, but it will be something. Give a little light. Warmth. But there's no snow in here, okay?"

"Okay," she whispered.

He smiled and began building a small fire in the far corner so the smoke would go outward instead of toward them. She was still cradling her backpack.

"You should probably eat one of your protein bars. Your blood sugar is bottoming out, which is making everything much harder on you."

"What about you?"

"I'll have one in the morning, but right now I'm fine."

She nodded. "I'll get out my sleeping bag, too."

"While you're at it, why don't you try your cell phone? I know you said you didn't have a signal before, but you never know, sometimes you can just catch the right spot and find a signal. I've already tried mine but it didn't work."

Maybe she would make it easy and call Freihof right here and now. Omega had provided a cell signal booster to this area and had an agent monitoring the local 911 dispatch. So if Natalie tried to call someone—hopefully Freihof—the call would go through, but a call to 911 would just disconnect.

It was option one in giving her time to contact Damien, and the easiest. He hoped she'd take it.

But she didn't.

"No, that's okay."

Now that the fire was going, their little dwelling was already becoming more comfortable. Ren took the sweater she'd given him and unwrapped it from his head. He tried to keep any annoyance from his voice.

"You don't want to even try? You never know. It's worth a shot."

She just shrugged and took a bite of her protein bar. "No, I don't have a phone."

What? "Not at all? Not even a really cheap one? Even eight-year-olds have a phone these days."

"Nope. Not me."

"Then how do you contact people? Your friends?" Maybe she'd ditched her phone before she left. Damn it, now he wished he hadn't told her his phone had no signal. He could've offered it to her to use to make a call.

"I haven't had one in years. I don't really like talking on one, I guess. And I don't have a lot of friends. I work a lot."

Ren didn't buy it. She either already had a radio-silence plan in place with her ex-husband or she didn't trust Ren and was hiding her phone until she could contact Freihof in private. Omega would intercept that call if it came.

"Wow, that's crazy, but I'll bet it makes your life more peaceful."

"Will your parents worry about you? Your brother? Since your phone won't work?"

"No. I don't check in with them every day. When they hear about the train, they'll worry. But like I said, it will be days before they backtrack to where the accident happened. And hopefully we'll be in civilization before then."

She got that worried look on her face again.

"Is there someone who'll be waiting for you?" he asked. "Worrying? Were you going all the way to Saint Louis?"

She shook her head. "No, there's no one who'll be concerned about me for a long time."

He crawled closer as she got the sleeping bag out and began to unzip it. "You should leave it zipped up," he told her. "You'll stay warmer that way."

"No, that means you'll have nothing. We'll share it."

Ren had to tamp down the unexpected pleasure that bubbled through his system at the thought of lying next to Natalie. His body didn't seem to care that she was probably a criminal and, if her ex-husband had rubbed off on her at all, she'd be able to kill him while he slept without blinking an eye.

No, his body wasn't interested in acknowledging that at all.

He distracted himself by getting some of the snow from outside and placing it inside her water bottle— a perk he hadn't planned on having this early, but was willing to take advantage of—so it would be melted and ready for consumption by the morning. He'd had a large water bottle stashed in the cave when they'd cleaned it out, but now they wouldn't have to use it and explain the sudden appearance of clean drinking water.

He helped her spread the jackets out on the ground so they could lie down on those and would be able to pull the sleeping bag over them. It wasn't going to be the Ritz, but it wasn't half bad.

"I'm feeling much better," she said as she settled next to him, close enough for their body heat to help each other.

"Do you want to tell me what the whole snow thing was about?" he asked.

He could feel her stiffen. "It's a long story. I just don't like snow. I've lived in California for six years so it hasn't been an issue. I guess I was just overwhelmed tonight. I still feel so off."

It had been a hell of a lot more than not liking snow, but Ren let it pass. "You'll feel better tomorrow. Let's get some rest."

He didn't say anything else, didn't give her a chance to say anything else. He just slid behind her on top of the jackets and put her between him and the fire. He reached down and pulled the sleeping bag over them both.

There wasn't much room in the cave, even less in their little sleeping pallet. Although they were both on their backs, Ren was pressed up against Natalie from shoulder to knee. Between the warmth, the exhaustion from what had happened and the drugs still in her system, she should've been asleep pretty rapidly. But an hour later, her stiff form announced that she was far from sleep.

"Peaches, what's wrong?"

She got stiffer. "I just…can't… There's so much… What if…"

When she couldn't get any more words out, Ren did what his body had been begging him to do since they'd lain down. He flipped her on her side so she was facing the fire, slid one arm under her so it cradled her head and wrapped the other around her abdomen and pulled her back until she was firmly tucked against his front.

And damned if her body didn't fit perfectly with his. He wanted to groan and curse at the same time.

"You've been through a trauma," he whispered in her ear. "Your body needs rest. I'm not going to let anything happen to you while you're asleep, okay?" He pulled her a little closer to his body. "Anything that's going to try to get to you has to go through me and that's…"

Ren trailed off. She was already asleep.

Chapter Seven

Damien walked from room to room inside the large Santa Barbara beach house.

Natalie—his Natalie—had been here. He breathed the air from the house deep into his lungs, as if he could inhale her very scent. Natalie was alive.

To discover this wondrous news after all this time was nothing short of a miracle. Ironically, he had Omega Sector, the very people he'd been trying to punish for taking his Natalie away in the first place, to thank for the information. Even though Damien's mole inside Omega was gone, he still had one small channel of information open to him that they hadn't found.

It was what had allowed him to discover and obtain the biological warfare canisters. He was sure they'd discover the tiny leak soon, but it didn't matter, because the most important information he could've ever discovered already had been.

Natalie was alive.

He'd gotten the canisters where they'd needed to go, then flew directly to California as soon as Omega agents—his old nemeses Brandon and Andrea—had been brought in to make contact with Natalie. He wasn't sure how long he'd missed them by, but it was long enough. Now he had no idea where Natalie was, again. He'd have to wait for another phone call to trigger more information.

Damien's fingers strolled along the top of the couch, imagining her sitting here with her feet propped up on the table. She'd always been sloppy like that until he'd come along and cared enough about her to teach her proper behavior. How to be the perfect wife.

Their marriage had been perfect, everything either of them could ever want. He'd helped her become a flawless model of what a wife could be and she'd loved him for it.

He wasn't sure exactly what had happened six years ago. Natalie had obviously been hurt—some sort of head trauma that had caused her to forget their marriage. Forget their perfect life together.

Because the alternative—that she'd run from him on purpose—was impossible.

He walked into the master bedroom, straight up to the bed, pulling back the covers. He bent low so he could smell the pillowcases, wanting to catch even the faintest hint of her essence. Did she still wear the perfume he'd picked out for her during their marriage?

He liked the thought of that. Maybe a subconscious urge she'd had that she didn't even understand because of her memory loss. But deep inside, her brain knew, because like her body and her heart it still belonged to him.

He sniffed again, ripping the pillows off the bed and throwing them to the floor when he couldn't smell anything remotely resembling his Natalie.

He stared at the bed. She had slept here. Without him. Had someone else joined her in it?

Rage rose in him like a savage wave. His teeth clenched as he forced himself to take a calming breath.

If someone had so much as even touched her, that man would die. And she would need to be punished. He didn't enjoy punishing her, of course. That would make him a monster. But he understood the necessity for it. It helped make her perfect. She'd always understood that, too.

He didn't know how long it would be before he received word of where Natalie was. And he refused to always be a step behind in something this important. So he would take matters into his own hands as he waited.

This house wasn't in Natalie's name, so it belonged to someone else. Damien would find them and have a talk with them about what they knew. Every single thing they knew.

And then he would find the love of his life once more. It would be like they had never been apart.

NATALIE WOKE UP SLOWLY, stretching her arm out above her. She'd dreamed of sheep farms and train crashes and caves and sleeping wrapped in…

"Careful there, Peaches. Don't want you to stretch too far and accidentally elbow me in the nose."

Oh. Sweet. Heaven.

It hadn't been a dream. And she was half-sprawled on top of Ren. The sun had come up and now she could very clearly see those clear green eyes of his staring out at her. He had one arm under his head, propping him up in a lazily delicious sort of way. Hair tousled. Smile charming.

Natalie felt her heart begin thumping harder in her chest. She immediately scooted back away from him.

What on earth was she doing—all but lying on top of a man she hardly knew?

But she couldn't deny—despite every reason why this shouldn't be true, and there were *many*—she'd slept the best she'd ever had since the first time she realized her husband was a monster who would cruelly punish her on a whim. Evidently her exhausted mind had had no trouble giving over her trust to an almost total stranger.

But now her mind wasn't exhausted and she wasn't just going to trust blindly. She had way too many scars to ever let that happen again.

She scampered back a little farther, ignoring the pang of loss she felt as his hand fell off her hip.

"Be careful," he said. "The fire is mostly out behind you but it might have enough heat to burn."

She stopped. "I'm sorry I was basically sprawled all over you."

That smile. Sweet mother of chocolate. "No worries. I can think of a number of things worse than waking up with a beautiful woman draped over me."

"Even in a cave?"

His smile faded as if he remembered why they were here. What had happened. "I'll admit, it isn't the best of circumstances. Are you feeling better?"

The fuzziness in her head was gone, she realized, and she didn't have any pain. So not a head injury, or if it was, not a severe one. "I'm feeling pretty great, considering everything."

"Good. Last night you were a little overwhelmed. The crash, of course, and some other stuff."

Snow. She knew he was talking about her reaction to the snow. But there was no way to be able to explain that easily so she wasn't even going to try. "Yeah, I just can't believe those people are dead. Do you have any idea what happened?"

"No. It was so chaotic. When I came to, everything was surrounded by smoke. I happened to hear you moaning, so that's how I got you out. The lady and the guy were... It was already too late for them."

"So what is our plan now?"

"The last thing I checked before we were out of cell tower range was weather. Mostly I was looking at Montana, but I happened to see an overview of here. It's not good. Snow, Natalie. Not quite a blizzard, but bad."

She could feel her teeth clenching. She was just going to have to overcome the snow. Mind over matter. She had control. Wasn't tied. Wasn't forced. Wouldn't need to beg.

"Natalie?"

Her eyes snapped to his green ones. "Yep. Got it. We have to walk through the snow and I have to not freak out."

"It's just..."

She nodded. "Yep," she said again. "I know. I freaked out a little last night. I won't let it happen again."

"Okay, then we should get on our way. Try to find better shelter than this before worse weather moves in. Or a town. Or cell coverage, or *something*. Are you sure there's no one you need to get in touch with who will be worried about you?"

How did you explain to someone who had multiple people who would be worried if he was a day late that there was literally not one person in the world who cared if Natalie dropped dead right now?

Maybe Olivia, the waitress from the bar who'd asked

Natalie to house-sit in her stead, would be worried. But honestly, Olivia had only asked Natalie because she was desperate to find someone who could take her place. In fact, Olivia had to confirm Natalie was actually her name before she'd asked her about house-sitting. Maybe Natalie's bosses would notice, but Natalie got the impression they were constantly surprised when she'd always shown up to work since she insisted on being paid cash, which, to them, said she was a flight risk.

She had spent the last six years not talking to anyone. Trying to make sure no one really noticed her. Obviously she'd been successful. And it pretty much made her pathetic.

"No, no one will miss me. I guess all my people are used to not hearing from me for a while. We'll make it somewhere before they get to the point of worry."

They shared a protein bar, agreeing that they needed to conserve as much as they could once they got moving, and drank some water through the filtered bottle. They scooted out of the cave into the trees and wilderness surrounding them. They both moved in separate directions to use the bathroom, then came back to wrap up as warmly as possible and were soon ready to leave.

Natalie looked at the snow. It was uncomfortable, it was cold, but she wasn't trapped in it. She could get out of it whenever she wanted. She felt much stronger and more in control.

She would be fine as long as she didn't think too hard about the fact that she *couldn't* actually get out of the snow whenever she wanted. There was nowhere else to go.

Focus, Natalie. Mind over matter.

"Which direction are we heading?"

"East." Ren pointed the opposite way from where they'd come last night. "If I'm not mistaken that should take us into a lower altitude and should be the most direct route to civilization and/or cell phone coverage."

Natalie figured he had just as much to lose—more since he had a business and family—as she did, and since she had no idea which direction they should take, his plan sounded as good as any. Plus, if he had plans to hurt her, he certainly could've done it by now.

But he hadn't. The opposite, in fact. It didn't take much to remember the feel of his arms—his whole body—wrapped around her, keeping her safe, warm, protected.

She forced the thought from her mind. "Sounds good. Let's go."

They began walking.

"Just let me know if you need a break, okay?" He looked over his shoulder since he was leading. "Don't let things spiral. If we need to stop, we need to stop. That's not a problem."

She nodded, a little embarrassed that he had to say it. She knew her paranoia, and not just about snow, sometimes got the best of her. Knew her mind was a little broken after what Damien had done to her. All she could do was try to keep everything in check for right now. Just this one minute. She'd survived that way before. She could do it again.

Chapter Eight

Ren wasn't sure exactly what sort of conduct he'd been expecting from Natalie as they walked. Based on last night's behavior, more distress as they'd walked through the wilderness and snow.

It wasn't easy hiking. Even his muscles were complaining, not to mention a couple of his wounds from his special forces days that tended to act up in the cold. But he knew exactly where they were going and how long it would take to get to the hunter's cabin that would be the crux of this entire mission.

If he was like Natalie and didn't know how far they had to go—if they would be able to find shelter before the weather turned worse, and had some sort of snow phobia—he definitely wouldn't be acting the way she had since they'd started walking.

Focused.

She hadn't muttered a single complaint since they'd left this morning, even though they'd walked for miles. She'd only stopped to drink water and eat a nutrition bar. Every time he'd glanced at her, she was doggedly putting one foot in front of the other.

The weather had been getting steadily worse, and since he knew there was shelter at the end of this little excursion, he'd had her take out the sleeping bag and wrap it around herself. If she insisted one more time that he take a turn with it, he was going to start feeling bad about leading her in circles in the icy wilderness.

"I can't believe it," he finally said as he led them exactly where he'd planned at exactly the time he'd planned it. He stopped staring at the small structure in front of them. Natalie peeked out from behind him and gasped.

"Is that a *house*?"

She made it sound like a ten-bedroom mansion. He chuckled. "I think *house* might be a bit too generous."

She stepped around him, giving him a grin. "It's got walls and a roof. That's a house!"

She beelined to the door, but he caught up to her before she reached it. "Hang on a second, let me check it first."

He grabbed the door and pushed it open. Inside was exactly like it had been when he'd seen it last week. One large room with a small kitchen on one end and a full-size bed in the corner on the opposite side. An old-fashioned metal wood-burning stove sat in the middle of the room with a couch in front of it.

Natalie was already pushing at his back. "Is it safe? What's it like? Please tell me the roof isn't leaking."

He stepped all the way in so she could follow. He expected a bit of disdain for the small, almost barren space, especially given the size of her Santa Barbara beach house, but she surprised him again.

"Is this not the most amazing place you've ever seen?" Her grin was ear to ear.

He shook his head. "You must really be glad to get out of the snow to think this is the best place ever."

She laughed. "Okay, it's not the White House. But what about that stove, right? And it already feels warmer in here."

"That's because the wind is blocked. But yeah, let's see about getting the stove to work."

They checked the two other doors in the room. One led to a large shed, stacked with wood in the back of the cabin, the other to a detached outhouse. Within fifteen minutes, Ren had a fire blazing and the cabin was warm enough that they had to remove their jackets.

Natalie wandered into the kitchen, gasping as she found cans of soup and vegetables in the small pantry.

"What is this place? Obviously it gets used. Are we closer to civilization than we think?"

Ren shook his head. "Actually, probably the opposite. This is a hikers/hunters cabin. For use when people are going to be away on extended trips." He pulled out his phone and made a show of checking it. "Still no signal."

She didn't look nearly as upset as he'd expected her to at the news.

"Well, at least we have shelter and a little food." She began counting and organizing. "Enough for today at least. I'll start dinner, I'm starving."

They worked together in the kitchen, finding what they needed to open the can of vegetable soup and a pot to pour it in. Ren also brought in some snow to heat over the fire so they could have drinking water through her filtration bottle.

"Tomorrow I'll go out and set some traps. See if I can catch us some food. Or there must be a river nearby since there are fishing poles in the corner."

"Do you think a storm is still coming in?"

He nodded. "The heaviness in the air when it's this

cold? Definitely more snow. We might be trapped here for a few days."

He was hoping the thought of being trapped would push her toward wanting to make a call. But he was beginning to believe her when she said she didn't have anyone to call. Maybe she and Freihof had a no-contact pact in situations like this.

Tomorrow he would be checking in with Steve Drackett and needed to have a plan. The problem was, the more time he spent with Natalie, the less confident he was that she was conspiring with her ex.

But he couldn't say for sure. That was the problem.

They ate, not nearly enough to be full, but enough to push away actual hunger pains. Afterward they washed their meager dishes in the faucetless sink with the now-melted snow Ren had brought in. Then Natalie searched the entire cabin and laid out everything that could be eaten, as well as anything that could be used to help them in other ways: tools, knives, the fishing poles.

She hadn't stopped moving since they'd arrived, and that was after they'd already walked nearly ten miles today in the snow. As the sun went down, she'd just gotten more frantic in her activities.

"Hey, Peaches, you want to sit for a while? We've had a long day and you haven't slowed down since the moment we got here." He patted the couch cushion next to him.

She turned from rearranging the supplies—again—and gave him a sheepish grin. "Yeah, sorry, I like to have things in order. Know where stuff is." She looked from the door to the cabin's two windows. "Just in case."

"Just in case what?"

She walked over to the door. "Just in case there's no

time to sort through stuff if there's an emergency. Better to be prepared."

"Okay, I think we're suitably prepared. Why don't you take a load off?"

She looked over her shoulder at him. "There's no lock on this door."

"No, there's not supposed to be. This cabin is open for anyone who needs it. We have a number of similar ones throughout Montana. Just for people who maybe get stranded and, of course, people who plan to use it. So, no locks."

"No locks," she whispered. She walked to the windows, checked them also.

Ren stood. What exactly was happening here? "No locks on those, either."

"Right." She gave a little laugh that didn't hold any humor. "Because why would you put locks on a window when you didn't have one on the door?"

"Exactly."

Her back was stiff again, and although she wasn't jumping straight into the deep end of a panic attack like she had with the snow, she was definitely becoming more tense.

"Natalie."

She didn't respond, just kept looking at one window, then the other.

He walked over and put his hands gently on her shoulders. She didn't even jump like he half expected her to. "Natalie. You're tired. Come sit down, okay?"

"It's dark out," she whispered. "I always check the locks. And the sticky notes won't help if there aren't any locks on the doors or windows."

He had no idea what the sticky notes comment was

about. He pulled her over to the couch and sat down with her, her hands in his. "You're tired, Peaches."

"I shouldn't be tired. It's still pretty early."

"Are you kidding? We walked for hours, then you made dinner, cleaned up and did your whole inventory of any useful items. You're tired."

She rolled her eyes, giving him the tiniest smile. "I work longer than this on any given day. I'm sure you do, too, on the farm."

The work she did in Santa Barbara couldn't be as hard as what her body had been through today. But it was a good time to press for details. "I do work hard on the farm when I'm there. What do you do?"

She glanced away. "I'm between jobs at the moment."

"I'll bet you were in business. At an office? I can totally see you as an executive."

"Ha. I wish. No such luck."

He smiled. "A secretary, then? No shame in that."

She tried to slide her hands back from his, but he wouldn't let her. He needed to get her to open up to him. He rubbed his fingers along her palms, trying to calm her, since she kept glancing back to the door and windows.

The texture of her hands didn't register at first. The hardened bumps where her fingers met her palms. When he realized what they were, he stopped his rubbing and turned her hands over.

Her hands had noticeable calluses. Ren recognized them for what they were because he had similar ones on his own palms. They'd been even worse when he'd lived on the farm.

They came from holding a wooden handle of something in your hands all the time. In his case it had been shovels or brooms, or even the horses' bridles. Days and years of hard work.

He wasn't ashamed of his calluses, and would never think poorly of a woman who had them, either—the opposite, in fact.

But for the life of him he couldn't figure out why Natalie Freihof's hands would have them. He'd watched her for the last week go to office buildings and a bar. Business meetings and parties.

Nothing that should have her hands in this shape.

She looked down at her hand resting in his. "Not so pretty, huh?" Her eyes immediately flew back to the door.

He didn't mention her hands again. He wasn't going to get any info out of her when all she seemed to be able to focus on was the fact that the door wouldn't lock.

It didn't make any more sense than her snow phobia did last night. But he could see she was on the path toward another breakdown.

"Natalie, look at me."

He could tell it cost her effort to look away from the door and meet his eyes, but she did.

"Can I tell you something I've realized about you in the short time I've known you?"

She nodded.

"You're strong. When you thought I might need help at the train, you were coming to do it, even though you were hurt. Today when we had to walk, you did it without complaint. Once we got here, you got to work doing what needed to be done."

"But now I'm freaking out," she whispered. "Just like I did last night. You have to think I'm crazy."

He pulled her closer. "No, I don't. But I do think a

body only has so much energy and it can only be utilized so many ways. You're completely exhausted right now, and because of that, your fears about the locks on the doors and windows are overwhelming you. If you weren't so exhausted you'd be able to handle it better, right?"

"Not always, but usually."

"How would you do that?"

She looked away. "I have a method of making sure I've locked the doors and windows. I use sticky notes. It's stupid."

"There's nothing to be ashamed about. You had a problem and you figured out how to work it."

She shrugged. "Doesn't help me much now."

"How about if we pull one of the kitchen chairs over and wedge it under the door handle? It doesn't exactly lock it, but it will be damn loud if someone tries to open it."

Her face was already looking more relaxed, so Ren continued. "We can't lock the windows, but we can close the shutters and put a broom handle across the bars. Again, it's not foolproof but it's definitely more fortified."

The relief that flooded her features was so pronounced it was difficult to look at.

After they'd made the cabin as safe as they could—he noticed she double-checked more than once—they washed and brushed their teeth as best they could and got into bed. Ren tried to ignore the fact that he wished it was colder in the cabin so that they'd be forced to get closer for heat. The bed wasn't that big, but it was bigger than their sleeping arrangements last night.

As he heard Natalie's breathing even out as exhaustion pulled her under, Ren lay for a long time trying to process what he had learned tonight about the woman lying next to him. Unfortunately he had more questions than answers. Questions that would affect every decision Ren made for the rest of this mission.

Why did she have calluses on her hands that suggested she'd been doing hard manual labor every day for years? Why was she fanatic about locking up and safety?

Because she knew that Freihof had a number of enemies who wouldn't hesitate to attack her to get to him?

Or because she was afraid of Freihof himself?

Chapter Nine

Ren woke up to a sleeping Natalie sprawled all over him again. She'd been that way most of the night. It hadn't taken long after she'd finally fallen into an exhausted slumber, secure in the knowledge that the windows and doors were as locked as they could be, before she'd snuggled into him.

He should've pushed her away, rolled over, hell, gone and slept on the couch. Curling her lithe body next to his while they both slept didn't do anything to advance the mission—she was asleep, so it wasn't affecting her. And if their closeness didn't advance the mission, then it shouldn't have interested Ren at all.

But damned if he'd been able to let her go all night.

He eased away from her now as dawn approached. He needed to go out, make the call to Omega, finalize plans.

Plans that were even murkier than they'd been when they'd started two days ago. Everything he learned about Natalie just made him more confused. He'd been so sure she was working with Freihof. But the calluses on her hands didn't lie.

The fear on her features last night, the panic at the

thought of not being able to lock the doors and windows, didn't lie, either.

But none of that gave Ren actionable intel. So he wasn't sure how to play this with her.

Even worse, he wasn't sure he wanted to play this at all. If time wasn't such a factor—with those damned biological warfare canisters—Ren would probably remove himself from the picture entirely. Obviously he was losing his objectivity when it came to her.

He looked down at her sleeping form, how she'd curled protectively into herself, even in sleep. As if her mind knew some sort of attack might be coming.

But from who?

Ren found a pen and paper and wrote that he'd be back soon and laid it on the bed where she would see it. He didn't want her waking up and thinking someone had gotten in the cabin because the door was no longer barred. She might wake up and not be thinking clearly at first.

He wiped a hand across his face as he realized that he wasn't just concerned—*again*—about the damage that might do to the mission. He was concerned about the damage it might do to her psyche.

He had to get his damned head in the game.

Grabbing the knife and fishing poles, he moved quietly out the door and made his way deeper into the forest away from the cabin. He came up to the river a few minutes later and cast a pole with a fly lure—might as well try to catch some protein to go with the canned food—then used a specially made cell signal booster to call Steve Drackett.

"Ren. Good to hear from you. How's camping?"

"We made it to the cave and then the cabin on schedule. Rest of the team make it safely from the crash site?"

"Yep. No problem, although now Philip Carnell is convinced he wants to work undercover full-time."

Ren chuckled. "That would at least get him out of your hair." Philip was known for his surliness and inability to play well with others. "Let him terrorize some criminals instead of your agents."

"Definitely something to consider. How's it going with Natalie? She give you anything useful yet?"

"Honestly, no, nothing. She hasn't panicked about not being able to make contact and wasn't interested in using my phone to try to call anyone."

Steve gave some sort of disgruntled sigh. "So what's your plan? Threats? Friendship? Seduction? Before you choose, there's been some developments you need to know about."

"What?"

"For one, Sean and Theresa Baxter."

"Why do those names sound familiar?" He knew he should be able to place them.

"They were the names on the deed of the Santa Barbara house where Natalie was staying. We were looking into them as a possible front."

"What did you find?" Ren asked.

"They definitely weren't a front. Were actually real-life people who legitimately purchased the house in 2003."

Ren didn't like how Steve was phrasing this. *"Were?"*

"They were both found murdered at a resort bungalow in Puerto Vallarta, Mexico, last night. Brutally. Tortured."

Ren's curse was nothing short of foul. Just when he

thought he was closer to getting a handle on things. "What the hell does that mean, Steve? Tying up loose ends? An enemy of Freihof's trying to get information?"

Could Natalie have ordered their deaths before she left to make sure they wouldn't be able to tell anyone anything about her? Not just killed, but tortured?

"We've been running info on the Baxters all night and haven't found anything to suggest they were linked to Freihof or Natalie in any way. Nothing."

"Which we both know doesn't necessarily mean anything. Not with a criminal of Freihof's caliber."

"True," Steve replied before they both dropped into silence. "So what's your plan?" Steve repeated.

"Until what you just told me, I was beginning to think that Natalie might be completely innocent in all this. A victim, like Brandon and Andrea said."

"But we can't deny that no one knew she was running except us and her. No one would know to tie up loose ends like the Baxters."

"Exactly. Plus, Lillian said Natalie mentioned Atlanta when she was trying to buy a bus ticket. That can't be a coincidence that it's Freihof's last known whereabouts." Ren ran a hand over his face. "Did you discover anything new about those office buildings she went to every day? That bar?"

"As far as we can tell, all the companies in both buildings are clean. Maybe some minor tax stuff, but nothing that would put them on any radars. If Natalie was using one as a front, she was damn good at it. And the bar has been family-owned for generations. I have no idea what she was doing there."

Ren thought of the calluses on her hands again. He

didn't know, either. And he was afraid the truth was going to make this mission even less simple.

"What does your gut say about her, Ren?" Steve finally asked when he didn't say anything. "You and I have been in the spy game for a long time. I would take your gut instinct over some incomplete intel any day."

What did his gut say? His gut said he was already too compromised to make an impartial judgment when it came to Natalie. That every time he looked into those endless blue eyes, it seemed impossible that she could be mixed up with Freihof. That she couldn't be a killer or be collaborating with someone who was.

But his gut also told him that those baby-blues, that tragic smile, even the panic, could all be part of a very specific ploy to fool him. That she could've been trained by Freihof for years on how to best manipulate a law enforcement agent. God knew there was no better teacher than Freihof when it came to exploitation.

"My gut says I need more time," he finally told Steve. "I need to be able to dig deeper into her and pick her apart."

"We don't have a lot of time. There's been another development."

Not what Ren wanted to hear. "What?"

"Because of the canisters, Homeland Security is breathing down my neck. They want to assume control of the op and take Natalie into custody."

"You know if they do that she'll be treated like a hostile subject and terrorist enemy of the United States." It would be illegal to torture her, but that didn't mean they couldn't make her incarcerated time extremely uncomfortable. "We don't have enough intel yet to even suggest she's guilty or knows anything about Freihof."

"That's what I told them and convinced them that you getting her cooperation voluntarily would be not only more efficient, but humane. Especially if she really is innocent in all this."

"How long can you hold them off?"

"Five days at the max, Ren. And that's with calling in every favor I have. If you don't walk into Riverton in five days, they're coming in to take her."

"And if I come out with no answers but Natalie's agreement to cooperate with the media blitz plan?"

"They don't like it," Steve said. "But they've agreed. As long as we're taking measurable steps forward."

A fish bit at one of the fishing lines and Ren leaned down to reel it in, but it had gotten away. Fitting. "Do you have everything set on your end for when we come out five days from now?"

"Yes. We'll have every major news outlet waiting in Riverton to cover the huge story of two lost hikers finding their way out of the wilderness. That tiny Colorado town will be packed with media, I promise. We'll spin the romance angle. It'll work."

Ren recast the line back out into the stream. "It's got to be big. Big enough for Freihof to hear about it wherever he is. If she doesn't know where he is, this will get him to come to us."

"Barring some international incident the news has to cover, we'll make sure this is top priority. That it goes viral. But, Ren, it won't work if she comes out all angry and refuses to get in front of the camera."

"She won't. I'll get her cooperation." He said it with a great deal more assurance than he felt.

"Like, you know, Brandon and Andrea both think she's innocent. They think that if you're honest with her, tell her about the canisters and what Freihof could do with them, that she'll help you."

Ren wanted to believe it. But he also knew that if he believed it and he was wrong, a lot of innocent people would die. Like it or not, Natalie was their best chance to catch Freihof, either by her telling them how he could be located or by using her as bait to draw him out.

"You've got five days to figure out the best way to use her," Steve continued.

Ren couldn't help his wince at the word *use*, even though he knew Steve was right. The softness of the woman he'd held in his arms the last two nights was secondary to what she could provide as an asset. Ren had to steel himself against any sort of tenderness toward her.

That was what he was known for, right? Getting the job done. Getting what he needed by any means necessary. Feelings had nothing to do with stopping a killer.

Ren could feel the darkness, the shadows he'd lived and fought in for so long, wrap around him a little more tightly. Another little piece of his soul gone.

"Five days," he said to Steve. "I'll have what we need. Just be ready."

The sound of cracking branches in the distance had him turning and slipping the phone into his jacket pocket. A few moments later Natalie came into view.

"Hi." She rushed in, then stopped, breathing a little hard. She was back in her jeans and sweater, the sleeping bag wrapped around her again. She looked around, then took a few steps closer. "I just wanted to make sure everything was okay. And then it sounded like you were talking to someone and I got excited."

Damn it. "I was talking to someone." He smiled, then

jerked his head toward the river. "This damn fish. Trying to coerce him onto my hook."

Ren swallowed a curse as her eyes narrowed like she didn't quite believe him. He let go of the rod and closed the distance between them until they were only a couple of feet from each other.

"I thought you'd sleep longer and not witness the lunacy that runs in my family in the form of talking to fish."

"I'm normally an early riser." She looked at the river, then back at him. "You were really talking to the fish?"

How much had she heard? "Did you hear what I was saying?"

"No."

He stepped closer. He had to get her mind off this, and there was only one way he knew how. "I was telling the fish I needed to catch him so I could take him back to the beautiful woman I found draped over my body again this morning."

"I was?" That flush. Damn, it was so adorable.

He reached out and grabbed the edges of the sleeping bag, pulling her closer. "You were. And just like yesterday I didn't mind it at all."

"I'm sorry. I don't know why I keep doing that… I just— I mean…"

He brought his lips down to hers, stopping her words.

The kiss was supposed to be a distraction. A way to stop her thinking about having heard him talking. Light. Fun. Hint of sweet flirtation and possible promise of more.

But the moment their lips touched every agenda he had vanished. What he meant to be sweet and soft immediately turned heated. Scorched air filled his lungs as she gave a little gasp at the attraction that crackled and danced around them.

He took complete possession of her mouth. There was no other word for it. His fingers slipped from the grip he had on the sleeping bag to slide around her back, wrapping low around her hips. The fingers of his other hand wound into the hair at the base of her neck, anchoring her in place so he could kiss her more deeply.

And he did. Over and over. Taking her mouth with a need he hadn't even known could exist, especially not in a situation like this. He moved her back against a large tree, pulling her closer as her arms entwined around his neck.

It was her soft sigh of something close to wonder that brought him back to reality.

What the hell was he doing? That kiss had left the distracting-her-from-almost-catching-him category within the first three seconds and had gone straight to...

Hell if he knew.

He stepped back, giving him some much needed distance, and found her clear blue eyes blinking up at him as if she couldn't quite figure out what was going on.

Know the feeling, Peaches.

He gave her a smile and moved away, trying—way too late—to make this more casual. And fighting the fear that this was going to leave them both bloody in the end.

Chapter Ten

Ren was showing her how to clean a fish.

Definitely not very romantic—although more romantic than teaching her how to skin the rabbit they'd caught a few hours ago—and yet, Natalie couldn't deny the closeness between them. An easiness that almost bordered on fun, which was crazy since they were lost in the middle of the wilderness.

But for her, not crazy at all. Not since she woke up this morning and realized she had nothing to fear out here.

Okay, maybe wild animals and blizzards. She could handle those. But the fear that she would turn around and possibly find Damien standing there was gone. For the first time she was one hundred percent certain he had no idea where she was.

Hell, *she* had no idea where she was. How could Damien possibly find her?

He couldn't.

That was the truth she'd come to grips with this morning. And that left Natalie with a feeling of freedom she hadn't known for as long as she could remember. A sense that anything was possible, even if she did have to learn to catch and cook her own meat in order to supplement what they had inside the cabin.

And then there was Ren.

If she had to be trapped in the wilderness, she couldn't have picked a better person to be trapped with. He knew how to hunt, fish, clean and prepare food.

And kiss.

That kiss. It hadn't been far from her mind since this morning.

She'd *never* been kissed like that. Not even before Damien had become a vicious monster. Never been kissed like someone wanted her more than he wanted his next breath. Like he might forget they were in the middle of the frozen wilderness and take her right there against the tree.

And Natalie was pretty sure she wouldn't have stopped him. Especially considering she hadn't even been able to remember her own name at that moment, had only been able to *feel*.

He hadn't kissed her again. Hadn't really touched her, except as needed when they were hunting and fishing. She would almost think she'd imagined the whole thing if it wasn't for the slight tenderness of her lips because of the onslaught from his.

"You ready to chop the head off?"

His words yanked her back. She made a face.

He smiled, rolling those green eyes. "You did pretty well earlier. I would think a fish would be easier."

"I was hungrier earlier." And the meat had been delicious. But she took the hatchet from him and quickly lopped off the head of the fish like he'd shown her and they began to clean it together.

Although she didn't particularly like doing *this*, providing for herself gave her a sense of accomplishment. Purpose. A couple of hours later they had a fish broth with canned potatoes. And damned if it wasn't one of the best meals she'd ever eaten. Because she'd been responsible for it herself.

After a lifetime of never being good enough at anything, some fish broth made by her own hands felt pretty fantastically rewarding.

"Did you do a lot of hunting and fishing on your farm?" she asked as they washed the dishes.

He looked at her for a long moment, as if he needed to decide something. He closed his eyes, tensing, and she hated that she had broken the easiness that had been between them all day by sticking her nose where it didn't belong.

"I'm sorry," she began. "I—"

"Actually, I learned most of my hunting tricks in the military. It was part of the wilderness and survival training I did during my time in the special forces."

She folded the towel in her hand slowly and hung it on the rack. "Oh, wow. I didn't know you'd been in the... I'm not sure which branch is special forces."

"In this case, army," he said. "I love the farm. Love my family. But I wanted to get out. See the world. See what else I was capable of."

That made sense. He had a quiet, understated strength and confidence about him that would've been honed in the military, much more than it ever would've been on a farm.

"Did you like it? Why did you get out?"

"I was good at it. But I liked being my own boss, not having to follow orders blindly. So I got out after six years."

She smiled as he gestured toward the living room, and they took a seat on the couch. "Did you get to see the world like you wanted?"

"I did. All over the place. The only continent I didn't make it to was Antarctica. I have this huge collection of postcards from all these different places sitting in a box at home."

"You didn't mail them to anyone?"

He smiled and it caused a bloom of warmth in her chest. Near her heart. "Some to my mom, but no, mostly I just collected them. Never really had someone I cared about enough to want to share my life with. How about you, ever married?"

The warmth immediately froze. It wasn't an unreasonable question. Funny, last week she wouldn't have even known how to answer without knowing if she was lying. Brandon and Andrea had at least given her that truth. "Um, yeah. Once. A while ago. It ended."

"I'm sorry."

She wasn't. "Some things die. Aren't meant to survive. Better just to let it stay buried."

How badly she wished she could let her marriage be buried. To put it truly behind her with no hold on her anymore.

Thankfully, Ren changed the subject. "So, you said you're between jobs. Relocating. To Saint Louis?"

"No." God, how much should she tell him? She didn't want to lie to Ren since he'd been so friendly, but if those Omega Sector people came to question him, she didn't want him to have any information. She would give him what she could without any specifics. "Honestly, I'm not sure. It was just time for a change. I'll get a job when I get to wherever I'm going."

"And what kind of job will that be?"

The same as before, she guessed. Whatever she could get being paid under the table. Dishwashing, cleaning, maybe lawn work. She shrugged. "Whatever I can get. I'm not really picky."

He smiled again, stretching his arm along the back of the couch, and her heart tripped over its own beat. "Not trying to become a millionaire?"

"No, money's not important to me."

"You sound pretty sure about that."

That was one of the few things she could say with absolute certainty. "Oh, I am. Some of the years when I was surrounded by the most money—a huge house, fancy cars and meals—were the most miserable I'd ever been in my whole life."

His fingers tucked a strand of her hair behind her ear. "I'm sorry to hear that."

"I always wanted to travel places, like you did. But… my ex-husband had other interests."

Ren shifted closer. "What sort of interests?"

She shrugged. To this day she still didn't know much about Damien or what he did business-wise. She knew he'd stolen money, and that was how he'd become rich, but by the time she'd figured that out she'd been too deep in his clutches for it to make a difference.

"His work."

"Was that bad? What did he do?"

She shifted in her seat. "I know this sounds so stupid, but I really don't know every pie he had his fingers in. I never did. I married him really young. I lost both my parents when I was eighteen and didn't have any other family. I was sort of lost. He swept into the art studio where I was working, made me feel like the most talented and important person in the world, then married me six weeks later."

And put her in a cast six months after that.

"He never traveled with you anywhere? Even with all that money?"

Not after he decided she flirted with everyone she came in contact with and that she needed to be kept apart from everyone else. Once he decided he would make her perfect.

She'd never been perfect enough. "No. He had his own priorities."

"Sounds like he wasn't any good for you and you should be glad the marriage is over."

Oh, she was. She just wasn't sure Damien would feel the same way if he knew she was alive.

"What?" Ren asked. "What was that look?"

She wanted to trust him with the whole story, tell him how she'd faked her death and was afraid Damien would find her and hurt her again. She'd carried this for so long alone. The fear, the exhaustion, the isolation.

But it wasn't Ren's burden to carry.

So she just smiled. "No look. Things just don't turn out like you thought they would, sometimes."

His green eyes studied hers. "I know."

She leaned her head back against the couch, against his hand still resting there.

"You ready to learn how to use the flint and make some fire with no matches?" he finally asked. It was one of the things he promised to show her. "The fire is down enough that I'll put it out and you can rebuild it. It'll be part of your SERE training."

She laughed, sitting up with him. "My what?"

"SERE. Survival, Evasion, Resistance and Escape. It's a military acronym for training they give us."

"I'm really only getting the S, so I don't know if the army would approve."

He chuckled. "Probably true. Let's hope you never need the other, anyway, seeing as it was a carry-over from soldiers who escaped and evaded Nazis in World War II."

"Yeah, I'm hoping not to be evading Nazis any time soon."

He showed her how to build kindling starting with the smallest and finest twigs she could find. When she had what looked like a tiny teepee in the stove belly, he stepped back.

"Okay, strike the steel against the flint like I showed you, close to the tinder, and you'll be all set."

He stood up behind her. Natalie stared down at the round piece of steel—it looked like it belonged on the bridle of a horse—in one hand and the flint, which looked like a plain rock you might find in any backyard, in the other.

She tried to get it to work, but couldn't. How hard could it be? Hitting one hard object against the other, getting a little spark and starting a fire? It certainly hadn't looked difficult when Ren had shown her.

Tension began strumming through her as she continued to try. Her aggravation was doubled by knowing Ren was watching this whole time, probably wondering why she was so inept. Tears stung her eyes at her inability to get such a simple task completed. He'd shown her more than once, given her understandable instructions, and she couldn't get it.

After another few minutes, sweat now dripping

across her brow, she saw one of his shoes come into her line of vision as he moved closer. She forced her arms to hit the flint harder, even though she was tired now and holding herself in this position was hurting her back.

How long before he lost his patience and started yelling? Or just pushed her out of the way and did it himself?

"Natalie."

She waited for the belittlement.

"Take a breath, okay, Peaches?"

She hunched her shoulders. "I can't do it. I'm sorry."

A moment later he was crouched behind her. "No need to be sorry. It can be tricky to use flint the first time." His arms came around her, his hand covering hers on the steel and stone. "Try hitting it at a slightly steeper angle."

He showed her again so she could get the feel for the motion. Then he let go, putting his hands on the stove, keeping her fenced between his arms. After a few more times she struck it again, and this time it worked.

Ren's hands trailed up her arms to her shoulders as he moved away from her. "See? Just needed to get a feel for it. Nobody gets everything perfect all the time."

Natalie looked away. When she thought about all the times she'd been *corrected* by Damien for not doing something right...which had usually involved his fists or worse. He'd demanded that she be perfect. Always perfect. In her life. In her art.

She never was.

"Whoa, hey, what's going on here?" He reached over and cupped her cheeks, wiping tears with his thumbs. "There's no crying in SERE training."

She tried to smile. "I couldn't get it. It wasn't right."

"Are you kidding? You've now built a fire that's so big we're going to have to crack a window."

"But..."

"Natalie, you did it. That's what matters. And hell, even if you hadn't been able to do it, you could've tried again tomorrow."

There had never been *try again tomorrows* with Damien. Only pain.

The urge to run now was strong. She needed to get away even from Ren, who'd never been anything but kind. Knowledge that she didn't have anywhere to go had panic lacing her veins.

"I—I need to go to the bathroom."

She flung herself by him and through the door that led to the attached outhouse. She had to pull herself together.

Ren was right. Perfection was not required here. Who cared if she couldn't get the fire started? Ren certainly hadn't. And more importantly, she *had* gotten it started.

She'd had such a peace this morning at the knowledge that Damien couldn't find her here. It wouldn't last forever; they'd have to leave soon—if not tomorrow, then in a few days, tops. She'd probably never have another place where she'd feel so secure again.

She wouldn't let the ghost of Damien past ruin her present.

Since she was there she used the bathroom, then walked back into the cabin. She expected to find Ren with eyes full of questions she wasn't sure she was going to know how to answer.

Instead, at first she didn't see him at all. Then he straightened himself from where he'd obviously been putting something on the ground near the wall at the other end of the room, by the front door.

He held his hands out in front of him in a gesture of peace. "Look, I wasn't snooping, but this morning I was looking through your backpack, trying to see if there was anything in there that could be useful, that you might have missed in the inventory you did yesterday."

She nodded. There wasn't anything she was hiding in the bag. "I don't really have anything."

"You have these." He motioned for her to come forward. After a few steps she could see what he'd laid out on the floor.

Her paints.

"I saw them this morning, but I didn't know if they were yours. Then a few minutes ago you mentioned working at an art studio so then I thought…"

She couldn't stop staring at them.

"Are they not yours?" he finally asked.

"No, they are. It's just—it's just… It's been a long time since I've used them. I've been carrying them around, but never used them."

"How about now?"

Her eyes flew to his face. "Now? Where? I don't have any canvas."

"I thought maybe a section of that door could be your canvas. You could give the owners of this cabin a nice surprise. And if they don't like it, it'll take them ten minutes to sand it down."

"But…"

He smiled, handing her a brush. "It doesn't have to be perfect."

She took the brush. It was time to take back part of what had been stolen from her.

Chapter Eleven

He awoke to the sound of Natalie's adorable snores against his neck.

This was the third day in a row he'd woken up to the feel of her in his arms. This morning she had a leg thrown over his hips and her arm wrapped around his stomach as she'd plastered herself to his side. Unlike the other two nights, she'd been completely relaxed all night. And although she hadn't started out in his arms, she'd certainly ended up there quickly. Not that Ren was complaining.

Although he was not complaining for the wrong reasons.

He should be happy that she was finally relaxed enough to roll into his arms because it meant she was getting closer to trusting him. Not because she felt damn near perfect in his arms.

He'd watched her paint for hours last night until she'd been too tired to hold her arms up against the door that had become her small masterpiece.

Had a hundred-dollar set of paints been the key to cracking Natalie from the beginning?

After watching her for a few hours, Ren was sure he could've saved a whole lot of time and money by just showing up at her door in Santa Barbara with an easel and encouraged her to do her best.

He wasn't sure why no information about Natalie as an artist had been in her Omega file. But the more she worked on the painting, the more evident her talent became. Like professionally good.

The sheer joy on her features as she worked—the utter serenity—was so intense it had been impossible for Ren to look away. Like she'd been waiting an unimaginable amount of time to do this, and then couldn't stop if she wanted to. And she very definitely hadn't wanted to.

Last night, painting by firelight, Natalie was almost the polar opposite of the woman who'd been frantically searching for a way to lock windows and doors with no locks the night before. She was serene, calm and utterly beautiful.

Actually, most of yesterday had been different. Except for the incident starting the fire, she'd been relaxed and helpful. She'd surprised him by wanting to learn how to hunt and how to prepare the animals to eat. Then surprised him even more at being so deft at it.

The more she did, the more he wanted to show her. The more they talked, the more truths he told. When he'd told her about his time in the special forces he knew he was in dangerous territory. But more and more he was finding it impossible to believe that she could be in with Freihof.

And if she wasn't, if there was nothing she could tell him about Freihof's location, then Ren knew he needed to end this. Tell her who he was, what was happening, and ask for her help. Lay all the cards out, talk her into helping, pack them up and leave.

He looked over at her painting taking up about one quarter of the cabin door. She'd be done by the end of today at the rate she was going. He'd let her finish. Partially because doing so would hopefully make her more agreeable to helping them hunt her ex-husband. But mostly because he couldn't stand to cut short the use of those paints that had brought such life to her so-often-haunted eyes.

He'd try to get more information from her today as she painted and was more relaxed. Maybe she knew something she wasn't aware of. Details that weren't important to her, but could be used for finding and stopping Freihof.

But one thing Ren knew for sure was that he needed to distance himself from her. Because, yeah, she was going to be mad when she found out he'd been deceiving her all this time. If he fostered any more closeness, it would just make the situation that much more difficult.

Natalie shifted slightly from where she was draped over him. He closed his eyes as her body squeezed more tightly up against him.

He needed distance just as much for his own sake as hers. Especially since he was the one who was undercover; and yet he was finding it almost impossible to lie to her.

For someone who had made a career out of lying to others, giving them whatever false information and security they needed in order to get what he wanted, not being able to lie to this woman was downright disconcerting.

Or maybe it wasn't that he *couldn't* lie to her, it was that he didn't want to. Just about everything he'd told her except for his last name—and even then, Thompson was his mother's maiden name—had been true. Telling her about his time in the special forces? Completely unnecessary. And yet…he hadn't regretted telling her.

He wanted her to know him. And when he asked questions, yes, he was always listening for potential info about Freihof, but he was also getting to know her.

And was liking it.

Which was possibly the most dangerous thing he could do. Especially given that nuclear kiss yesterday morning.

Distance. It was the best tactical move he could make right now. He eased himself out from under her—ignoring his body's demands that he stay exactly where he was—and got out of the bed.

He needed distance.

NATALIE COULD HONESTLY say she'd never seen a door be used as an actual canvas before. Her face broke out into a grin as she leaned back in to complete the section she was working on. Who cared if it was untraditional, if the paint soaked in more than it would on canvas? It still worked.

And she was painting. It had been years since she'd held a brush. Since she'd felt the calm flow through her body that she only got when painting.

She was painting the view of the Pacific from the beach house. It was an unusual choice for a cabin in a landlocked state, particularly in the middle of winter, but she liked to think the owners would come and be surprised and like it.

Although they couldn't possibly like looking at it as much as she'd liked painting it. She'd started again as soon as she'd woken up this morning, after eating the breakfast Ren had already graciously fixed, and had been at it most of the day. She'd only stopped when her arms or back—unused to this type of abuse since it had been so long since she'd painted—had begun to protest too loudly.

She painted in another section of blue that morphed into teal. The colors blended beautifully in front of her, the image from her mind taking formation on the wood. This was what she was meant to do. Had always been what she'd been meant to do.

She couldn't believe she'd allowed this to be stolen from her for so many years. During her marriage—when none of her paintings had ever been perfect enough for Damien—but then also after. She'd been so busy making sure she was ready to run, able to hide, that she'd forgotten to live.

"Is that an ocean view?" Ren asked now that the picture was really starting to take shape, the lines of blues and greens clearly the ocean.

"Yep."

He'd been in and out of the cabin all day. They had eaten dinner, which he had prepared—more small game with mixed canned vegetables this time—and she tried to do the cleanup but he'd insisted she spend her time painting. She'd been happy to agree. Now she was back to painting by firelight, like she had last night. Normally that might be frustrating but she didn't care.

"You drawing that from your imagination or from a place you've been?"

She smiled at him over her shoulder. "Believe it or not, this was the view from my back door in Santa Barbara. The Pacific."

"Really? Wow. I can't believe you even pretended to

have interest in my family's farm if you had that view to wake up to every day."

She turned back to the painting, laughing. "Well, it wasn't actually my house. I wish I had that sort of money. I'd just been house-sitting for a couple of weeks before I left."

"House-sitting?"

She added another patch of blue that would blend into the gold of the shoreline. "Yeah. Honestly, I don't even know the people who live there. It just fell into my lap. A lady I worked with was supposed to do it but then had to go out of town on an emergency. Next thing I knew I had a close-up view of the Pacific."

Not that she'd taken advantage of it. And she hoped Olivia didn't get in trouble with the owner since Natalie had left so abruptly.

"Really? You were house-sitting?"

Ren's voice sounded strange. Half-strangled. She turned to look at him. "Yeah. Do they not have a lot of house-sitting in Montana?"

"Not really." He shook his head, looking a little strange. "I guess you were lucky your friend thought of you for the house. What did you guys do together at your job?"

She turned back to the painting. He was fishing for info, as he had been all day. Questions about her childhood, her past, her friends and plans. That should make her nervous, but instead it spread a feeling of warmth through her.

Ren wanted to know more about her.

This sexy, intelligent, insightful man wanted to know more about *her*.

She knew that didn't mean anything, that this…attraction between them couldn't lead to anything permanent, or any sort of serious relationship.

But he wanted to know stuff about her. What harm could there be in telling him about herself? So she had. Not everything, of course, but some. It wouldn't hurt her to tell him about a job she was never going back to.

"Olivia and I worked together at a bar. She waited tables. I did other stuff. Washed dishes, bussed tables, cleaning."

"Living in California on a dishwasher's salary couldn't be easy, even with house-sitting."

She shook her head without looking away from the door. "You're not kidding. I actually worked two other jobs. Nothing very glamorous, just cleaning office buildings in the mornings. Between the three jobs, I was able to make ends meet." She laughed a little. "Barely."

"Why stay in California at all? It's so expensive there, especially in Santa Barbara."

She shrugged. "Honestly, I was avoiding someone. My ex." There. She'd said it. It hadn't been so hard. "He once said he never wanted to step foot in California ever again. I was sort of hoping that was true."

"How long has it been since you've seen him?"

"Six years."

"He never tried to get in touch with you in all that time?"

No, because he thought she was dead. That was too complicated to even begin telling. "I kept a pretty low profile."

"Sounds like you wanted to stay away from him pretty badly. You had to take some pretty drastic measures."

Oh, God, how had he known that? Had she slipped

and said something she shouldn't? She turned slowly. "What do you mean?"

"Even for a farmer who knows what it's like to work seven days a week, working three jobs just to avoid someone is pretty drastic."

If Ren thought that was pretty drastic, telling him how she pretended to be dead would definitely seem like overkill, pardon the pun.

"He was worth avoiding."

She didn't want to talk about Damien. Didn't want to think about him. Out here in this cabin in the middle of nowhere, in this dream where she was doing what she loved to do, with a sexy man watching her and talking to her, Damien had no part.

Ren was already in bed—she'd been so focused she hadn't even realized it—by the time her arms refused to let her do any more work. She was at a good stopping place. Tomorrow she'd finish it.

Then it would be time to get back to the real world. Or at least out of this dream house.

She put away her paints and cleaned her brushes as best she could before turning to her own personal hygiene. She slipped out of her jeans and sweater and into the pajama pants and tank she'd been sleeping in, wishing it was something sexier.

Because she'd already decided that if her time was running out here in the dream cabin, then she wasn't going to waste the time she had left with Ren.

She was going to seduce him, right now.

Chapter Twelve

Of course, wanting to seduce and actually knowing how to seduce were two very different things.

Natalie crawled onto her side of the bed and pulled the covers over herself, staring up at the ceiling without touching him. How come her sleeping body never seemed to have any problem plastering itself all over him, but awake she couldn't even force herself to touch him at all?

Then Ren moved in his sleep, rolled toward her, the shift in the mattress causing her to slide toward him.

Then she just let herself fall the rest of the way into him.

She trailed her fingers across his naked chest, since he just slept in a pair of sweatpants they'd found. She loved touching him, his muscles so defined, yet had never once been used in any sort of violent way against her. The opposite, in fact. Only used to help make her feel secure, safe. Her fingers trailed slightly lower, over his abs. They tensed just the slightest bit under her touch.

"You're awake," she whispered.

"From the second those fingers touched me."

She snatched her hand back. "I'm sorry. You were trying to sleep. I don't know what I'm doing. I—"

She stopped abruptly as he reached out with his own hand and brought hers back down to his chest. "I wasn't complaining about your hand being there."

He slipped his other arm under his head, giving her room to move in a little closer to him. In the soft light of the dying fire he looked so relaxed, half smiling at her with drowsy eyes.

She was never going to get another opportunity like this.

She didn't let herself think about it too much, she just reached in and kissed him. She was tentative, unsure how to show him how she wanted more.

She needn't have worried.

At just the slightest bit of persuasion from her, Ren's mouth was hot and open against hers, his tongue sliding inside, coaxing *her* for more. It was different than the kiss outside in the snow. Slower, less frantic, more exploratory. But no less passionate.

His tongue skimmed across her bottom lip slowly before nibbling on it, like he had all the time in the world to taste her and no plans to ever move from this bed.

Natalie couldn't help it—she sighed into his mouth, wanting him closer.

Then the kiss changed. Every part of her hummed with excitement as he pulled her hard against him, his hand curving around her nape to hold her there. He moaned against her skin as his lips worked their way from her ear down her jaw to her neck.

He grabbed the hem of her shirt like he was going to pull it over her head—something she desperately wanted—but then paused.

They were both breathing hard as he leaned his forehead against hers.

"Natalie...we should stop."

"Oh. This isn't what you want?" She'd been such an idiot. Just because she'd been attracted to him and wanted to take advantage of this time for intimacy didn't mean he did. Maybe he'd just kissed her so she wouldn't feel bad. She shot back from him. "I'm so sorry. I—"

"Peaches." His voice was guttural as he grabbed her and pulled her back against him so her fingers were once again touching his chest. "Believe me, I want this. But there's stuff about me you don't know. Important stuff."

He had things he hadn't told her. Logically she already knew that. But they couldn't possibly be as big as the ones she hadn't told him. Her fingers curled into his muscles.

"Is there someone waiting for you at home who will be upset if we do this?"

He gave a shake of his head against the pillow. "No. Nothing like that."

Really, that was all Natalie needed to know. She leaned back in to kiss him, but he stopped her again, holding her by the upper arms while his thumbs drew gentle circles on her shoulders.

"Natalie, you still need to know—"

She cut him off with a finger to his lips. "You know what? There's stuff about me—also important stuff—you don't know. We've both got secrets. But just for tonight, let's leave them out in the snow, okay? For tonight, it's just you and me inside this place. Nothing else. No one else."

His eyes were burning, tortured. "Peaches—"

She brought her lips up to his, replacing her finger, knowing he didn't know how much it was costing her to put herself out there like this, how much his rejection would completely crush her.

"Ren, the only question I need answered right now is whether or not you want me."

He didn't answer her in words. He didn't have to. Instead, his hand gripped the hem of her shirt and pulled it over her head, throwing it to the side. He fisted a handful of her hair as his lips ravished hers, his tongue licking deep into her mouth as if he couldn't get enough of the taste of her.

A hot wave crashed in her chest. She had never felt like this. *Desired* like this. She was drowning in it.

Ren's other hand slid down to her hips, pulling her up against him. Leaving her zero doubt that he did, in very definite fact, want her.

It was amazing and overwhelming. She'd only ever been with Damien and that had never, ever—even at the best of times—felt like this. Like she could gladly stay in this bed for the rest of her life and that would be just fine.

Ren was big and strong and domineering, holding her tight against him as they nestled side by side on the bed, keeping her where he wanted her. But when he rolled over on top of her, covering her with his big body, despite how much she wanted him, wanted this, all her mind could remember was Damien holding her under him. Forcing himself on her even when she didn't want anything to do with him.

She tried to keep kissing Ren, to just push past the ugly memories that tried to creep in, but he noticed.

He sat up, holding his weight on his elbows on either side of her head, using his thumbs to brush her hair off her cheeks. "Hey," he whispered. "What's going on? Did you change your mind?"

She tried to force words out, but they wouldn't come. As tears slid down her temples, he caught them with his fingers.

"Peaches. If you've changed your mind, that's fine."

"I—I got a little overwhelmed." She finally got the words out. "It's been a long time for me. And even before that it...wasn't good."

Anger burned in Ren's eyes but Natalie knew it wasn't directed toward her. Somehow he understood about Damien, had read between the lines, or maybe she hadn't been as secretive as she'd thought when she talked about her past.

Ren rolled his weight off her, and all she could feel was a crushing defeat. All her talk about it just being the two of them inside the cabin and she'd gone and ruined it all. When Ren sat up she knew he was pulling away and the moment was over.

But instead, he pulled off his sweatpants and lay back down. He put both arms back behind his head, which caused the muscles in his arms and shoulders and chest to ripple.

By the time her eyes made it back to his face he was smiling, his eyes just as smoldering as they'd been a few minutes before.

"Oh," she whispered. "We're not done?"

"Peaches, I've been thinking about you and your soft skin and crystal eyes and haunted smile from the moment I laid eyes on you. Longer, it feels like."

Something dark crossed over his face so fast she

couldn't quite decipher it. But whatever it was, he pushed it away and his smile was back.

"Right or wrong, good or bad, smart or stupid, I want you right now more than I've ever wanted any woman. I want to kiss you all over and see if your skin is just as sweet as the peaches and cream my mom used to give me."

She couldn't stop the hitch in her breath. "I want that, too. More than anything. I'm sorry I freaked out."

"No need for apologies. We just need to slow things down. Get it to a speed you're comfortable with." He reached over and grabbed her wrist, giving her a tug so she was once again sprawled on top of his chest. His lips found hers, and all the passion was still there, but with a slow, lush burn this time.

"I've woken up with you like this every morning since I met you. Under you is very quickly becoming my favorite place to be in the world." His thumb brushed along her jawline, sending a rush of sensation skimming across her flesh.

"I thought men wanted to be on top." Damien would've never dreamed of doing anything but dominating her with his body.

Ren's smile was wicked, his hands trailing down her throat, over her chest and breasts, before coming to rest on her waist. "A *real* man wants to be wherever is going to help his woman get what she wants."

"I don't know that I know what I want."

He pulled her more fully on top of him. "Peaches, we've got all night to figure that out."

And they did.

Chapter Thirteen

After their amazing night of lovemaking, trying to tell Natalie the truth hadn't gotten any easier. The entire next day—for the couple hours he let her out of the bed—he'd peppered her with more questions about Frei-hof, trying to get any info he could.

Justifying to himself that once he told her who he really was she'd likely clam up for good.

She'd opened up more about her marriage and the hell it had been. She'd admitted to running from Frei-hof, although she hadn't said anything about faking her own death. And finally mentioned that the reason she'd needed to work three jobs was because she was being paid under the table and therefore much less.

Ren had been forced to keep his questions more neutral than he'd wanted.

"You really felt like you couldn't get a regular job? That your ex had the means to find you no matter where you were?"

She glanced away. "Maybe not himself. But Damien has uncanny skills when it comes to getting people to help him. He just has this way of making people believe that he can meet their needs. So I wouldn't doubt for a second that he had someone checking the grid for me every once in a while."

Ren was just beginning to understand the pressure and isolation Natalie had been under for the past six years. He had no doubt she was innocent and that they'd be moving on to the media blitz plan in two more days. The only question now was if she had information locked away inside that could help them.

Before she learned the truth and stopped talking to him altogether.

"What did your ex do for a living?"

She almost seemed to shrink in on herself. "You're going to think I'm an idiot, and I was. All I knew when I got married was that he was a businessman, and had enough money for us to lead very pampered—and isolated—lives. Enough money to pay people to say and do whatever he wanted."

"You never asked later?" Ren realized he probably knew more about Freihof's "business" actions than Natalie ever did. That he'd made his fortune through blackmail, weapon sales and trading of information.

"I learned after he dislocated my shoulder to never ask him anything that might be considered too inquisitive. After he broke my fingers, I learned never to ask any questions at all."

What? Ren walked over to where she was still painting and took the brush from her hands. "He broke your fingers?"

She shrugged, still not looking at him. "It's not a particularly exciting story. He wanted me to be perfect. Was obsessed with me being *perfect*." She all but spat the word. "Whenever I did something that wasn't, there was a punishment. Sometimes my hair wasn't perfectly styled and that garnered a slap."

She began shaking, swallowing hard. "One day after he saw my latest finished painting and disapproved, I asked whether perhaps someone else would like it even though he didn't. He broke every finger on my right hand." She let out a shuddery breath as Ren pulled her into his chest. "I couldn't hold a paintbrush for months. As a matter of fact, I haven't held one since, haven't painted, until now."

He'd lifted her fingers to his lips so he could kiss them. Then took her back to bed. Just to hold her and let her rest, knowing that when she woke up it would be time to tell her the truth. To explain what was really going on and how much they needed her help. Doubly now. One, because she was their best shot, and because of what Homeland Security would do to her when they came barging in here in less than three days.

Hell if Ren was going to allow Natalie to be taken into custody as a hostile informant, suspected of aiding a terrorist. Especially since Ren had been the one to so adamantly argue that to be true three days ago. His judgments about her were what had landed her on Homeland's watch list in the first place.

Now he knew there was absolutely no way. Even if Freihof hadn't done all the terrible things he'd done to her, there was still no way she would assist him. Ren was confident she would be willing to help them make sure Freihof was arrested. Certainly that was in her best interests, but also because it was the right thing to do.

Natalie would need protection after they were out of the wilderness, and not just from Freihof. Obviously someone knew she was alive, or suspected it, based on the deaths of the Baxters. Some enemy of Freihof's, hoping to take her and use her to find him? They'd also put a protective detail on her friend Olivia, just in case someone came after her.

When Natalie woke from her nap, which was plagued by bad dreams, Ren still couldn't find it in him to tell her right away who he was.

Because he knew it would be over. That the sexy, generous woman who'd spent last night and most of today in his arms—hell, even the courageous, friendly woman who'd spent the last two days talking with him—would be gone.

But he had to tell her. He had less than thirty-six hours to get her to understand and ensure her cooperation with the media blitz plan.

He wanted to show her somewhere first. A low overhang that looked out over the river. He could admit it was because he was hoping she would paint it one day.

Not that he'd ever be there to see a finished piece in the future. But he was hoping some part of this place might inspire her to continue painting. Ren and the rest of Omega were going to make sure Freihof never hurt her again.

Broke her damn fingers. No doubt specifically so she couldn't paint, to steal away the obvious joy she derived from it.

That bastard was going down. Ren was willing to pay whatever price it took to make that happen. Had been willing to for a long time.

But he'd never dreamed the price would be the special connection blossoming between him and Natalie. Had never dreamed that would even exist and be so precious to him.

"Ren, where are you taking me?" The exasperation was clear in her voice. He'd made her stop painting, even though she was so close to being finished, and was walking her to the overhang. To share the breath-taking view.

As if that was going to make what he had to tell her—how he'd deceived her—all okay.

"A view. You have to see it for yourself. I think it's right up there with your beach house view."

"You know I don't like snow," she grumbled, but kept walking.

She still hadn't told him why, and he hadn't pushed. He had no doubt it was horrific. "It'll be worth it."

The smile she gave him said she absolutely trusted him to be telling the truth. And his gut clenched even as he wrapped an arm around her and pulled her close.

Beautiful view first, relationship-ending talk after.

He knew the moment she saw it. "Oh, my gosh, Ren!" She hurried up to the edge, looking down over the river just ten feet or so beneath them from here. Most of the edges were frozen but the middle still flowed, giving the entire area a surreal, unearthly look.

"I was hoping you might paint it someday."

She grinned back at him over her shoulder. "Are you kidding? Absolutely. I wish I could paint it right now!"

"I know it's snow, and how much you hate that, but I thought the beauty of it all could trump that."

She spun around to face him. "It does. More than, it…" Her words trailed off as blood drained from her face at something behind him. "Ren, it's a…"

He spun and found a mountain lion just a dozen yards behind them. A huge one. Maybe close to eight or nine feet long. He knew these big cats didn't hibernate and they normally weren't aggressive toward humans. Only under extenuating circumstances like protecting young or...

Then Ren saw it. The animal's slight limp in the back leg as it took a step forward.

He immediately pushed Natalie behind him. "Mountain lion. It's injured or it normally wouldn't be anywhere near us." Ren unzipped his jacket and opened it.

"We need to make ourselves look as big as possible." He wished like hell he had his Glock. He wouldn't have shot the cat unless he absolutely had to, but even firing above his head would probably scare him off.

Natalie was opening her jacket and standing beside him.

"Peaches, get back behind me."

"No. If being big is what will scare him off, two of us looking as big as possible has to be better."

She was right but he didn't like it. He began yelling loudly and clapping his hands, which also should've scared the animal away. It was definitely not behaving in a normal way. Ren began shifting Natalie slowly toward the side, providing more distance from the cat, yelling the whole time. If they could make it to the set of trees near the edge, Ren could at least use a branch as a weapon if the mountain lion attacked.

When it attacked. If it was going to flee it would've already done so.

He had to turn to use both hands to break off a branch and that was when the giant cat pounced. Natalie let out a terrified scream as he pushed her to the side.

Ren ripped the branch the rest of the way off as the cat landed on him, the force knocking him to the ground. He swung as best he could from the side, but couldn't get much momentum. He felt his jacket and skin rip from the mountain lion's claws.

And then another branch hit it from the side. Natalie, screaming like a banshee, struck the cat as hard as she could. The animal jumped closer to the ledge, dragging Ren with him when its claw got caught in the fabric of his thick coat.

Ren felt the ground beneath him and the cat begin to give way. Natalie was rushing forward to hit the cat again.

"Natalie, no! The ledge is breaking!" Her weight would definitely cause it to fall.

Her eyes were huge as she froze, but it was too late. With a loud crack, the ledge broke away, sending him and the cat into the river ten feet below. The mountain lion jumped away, ripping more of Ren's skin.

Natalie screaming his name from ten feet above was the last thing Ren heard as the icy water of the river sucked him under.

Chapter Fourteen

Natalie screamed Ren's name as he fell from out of her sight and she heard a splash below. She turned and ran as fast as she could to a place where she could slide down to the riverbank, praying the whole time that he was okay and she'd be able to find him.

At the bottom she saw the cat running in the opposite direction, thank God, limping more severely.

"Ren!" she screamed again, looking for him in the sea of white. His head popped up out of the water just a few yards away.

"Oh, my God, Ren!"

Natalie grabbed a branch and skimmed across the edge of the river until she got to a large flat rock that cut into the water, that would put her within just a few feet of him. She wasted no time crawling out on her belly, careful to keep her balance. If she fell in the water, they would both die out here. There'd be no way they'd be able to get back to the cabin.

As she got to the edge she could see Ren's green eyes looking back at her, conscious but in agony as he swam toward her, cold making him sloppy. She threw the branch out to him. He grabbed it as best he could and she pulled him in.

She hooked her arms under his armpits and pulled, using gravity and her own weight to help hoist them backward, and was finally able to drag him out of the water and on top of her. Violent shudders racked his frame and she had to wrap her arms and legs around him to keep him from falling off the rock.

They subsided a little and she got herself out from under him, ignoring the discomfort of her now-wet clothes turning icy. It had to be much worse for Ren.

And if she didn't get him to the cabin and warmed up quickly, his body was going to go into shock. Then shut down.

Reaching under his arms again, she hefted him until they both were on the shoreline.

"Ren!" She rolled him over onto his back and tapped his face with both hands when his eyes began to close. "Come on, solider. I need your help to get you to the cabin."

"Na-Natalie…"

She kissed him hard on the lips. "Yeah, it's me. Now we've got to move before you lose all control of your body." His eyes started to close again. "Ren! I need you to stay awake. We've got to get you on your feet."

Those green eyes looked back at her, glazed with pain.

"I know it hurts," she whispered. Oh, how she knew. "I know everything hurts. Damien used to leave me out in the snow naked, as punishment."

She knew exactly how god-awful the burn was from freezing. Like your whole body had been lit on fire with no chance for relief.

"Ba-bastard."

"He was. Trust me, he was. But I survived and you're going to also. Now I need you to stand."

He nodded jerkily, and she got him to a sitting position. She wrapped one of his icy wet arms around her shoulders, her other arm gripping his waist.

"On three, here we go. One, two, three!"

She used every bit of strength she had, pushing through her legs to get them off the ground. Ren groaned but made it to his feet. She immediately began walking them in the direction of the cabin.

A half mile never seemed so far away.

Ren's face was colorless after just a few steps and she realized he was bleeding from where the mountain lion had mauled him.

They walked slowly but steadily toward the cabin, Ren leaning heavier on her with every step. He wasn't shivering anymore, which she knew was a very bad sign. Natalie was using all the strength she had just to propel them in the correct direction.

"Come on, solider," she said through choppy breaths. "Left. Right. Don't you give up. I'm not leaving you here, so if you stop, we're both going to die. Keep going."

She had to give it to him; he moved one foot in front of the other for a long time. But about halfway there she felt him collapse. It was all she could do to keep him from falling face-first into the snow.

"Ren!" She crouched down and tapped his face lightly again and again but he didn't move. She couldn't even tell if he was breathing. Panicking, she ripped off her gloves and held her fingers to his icy neck, nearly sobbing with relief when she felt his pulse, thready but there.

They weren't far from the cabin but there was no way she'd be able to carry him the last couple hundred yards. They might as well be miles away.

She put her gloves back on and yanked off her jacket, rolling his torso onto it. Then she grabbed it by the collar and pulled, once again using her weight and gravity to her advantage. Every time she pulled him forward it was by crashing herself into the ground, but at least it moved him.

The progress was slow and agonizing. She had to fall into the snow each time just to get him to move one or two feet. It wasn't long before the cold and exertion was stealing all her strength.

She fought to keep her mind in the present as the agonizing burn of the cold tried to throw her back into the past. When she was helpless. At Damien's mercy.

As the flames of cold licking her skin receded to the blessed numbness, her mind wanted to hide. From the pain, from the exhaustion. To just curl up in the snow and let everything float away.

But if she did, she and Ren would both die. And damn it, she wasn't going to let that happen.

They were less than fifty yards from the cabin—she could see it, for heaven's sake—when her coat ripped under Ren's weight. Sobbing, she stumbled up to the house, grabbed a blanket from the bed and ran back down to Ren.

She laid the blanket out on the ground and used her legs—there was no way she'd be able to do it with her arms—to roll him face-first onto it.

Reaching for an inner strength she didn't know she had, past all the pain of getting them this far, she got them the last few yards and into the house, kicking the door closed behind them. She fell next to Ren on the floor, breaths sawing in and out of her chest.

She just wanted to lie there, but knew she couldn't. They weren't out of the woods yet. Leaving Ren where he lay, she crawled over to the stove. The fire had gone out so she built a new bundle of tinder like he had taught her.

Using the flint with numb, exhausted fingers was even more difficult, but—thanks to Ren and his patience—she knew she could do it. Finally, a spark caught the kindling and a flame began. She built the wood on top of it and opened all the vents on the stove to allow as much heat out as possible.

She pulled off her own clothes, now just as soaked as Ren's, wincing at the pain down the entire back of her body after throwing herself onto the ground time after time to move him. She wrapped herself in a second blanket, crawling back to him. She got his wet clothes off as quickly as her numb, trembling fingers would allow, and wrapped his wound with a T-shirt to stop the bleeding. She threw all the frozen clothes and blanket she'd used to pull him into a pile by the door, just under her painting.

With the last of her strength she grabbed a quilt resting over the back of the couch. She crawled back to Ren where he still lay on the floor, pulled his naked body to hers and wrapped them both as best she could in the blankets. She knew she should try to get him to the bed or closer to the fire, or do more with his wound, but she couldn't. Her strength was gone.

She pulled his icy hands under her armpits and his

toes between her calves. She was so cold the difference in temperature barely registered.

She'd done all she could do. She prayed it would be enough.

Blackness claimed her.

EVERY PART OF him was screaming in agony. Ren fought back a moan of pain, years of ops kicking in, not sure where he was and if it was safe to make any sound.

Slowly, awareness came back to him. That damn mountain lion and the icy bitch of a river as it had stolen every bit of breath he had.

But now he was in the cabin with Natalie, lying on the ground, naked with her in his arms. How the hell had they gotten here?

He shifted, and pain blistered up his shoulder. He moved cautiously, glancing down at the wound. That cat's claws had gotten him good. It was going to need to be stitched.

Natalie rolled, moaning, and her blue eyes blinked open.

"You're awake," she whispered, before her eyes closed again briefly in relief.

Then she frantically sat up and began examining his fingers and toes. "You were wet for so long. I was worried about frostbite but I didn't know what to do and once I got you here I just ran out of steam."

He could feel her poking at his hands and feet as she continued talking. "But they look okay. Thank God." Her hands moved to his shoulder, her voice becoming more and more distressed. "Oh, no, your wound. I knew I needed to do something about it, but I—"

He put his finger to her lips to stop her stream of

words, his body burning. "I'm okay. You did great. How did we even get back here?"

"I got you out of the water and you walked part of the way." She shrugged. "Then you lost consciousness and I pulled you the rest of the way on my jacket, then a blanket."

She said it casually as if she hadn't just gone beyond, way beyond, what most people would've been able to do, and saved his life.

He pulled her lips down to his with his good arm. "Thank you. You saved my life."

"I should've done more. I should've—"

"You did enough."

She helped get him up and to the bed. He was barely able to walk, and dizziness assaulted him immediately. Once there, she removed the T-shirt she'd used to stop the flow of blood.

Looking at it, he realized the wound was worse than he'd thought. Skin ripped open and still bleeding. It was already swollen and ugly. Infection was going to be a real worry.

The game was up. He needed to call Omega and get some medical attention out to them. They could have someone here on Jet-Skis within twenty minutes.

Natalie's concerned face was already going in and out of focus. Hell, how was he going to explain this to her?

"I need my phone," he croaked out. She'd covered him with a blanket, but he kicked it off, feeling too hot.

"Ren, we don't get a signal, remember? You've already tried."

He shook his head, the movement causing him to fall

back with a groan. "I have to tell you something. But I need my phone first. Pants pocket."

She moved to the pile of clothes by the door, hanging them over the couch to dry as she came back, but was shaking her head. "I'm sorry, it's broken. The fall in the river and then probably as I dragged you back to the cabin."

When she handed it to him, he realized it was true. There was no way to make a call with this phone. Damn it, they were going to need to walk out of here. As soon as possible.

"You're going to need to stitch this," he told her, struggling to stay upright as everything pitched around him. "There's a first aid kit in one of the kitchen cabinets."

She got it and came back. Ren already knew it was fully stocked, including some supplies for sutures.

She cleaned out the wound, wincing as he bit off a curse at the pain.

"I don't know if I can do this," she whispered as he showed her what she would need to do and helped her prepare the sutures.

"You can." He tried to smile at her but everything was so blurry. He could feel fever beginning to course through his body. "It doesn't have to be perfect. We just need to get it closed before infection sets it."

Although he was pretty sure it already had.

His breath whistled out his teeth as the needle pierced his already inflamed skin. But he swallowed all signs of pain when he saw the tears leaking out of Natalie's eyes.

"You're doing great. You're the most amazing woman I have ever met," he told her after what seemed like hours later when she was almost finished. Her face had long since blurred into an unrecognizable blob as his eyes glazed over from pain. The sound of her voice— the sound of *everything*—starting to seem farther and farther away. He fought every second to stay conscious.

He needed to tell her. Tell her how close they were to civilization. Less than four miles. What if something happened to him and he couldn't lead her out? She could make it. This wasn't just about Freihof anymore.

"Nat, you need to know… I have to tell you…"

"Ren?" Panic was clear in her voice.

And then there was nothing.

Chapter Fifteen

By the time she'd tied off the stitches like he'd shown her how, Ren was completely unconscious.

And burning up with fever.

She touched his forehead but she didn't even have to know for sure how high his temperature had climbed. His face was already a bright red and he'd kicked all the covers off his body. She spent the next few hours alternating between trying to cool him down with a wet washcloth and attempting to get some ibuprofen in him by grinding it into powder and mixing it with water.

Nothing seemed to help.

When the heat in his body turned to chills, she wrapped him in her arms, covered them with a blanket and held him.

"I know you had something you wanted to tell me, so I need you to wake up and try, okay?"

Her voice seemed to soothe his fever-ravaged mind and body so she kept talking.

"You call me Peaches. Did I ever tell you how much I like that? I never would've thought I would, but I really do. It makes me feel…special. Cared for."

His body shuddered again, and she pulled him closer,

hooking her leg over his hips to bring him even closer, kissing his forehead.

"I know you've been talking to me and asking me questions. Trying to get to know me. And I know I avoided them a lot."

She knew there was very little chance that Ren was understanding her, but she still wanted to get it all out.

"But I'll tell you, anyway. I married a monster. I was nineteen years old, pretty much alone in the world, and fell for the first guy who showed me attention."

She brushed hair off his forehead.

"You asked me if I knew what he did. I didn't. I really didn't at first. But it didn't take long for me to put it together. He was a criminal. Sold things on the black market. I'm not sure exactly what. Weapons, I think, maybe? Technology.

"I should've gone to the police. The first time I suspected something, or at the least the first time he hurt me. But I had nowhere else to go. He convinced me that nobody would believe me about the abuse."

Talking about this hurt so much.

"But I think maybe he knew I was going to go to the cops, anyway. Before I even knew that was going to be my plan. That's when he changed everything. He fired all the live-in staff who worked at the house, so there was no one around but us.

"Then he told me he was going to train me to be perfect. Teach me how to be the perfect wife. For two and a half years I never saw another living soul but him in that house in Grand Junction. I never stepped foot outside it unless it was some sort of punishment. Like…like the snow. Buried in the snow until I was sure I would die."

She wiped the tears that leaked from her eyes.

"That day it was because I'd forgotten to put the lid back on the toothpaste and clean out the sink. But really that was just an excuse for him to torture me. If it hadn't been that, he would've found something else."

She rubbed her hands up and down Ren's arms. Arms that had never once been used to do anything but bring her pleasure and comfort.

"Eventually I just gave up. Gave in to him. He wanted the perfect puppet, I realize now. Damien's always been the master puppeteer, getting people to do what he wants. I became an empty shell of a person filled up with the desire to be perfect for him."

Ren stopped shuddering. She almost hoped he could hear her, could process what she was saying, so he would understand. Even though she knew it was probably better for him if he didn't know anything about Damien if the police asked him.

Or, God forbid, Damien coming after Ren himself.

Because telling him this didn't change anything. Didn't change the fact that if Damien discovered she was alive, he would search the world over for her and kill anyone who got in the way of bringing her back to him. Ren included.

"I completely lost myself. Didn't know who I was anymore. Once I was that perfect shell, he could start bringing me places again. A restaurant. The opera. I never talked to anyone, and just sat by his side, the perfect dutiful wife. One day he took me to the bank with him.

"For most people, getting caught in the middle of a bank robbery, getting grazed by a bullet in the head, would be the worst day of their life. For me, it was the best.

"I still couldn't even tell you exactly what happened that day in the bank. Robbers. A SWAT team. Yelling, shooting. I got shot. Well, a bunch of people got shot, but I think my wound actually came from the good guys. Or at least Damien was screaming something like that."

She trailed her fingers along the gauze covering Ren's wound.

"There was blood. So much blood everywhere. Even more than what you lost today. I thought I was dying. Everybody thought I was dying. Damien jumped on a SWAT team member and started hitting him and then got detained, although he didn't get arrested."

If they had arrested and processed him, they would've realized what a criminal they had on their hands. But they'd thought he was just a guy hysterical that his wife had been shot, so they'd let him go.

"Miracle of all miracles, I got brought to the wrong hospital. The closest, but one that was having some sort of biological pathogen scare and was turning away patients. The CDC had been called in and it was complete chaos. I was just sitting in a corner of the ER since everyone had bigger problems than me. I'd stopped bleeding and obviously wasn't going to die. CDC personnel stopped right in front of me, discussing how anyone who had died in the last four hours in the emergency room needed to be immediately cremated because of contamination concerns."

She could swear she almost felt Ren's arms tighten around her. His shuddering had completely stopped. She kicked the blankets off them a little so neither of them would overheat.

"I was sitting there with my own medical file in my lap and knew this was my only chance. Nothing like this was ever going to happen again. I saw the CDC guys tell an orderly to take a woman I was pretty sure was dead, somewhere, and I followed. To make a long story short, I looked at her chart, copied what was said about needing to be cremated. Put my medical file and jewelry in a metal box next to hers and ran."

She rubbed his hair off his forehead again.

"It worked. Everyone assumed I had died in the shootout—I was reported on the news as a victim—and the hospital confirmed they had ordered cremation of all bodies at that time."

She sighed, lying back farther. "That was six years ago. I've been running and hiding ever since. Scared of everything. Haven't even painted. I let him steal so much from me, Ren. Not only the three years I was married to him, but the six years since. Nearly a decade of my life.

"It wasn't until I met you that I realized it was time to stop. Not stop hiding. I'm never going to be able to stop hiding. But stop being his puppet. Stop letting him dictate and control my every move."

She reached over and kissed his forehead, pulling him closer. "You taught me that, Ren. And I love you for it."

IT WAS THIRTY hours before Ren finally woke up. Natalie had bathed him with cool washcloths when he got too hot, held him when he got too cold, fed him as much broth as she could get him to take.

And talked to him through the whole thing.

She realized talking about her life with Damien had been more for her than it had been for Ren, especially since Ren wasn't going to remember any of it anyway.

There was so much she'd pushed aside. Feelings of anger, inadequacy, helplessness, pain.

Maybe she was never going to ever truly stop running from Damien physically. But she could stop running every other way.

She was done letting him pull all her strings. Done being a puppet.

Looking at Ren now, watching his body wake up— his temperature back to normal, the sickly pallor gone, even his shoulder wound looking much better—was like a physical caress.

Natalie knew she hadn't known him long enough to call what was pressing inside her chest legitimate. Knew they were brought on by the dangerous and adrenaline-inducing circumstances that they'd found themselves in. But she didn't care.

She hadn't known she was starving until she'd tasted him.

She wasn't a fool; she knew things would always be complicated at best. But maybe a relationship with him could possibly work. He lived in Montana on a farm, for crying out loud.

A farm that sounded like everything she'd ever wanted in the world.

Why would Damien ever look for her on a farm in Montana? He wouldn't. She could explain everything to Ren, and then stay off the grid there. Take shelter in him. In *them*.

Give in to these feelings that had been wrapping themselves around her heart since the first moment she saw him on the train. And hope he felt the same way.

His green eyes blinked open right then. She saw confusion light his eyes, then knowledge as he remembered where they were.

Then heat—so much heat—as he focused in on her.

"You're so damn beautiful," he whispered. "From the beginning it has hurt me to look at you."

She felt her face—and other parts of her body—begin to burn.

"I think that might be some residual fever talking there, soldier. You've been pretty sick for a while."

In a heartbeat his face changed, a cool focus washing out the passion that had just crackled between them.

"I've been unconscious?" he asked briskly, already starting to sit up. "How long?"

She moved to help him, but he'd already made it himself. "A few hours."

He pinned her with his eyes, moving his shoulder, testing it. "How many hours? Twelve? Eighteen?"

"Probably closer to thirty. It was sunset two days ago when you fell in. You woke up and helped me stitch you the next morning, and then you were out all day yesterday and a lot of today. It's midafternoon now."

She wasn't expecting the muttered curse that fell from his lips.

She laughed nervously. "Got a big date that you're missing?"

He began patting around the bed. "I need my phone. Do you know where it is?"

"It's broken, remember? You were asking for it before the fever." She got the pieces from the table and brought them over to him. "It got crushed in the fall or the river."

He muttered another curse before standing, completely naked and a little unstable, and walked to the window.

"It's too late. Damn it. I didn't expect this."

Natalie had no idea what he was talking about. "Expect what?"

He didn't answer, just rolled his shoulder and stretched his arm as if to test the usability. It had to have hurt him, but he didn't complain. Then he walked over to the couch where she'd hung his clothes—getting steadier with every step—and got dressed.

"Ren, what's going on?" Obviously she was missing something important. She struggled to keep her voice calm.

He walked to her and cupped her face in his hands. "We have to go. We're going to be walking out this afternoon."

"We are? Why? Where?"

He closed his eyes like he was in pain. More than just the pain in his shoulder. Something deeper. "We're closer to a town than we originally thought. I saw some smoke a few miles away before I fell in the river. So get together whatever you can so we can walk out in about thirty minutes."

"Are you sure we're that close to civilization?"

He walked over to her and leaned his forehead against hers. "Yes. I'm positive. I just wanted a little more time with you alone before giving you back to the rest of the world. And then the mountain lion…"

He still looked pained. She knew he wasn't telling her everything. But what he was telling her was enough.

She smiled and kissed him softly. "I don't think I

wanted to go back to the rest of the world, anyway. Go do whatever it is you need to do. I'll be ready in thirty minutes. I trust you."

Chapter Sixteen

I trust you.

The words echoed through Ren's mind as he stepped outside the cabin and moved quickly through the trees where he kept the lockbox with items he thought he might need: his Glock, Omega badge, a set of handcuffs.

Another phone right now would be pretty damn handy, too. Although it would be too late to call off the agents Homeland Security had sent.

He'd run out of time while he was unconscious. He knew they were here to take Natalie. To confine her in a windowless box of a room and force her to tell them every single detail about her life with Damien Freihof.

He remembered parts of what she'd said to him while he'd be in and out of delirium with fever.

I married a monster.

Buried in the snow.

Perfect shell.

I love you.

He slammed the bottom of his fist against the tree, gritting his teeth at the reverberations that coursed through his arm and wounded shoulder. It was no less than he deserved.

Natalie was completely innocent. She was good and

gentle and kind. Brandon and Andrea had tried to warn Ren of that from their first meeting with her, but he hadn't wanted to believe it.

And now Homeland Security wanted to take her in and break her. Not through physical torture, but they wouldn't need to use that. Because there were so many ways someone as gentle as Natalie could be broken.

Like learning she'd given her heart to and trusted the wrong person.

He clamped down on the howl that wanted to rip from his throat. Because at the end of it all, it wouldn't be Homeland Security's brutish methods that would break Natalie.

It would be Ren's attention and kindness.

But hell if he was going to let them take her. She might be heartbroken by the time this was all done, but he wasn't going to let her mind and spirit be crushed by what they would do to her. And he knew agents were out here right now, preparing to seize the cabin and take Natalie in.

He stayed low, moving outward toward the higher ground that would give him the tactical advantage. If he had to guess, there were probably two or three agents out here for the arrest. Two who would knock openly on the door—especially since they thought they had another law enforcement officer inside who would help with the arrest—and a third who would stay hidden and make sure there were no surprises.

Ren would take out that third agent first.

From up on the ridge he could see the snowmobiles they'd used to get here, leaving them parked half a mile away to keep sound from traveling to the cabin. He would need to work quickly to disarm the first guy before the other two burst through the cabin door. And do it all without killing or seriously injuring the other law enforcement officers.

He spotted them—three just like he'd thought—as they were splitting off from one another. All three already had their sidearms out, which meant they were definitely taking this seriously.

Ren moved quickly in the direction the backup man had gone. He estimated he had about five minutes to disarm and subdue this one before the other two entered the cabin.

Ignoring the pain from his injuries and weakness from a day and a half ravaged by fever, Ren moved silently between the trees. He kept his own sidearm holstered at his waist. No matter what, this couldn't become a shootout.

Ren knew these woods much better than the agents, and they weren't expecting anyone to be out among the trees. Agent Three was looking in the direction of the cabin when Ren moved up behind him, got out his weapon and knocked him on the back of the neck.

The man crumpled to the ground without a sound. Taking out his handcuffs, Ren bound the man around a small tree, then used a ripped part of his shirt as a gag. He hadn't hit him that hard; the guy was already groaning and would be awake in a couple of minutes.

"Be back with your friends in just a second, buddy," Ren whispered, then ran toward the other two agents.

One had just peeked through the window to see what was happening inside the cabin, and was signaling to the other. Ren needed to get them far enough away that there wouldn't be any chances of Natalie hearing them.

"Hey, fellas," he called softly from behind them, Omega ID already in hand, praying this would work.

They swung around with weapons raised but he'd been expecting that. Ren kept his credentials out toward them, while raising a finger to his lips.

"Ren McClement, Omega Sector. Been waiting for you guys to get here for a while."

They lowered their weapons exactly like he'd wanted them to do.

"McClement, what are you doing out here rather than in there with the suspect?" Agent One asked.

Suspect, not witness. Not informant. That confirmed everything he needed to know.

"We were told that Omega didn't necessarily want us butting in," the second man said, the look they gave each other clearly stating they didn't care what Omega Sector wanted. The two law enforcement organizations were independent of each other, neither under the other's jurisdiction. Generally, they were after the same bad guys and it rarely caused conflicts.

Today there would definitely be conflict.

Ren motioned them closer to him, farther from the cabin, and they came. When they got close enough, he stuck out his hand like he wanted to shake. "Like I said, I'm Ren."

"Mark Jaspers," the first guy said. "And this is—"

Ren didn't wait for the second introduction. He grabbed Jaspers's outstretched arm and yanked, pulling him forward and into a vicious punch to the jaw that knocked him to the ground.

Not-Jaspers witnessed it, and was in the process of pulling his weapon back out when Ren swung around and roundhouse kicked him, knocking the gun into the trees. An uppercut to the jaw had the other agent stunned and stumbling backward.

"What the hell?" Jaspers croaked from the ground as Ren grabbed not-Jaspers by the collar and threw him down next to Jaspers, pointing his Glock at both men. "What the hell are you doing, McClement?"

"Sorry, guys, but I'm not going to be able to let you take Ms. Anderson today." There was no damn way he was calling her Mrs. Freihof.

"Are you in on it with her?" not-Jaspers asked. "Working with Freihof?"

"No," Ren spat. "But neither is she. And she doesn't know where he is. She's running from him."

Jaspers tried reason. "Why don't you just let us take her in, make that clarification for ourselves? I'm sure if you've found it to be true, we will, too."

"No offense, guys, but I've seen the tactics you use when questioning someone you consider to be hostile." Never quite enough food, water, sleep. No bed. Sitting in hard chairs in windowless rooms for hours upon hours. Ren had never felt bad about it when it was someone who knew something that law enforcement needed to know in order to save lives.

But it damn well wasn't happening to Natalie.

"Omega has a plan in place to draw Freihof out," Ren continued.

"You missed that deadline this afternoon, McClement," Jaspers said. "You didn't report in, didn't show up. You missed your chance."

"There were circumstances that couldn't be helped. The plan will still work. So I'm just going to keep you guys here a few extra hours until I can get her out and in front of the media. Freihof will come." Ren knew that for an absolute fact now that he knew what had happened between them. How Freihof had tried to control every part of her life. Letting Natalie wander free without him wouldn't even be an option.

"You do this, your career is over," not-Jaspers said. "It won't matter if it's for the greater good or not. Your time with Omega will be done."

Ren already knew that. Had known it as soon as he'd come up with this plan. But he didn't grieve the choice. It was time to stop living in the darkness that had been his constant companion for so long. Step into the light.

Natalie and her innate generosity of spirit and kindness had shown him that in such a very short time. He prayed there would be some way to get her to forgive him for what he'd done, what he was about to do. Some way to get her to share the light with him, once they had taken Freihof out for good and he could never hurt her again.

He brought Jaspers and his partner into the woodshed and tied them, before going back to get Agent Three—now conscious—and brought him back also.

"There will be someone here to release you guys in the next couple of hours. Just don't get yourselves killed in the meantime."

"You're done, McClement," Jaspers bit out. "Your entire career washed down the drain. I hope she's worth it."

Ren moved a gag over the other man's mouth.

"She is."

Ren took a phone from one of the agents and stepped outside, immediately calling Omega.

"Steve Drackett."

"I'm going to need a Homeland Security cleanup in aisle four."

"Damn it, Ren. You missed the deadline. What the hell is going on? I was about to send agents in there myself. What happened?"

"It's a long story involving a mountain lion and near death."

Steve actually chuckled. "Doesn't it always?"

"Are we too late for the media blitz?"

"I can maybe keep the press here in Riverton for thirty more minutes." Steve's voice was tight. "They passed restless two hours ago."

Ren grimaced. They would need to take a snowmobile. He would move the other out of her path and tell her he ran into some hunters. But this meant more lies to Natalie and not enough time to explain about the whole plan.

Who Ren was. What he needed her to do. She'd be blindsided.

But there was no other way. He had to get her in front of the cameras. Once that happened, Homeland wouldn't take her out of play if she was the best bet of luring Freihof in.

"Do it. We're on our way. We'll be there in twenty-five."

"Please God, tell me there are no dead Homeland Security agents at that cabin."

"No, but some very pissed-off ones. You need to send someone to get them in the woodshed."

"You know those guys can make your life hell, right? We may not work for them, but they have the ear of pretty powerful people."

Ren took a calming breath. "I know. I crossed a line. I'm done."

The other man said nothing for a long second, then ironically echoed Jaspers's words. "I hope she's worth it, my friend."

His answer was still the same.

"She is."

Chapter Seventeen

Like she promised, Natalie had all their stuff returned
to the backpacks, and had even cleaned up as best she
could, when Ren arrived back a little over thirty minutes later.

He strode through the door and walked right up to
her, lifting her in a one-armed hug with his uninjured
limb.

"What?" she said as he kissed her, ignoring the pain
from her hurt back. There was a desperation to him
she'd never seen before.

"We have to leave right now."

"Oh." She'd known that was coming but had hoped
he would come back and say they had more time. She
liked it here. Just the two of them and her painting.

He closed his eyes for a moment, almost like he was
fortifying himself before reopening them. "I ran into
some hunters. They gave me a snowmobile to use to get
us into town. But we've got to go right now. My family got word of the accident and they've been frantic. I
need to get in touch with them right away."

She felt terrible. Of course they needed to go. "Sure.
I'm ready."

"Peaches. I…" He stepped away from her, eyes tortured. "When we get there, everything will change."

"I know." She'd always known that. "The real world. It's okay."

He looked at the phone in his hand. "Damn it, we've got to go right now." He rushed over to the door and ushered her out. "Just, once we get to Westwater, stay near me, okay? I promise I will explain everything as soon as I can."

Westwater? That was the nearby town? Natalie forced herself to breathe down the panic. She'd known they were somewhere in or near Colorado, but had no idea they were so close to Grand Junction where she'd lived with Damien.

It didn't matter. She would get out of here as soon as she could. Maybe she wouldn't be able to go to Montana with Ren right away, but she could meet him there later. There was so much they needed to talk about.

Ren got her situated on the snowmobile, before sitting behind her, surrounding her with his warmth.

"We'll need to talk," he said. "I ran out of time, and that's on me, but just promise me we'll talk when we get there. That you'll give me a chance."

She turned to look at him over her shoulder and smiled. "Of course." There was nothing she wanted more.

He didn't smile back, that tortured look still in his eyes as he put the only helmet over her head, started the machine and soon had them flying.

The faster they sped, the more worried Natalie became. Something must be pretty desperately wrong for him to move them at such a reckless pace.

Less than twenty minutes later he stopped them. She

could see the lights of the town a few hundred yards away, but he didn't drive the snowmobile all the way in, even though it probably wouldn't even be that uncommon.

He stood and helped her take off her helmet.

"Why did we stop? A lot of Colorado towns allow the use of snowmobiles on the street."

He began walking, holding her hand. "We have to walk the rest of the way and there are things you need to know before we make it into town."

Her gut tightened, but she kept up her steps with him. "Okay."

"Natalie, I haven't been completely honest with you."

"About what?" She almost stumbled over a root sticking up on the uneven ground but he held on to her arm, righting her.

He grimaced, continuing to propel them forward. "About a lot. I need your help. It's important. Bigger than you or me. Or even us. A lot of lives are at stake."

"Ren, what's going on?" she whispered.

He stopped and ran his hand through his brown hair. They were just on the outskirts of town. "God, Peaches… Natalie… I never meant…"

"McClement!" A woman rushed into the woods. "Thank God. You guys have got to move right now. We're going to miss our window to hit the evening news if you don't."

Natalie just watched as Ren turned to the woman, not correcting her at the wrong name.

"Lillian, I need a few minutes. Natalie doesn't know what's going on."

He knew this woman?

And what was it that Natalie did not know? Evidently a lot.

Lillian just shook her head. "What the hell have you been doing in that cabin for the last five days if not explaining what we need?" She looked back and forth between Ren and Natalie. "Oh."

The petite woman who sounded vaguely familiar turned to glare at Ren as she obviously figured something out. Something Natalie still couldn't. "Damn you, McClement. But we're still out of time. We've got to go."

As she came closer, Natalie realized this was the same woman who had sold her the ticket for the train. Why would she even be here?

Natalie grabbed the woman's arm gently. "Why are you here if you work for the bus company?" Maybe the train and bus company were owned by the same corporation or something.

The compassion—*pity*—in the other woman's eyes made Natalie's heart sink more.

"You just need to come with us," Lillian said, taking another moment to glare at Ren. "Don't say anything, okay? Just let Ren do the talking."

"Do the talking to who?"

Neither Lillian nor Ren answered. Lillian just wrapped an arm around Natalie's waist and led her toward the town.

Just before they made it onto the streets, Lillian grabbed a walkie-talkie from her waist and spoke into it. "Sheriff, I found them! They're here on the west side of town near Mill Road! Going to need medical, but they're both alive and relatively unharmed!"

The excitement in her voice was in direct opposition to the anger in her eyes for Ren.

"Damn it, I told everyone to use the private channel if we learned anything." The sheriff came back on the walkie-talkie a moment later. "The press is on this channel."

"Oopsies," Lillian said. "Sorry, Sheriff. I forgot."

She most definitely had not forgotten.

"I don't understand what's happening," Natalie whispered. Every second her heart sank lower in her chest.

"Congratulations. You and Ren are hikers who have been lost for nearly a week and have somehow miraculously survived."

Natalie shook her head. "But we weren't hiking. We were on the train. The train you sold me a ticket to."

"Natalie…" Ren reached for her, but she took a step back.

She could see people rushing toward them now. A lot of people. People with lights and cameras.

"What have you done?" she whispered. Not wanting to believe what she was finally beginning to understand. Ren had been using her.

"I've got to go," Lillian said. "I can't be in any of the press footage. Freihof knows me."

Lillian knew Damien.

Ren knew Damien.

Natalie fought to hold on as the whole world spun around her, the snow seeming to rise up and swallow her whole. She couldn't fall. Couldn't allow it to bury her.

Because this time no amount of begging was going to get her out.

THE NEXT HOUR passed in a blur for Natalie. Just before the press had completely descended on them, Ren had ripped his jacket open just a little farther so his wound was more noticeable.

They'd been led to the high school auditorium, quickly checked out by a medic, then sent in front of the cameras. Ren kept Natalie plastered to his side. When it became obvious she wasn't interested in—or capable of—much response, the reporters had turned all their questions to Ren.

He answered them with practiced ease.

They were two hikers whose GPS had failed and then they had gotten caught in a freak storm. No mention of a train crash at all. When Natalie glanced over to the side and saw the young man with the sandwich who had hit on her on the train, still very much alive, she realized the extent of what was going on.

It had all been a setup. From the very beginning. The moment she'd set foot in the bus station. She couldn't even fathom the resources it had taken to fool her to such a degree.

Ren answered more questions as Natalie glanced the other way and saw Brandon and Andrea, the Omega Sector agents who'd come to her house, standing in a darkened corner. Andrea smiled gently at Natalie, an obvious attempt at some sort of apology for what was happening, but Natalie just ignored it. They were all working together. Every single event and action of the past week had been in careful deliberation to get them right here in front of dozens of news cameras.

Where Damien would be sure to see her.

Ren, or Warren Thompson, as he'd been introduced, was great with the reporters. Charming. Handsome. So photogenic that every producer in the country probably couldn't wait to get this happy-ending story in front of as many viewers as possible. Ratings through the roof.

"A mountain lion, not behaving normally because it had been injured, became aggressive and attacked me. If it hadn't been for Natalie…"

The reporters launched into more questions that he answered.

"Natalie pulled me out of the river.

"Natalie amazingly managed to get my unconscious half-frozen carcass to the hunter's cabin.

"Natalie was able to stitch me up.

"Natalie is very definitely the reason I'm still alive and we're both here."

She realized he was saying her name over and over for a reason: to draw attention to it. So that any sound-bites that were used had a better chance of including her name.

"Natalie and I are truly touched by the onslaught of support and thankful to be alive. But I'm sure you can appreciate how tired we are and our need to be more thoroughly checked out by medical professionals, but we will definitely be here for at least three or four more days, until we're cleared to travel. On behalf of both Natalie and me, thank you."

Her name again. They were throwing her in Damien's face.

She was bait.

And she had no doubt at all that Ren had just signed her death warrant.

Chapter Eighteen

Natalie was alive.

After talking to the people who'd owned the Santa Barbara house had proved to be a dead end, Damien had been forced to wait, wondering if it was all true. Until he could see her with his own eyes, he wouldn't be able to believe it.

Waiting for another call to come in concerning her on the tapped phone had been agonizing. And even when it had come, the information hadn't quite made sense. But it had gotten him the information he needed: something was happening in Riverton and it concerned Natalie.

He'd had to keep a very low profile since this tiny little town had been crawling with Omega agents for the last day and a half. He'd seen Brandon and Andrea Han, not to mention SWAT team members Lillian Muir and Ashton Fitzgerald. All people he'd battled in the past.

It would've been so easy to take them out one by one. But that would've cost him his chance to see Natalie. To see if it was really Natalie they were so convinced was alive.

He had no doubts now.

He could feel rage crashing through his system. It was all he could do to remain behind the large video camera in the high school auditorium, careful to keep his face hidden, rather than run up onto the stage, grab her and escape.

Natalie was alive.

Not only that, she was fully aware of who she was and what she was doing. Which meant only one thing: she had deliberately run from him six years ago. Deceived him.

Defied him.

His fingers clenched around the edge of the camera until he felt pieces of plastic break off in his hands. He forced himself to breathe in and out deeply, to get his rage under control.

There would be plenty of time to correct Natalie's behavior. To punish her. To teach her that her conduct was unacceptable.

He looked at her tucked up against the man who was speaking. This Warren Thompson fellow who seemed to have the press eating out of his hand. Was he a member of Omega Sector? Damien didn't know, had never seen him or heard his name, although he'd spent extensive time studying the organization.

It didn't matter. He would have to die, of course. He dared to touch the perfect Natalie? The man must die.

Sadly, it was probably time for Natalie to die, as well. If she was willing to deceive Damien in this way, to throw away their perfect marriage, then she obviously was broken beyond repair.

Maybe with enough correction, enough punishment, she could be fixed. Probably not, but he wouldn't know until he tried.

Omega Sector once again was putting themselves between Damien and what belonged to him. And Natalie did belong to him whether she wanted to accept it or not.

No matter. Omega would soon be so busy trying to clean up the mess he'd made with his handy-dandy biological canisters that Natalie would be the last of their worries.

Couldn't she feel it? The pull between them? The connection even from across the room? Not once did she even look up, so he had to assume she'd lost touch with what had been so special between them.

It was a shame Natalie would have to die, but it couldn't be helped. As a matter of fact, his lovely wife had just helped him make the decision about where to release the biological contaminants.

His perfect wife was gone. He would punish her, then bury her.

And this time when she died, she would truly be dead.

Chapter Nineteen

An hour later Ren was calling himself every foul name he could think of. He'd expected Natalie's anger. For her to fume, scream, throw a few punches at him.

He would've gladly taken them over her blankness.

He hadn't been making it up when he'd told the press they'd needed a thorough examination by the medics. The doctor had winced at the ugly sight of the stitches in his shoulder, but had declared that they would do the job. It would just mean that Ren would always have a scar there, much more pronounced than it would've been if he'd been stitched by a professional in the hospital.

Ren had a feeling he was going to have much more than just this one scar by the time this mission was over.

The doctor had given him an antibiotic shot to help fight off any remaining infection and declared him in fairly good health, all things considered.

Ren had demanded to see Natalie immediately. He needed to talk to her. To explain.

As if she hadn't figured it out already by herself.

Panic had him entering the room where she was being examined immediately after knocking. Like him, Natalie had been given a new set of clothes. She was facing the opposite direction, pulling a sweater down over her back.

A back covered in bruises.

"What the hell is wrong with your back?" he growled.

Natalie pulled the sweater the rest of the way down, spinning toward him.

"I realize you're in charge of this operation, Agent McClement," the Omega medic said. "But please wait for permission to enter an examination room in the future."

Ren ignored the doctor. "What's wrong with your back?" he asked Natalie.

Her eyes just stared at him. No anger. Just blankness. Totally withdrawn. She sat down in a chair and began putting on tennis shoes that had been provided for her.

She obviously wasn't going to answer so he turned to the medic. "What happened?"

He didn't look like he was going to answer, either, so Ren took a quiet step forward. "You can either tell me now, or I can read your report in an hour, which will be your last here before you start looking for a new job. If she's injured I need to know about it for this operation."

And because how the hell had he not known she was hurt?

"Ms. Anderson has extensive bruising on her back, shoulders and hips from repeated contact with the ground. Painful, but nothing that won't heal in the next few days."

Ren turned to Natalie. "How did you come in constant contact with the ground enough to bruise that much?"

She didn't answer, just kept messing with her shoelaces like they contained the answer to every mystery in the universe, although she still hadn't tied them.

He turned back to the medic.

"Evidently it took concerted effort to get you from the frozen river, back to the cabin. Ms. Anderson didn't have the strength to get you there on her own, so she used momentum and gravity to move you forward. Unfortunately that meant throwing herself onto the ground over and over. So…extensive bruising."

Ren ran a hand over his face. "Thank you."

He moved to crouch down in front of Natalie, who was still messing with her shoelaces. Gently brushing her fingers aside, he tied her shoes for her, then placed his hands on her ankles until she finally looked at him.

What rested behind those blue eyes was just as bruised as her back and hips, if not more so. He had known it wouldn't be easy to explain what he'd done, why they needed her help to catch her ex.

But he never dreamed it would put this look in her eyes. Haunted. Empty.

Bruised.

"Peaches…"

She shook her head. "No." Her voice was hoarse as if she'd screamed until it had broken. "Don't you dare call me that."

Ren turned back to look at the medic. "Are you done here? Can she and I talk alone?"

The man nodded and walked out. Ren stepped back and leaned against the table.

"I work for—"

"Omega Sector. Yeah, I figured that part out already."

"How?"

She looked at him before turning to study the wall. "I saw that couple, Brandon and Andrea, who were at the Santa Barbara house last week, during the press conference. I saw the guy who hit on me on the train there, too, so I'm assuming it was all a setup. No real train accident."

He nodded. "Yes, that's correct."

"I suppose I should be glad nobody died. Although I've been so caught up getting laid that it wasn't like I really cared, anyway."

Ren gripped the table forcefully. "Don't you dare talk about yourself—what we shared—that way. You thought you were *surviving*. There was no shame in what you did or how you reacted."

"I'm sure you see it that way," she whispered, looking away.

"I mean it. You want to be mad at me for what I did, how I deceived you, that's fine. You have every right. But you did nothing wrong."

He wished she would get mad at him. Anything would be better than this blankness. A shell of the woman he knew.

I completely lost myself. I was the perfect shell.

Tendrils of memories flowed through his mind. Words she'd said while he was in and out of the fever.

"Natalie, Omega Sector is a powerful law enforcement agency. The best of the very best. We're going to protect you."

She just shook her head.

"Three weeks ago your ex-husband was part of a plan that would've killed tens of thousands of people if Omega hadn't stopped him. Freihof has also been responsible for the killing or wounding of multiple agents and civilians over the last few months. When we discovered you were alive we thought we might be able to obtain a clue about his whereabouts."

Now she looked at him. "I don't know where he is. I've spent the last six years hiding from him in case he figured out I was alive."

"I know that now, but I didn't at the time. You were staying in a million-dollar beach house, going to work in fancy office buildings each day. It looked like maybe you were either working with Freihof or providing for him in some way."

"I wasn't," she whispered.

"I know," Ren repeated. He could feel his heart ripping in two. "And we were going to follow you, talk to you, see what happened and how you might possibly help us catch him. Then we discovered that Damien had obtained biological weapons. We were out of time. We needed to use any and all means necessary to find him."

"Including this elaborate plan involving me."

"Especially you. He's always been obsessed with you. His attacks on Omega Sector, killing agents and their loved ones, were in direct retaliation for what he thought Omega SWAT did to you at that bank six years ago. They were the ones who came in to fight against the robbers."

Her fingers covered her eyes. "That SWAT team saved my life by nicking me in the head. I have no doubt I'd be dead right now at Damien's hand if not for what happened."

It was time to tell her everything.

"Andrea and Brandon came to see you, to ascertain if you knew anything, or if you'd be willing to help. They still weren't sure if you had ties to your ex when they left. But mostly we put them in play to get you to run. To shake you up."

She laughed, the sound hollow. "You certainly did that."

"We set up the crash to see if you would call Freihof when there was an emergency. When you were sure there wasn't anybody following."

"Except you."

He nodded. "Except me. I was hoping I'd come across as a nice enough guy that you wouldn't worry that I was law enforcement."

"That I would accept that you were just a Montana sheep farmer." She laughed again, hysteria lacing the sound. "God, I'm the biggest idiot on the planet."

Ren crouched down at her feet again. "No. My parents do have a sheep farm in Montana. I don't work there, but—"

"Is your name even Ren?"

"Ren McClement. Just Ren, not Warren. Although many people assume it's a shortened name. Thompson is my mother's maiden name." He touched her ankles again, then let them go when she flinched. "It didn't take me long to figure out that you had nothing to do with Freihof or his actions."

"And once you did that? Then what was your grand plan?"

He strung his fingers through his hair. "First, I wanted to make sure you didn't know anything—details—subconsciously. So I just tried to talk to you."

"While I was painting."

"Yes. Then—I swear, Natalie—I was taking you out to show you that river so you could see something beautiful, a place I would always remember and wanted you to remember, too. Wanted you to paint, before I told you what we needed you to do back here with the press. But then that damned mountain lion and the fever…"

"You should've told me, Ren," she whispered. "Once you woke up. You should've told me."

"I know. I wanted to. But we were out of time. I had been unconscious much longer than I'd thought. Homeland Security was sending agents out to detain you as a hostile subject. They would've thrown you in a cell."

"But I have nothing to do with Damien!"

"It wouldn't have mattered, not to them—they would've detained you indefinitely. There were three agents already at the cabin when we left. They should be getting rescued from the woodshed where I tied them up right about now. I couldn't let them take you. And then I had to get you here in front of the cameras so they couldn't arrest you, because now the plan is already in play."

She just shook her head and looked over to the side. Ren stayed where he was, crouched down in front of her, unable to bear to put distance between them, afraid they'd never be close again.

Not that he could blame her.

"I would've told you, Natalie. I promise. I just ran out of time. We needed your help. Freihof has to be stopped before he can use those biological weapons."

"And the lovemaking? Where did that fall in your great scheme? Since it seems like you planned everything down to the letter."

The time for lies was over. "It was always a possibility if that would help me get closer to you, to get you to contact Freihof. He's going to kill thousands of people if we don't stop him. I was willing to do just about anything, including faking intimacy with the woman I thought might be in league with him."

He moved slightly closer to her, not expecting her to respond. "But it didn't take me long to figure out you weren't working with him. The opposite—you were running from him. It didn't take me long to see the brave, kind, smart woman you were. I made love to you purely for selfish reasons. Because I couldn't stay away from you. I had to know how you felt, how you tasted."

He touched her ankles—hell, he would stay here perched at her feet forever if it meant she would listen to him, forgive him, give them another chance—his heart swelling when she didn't flinch away again.

"I did everything wrong with this case, Peaches. Everything I told you, all the stories, facts about my life, almost every single part of it was true. I wanted to get to know you, and I wanted you to know the real me."

"Family farm?"

"True."

"Special forces?"

He nodded. "Also true. These are all things I never should've been honest about in an undercover operation. If you'd been playing me, you would've known things about me—about my family—that could destroy me and them. But I couldn't stop myself from telling you. Just like I couldn't stop myself from asking about all of you. Not just the stuff that might possibly help us catch Freihof."

"So plan B or Q, or whatever derivative you ended up at, was to ask me to out myself. To give up the tiniest bit of safety I've had for six years and rub the fact that I'm alive in his face. To be bait."

"We will protect you. He won't get anywhere near

you. We just needed to get him to show up where we are ready, for him to go on the defensive." He moved closer. "I would've asked you, Peaches. Begged you to help, if needed. Explained about the biological weapons and how many people he could kill indiscriminately."

"I already knew Damien was a monster. Did I ever tell you about how one of his favorite games when I didn't do something right, didn't do something perfect, was to choke me until I stopped breathing and then revive me? Or leave me trapped in a cage while he left the house? Sometimes for days?"

She moved her legs away from his touch, but her voice held no emotion as she said the words. No anger. No fear. She should be screaming, railing, not sitting there in the chair like she was discussing the weather.

She was in shock. He needed to give her more time to adjust to what he was, who he was, what had happened. It was unreasonable to expect her to just be okay with it.

In many ways he wished she was furious at him, even hated him, screaming that she would never forgive him. That would be better than this despondency.

He put his hands on the outside of her chair, trapping her in his arms in the only way he knew how. "I'm sorry, Peaches. Sorry that I didn't think there was any other way to do this. Sorry that you were too damn gorgeous and delicious for me to resist in that cabin, even though it broke every rule I've ever had. Sorry that I blindsided you with the press when we got here. But I knew, deep in my gut, that you would help us. That you would play the role you needed to in order to help us draw Freihof out. To save so many lives."

She stared at him with those bruised blue eyes for

long moments. "Yes, you're right. I've always been the perfect puppet."

"Natalie..."

She stood, and he stood with her. He wanted to pull her into his arms, to just hold her. Not that it would make everything okay or even bring her closer to forgiving him, but because she looked like she was about to crack into a million pieces.

"No." She held a hand out, stopping him. "You can't touch me. Not right now. I'm sorry."

"Don't be sorry. I understand."

She gave a self-deprecating shake of her head. "You're right. I shouldn't be sorry." She walked toward the door, turning back as she reached it.

"You were right, Ren. Your gut was right. I would've helped you draw Damien out. Maybe not at first, like when Brandon and Andrea came to talk to me. But once I understood the true scope of the situation, I would've helped."

"I know," he whispered, feeling his heart crack a little more in his chest.

"You're a good man who had a job to do that I happened to be part of. I know that. You had to do what you had to do. Me included."

He couldn't help it—he was at her side of the room in seconds, arms trapping her once again as he brought his forehead to the side of her head. Breathed in her scent.

"Nothing about us was fake, Natalie. Not being able to keep my hands off you was the truest thing I've ever felt. I regret that I wasn't able to be honest with you, but I'll never regret the days we spent together in that cabin. Getting to know you. Getting to taste you. Getting to love you."

He felt her suck in a shuddery breath, leaning into him just the slightest bit.

"Then I'll tell you what I would've told you if we'd come at this problem together from the beginning. If I'd been working with you and had agreed to all this."

"What?"

"I won't blame you for what happens. And you shouldn't blame yourself."

"What do you mean?"

"When Damien finds me and takes me…" Her voice cracked. "Whatever it is he ends up doing to me, it's not your fault."

His teeth ground in his jaw. "Not. Going. To. Happen."

Now she turned completely to him, stepped closer and rested her forehead on his chest.

"You trust your gut. It's what makes you a good agent. Made you a good solider. Your gut told you this plan was going to work and I was going to help you."

He kept his arms braced on the wall even though her head was touching his chest. He knew she didn't want to be pulled to him. "Yes. I trust my gut."

"I trust my gut, too. And my gut says that Damien is going to find me and he's going to kill me."

Chapter Twenty

"By now Freihof will have seen the footage of Natalie. Our best estimates based on where he was last seen in South Carolina are that he will be here in twenty-four to thirty hours," Brandon Han said. A big chunk of the Omega Critical Response team—including Brandon's wife, Andrea, Steve Drackett, Lillian Muir and Aston Fitzgerald—were all sitting around the kitchen table of the safe house on the outskirts of Westwater.

These were the people who had faced down Freihof in the past, who had, or very nearly had, lost everything to him. The ones who were most invested in catching him.

"So we give him twelve hours tops before we're on red alert," Fitzgerald shot back. "Because we all know that Freihof is always at least one step ahead of where we think he is."

Ren was listening to the team but his eyes were on Natalie. He'd tried to talk her into sleeping. Even had Andrea try. Natalie had rested for about twenty minutes, but had been up wandering around the house for the last half hour.

"We have law enforcement at every major airport looking for him. Hopefully he is so desperate to get to her quickly that he'll decide air travel is worth the risk," Steve said. "We've also got all smaller regional airports on alert. If anyone files a sudden flight plan to any of the airports within a hundred and fifty miles of here, we'll get a notification. But our guess is he'll probably drive, rather than risk detection."

"I'll still be ready with my sniper rifle by dawn," Ashton, one of the best marksmen in the country, assured them. Freihof had dared to bring Ashton's beautiful toddler daughter into this bloody fight, a fact Ashton wouldn't be forgetting any time before ever.

Natalie walked to another window, looking out it, her arms wrapped protectively around her middle. No amount of words had been able to convince her that they weren't going to let Freihof get to her.

Brandon looked in Natalie's direction also. "We'll do one more press interview with Natalie in the morning. Just to make doubly sure she's seen, then we'll get her to Omega HQ for safety."

She had to be able to hear them, but nothing changed about her demeanor to indicate that she was listening at all. She just walked over to the door and stood looking at it. Then began to gently rock herself back and forth, just like she had...

Damn. Ren was out of his chair and over to her in an instant, her face confirming what he'd feared. She hadn't been just wandering around the house. She was panicking over the door and window locks like she had in the cabin.

Her face was devoid of color. Her nails had dug into the skin at her elbows until they were bloody. She was staring at the locks on the windows.

He had done this to her. By selfishly using the time

they had to be physically close to her rather than prepare her for what was coming—this battle with Freihof—he'd tossed her back into this fight with no warning and no mental weapons.

"Natalie."

She didn't blink. He gently pried her hands from her arms. "Peaches."

She finally looked at him. Explaining to her again that they weren't going to let Freihof get to her wouldn't help. Instead, he drew her closer to the window.

"C'mon. I'll check the locks with you, okay?"

"I already know they're locked. But I can't stop checking. I know it's stupid, but I can't…"

He wrapped an arm around her and pulled her forward. "Sometimes we fight our demons. Sometimes we just learn to live with them. Either way, it's okay." They stepped forward and tried the lock of the first window together.

When they made it over to the second, he stopped her. "We'll finish checking all the locks, but before that, I want to give you something. Maybe it will help you feel better."

He pulled out the tiny piece of equipment Steve had given him. It was flat and not much larger than a dime, sticky on one side.

"This is a tracking device. Omega Sector agents often use something similar when they're on undercover missions. I'd like you to keep it on even when you get to Omega HQ tomorrow. That way I'll always be able to tell where you are."

"Will you be able to hear what I'm saying?"

He swallowed a smile at her natural inquisitive nature overtaking her fear for just a moment. "No, location only. It's not a communication device, so you can't hear me and vice versa."

"Where do I put it?"

He gently lifted her beautiful mane of blond hair from her shoulder and placed it behind her ear. "We've discovered this is the least obtrusive place for an agent to put it. If it becomes unsticky, just get it wet to reactivate the adhesive."

"Okay."

He reluctantly let her hair fall and moved his hand away from her neck with one more soft caress.

"And I have a phone for you, too." He handed her the little red device. "It doesn't have any bells or whistles, but you can use it to call me anytime once you get to Omega. Anytime. For any reason. It's going to be okay."

She tried to smile, but all the fear was back. "I know you believe that. I hope I'll be able to believe it soon, as well." She glanced back at the windows, tension once again strumming through her lithe body, and he knew her need to check them had returned.

"Let's finish double-checking the locks. Maybe then you can get some rest."

"I've already double-checked them," she whispered. "It will just get worse from here. I can't help it. I move from lock to lock, rechecking them even though I know I've already made certain they're secure."

He wanted to take her into his arms more than he wanted his next breath, but knew she would resist. Knew fighting him would just add to her burden.

"Can I help with anything?" Andrea stepped up next to them and asked.

"Do we have any sticky notes? Or even just paper

and tape?" he asked her. "Natalie uses them to keep track of what locks she's checked."

Her face crumpled. "It's stupid, I know."

Andrea touched her on the arm. "Actually, it's a pretty smart coping mechanism that helps you keep situational OCD under control. Did a psychiatrist suggest it to you?"

"No, I came up with it on my own."

Andrea smiled. "Then I think it's even smarter. Let me see what I can find, then I'll help."

Ren turned around and found the rest of the team there.

"We'll all help," Steve said.

Natalie just stared at them. "B-but I'm your enemy," she finally stuttered.

"No, you're not." Ren kept his arm wrapped around her. "You've lost more than all of us at Damien's hands. And you're never going to fight him alone again. Now you've got a family who will fight with you."

"Let's get those locks checked," Steve said. "Because that's how family gets through things. Together."

NATALIE FINALLY FELL asleep on the couch with the lights on and everyone sitting and talking around her.

That was fine with Ren; he was going to have trouble letting her out of his sight until Freihof was caught. Even once she was at Omega HQ it wouldn't be easy for him.

Everyone had moved the conversation into the kitchen to give Natalie some quiet. Ren had stayed. Watching her from the chair next to the couch, wishing he had the right to scoop her up in his arms and hold her while she slept.

"I would say you've got it bad, brother, but I think you already know that." Steve, one of Ren's oldest friends and colleagues, took the chair across from him.

"That doesn't mean she's going to forgive me for what I did."

"Maybe. Maybe not. But at least at the end of the day, she'll be safe."

Ren nodded. If she couldn't forgive him, couldn't trust him again, he'd have to find a way to live with that. But Steve was right. At least he would know she was safe.

"I just got a call from Homeland."

Ren rolled his eyes. "Knew that was coming."

"We'll fight it. All of us. Everybody knows things happen in the field that are unexpected. You have to make decisions on the fly and sometimes—"

"I'm out, Steve." There wasn't any point in anyone taking a political bullet for him.

"Is that what you want?"

Ren shrugged again. "It's what I need. I've been under too long."

Steve studied him for a long minute. "Got other plans? Hell, Ren, you basically started Omega. It's been your baby all these years."

"Might be time to have a different kind of baby. I do believe you know a little something about that."

"Don't force me to get out pictures. My son is three months old now and I have at least one for every day of his existence." Steve chuckled before turning serious. "What will you do?"

"Go back to Montana, I think. I miss it. It wasn't until I was talking in such detail to Natalie about the farm that I realized how much."

Ashton stuck his head in from the kitchen. "You guys, we've got problems. This town isn't really equipped for the number of people we brought here with all the press, not to mention gawkers. There's a fight at the one bar in town and a fire has broken out at the hotel. Locals are asking for assistance."

Ren shot a look at Steve. "I'm not leaving Natalie."

"I'll send Brandon, Lillian and Ashton. This may be just what it seems like, too many people in a town with not enough amenities. But it doesn't change our overall mission. Freihof is the priority."

Ren looked over at Andrea, who wouldn't be going, and she just shrugged. "I'm not like Lillian in a fight—I'm more of a liability. And it would split Brandon's focus. He worries about me."

When the team left it was Ren's turn to pace from window to window—sidearm in hand. Dividing and conquering was definitely one of Freihof's MOs. Fire was, too.

But Ren would stand guard over Natalie while she slept. The magnitude of the fact that she trusted him enough, at least subconsciously, to sleep was not lost on him. Her brain had accepted that it was okay to shut down, that Ren wouldn't let anything happen to her.

And it was one hundred percent correct.

A couple hours later, looking a little worse for wear, the team returned. Yes, there had been fighting. Yes, also a fire. But nothing that suggested there was any further nefarious intent behind them.

Ren still didn't sleep. Even with the tracking device on her he wasn't sure he'd be able to sleep until he knew Natalie was safely within the fortitude of Omega HQ's walls. Nobody got in there.

He hated to wake her up a few hours later, knowing she needed the rest, and her body, which she'd abused so badly saving his life, needed to heal. But it was time. They were doing one last press conference before she was taken to Omega. After that, an agent of her general build and coloring would stay here for a few days to see if Freihof took the bait.

Ren didn't even want to think about what would happen if Freihof was more cautious than they gave him credit for. If he didn't come after Natalie—or who he thought was Natalie—over the next few days. If he decided to bide his time, wait for their guard to drop.

It would eat at Natalie's very sanity. And there wouldn't be a damned thing Ren could do about it except continuously put her in danger in hopes of luring Freihof out.

The entire team was exhausted but on high alert as they entered the school auditorium once again to meet the press. The county had given the kids the day off due to all the hoopla, but the school was packed with media and townspeople.

Ren kept his arm around Natalie as the mayor of Westwater introduced them. Ren stepped up to the podium, giving everyone his most charming smile. Their plan had to work this time. They needed to draw Freihof out.

"Thank you all for coming. As you can see, Natalie and I are alive and well." Out of the corner of his eye he saw her flinch at his use of her name. She was on to the fact that he said her name as much as possible. "We appreciate you even thinking we're newsworthy—"

"We don't!" someone screamed from the back of the room. "Get out of our town!"

Then Ren threw Natalie to the ground as shots rang out in the air and people began screaming.

Chapter Twenty-One

Natalie wasn't sure what was happening as Ren's weight rested on top of her, his hand keeping her head pinned protectively to the ground. She could vaguely hear panicked screams after a couple more shots were fired.

Ren kept them behind the large podium. A few minutes later Steve Drackett crawled over to them.

"Is it Damien?" she asked, trying to keep panic at bay.

"Not according to the sheriff." Steve kept low, like them. "Looks like it's some local troublemakers. Definitely heard shots fired from multiple locations, so that would make sense."

"We need to get you out of here. Back to the safe house," Ren said. "Then preferably immediately to Omega HQ. This little stunt—if it is, in fact, some local yokels—may change everything. May spook Freihof."

"It will definitely get a different type of media coverage now."

They crawled over to the side of the stage and then out the door. Ren and Steve kept her sandwiched between them, both of them with their guns in their hands, Ren with his arm wrapped firmly around her once they got off the stage, as they rushed to the side entrance.

A police car was waiting there in the small covered alley, as well as two police officers in their tan uniforms. Ren and Steve obviously already knew them both.

"Levell, Stutz, we need you to get Ren and Natalie back to the safe house and stay with them," Steve instructed the two younger men before turning to Ren. "I'm going to stay here. They'll need help with—"

A call came through loudly over Levell's police radio. "We've got a confirmed sighting of Freihof on the north side of the building. Exit that leads out to the playground!"

Natalie felt bile rising in her throat.

"That's Jensen," Stutz said. Both men looked ready to burst into action.

"No." Ren stopped them. "You two get her to the safe house. You don't leave her under any circumstances, you got it?"

He turned to Natalie. "We're going to catch him. Right now, okay? This is all going to be over soon." He threaded his hands into her hair and kissed her hard and fast. "And then I will find some way to make you forgive me and give us another chance."

Before she could say anything, he and Steve were gone. Sprinting in the direction of where Damien had been seen.

Desperate fear clawed up her belly. What if Damien killed Ren? She knew firsthand how diabolically brilliant her ex was.

"I can't believe we're this close to the action and have to be on babysitting detail instead," Levell said as he opened the squad car door for Natalie. "No offense."

"I think you're quite a bit closer to the action than you think."

Her whole world spun in a spiral of grayness as she heard the voice that haunted her nightmares. The one she hadn't heard in six years.

Damien.

She spun in time to see him raise a gun with a silencer on it and shoot first Levell, then Stutz, in the chest. Both men fell to the ground, not even able to draw their weapons. "Allow me to take over babysitting duty of my wife."

He turned to Natalie, smiling. "Hi, honey."

She opened her mouth to scream, but he brought the gun and placed it close to her cheek. "One sound and you'll be as dead as they are, wifey. Get in the car."

She stood rooted in place. If she went with Damien, she knew her life was over.

His eyes narrowed, the promise of violence clear in them. "If you don't get in the damn car right now, I will hunt down every single person in your beloved Omega Sector team and kill them slowly in front of you. You will do what I say, Natalie. You know what happens when you disobey."

She could feel the past coming back to crash over her, drowning her. His rules. His command. The knowledge that she had to be perfect like he wanted her to be or the pain would come.

She had to avoid the pain at all costs.

"Yes, sir." She got in the car; he followed, snatching her phone from her and keeping his gun trained on her.

"That's more like my perfect beauty."

They drove out of Westwater, Damien providing directions, Natalie following them. Once they were a few miles outside of town he had her pull over in a parking lot and change to a car he'd parked there. He put her in the passenger seat, zip-tying her wrists together, and got in behind the wheel.

She kept herself as far away from Damien as she could, huddled over against the door. Trying to get her mind to work through the fear that seemed to swallow her whole.

"Looking at you last night, I thought all our training, our attempt to make you into the perfect wife we always knew you could be, had gone to waste." He reached over and stroked a finger down her arm. "But now I'm thinking maybe with some correction you can once again be trained to be perfect."

He hadn't touched her up to this point. The feel of his skin on hers tore something open in her.

"Do. Not. Touch. Me." She spat the words, dragging her arm away from his fingers.

He didn't even stop driving as he backhanded her. Natalie's face slammed into the window and she tasted blood.

"Evidently it will take a good deal more training to get you back to where you were. The perfect wife. I daresay I am up for the challenge."

"I was never your perfect wife. I left you. I ran away."

He shook his head. "You became confused. I'm willing to overlook that. You'll have to be punished for it, of course, but I am willing to give you another chance."

Something inside Natalie snapped further. No. She would not go with him. Ren and the rest of the team would've figured out she was gone soon if not already. She had to slow Damien down.

"I pretended I was dead for six years rather than live one more minute with you, Damien. I wasn't confused."

That earned her another slap on her abused face. "You'd been shot by those careless bastards at Omega Sector. I saw all the blood. You couldn't have known what you were doing."

She reached up and wiped blood from her split lip. "Oh, but I did, Damien. I took the opportunity to run as far and as fast as I could from you. I knew exactly what I was doing when I made sure you would think I was dead and I hoped I would never see you again."

She saw his fists tighten on the steering wheel but she didn't care.

"I pretended to die to get away from you, Damien. I'd rather die for real than go back to being married to you. Omega Sector is going to find you and they're going to stop you."

Damien pulled over to the side of the back road and slammed on the brakes. He grabbed her hair and yanked her over until she was just inches from his face.

"Your precious Omega agents are going to have way too much on their hands to be worried about you. They're going to be busy dealing with the fallout from their own ineptitude."

"With your biological warfare canisters? Yeah, they know all about that."

He rolled his eyes. "I would hope so. If I'd made it any more obvious that it was me who had them, it would've had to be with engraved letterhead. But they don't know when and they don't know where, do they?"

He yanked her hair again, before letting go and starting the car once more. She reached up to touch her tender scalp and felt it. The tracker Ren had put at the back of her ear. She'd forgotten about it.

And Damien had no idea it was on her. All she needed to do was keep near him and it would lead the team right to them.

But Damien was never going to let them have her. She knew that. He would kill her before he would let her go, even if he was going to die, too. But at least they would stop him from whatever mad destruction he'd planned.

"The canisters are in the car even as we speak. I hadn't planned to use them all at one time in one location, but you helped me realize there's a blot in my past that needs to be erased. From now on, when I think of this place, it won't be because it was where you legally became mine, but because of what I did here today."

Natalie looked around more closely. "We're going back to Grand Junction?"

"Yes, to city hall, where we were married. To love and to honor. A vow you've decided to forget."

Just like he'd somehow forgotten *cherish and protect* when he'd broken all her fingers.

But as much as she wanted to stand up to Damien—and for the first time in her life she really did—she needed to lie. To remain docile. To distract him until Ren and his team could get here and stop him.

They drove in silence, Natalie struggling to figure out what to say, what to do, in order to stop Damien. Cry? Beg? He would love that. Could she do it? Maybe to save lives.

As they passed the city limits sign for Grand Junction, she knew she had to do *something*.

"Part of me missed you," she whispered, trying not to choke on the words.

"Is that so? Evidently not enough to return to me where you belong, even though you were my wife."

"You married someone else." Dissolving their marriage. Thank God.

"She looked like you. I thought she would be a better model, more easily trained. But when she decided to betray me, she had to be eliminated."

Natalie didn't even know how to respond to that. To the fact that he'd killed another woman who couldn't live up to his sick standards.

Damien drove in silence for many minutes.

"Tell me, Natalie. That man you were with out in the woods, the man you were hiking with, Warren Thompson. Were you intimate with him? Did you allow him to touch your body, which should've only ever belonged to me?"

"Damien..." Telling him the truth would only bring pain.

He shook his head as if overwhelmed by sadness. "You are not the person I'd hoped you'd be, Natalie."

"Can we go somewhere and talk? I don't want to go to city hall."

He looked over at her and smiled. "Yes, we can go somewhere. And I have no intention of taking you to city hall."

Good. That at least bought her—bought Ren—more time.

They drove to the other side of town and out of the most populated area. He turned into what looked like a field, driving through a gate, and down a paved road of some sort of park.

Then she realized what it was. A very high-end, private cemetery. "Damien, what is this place? Why are we here?"

"I want you to see your final resting place, my dear. The place where I buried an empty casket. The place I came to grieve my dead, perfect wife. I realize now that my wife did die six years ago. My wife would've never let another man touch her. I have no wife. And soon that casket won't be empty."

Natalie blanched as the truth hit her. There was no more time. He'd brought her here to kill her. She had to get away from him right now. Not even thinking about the consequence, Natalie reached over, yanked open the door and threw herself out of the car.

She cracked the ground with a bone-rattling thud and struggled through the pain to get up, her restrained hands hindering her. She heard Damien stop the car and forced herself to begin running toward the trees. As soon as she was off the road her feet became bogged down in snow.

She knew there wasn't any use. Damien was bigger. Stronger. Faster. But she pushed herself as fast as she could go. He still had her phone, so she'd have to pray the tracker would work.

And that she was buying Ren enough time to get to her.

She screamed as a hand grabbed her shoulder, jerking her down into the snow. The icy whiteness permeated everything.

"Thank you for at least running in the right direction," Damien said. He reached down and grabbed her by the hair, yanking her forward. She stumbled to keep up with him, since it was either that or be dragged.

"The minute you let someone touch your body you should've known you would never be worthy of me again. Now I'm grateful I had the foresight to buy such a private burial plot for you six years ago. Nobody ever comes out here."

He continued marching forward. She threw her hands up to his wrist to ease the pressure of the pull on her scalp. Finally, he stopped and threw her down and into the snow.

Right in front of a casket that had obviously just been dug out of the ground.

"Ironically, Omega Sector were the ones who dug it up. I guess it confirmed that you were alive. I can't believe you would choose them over me. I gave you a home. A life. Everything."

His foot came up and crashed against her midsection in a vicious kick. The shock hit her first—she couldn't inhale—and then the pain exploded. She curled herself in a ball, the cold seeping in everywhere.

"Remember how you used to beg me to let you out of the snow during your punishments, Natalie? I shouldn't have. I should've let you suffer and die out there. But now I'm going to let you suffer and die out *here*. You're going to be inside that casket, knowing that no one is ever coming for you."

"Damien, please…" She finally got words out. Her begging now wasn't to buy more time. It was in a desperate attempt to save her own life.

Could Ren possibly get here in time?

"I would love to stay here and watch you suffer, but I have a limited window of opportunity at city hall. I've got to give your Omega friends something to do with their time. A few thousand dead bodies ought to do it."

He leaned down and whispered in her ear. "But don't worry, darling. I'll come by and visit your grave site often. Especially now that there will be a dead body to mourn."

Natalie closed her eyes, facing the facts. If Ren used the tracker to find her and she was already dead, they'd never be able to find Damien and stop him.

Thousands would die.

If she put the tracker on Damien now, the team would go straight to him. Maybe they would be able to stop him.

But Natalie would die.

Silently, she wished she'd had the strength to tell Ren last night that she would've forgiven him. That she wished they'd had more time.

But now she would never have a chance.

She opened her eyes, reaching behind her ear and picking off the tracker. The wetness from her fingers immediately made it sticky again.

"One kiss?" she whispered to Damien.

She leaned in close and placed the tracker on the back of his neck as she touched him. She prayed it would be enough.

His lips touched hers and for once she was thankful the snow had numbed her and she couldn't feel a thing, especially his touch on her lips.

"The kiss of death," Damien said, smiling.

He picked her up and put her in the casket in the hole in the ground. She tried to keep her composure, her strength, her pride. Tried not to let Damien know the depths of her terror. But as the lid closed and she heard the thumping of earth being poured over her, she began to scream in terror.

She could hear Damien's laugh over it all.

Chapter Twenty-Two

Ren and Steve sprinted toward the north side of the school. Getting through the auditorium was nearly impossible with the pandemonium from the gunfire a few minutes ago. Chairs had been thrown everywhere. A few people had been hurt in their desperate need to evacuate.

They didn't stop. Unless someone was dying, they would have to wait for other assistance.

"Sheriff, tell your man not to engage Freihof," Steve was shouting into his walkie-talkie as he ran. "He is to be considered extremely dangerous whether he looks armed or not."

They burst through the door on the other side of the building, bringing them outside. Jensen, the deputy who'd called in the Freihof sighting, was waiting there, walkie-talkie in one hand, his phone in the other.

"Freihof ran off toward the trees." He looked down at his phone again. "Hurry, maybe we can still catch him."

He and Steve bolted toward the trees, the deputy right behind them.

"Lillian—" Steve got on the walkie again "—Freihof's headed into the woods from the north side of the building."

Ren heard her curse. "Okay, Ashton and I are switching directions and heading straight into the woods from the east side. We'll try to cut him off."

"Do these woods lead anywhere? To a road? Another town?" Ren asked Jensen.

He shook his head. "Just more woods. It's all part of the McInnis Canyon National Park."

"He could be waiting to pick us off, Steve," Ren said as they slowed down, taking cover in the trees. Shooting from long range would be a little anticlimactic for Freihof, but Ren wouldn't put it past him.

"I can't figure out why he would even run in this direction at all." Steve said. "He's always used people for cover to get away, not nature."

Ren nodded. "Or why he wouldn't be in disguise. It's not like him to just rush into a situation where he can be easily identified."

They each kept a very careful eye for movement in the trees, progress frustratingly slow. They didn't want to give Damien room to circle back around.

Eventually, they met up with Lillian and Ashton, who'd been coming from the opposite direction.

"Nothing?" Ren asked.

Lillian shook her head. "He didn't cross by us. He's either hiding or has gone farther out into the woods."

Brandon's voice came over the walkie-talkie. "I've got confirmation that it was definitely the Sheffield cousins, well-known troublemakers in this county, who were responsible for the shooting this morning. No one was hurt—they were just trying to create chaos because of, and I quote, 'All them peoples who think they can just piss on Westwater had another think coming.'"

Steve rolled his eyes. "Great."

"But I got hold of one of the Sheffields as he was being arrested and it ends up that it was someone matching Freihof's general description who gave them today's brilliant idea in the first place."

Ren stopped moving forward. "It was a brilliant idea to shake things up. To separate us. But not if he was just going to run into the damn wilderness. Only if he had a much bigger plan…"

Like separating him from Natalie.

He turned and looked at the deputy who'd led them this far. The man was sweating well beyond what should be normal for the slower speed they were moving and the man's overall fitness level.

"What did you do?" he asked, fear closing around his throat so tightly he could hardly breathe.

"I'm sorry." Jensen began to cry. "He sent me a picture of my wife and daughter, tied up. Said if I didn't tell you I'd seen him run into the woods he'd kill—"

Ren didn't wait to hear the rest; he turned and began running as fast as he could back toward the school.

"Levell, Stutz, come in," Steve yelled into the walkie-talkie. "Report. Sheriff, we need a report right damn now from Levell and Stutz. We left Natalie with them."

There was not a sound from them. Ren didn't even slow down to curse, just pushed his body faster than he ever had. He could hear Lillian and Ashton right behind him.

"I need any available officer to the south side of the auditorium," Steve was yelling into the walkie through panted breaths.

As Ren rounded the corner of the high school, someone stepped in front of him and he had to dodge to keep from knocking the guy over. He didn't so much as pause. Every fiber of his being was focused on getting back to Natalie.

He ripped open the door on the far side of the auditorium, leaping over fallen chairs and broken camera stands, bolting up to the stage and out the back door where he'd taken Natalie not thirty minutes before.

Weapon still in hand, he burst through the outer door that led to the alley.

His worst nightmare met him there: two fallen officers lying in puddles of blood and Natalie nowhere in sight.

He planted himself on the ground beside Levell to check for a pulse while someone else did the same on Stutz.

Ren shook his head. There was nothing. Levell was dead. Kid hadn't been wearing his vest.

"I've got a pulse here," Lillian said, reaching in to put pressure on the wound. "But tell the ambulance to hurry the hell up."

Ren stood and looked at Steve. "I gave Natalie the tracker last night. We can follow her, but I've got to get to the safe house to get the computer with the program."

Steve nodded, still talking to emergency services. Lillian stayed with Stutz, but Ashton took off running with Ren. They were in the house, booting up the laptop, when Ashton spoke.

"If Freihof was talking to those jerks last night, inciting them to riot this morning, then he either got exceptionally lucky or he already knew about this little plan."

He'd known. The bastard had known they were coming to Westwater before they'd even gotten there. "I think he has some sort of tap on Steve's Omega phone.

It's the only means I've used to communicate anything about Natalie. Freihof is the one who tortured and killed the owners of the Santa Barbara beach house, probably to try to get answers for what info was missing from the phone calls. But he definitely knew Natalie and I would get here last night. Steve and I talked about that specifically."

"You think the fire and fight last night were instigated by him, too?"

Why the hell was the computer taking so damn long to boot? "Undoubtedly."

"We're going to get her back," Ashton whispered as they both stared at the screen.

Had someone told him this when Freihof had taken Ashton's wife, Summer, and her daughter, Chloe? Ren hoped it had worked better than the words of comfort were working on him right now.

He knew what Freihof was capable of. Knew the ways he had tortured Natalie.

Knew she had to be scared out of her mind right now. Freihof had nearly forty-five minutes on them.

The ways someone could hurt another person in forty-five minutes had Ren breaking out in a cold sweat.

The computer finally booted and Ren started the program that would track Natalie, breathing a sigh of relief when he saw the dot on the map was still moving. Movement meant life.

He connected the 4G from his phone to the laptop. "Let's roll. We'll be able to get a more accurate location as we get closer."

Ashton jogged with him to the car. "Where are we headed?"

"Grand Junction."

"Anything special about that place?"

"Definitely to Freihof."

REN CURSED UNDER his breath when the tracker stopped. Ashton was already driving well over one hundred miles per hour. The rest of the team—Steve, Lillian, Brandon—were five minutes behind them. A number of other Omega Critical Response team members were on their way to Grand Junction via helicopter.

Damien Freihof was going down today. He would never hurt anyone else again; these agents were going to make sure of it.

Ren just prayed it was in time to save Natalie. That she—who had suffered the most at Freihof's hands already—would not be his last victim.

Before they could home in on an exact location, the tracker began moving again. A few minutes later it stopped again. And stayed stopped this time. When Ren realized where it was he cursed out loud.

"What?" Ashton said.

"They're at city hall."

"Why would he go there?"

Ren grimaced. "That's where he and Natalie got married nearly ten years ago." He called Steve and put it on speakerphone.

"The tracker stopped at city hall. I think Freihof is trying to make some sort of sick romantic gesture, marry Natalie again."

Over Ren's dead body.

"How far out are you?" Steve asked.

"Maybe six minutes," Ashton responded, never letting up on the speed.

"Okay, we're right behind you. Everybody get your comm units on, channel one."

"Steve." Ren couldn't hide the desperation in his voice. "He's not going to let her go willingly. If we go barreling in there, we might get Freihof, but we'll lose Natalie."

"That's not going to happen. Neither the barreling nor the losing Natalie. Ashton, city hall probably isn't going to have a lot of windows, but see if you can find a vantage point on a neighboring roof once we know what room they're in, in case it comes down to a long-distance shot."

"Roger that, boss."

"We'll get Lillian up in an air duct," Steve continued. "Nobody ever expects the ass-kicking midget dropping out of the ceiling."

In the background, Ren could hear Lillian's choice words at that description.

"We've got Roman and Derek coming with heavier firearms and expertise on explosives. And even Joe Matarazzo, just in case negotiations will help."

In other words, the entire Omega team.

A few minutes later, they were pulling up in front of city hall. Steve was still giving out orders as to who would handle what, since a priority would be clearing the building as much as possible before anything went down.

This was Steve's team. Ren may have been the one who originally created Omega Sector, but Steve had turned the Critical Response Division into a well-oiled machine.

"She's in an office in the southwest corner of the

building," Ren said, reading the information from the tracker into the comm unit.

"According to building plans," Derek spoke from the helicopter, "that's the wedding licensing section."

Ashton grabbed his sharpshooter rifle and sprinted toward the roof of the building next door.

Ren waited for the rest to arrive, ushering civilians out and away from the outside of the building. It went against his every instinct not to burst in on his own. But Steve was right; if there was anything that Freihof had taught Omega Sector in his attacks over the past few months it was that their greatest strengths were in how they worked together.

Within a few minutes the rest of the team was there, moving into position with a silent nod at Ren. Immediately, they began to get as many people out of the building as possible. Local police were showing up to help, setting up barricades. Seeing the team, how capable and functional they all were, Ren had his first sense of true hope.

Until Ashton spoke into the comm unit from his spot on the roof.

"Uh, guys, I've got eyes on Freihof and we've got some bad news. He has a pressure switch in his hand. If I take a shot, whatever he's rigged to explode is going with him. And given that he has multiple canisters of that biological contaminant, I'm going to assume that's what he has planned to go."

Ren cursed under his breath. "Is Natalie okay?"

"Natalie's not with him at all."

Chapter Twenty-Three

"Are you sure she's not with him?" Ren asked.

"At least she's not in that room," Ashton responded. "It's got big windows with no curtains, so I've got a pretty unobstructed view."

"I can confirm," Lillian chimed in from her location. "Damn it, I can't get all the way over to that set of offices from this air duct, but I can see them from this vent. Freihof is just standing here, like he's reminiscing. And no Natalie. But, Ren, I think in Freihof's other hand is Natalie's red phone."

Ren cursed under his breath. How the hell was the tracker in the room if Natalie wasn't? If she wasn't there, where the hell was she?

"Lillian, do you think he's about to blow the whole building?" Steve asked.

"I don't know. But we need to do something fast. Because clearing the building if he uses that biological weapon is not going to help. It will spread. Radius will be devastating."

Ren turned to Steve. "I'm calling him on Natalie's phone. If he's about to release that pressure trigger, we need to do something to distract him. He doesn't know we're here, and I won't let him know. Let's just get as many people out and back as far as possible without causing a panic."

Steve nodded, and the rest of the team immediately began moving fast around him.

"I'll keep trying to find a way to get closer so I can get the drop on him," Lillian said. "It might mean crawling back to the other side of the building and coming in from that direction."

Ashton added, "Ren, I need a word or phrase that lets me know to take him out. I don't think a direct shot is a good option with the pressure trigger, but we need one, anyway. I'll aim for the chest."

"Let's go with 'reign of terror.'"

"Appropriate. Roger that."

"Get him mad," Brandon came on the line and said. "He won't take himself—and hopefully everyone else—out if he's angry at you. Make him mad enough that he wants to live to come after you."

Ren pulled out his phone and dialed the number for the one he'd given to Natalie.

"Who's this?" he asked when Freihof answered, like he didn't already know.

"Who's this?" Freihof responded in kind.

"Let me talk to Natalie."

"I'm sorry. I'm afraid Natalie isn't here right now."

"And this is?" Ren wasn't sure exactly how to play this most effectively. Did Freihof know about Ren? That he was part of Omega?

"I'm Natalie's husband, Damien. You must be her... friend, Warren."

"I think you mean ex-husband, right, Damien? Since you remarried and all?"

"I never would've remarried if I had known my Natalie was alive. So as far as I'm concerned, that means we're still married."

Ren sighed dramatically and walked inside city hall. He didn't want Freihof to hear any activities or sirens and become suspicious. "Well, as far as the law—and every logical person on the planet—is concerned, when you signed a divorce decree from her, you officially became unmarried. No matter what you want."

There was a long moment of silence. "And why does it matter to you, Warren?"

"Because she's mine now, Damien. She's done with you and she's chosen me. That's just the way it is."

"No, that's not how it is at all." The words were bit out. "Not at all."

"Why don't you just let me talk to her, okay? Or maybe the three of us can meet somewhere and figure out the answer to this. Nobody has to get hurt. Just put Natalie on the phone, okay?"

"No, the choices have already been made. Natalie knew if she didn't choose me, then she wouldn't be choosing anyone."

Ice formed in Ren's veins. Was he too late? Was Natalie already dead? Or stuffed in a closet somewhere here, hurt? He hit the mute button on the phone and spoke into the comm unit.

"Steve, make sure your people are checking the utility closets and small spaces where he might have put Natalie."

"Roger that."

Ren unclicked the mute button. "Tell me where she is, Freihof."

Natalie had put the tracker on Freihof, so that gave Ren a measure of hope. She had to have been alive when she did that. But it could've been moments before her death, realizing Damien would leave once she was gone, and Omega would have no way of knowing where. That they would come to her rather than follow him.

And it was true. If Ren knew where Natalie was right now, he would leave this situation—damn the consequences—and find her. He refused to believe she was dead.

Freihof just laughed. "You know, I came to this place because it held special memories for me. Memories of a time before my relationship with Natalie became so tainted. She was so innocent when we first got married, do you know that? I thought she could become the perfect wife. I tried to teach her that."

"By abusing her?"

"Now, Warren." Freihof tsked. "You weren't there. You don't know. Some people might think my methods were a little harsh. But they were necessary. I was trying to make her *perfect*. Isn't that what everyone ultimately wants? Natalie would've thanked me eventually."

"Instead, she pretended she was dead and ran away and hid. Doesn't sound like thanking to me."

Freihof sighed. "I was feeling sad when I got here. Feeling that now that I was never going to see Natalie again, maybe it was time for me to die, too. That I would also just go out in the chaos I create."

Ren felt like all the oxygen had been sucked from the room. "Freihof…"

"But the good news is, talking to you has made me realize that it's not my time yet. That I want to see the fallout of my actions and how they affect Omega Sector. After all, they are the ones who took Natalie from me in the first place. She may have chosen to stay away from me—a sin she is currently regretting, at least for a little while longer—but Omega is what gave her the opportunity to run. You've made me realize I need to stay my course. It is not my destiny to die here today."

"Where is she, Freihof? If she's not with you, tell me where she is."

"No, Warren Thompson, you tell me *who* you are. I could find no record of you at all inside Omega Sector. No pictures in the files. You're so unimportant that you don't have a significant file yet. So, honestly, I'm not sure you're worth my time to talk to."

Ashton's voice came in Ren's ear. "Freihof's getting agitated. If he moves out of this office I might lose the shot."

"She chose me, Freihof. This whole plan in the woods may have started just with the intent to catch you, but we fell for each other. She chose me. Natalie is mine."

"No!" The word came through so loud Ren had to hold the phone away from his ear. "Natalie is *mine*."

"No, she's not, Damien. And you've always known that, haven't you? Tried to make her into something fake. Called it 'perfect' so you could justify abusing her. She chose me, you bastard."

The phone line clicked dead in his hand.

"Okay, it's working." It was Ashton's voice again. "He's taking off his explosives vest and placing it on... Oh, hell, there are the canisters. The biological contaminant canisters are definitely in the room with him. It looks like he's setting some sort of timer, but he's still got the kill switch in his hand."

Ren had to make his move now. "Steve, I'm going in. I've got to stop him. If he gets out we'll lose our shot and he'll blow the canisters, anyway. Ashton, be ready."

"We've gotten most of the civilians clear and locals are getting them back to the safety point. Every hazmat team in the state is on their way here," Steve said.

"Did anyone find Natalie in the building?"

"No, brother. I'm sorry."

"Okay, get your team out. Once I'm close enough to grab the pressure trigger and give Ashton the signal, he'll take him out. But we don't need to risk more lives."

"I'm staying," Lillian piped in.

"Me, too." That was Derek Waterman, SWAT leader.

One by one, the rest of the Critical Response unit chimed in. None of them would be leaving. They'd lost too much at Freihof's hands.

"I think you've got your answer, Ren. We take this bastard down together."

Ren dialed the number again as he walked down the corridor of city hall toward the office where Freihof was located.

"Warren," Freihof said as he answered. "I'm busy. I don't have time to talk to you anymore."

"I think you do, Freihof. Especially since I haven't quite been honest with you."

"Oh, yeah, about what?"

Ren opened the door to the office and ended the call. Freihof spun around, eyes wide.

"The fact that I'm here in city hall, for one thing," Ren said.

Freihof immediately held out the pressure trigger in front of him. "Stay back. If I let go of this trigger, this entire building is going to blow. So if you decide to shoot me, we die together."

Ren took out his sidearm and laid it on the ground,

then did the same with his ankle holster. "I'm not going to shoot you." He kicked them both away.

"How did you know where I was?"

He needed to convince Freihof that he really was just a peon in Omega and he was here alone. "I figured it out when you said that you were somewhere that was special to you and Natalie. I know you got married here."

"And all your Omega buddies?"

Ren took a tiny step forward. "You're right. Nobody is very interested in hearing what a peon has to say. They're all out searching your previous property and places you were known to go. I told them I was coming here but none of them would listen."

Freihof scoffed and relaxed just slightly. Ren took the opportunity to take another step toward the man.

"That's the problem with Omega. They're so gung-ho for action. Always with the working harder rather than smarter. Don't truly think like a *team*."

"Oh, I think they can when it's truly important. I just don't think I'm part of the team." Another half step. He was about eight feet from Freihof now. "Where is Natalie? That's all I care about."

"I'm afraid my wife will no longer be available to play the whore for you, Mr. Thompson."

"Is she dead?"

Freihof looked down at the phone in his hand and Ren quickly took another step forward.

"She's not dead yet. Although right about now I'd say she's probably wishing she was."

Ren swallowed the fear and fury Freihof's words ignited. "Tell me where she is and I'll let you go."

The other man laughed heartily. "See, this is the problem with newbies. You think you have control of the situation, but you don't. You don't get to tell me when I go or don't go, because I'm the one holding the pressure trigger." Freihof put the phone down on a chair next to a wall and picked up one of the guns Ren had kicked away. "And now I'm holding your gun. So I'm afraid I'm going to walk out of here right after I shoot you."

"Ren?" Ashton's voice was in his ear. "I've still got the shot."

Ren gave a slight shake of his head.

"Ren says no." This time it was Lillian's voice in his ear. Ashton would only have his sights trained on Freihof, and wouldn't be able to see Ren.

It wasn't time yet. Now that Freihof had weapons, he was feeling more secure. Ren was able to take another step closer under the guise of dejection. He was almost close enough. Would almost be able to take the leap and catch the pressure trigger once Ashton took his shot.

"Holding until the go phrase is given," Ashton muttered. "But hurry up or he's going to shoot you, Ren."

"My name isn't Warren Thompson." Another step.

Freihof's eyes narrowed. "So? I don't really care what your name is. Soon you'll be dead."

"My name is Ren McClement."

"I've still never heard of you."

Ren shook his head. "No, you wouldn't have. I'm not part of the Critical Response unit. I'm not part of any official Omega unit. Look at me, Freihof. Do I look like I'm a newbie?"

There. The last step he needed. Freihof actually took it for him.

For the first time Freihof didn't look totally in control. "Wh-what?"

"You're trying to finish Omega Sector? Then it's probably fitting that you meet me as you go down. I *created* Omega Sector, and it will not be destroyed by the likes of you. Your reign of terror is over."

Ren didn't wait to see if Ashton would shoot at the agreed upon words, just knew he would. Ren dove toward Freihof's arm that held the detonator, his hands closing over it as the force of Ashton's bullet ripped through Freihof's torso. They both ended up lying on the ground.

Blood was pouring out of Freihof's chest but he still brought the gun in his other hand up and pointed it at Ren, smiling. Ren couldn't let go of the trigger device to save himself.

But then another bullet hit Freihof's hand and knocked the gun out of it, at the same time yet another bullet came from a different direction. Freihof screamed, his arm falling to the side, useless.

Lillian lowered herself from the air-conditioning vent. "Nobody ever expects the ass-kicking midget dropping out of the ceiling."

"Or the really pissed-off SWAT member waiting outside the door," Roman Weber, whose shot had hit Freihof's shoulder, said. "I was in a coma for over a week because of you, you bastard, and you sent my pregnant woman to what would've been sure death."

The blood flowing from Freihof's wounds left him with just a few more seconds left to live. The rest of the Omega team filed in, but Ren ignored them.

"Where is she, Damien? This is over. Tell me where Natalie is."

Ren could hear the pleading in his voice, but he

didn't care. He would beg, threaten, grovel…whatever would get him Natalie back.

"My perfect wife. She wouldn't have wanted to live without me." His breaths wheezed in and out of his chest as more blood pooled on the floor. "I had nobody to bury last time. But this time I did. You may have saved your precious Omega, but you won't save—"

Freihof's eyes closed and his body went slack.

"No!" Ren screamed the word. Steve's hands closed over his and took the pressure trigger from him as Ren grabbed Freihof by his shirt. "Tell me where she is, damn it! Tell me."

But Freihof would never be telling anyone anything ever again.

And Natalie, his first victim, would also be his last.

As the team began preparing the canisters for containment, Steve put his hand on Ren's shoulder.

"She could be anywhere," Ren whispered. "If she's still alive at all. He could've buried her in the snow, like he used to do to torture her."

Although this time there wouldn't be anyone to let her out when she begged for mercy.

"She could be at his house. The house they lived at."

Steve nodded. "We're sending locals over there right now. They'll search every inch of that property."

Brandon Han burst through the door. "Andrea figured it out. It's Freihof's last words about not having a body to bury the first time, but now he did. We had the grave site exhumed two weeks ago when we found out Natalie was alive."

"Where?"

Brandon gave the address.

Ren didn't even respond, just sprinted out of the hallway and to his car. He knew beyond a shadow of a doubt that Brandon and Andrea were correct.

Damien had buried Natalie in her own coffin.

Chapter Twenty-Four

At some point Natalie's screams died off to raspy whispers. She had no idea how long she'd been inside the casket—minutes? Hours?

Eternity?

She'd tried to have the presence of mind enough to push at the lid. To attempt to bring her legs up so she could use them as leverage to push. But no matter what she did, it wouldn't budge.

She tried not to think of all the dirt and snow piled on top of her. Because now when she screamed with her broken voice it was just silent, which was somehow worse.

She had lived silent and alone and broken for so many years and now she was going to die silent and alone and broken.

She faded in and out; the moments of nothing were pure bliss that ended too soon. When she would come to, she would have a moment of trying to fight the panic before it would overwhelm her. She ripped at everything. Her clothes. Her hair. The skin of her neck. She knew when her fingers came away wet she had drawn her own blood.

She wished so badly she had kept the tracker on

her own body rather than put it on Damien. She didn't care how selfish it was. Then Ren would've found her. Would've gotten her out of here.

Finally, everything began to fade to a distance. She felt like she was floating. Almost swaying. Maybe she was running out of oxygen. How long could one survive buried underground?

Through the fog she swore she could almost hear somebody calling her name, but knew that couldn't be right. Her brain had finally broken completely and was playing tricks on her. The movement she felt had to be her own shudders. Surely this had to be near the end.

"Natalie, can you hear me?"

Yes, Ren, I can hear you. She didn't try to say the words since her voice was so wrecked. Plus, he wasn't really here, anyway.

"Hang on, Peaches, I'm coming."

The noises got louder. The jolting more pronounced. And then Natalie saw something she thought she was never going to see again.

Sunshine. She had to blink against the brightness of it.

"Oh, my God." Ren's hands were in her hair, over her heart, running up and down her arms. His lips were all over her face, her cheeks, her eyes, her hair. When he drew back his hands he stared at her blood.

He sat back up and yelled over his shoulder. "She's here. She's hurt. Get an ambulance."

His deep, strong voice broke on the last word. She wanted to tell him that she was okay. That she'd done that to herself in her panic.

"Ren…" Her voice came out in a whisper. She couldn't say anything else even if she wanted to. She slipped her arms around his neck as he lifted her out of the place she'd known she would die.

He stayed next to her as the paramedics placed her in the ambulance, answering questions she wasn't able to answer. Stayed with her as the doctors checked her at the hospital, explained about the damage to her vocal cords that would eventually heal and bandaged the superficial damage she'd done to her neck with her own fingernails.

Ren explained that Damien was dead. And the next day, as morbid as it sounded, he'd wheeled her down to the morgue so she could see the body for herself. And know there was no chance Damien was ever coming back.

Ren stayed by her side the first night in the hospital, holding her hand as he slept in a reclining chair beside her.

And through it all she hadn't said a word to him.

She couldn't talk to Ren. And not just because of the damage to her voice.

She couldn't talk to him because she needed space. Needed to find herself. Needed to know what her life was on her own without the constant companionship of fear and panic.

It had nothing to do with not trusting Ren and everything to do with figuring out a way to trust herself.

When Ren went out to talk to Steve and some of the other Omega people the second day, Andrea slipped in to say hello.

"How are you?" she asked. "I know you can't really talk. But I just wanted to say that I'm glad you're okay. I don't know how much anyone told you, but basically Omega has been under siege by Freihof for months. In my case, longer. So we're all glad he's gone and we're truly thankful for the role you played in taking him down. Putting that tracker on him under those circumstances was an exceptionally brave thing to do."

Natalie just shrugged, given how she'd cursed herself for that decision.

"Is there anything I can do for you?" Andrea asked. She stepped in closer. "Natalie, I'm not just talking get-you-a-soda type stuff, although I'll certainly do that. I know what it's like to feel like you have nothing. To need a chance to find yourself before you can do anything else."

Natalie took the pad of paper next to her bed that she'd been using to communicate.

> I'm not trying to hurt Ren. I'm not angry. But I just can't be with him right now.

Andrea smiled, understanding and sadness tinting her eyes. "You need to heal. Nobody would begrudge you that. Least of all Ren."

Andrea sat down next to her, and together they worked out a plan.

Six months later

NATALIE SAT ON the deck of another beach house in Santa Barbara. This one was quite a bit smaller than the one where she'd house-sat months ago. And a couple of blocks from the beach itself. Andrea and the Omega Sector team had helped her find it and, using money confiscated from accounts linked to Damien, had bought it outright for her.

Combat pay, they'd called it.

The house had become her saving grace.

It was here that she'd cried her eyes out for the teenager she'd been who'd made such a bad decision in who she'd married and paid such a steep price for it in the years to come. Here that she'd ranted and slammed dishes on the ground when she thought of the six more years of her life that she'd lost by running and hiding and living in terror.

At first she couldn't even look at a pack of sticky notes without feeling shame. But then Andrea, who had become a regular visitor, had pointed out—for both of their cases—that someone never needed to apologize for the way they had chosen to survive. And more importantly, that Natalie didn't need the sticky notes any longer. That was the most important thing.

Other members of Omega Sector had come by to visit also those first few weeks, some Natalie had seen before, others she hadn't.

Roman Weber, a member of the SWAT team, brought his very pregnant soon-to-be-wife, Keira, also a good friend of Andrea's. They explained how Freihof had nearly killed them both—on two separate occasions—and thanked her for what she'd done to help stop him.

Tiny, tough SWAT member and occasional bus-ticket-saleswoman Lillian brought her man, Jace, by. They told her the story of how Damien had almost blown up a huge chunk of Denver, and brought Lillian's worst nightmare back into her life. They thanked Natalie for making sure they would never have to worry about Damien again.

And sharpshooter Ashton, whom Natalie had found out was the one to put the bullet into Damien, brought his new wife and adopted toddler daughter, Chloe, by. She'd played with the adorable little girl for hours on the beach and then set up a little easel for her to paint when she'd expressed interest in Natalie's own pictures.

"Because of your strength and courage, the world is a better place," Ashton had said in her ear the next day as he'd hugged her goodbye. "You're part of the Omega family now. You and Ren both, even though he's not working there anymore."

"He's not?" She couldn't stop herself from asking, the same way she hadn't been able to stop herself from thinking about him or dreaming about him.

"Nope. Went back to work on some sheep farm in Montana. Go figure. Said it was where half his heart was. And that he was hoping the other half would get there soon."

Steve Drackett showed up the next day, a small dog kennel in one hand. He did not look amused.

"I've known Ren McClement for more than fifteen years. He's saved my life more than once. Please tell him when you see him that, after this little stunt, I consider my debt to him well and truly paid."

He set the crate on the ground and opened it. A puppy came bounding out.

A damned Old English sheepdog puppy.

A *sheepdog*.

Steve handed her a card.

This little guy might look out of place in Santa Barbara. But he'd be perfect in Montana.

Natalie grabbed the tiny ball of white fur and pulled him up into her arms, giggling as he licked her face over and over.

"Aren't you just the most adorable thing I've ever seen? I shall call you... Cream."

Steve had just rolled his eyes. "Damn thing howled the entire way here. Tell Ren that next time he has to do his own dirty work."

But Steve had winked at Natalie, so she knew he wasn't truly mad.

Cream became her constant companion, his unconditional affection helping to heal Natalie in ways she hadn't even known she had been broken. She wanted to write Ren, call him, something. But couldn't quite make herself do it.

The next month the first postcard arrived. It was obviously over ten years old and had a picture of sunny Barcelona, Spain, on the front.

> I realized I'd never sent these while I was in the army because I never had someone I wanted to share my life with. You are that person. Yours, Ren.

A couple days later another old postcard, this one from Istanbul, Turkey, showed up.

> Growing up, I loved to read but my friends teased me about it, so I used to hide it, only reading while I lay under the covers at night. Yours, Ren.

Every few days, another postcard from his collection would arrive. And on the back, some small truth about his life that would help her to know him better. Some funny. Some heartbreaking. But always honest.

Day sixty-two. Tallinn, Estonia.

I want to give you new memories of the snow. To teach you how to make snow angels. Yours, Ren.

Tears leaked out of her eyes as she read this one, and then them all, over and over again. How could she explain to him that she had long since made peace with the fact that he'd just been doing his job when he'd tricked her. That after talking with the people from Omega—and having experienced Damien's horrific violence herself—that she understood that Damien had to be stopped no matter what.

She was just afraid she was too broken to ever be the woman Ren deserved to have.

Day one hundred and five. Bari, Italy.

We don't have to have all the answers now. We will figure them out as we go. Yours, Ren.

She painted. Day in and day out. Scenes of the ocean. Of Cream. Of people. Of storms she witnessed. But mostly of that beautiful spot in the wilderness looking down on the river. When she finally got enough guts to show them to a gallery they surprised her by immediately wanting to put on a private show of just her work.

The show came and went the next month and Natalie was flabbergasted by the fact that nearly every single piece had sold and at quite a hefty price.

She was going to be able to make it on her own.

And that was when she realized she didn't want to. She wanted to be beside Ren—to share every part of her life with him. She could paint anywhere. And where she really wanted to paint the most was at a farm in Montana that she'd never seen.

It was time.

The next day she sent *him* a postcard.

Santa Barbara. Montana. Any of the places on your postcards. As long as it's you and me together. Yours, Peaches.

When a knock came on the door that night, she opened it, never expecting it could be Ren. But it was.

"What— How— I just sent the postcard this morning!"

His fingers were in her hair, pulling her close. She breathed in his scent, arms slipping around him.

"I ran out of patience—and postcards—last week. I was here to beg, grovel, do whatever I needed to do to get you back into my life. We can take it slow, or we can drive to Vegas tonight and get married. But please, Peaches, just tell me you will be with me."

She smiled. "Yes. Like you said, we'll work out the details as we go. But…yes."

His arms wrapped around her hips, pulling her up to him so he could kiss her. Gently. Reverently. Kisses that stole her breath. Stole her heart.

"As much as I'd like to stay here doing this for the rest of the night—hell, the rest of my *life*—there's something nibbling on my ankle."

Natalie giggled. "That would be Cream. I think you're to blame for him."

A smile full of reverence softened his face. "I'll take the blame for anything that causes you to make that sound and your face to light up like that. I plan to take every bad memory you have and replace each one with a dozen new good ones."

He set Natalie down so she could pick up Cream. "That might take a long time."

He kissed her. "That's okay, Peaches." Then smiled at the pup who was busy licking both their faces. "And Cream. We've got forever."

* * * * *